Grendel Rising

Grendel Rising

Gordon Phillips

GRENDEL RISING

All Rights Reserved © 2023 by Gordon Phillips

The story within is a work of fiction. All events, institutions, themes, persons, characters, and plots are completely fictional inventions of the author. Any resemblance to people living or deceased, actual places, or events is purely coincidental and entirely unintentional.

No part of this book may be reproduced or transmitted in any form or by any means, graphic, electronic, or mechanical, including photocopying, recording, taping, or by any information storage retrieval system, without the permission in writing from the author and publisher.

JMS Books LLC
PO Box 234
Colonial Heights, VA 23834
www.jms-books.com

Printed in the United States of America

ISBN: 9798387848537

For David E., my own Grendel.

Chapter 1
Halloween

I GOT DOWN on my hands and knees and peered under the bed.

The eyes that regarded me from the shadows were steady, unblinking, and defiant. After a long silence, I sighed—which produced a noncommittal blink from the eyes.

I blinked myself. I was acutely aware of a sense of impotence. It was a stand-off, pure and simple and, as I remained there unmoving, the only development was my knees began to hurt. So, I sighed again, but more deliberately this time, and got slowly to my feet.

"Oh well," I said as I walked out of the room, then in a louder voice when I reached the top of the stairs, "I guess Jake doesn't *want* to go for a walk."

Nothing.

I shook my head and began to descend the stairs, slowly. When I was standing just inside the front door, putting on my jacket, I tried one last time.

"Oh well!" I said loudly and unlocked the door.

That did it.

A moment after the lock clicked, there was a skittering of claws on wood above, followed by a plop, plop, plop, and Jake appearing, rapidly descending the stairs. I smiled to myself as I took the halter and leash from their wall hook and turned to face my dog.

Jake, my beloved Jack Russell terrier, was standing facing me, just out of reach, and wagging his tail tentatively. I squatted down and held out the halter and was puzzled by the fact that he didn't move. He was clearly in the grips of a strong canine conundrum.

I blinked as I contemplated this very odd behavior. I must have been distracted—I had been doing an evening session in my second-floor home office, finishing up elements of the software contract due in two days. Apparently, I had not really come out of work-mode when I called Jake for his evening walk, and he had gone under my bed. It was only now it hit me.

It was *Halloween*!

❖

I HAD GOTTEN Jake, as a three-month-old puppy, just over a year ago, in August. And during my first weeks with him I had been impressed with how well he took new experiences—larger dogs, moving cars, and the occasional cat sighting. Though at times cautious, he never seemed afraid, and I concluded Jake was a courageous and stoic little dog.

So, when Halloween came around, I had the brilliant idea of greeting Halloween trick-or-treaters with a candy bowl *and* my new puppy—on leash of course. I prepared the candy jar, put it on a chair just inside the front door, out of reach of Jake's obvious interest, seated myself and waited. Jake's leash was tied to the newel post of the stairs, and he sat, looking up at me, puzzled, while I told him how exciting this was going to be.

Turns out, I had underestimated this.

When the doorbell rang with the first trick-or-treaters, Jake gave his usual challenging bark. Only that, one bark—providing I was around and responding to the doorbell. Seeing me rise to open the door now, he was content to wait and see who it was before further action. I grinned down at him and said playfully, "Now, who could *that* be?"

He was wagging his tail slightly in anticipation as I opened the door.

"*Trick or treat!*" screamed a trio of small monsters happily into our faces. They were a ghost, a witch and a vampire, all about six or seven years old. I was just turning to reach for the candy jar when Jake, to put it baldly, simply *lost his mind!*

I had tied his leash so he couldn't go beyond the door, but now he didn't advance at all, but simply stood there in the middle of the hallway, legs braced, hackles up, and barked his head off! I jerked my head around in astonishment, and for one instant I saw him as a monster too, a creature that was all teeth and aggression. Then I was brought back to the situation by the terrified screams of the kids as they fled from my door.

"*Sorry!*" I called to the parents who, having come forward from the sidewalk, comforted their offspring while scowling fiercely at me. I shouted apologies to their retreating backs, then stepped back and closed the door.

Sitting in the hallway, Jake licking my hand, I finally recovered enough to reach up and shut off the outside front light. Then, I took Jake into the living room, petting him reassuringly. It wasn't his fault. I lifted him so he could peer through the front curtains at the other trick-or-treaters who were coming out now in the dusk. Being safe in my arms, he stiffened, but his only utterance was a growl deep in his throat.

"See?" I said, putting my head against his side. "It's just—well, it's a game we humans play."

I stood there for some fifteen minutes and gradually his growls diminished. They didn't disappear altogether, however, so my half-formed intention to try the experiment again died a quiet death in my heart. I turned off the lamp in the living room and, putting Jake down, retreated to the kitchen at the back of the house. I closed the door to the hallway and made a late dinner, listening to the radio while Jake, having been fed earlier, went to his kitchen doggie bed and curled up.

THAT HAD BEEN Jake *last* Halloween. Since then, he had grown from a puppy into a confident and intelligent—I would even say *wise*—dog. But I hadn't forgotten that traumatizing experience, and when Halloween came round again, I had decided to avoid any possibility of a repetition. So, as dusk approached, I closed the living room curtains and didn't turn on any lights in the front of the house. I fed Jake, let him outside in the backyard for several minutes, and then went upstairs to work.

I became so engrossed in what I was doing, accompanied by music on my headphones and Jake curled up in the doggie bed in my office that, when I realized it was dark outside, I thought of our evening walk without reflection.

So, here I was, quite helpless in a squatting position, holding out the halter to Jake, and Jake *wanting*, I knew, to come and get hooked up, but unable to do so. Like I said, a canine conundrum.

Something about the situation made me feel helpless, too. I let my head fall forward and gave another sigh, a genuine one this time.

Perhaps it was the sense that I had genuinely given up, was at the end of my tether, so to speak, that did it—for after several seconds I felt the gentle warmth of air on my ear, and the touch of a wet nose. I smiled and, without raising my head, reached out and gently stroked my dog.

Once I had done this he didn't try to get away, and when I finally raised my head and looked at him, his expression was definitely penitent, one of *sorry, Dad!*

"That's okay," I said smiling and scratching him under the chin while I reached for the halter with the other. I slowly brought the halter around and slipped it over his head, but he never moved.

"Good pup!" I murmured gratefully as I got to my feet. Jake, now recovered from his anxiety, went to the door, his tail wagging. But I noticed it was not in his usual eager and excited manner.

"Okay," I said. "Here we go." I opened the door.

Stepping out into the cool October night, I paused at the top of my front steps and looked around. Delightful! It was full-on dark now, and as I breathed, I smelled that wonderful odor of fall comprised of dead leaves and a slight crispness in the air.

Grendel Rising

"Oh, man!" I murmured. "I *love* this weather!"

Looking down at Jake, I noticed he was keeping close to my leg as he surveyed the empty street suspiciously. I suppressed a laugh and reached down to pet him.

"All gone, boy," I said reassuringly after surveying the now-deserted street. "They've all gone home to feast on their hoards of candy." Images of this activity were displaced by the parties of costumed teenagers, gathered in the rec rooms of their parents' houses. I shook my head and smiled. It was the suburbs, after all.

"C'mon, Jake," I said.

Walks with Jake were always accompanied by pleasant mental meanderings. Tonight, I remembered the Halloween parties had I been invited to. There had been two in high school—not very successful from my point of view—and three in my early twenties. That had been enough to teach me parties were not really my thing.

Square was what I had been called, and probably that was fair enough. I had done drugs in college but hadn't really found any real joy in them. Besides, hadn't it been that famous gay man, Noel Coward, who had said: *Work is more fun than fun?*

The truth was, I liked my job—my *career*—having my own one-man company. The puzzle of developing software for clients had always been a delightful challenge, and something I was good at—enough that I was able to buy the detached house I now lived in, while *still* in my twenties!

Before that, I had tried living in the downtown gay village. Sure, it had been fun and exciting—at least at first. But after several years all that had begun to pale. Occasionally the neighborhood had been just a bit *too* exciting; and after the *third* time my place had been robbed, I began seriously to think about moving.

My appreciation of green lawns and quiet streets had been learned in my early childhood, when my family was still together. I was only five when my father left us, and my mom and us kids had had to take lodgings in a less-than-opulent area of town, so I guess I remembered that suburban world with bucolic nostalgia. Certainly, I dreamed about it often enough. So, when I began to have success as an adult, I directed my habitation interests to the greener and quieter suburbs of our city—and finally bought my first house—and two months later got Jake.

And so, I was to all intents and purposes, settled.

Friends were not so approving. "What about a boyfriend?" they asked. "You're not going to find Mr. Right out there in that middle-class, heterosexual wasteland."

My response, because I wondered that myself, quickly became a dismissive,

"There'll be time enough for that."

But now, as I was led by Jake along his favorite route through the quiet, curving streets, illuminated by streetlights and curtained windows, many with candlelit jack-o'-lanterns in them, that challenge of finding love came back to haunt me.

What about it, Ken? I asked myself. *What about finding, as the song says, "somebody to love?"*

Jake brought me back from these fruitless ruminations when he stopped, frozen in place, staring into the dark shadows of a front yard. I shook my head to clear my mind and looked where he was staring. Nothing. Yet, Jake's hackles were raised, and he was growling, which I knew meant *something*.

Still, I was puzzled. There was no Halloween decoration visible, no jack-o'-lantern in a window, nor a stuffed figure of a witch peering around the column on a front porch. We had encountered the latter on previous nights, when Halloween decorations had gone up prior to the day itself. Jake's reaction had been the same each time. He froze, stared for several seconds, and then erupted into a fusillade of barking. I had reassured him each time and made a point of letting him sniff each decoration. After this, he seemed to recover, and I thought him more or less inoculated by this point.

Yet, here it was again, that reaction. Yet I could see nothing.

"What is it, boy?"

I held onto the leash as I stepped forward to where he was, the thought in my mind being: skunk. We had already had one close call, and I didn't want to have to deal with a skunked dog, either the trauma to him or the cleansing.

I had just reached him and was about to squat down to pet him reassuringly, when he lunged forward a foot and simply *exploded* with a burst of furious barking. I pulled back on his leash, stepped forward and knelt down, putting my arms around him and breathing "*Shhhh!*" in his ear.

It wasn't late, but still, I didn't want Jake to get a reputation for too much barking.

Usually, this tactic worked. But *this* time, while his barking died down, it was replaced by a kind of whining I couldn't seem to stop.

So now *I* was curious. I stood up and, holding him firmly on a short leash, moved forward. I noticed Jake was not pulling now. He was staying right beside me, but still making odd anxious noises.

I continued to peer into the darkness of the yard but could make out nothing. On the right was a large shrub, and on the left, along the line of the front walk of the house, a hedge. I was alert for the telltale sign of movement that would indicate an animal, but there was nothing.

After taking another step, however, I was just able to make out something—or, rather, *several* somethings—amid the grass lawn: a larger something in front, and two smaller somethings on either side and back somewhat, in a triangular configuration.

I stared, trying to figure out what I was looking at. Then it came to me, and I experienced a *frisson* of real terror.

It froze me for several heartbeats as I stared, incredulous but horror-stricken, at what apparently was a huge face—a nose and two eyes just barely protruding above the grass surface.

It only took that long for my rational mind to override this impression, and I chuckled shakily with relief. I had seen something like this before—in daylight, a week previously: an artificial nose and eyes, placed on a front lawn to suggest a buried head. I had been walking Jake, but because I had spotted the thing from across the street, Jake had not noticed it. I was careful afterwards to avoid that particular house. But that was several streets over. This one I realized must be new. Very new, in fact, for it certainly hadn't been here as recently as yesterday.

I looked down at Jake, who was still standing stiffly next to my leg, staring at the thing.

"It's okay, boy," I said, reaching down and petting him.

Something in my voice must have reassured him, for after looking up at me anxiously, he made no further utterance.

"It's just a Halloween decoration," I continued soothingly. "C'mon. Let's go check it out."

I took a step forward, and then another, and was surprised at how cautious I was feeling, more than seemed reasonable. I chided myself: this was not the way to reassure one's dog! I took another deliberate step. Now the three elements were quite clear: the nose and two eyes. And wasn't there something beyond the eyes? I ridge of sorts? I frowned, then squinted to blur the image and get an overall picture. Immediately, I saw this fourth element might be the eyebrow ridge on the forehead of the buried face!

I was impressed. This was of higher quality than the other so-called face had been. No wonder Jake had been fooled! What was the scale? It must be about three times human size. The nose was very well-formed. It was the *size* that made the buried face so frightening. Perhaps it triggered a long-buried instinct. A fear of dinosaurs, perhaps? No. Those were long gone when humans evolved.

Still.

Jake was no longer straining, so I eased my hold on his leash. He was still staring at the decoration and remained next to my leg. I squatted down and petted him again.

"It's okay, boy. This is just another silly thing we humans do."

He looked up at me, his expression still slightly anxious, which made my heart twist. I didn't like my dog being afraid. So, I decided to help.

"Here," I said. "I'll show you."

I stood up and took another step forward. Jake remained where he was.

"It's okay!" I said quietly. He looked at me but didn't move. I laughed gently. "I'll show you."

Taking a deep breath, I stepped almost right up to the nose, and looked down again at the face. From this proximity I felt even more impressed with the realism of the features. There were actual eyebrows on the ridge of forehead, and eyelashes on the eyes. It all looked quite genuine, except for the blank look in those eyes, which clearly gazed at nothing.

And that nose! Probably Styrofoam. It stuck up, several inches above the grass. I was about to nudge it with my sneaker, but instead I stepped to the side and half turned, so I could see both Jake and the nose. Then I squatted down and touched the nose with a fingertip.

What?

I leaped back, toppling onto the grass. Immediately, Jake was next to me, licking my face in concern. I put my arm around him and pulled him close, then just lay there, unmoving, while I caught my breath.

But when I remembered *why* I had fallen, I sat up hastily, ready to scramble to my feet as I stared at that nose thing, I could feel the hackles on *my* neck stand up.

That nose was *not* Styrofoam; it had felt distinctly *warm*.

I looked at Jake, who was still watching me anxiously.

"Maybe we should leave," I murmured.

But something in me wouldn't allow that. I was unnerved, but still—I wanted to *know* what it was. And besides, the idea of fleeing from a *lawn ornament*—

My mental use of the term brought me back to some sense of reality. *That's right*, I told myself. *It's just a damned Halloween ornament—meant to scare little kids.* That made me feel a little better. But it *had* been warm, had in fact felt *very* lifelike. But how could that be?

Then, it came to me: *heated* of course! That seemed odd, but maybe that was to make it scarier? Did that make sense? I wasn't sure but decided that must be it. Perhaps it was just another aspect of the detailing.

I shrugged, and murmured, "Okay."

So, squaring my shoulders, I faced the display, looked at each of the four elements, and then at them together. My eyes had by now adjusted to this deeply shadowed part of the yard, and *still* the effect was startlingly realistic. I was even *more* impressed. I thought of the scare both Jake and I had had, and chuckled. That was what Halloween was all about, after all.

I looked down at Jake. He was standing next to me, still staring at the ornament, but no longer looking frightened. Perhaps my touching the thing, even with my subsequent tumble, *had* reassured him.

If only it had reassured *me*!

But I tightened my jaw. "You're made of sterner stuff," I murmured, and took a step forward again. Then another. A foot from the nose, I squatted down to examine the object, the smooth, curving shape of the thing; so fleshy. Then, an image came to me of the hypothetical rest of the form, at the same scale. The image of so *much* flesh—I found myself getting slightly aroused.

The simultaneous amusement and mortification that this produced helped my state of mind. *Was* it a male nose? I decided it was, somehow. And its curves really *were* quite beautiful. Majestic. I felt another tingle of sexual excitement, and chuckled.

I squatted down, examining the nostrils—and received another shock. There appeared to be actual nostril hairs. *More detailing?* I reached out toward the nostrils but hesitated to touch.

A moment later I drew my hand sharply back, as if I had been burned.

I experienced a swooping sensation in my stomach, and I had to bite my lip to stop myself from crying out. A veritable orchestra of symptoms afflicted me now: creeping flesh, icy chills and my hair standing on end.

Deliberately, I turned my head and shoulders so I could see the sidewalk, the street, the overall peaceful look of a night in the suburbs. It was reassuring.

Even so, it took nerve to turn back to that nose again. Those well-formed, oval nostrils. What I had felt was a slight but definite flow of warm air coming from them.

As if from breathing.

I slowly stood up and took a step backward. It really was getting late, and I should probably get Jake home. I had taken several steps toward the sidewalk when I thought, with a stab chagrin: *What a coward!*

I turned back and looked at the ornament, frowning. A moment later, I clapped a hand over my mouth to stifle a real scream of terror. The eyes had blinked. Moreover, they had lost their blank look and were now quite definitely *gazing directly at me!*

Chapter 2
Excavation

OH MY!

I staggered. It really felt, for just a moment, as if the whole earth had moved under me. But I planted my feet further apart to reestablish my sense of being on solid ground. I looked around. Nothing had changed. There had, of course, been no earthquake. It had just been me. So, I took a deep breath, and turned back, to look at those enormous eyes.

This took some effort, and a momentary shudder went through me when I faced them, for they really *did* seem to be looking straight at me.

Effective! I thought, and all at once I was viewing this experience merely as a Halloween scare. An effective one, certainly—but still, only a scare. Immediately, I felt reassured. And curious. I wanted to discover how the scare was done. Then, part of me thought: *If I do that, then the magic of the effect will disappear.* I realized that would be a real loss; the effect was so delightfully—*scary!*

Again, I felt the urge to leave without pursuing further inquiry. But Jake, I noticed, was still interested in the objects. He was at the end of his leash, *sitting*, facing the thing at a distance of several feet. *Just*, I thought, *like he's waiting for something.*

That did it. I took several steps back toward the ornament and stood there, staring at the eyes—that were still fixed on me. Which meant, of course, a change in gaze direction. *Odd!* I thought. The gaze of those eyes seemed to be having an effect on me, on my sense of being. It was a definite sense of being—*watched*. And the odd thing about it was how *definite* it felt, strong enough, in fact, that it made me feel slightly giddy.

What?

I remained there, looking at those eyes, while I examined my own feelings. It was, I decided, the first time I had ever felt so completely the object of attention. It was disconcerting, yes, but in a pleasant way. In fact, the word *attention* wasn't quite the right. *Interest*, I decided was better. I was of interest to those eyes.

I felt flushed and, breathing in sharply I touched the tip of my tongue to my upper lip with sensual self-awareness and a slightly intoxicated sense of coquettishness—which was *certainly* not normal for me! But now it seemed that *interest* too wasn't quite right. In fact—and my heart fluttered at the thought—it *felt* as if those eyes were *appreciating* me! Drinking me in. And now a wash of physical arousal passed through me—settling, warm and disturbingly pleasant, between my legs.

I felt hot and cold at the same time, disoriented, and as if the entire world had changed. And my pulse was racing. And, interestingly, I no longer felt *any* fear at all!

Words for my state started to go through my mind. *Appreciated. Intoxicated.* Perhaps even *fascinated?* But that could be a disturbing idea. Fascinated like a bird before a snake? Was I, in fact, unable to move? But no, I had no desire to flee. What I wanted was to *know*, to *engage*—somehow. *Physically.*

I squatted down and felt the cool grass with my fingers. This was reassuring. I was feeling around for some kind of trigger device, a wire perhaps, that might make the eyes alter their direction as one approached them.

There was nothing, however, and finally I knelt forward and, reaching out, touched the rounded tip of the nose with a fingertip, pushed against it. It gave just like flesh. And it *felt* delightful: smooth, warm, and slightly spongy. I tweaked the nose, squeezing it between thumb and forefinger, which felt even more like flesh.

I shook my head and looked at Jake. He was sitting right beside me, watching my actions with curiosity. I looked back at those eyes and got a *new* shock.

They were still looking directly at me! That is, their direction of gaze had shifted toward my lowered position. And—which made me whimper with renewed fear—were even slightly cross-eyed, due to my close proximity.

Slowly, I rose to standing position, and moved backward, all the time keeping my gaze on those eyes. I saw—sickeningly—they followed me exactly.

I closed my eyes to get away from that gaze and thought furiously.

Optical illusion? Like those portrait paintings whose gaze seem to follow you? I couldn't quite buy that. Then: *Mechanism!*

Oh! My rational mind leaped in to save me. Simple! I only had to look for a mechanism—something that—directed the eyes according to some—position sensor. Admittedly, this seemed a little incredible—even for an expensive, top-shelf holiday decoration. And yet, it *had* to be the case!

Didn't it?

I looked away and then back, toward the face—and saw it even more clearly *as* a face. The elements seemed so *obviously* part of one unity. And then, there was that *gaze*. As I stared at it, that feeling of being appreciated began to return, like the weaving of a magic spell. And, not just appreciative. *Interested. Very.*

Memories came to me of the times when, in a bar some guy was *seriously* cruising me. Yet, incredibly, this was stronger, *and* more exciting. I began to get a hard-on.

I looked at Jake and he, perhaps sensing my change in mood, walked forward, right up to the nose, sniffing it while his tail wagged tentatively. Then he turned his head and looked at me, giving a gentle whine.

"It's okay," I told him, taking a step forward. The gaze of those eyes followed me, their sense of interest more pronounced than ever. My arousal was greater as well. A tingle crept along my skin, and I became acutely aware of how my clothes touched my skin—especially my undershorts, which I now conceived of as a garment that *contained* my lower abdomen and upper thighs, its crotch cupping my hardening cock and testicles. It was intimate; hell, it was almost pornographic!

And now I decided to try something.

I took several steps backward and stood, focusing on the face in its entirety. After hesitating, I cleared my throat and said, in a tentative voice, "Hello?"

There was no answer, and after a moment or two I laughed quietly with embarrassment.

Of *course*, there was no answer! I thought, my mind shifting back to rationality. Now, looking at the elements of that huge face, I saw it as completely inanimate, despite those eyes watching me. I shook my head.

It was *a mechanism!* I told myself. *Of course! Of course! Of course!* Images of wires, sensors, heating coils filled my relieved mind when, all at once, the deep stillness of the night was broken by a low sound.

"Hmm-mmmm!"

It was a low rumbling noise, accompanied by a slight vibration from beneath my feet!

I leaped aside without thinking, my heart pounding. My hair was standing on end again as I stared down at the spot where I had been standing. My heart was pounding, my brain in a whirl. Jake, who was now next to me, looked anxious.

"Hmm-mmmmm!" came the sound again.

It was exactly like the previous sound, and automatically (and somewhat frantically) my rational mind spoke the words: *audiotape sound-effects*. But I had not felt the vibration in the ground this time, which reassured me somehow.

I looked again at those eyes. I saw their gaze had shifted *again*. They were *still* looking directly at me!

I gave a slight groan, feeling like a rat in a very complicated maze.

Grendel Rising

As I looked at those eyes, it struck me the *quality* of that gaze had changed. It was more—what? Appealing?

What?

Then the sound came again, louder this time.

"*Hmm-mmmmmm!*"

I frowned, thinking. The sound was definitely suggestive of muffled speech. But now it now had an insistence to it, as if that muffled voice was crying out—to me.

Hmm-mmmmmm! I replayed the sound in my mind—and *had it!*

The sound's cadence was exactly that of the cry: *Help me!*

Suddenly convinced of this, my reticence and incipient fear disappeared completely. I felt only concern for—whoever, *whatever* this was. My heart racing with urgency, I thought furiously of what I should do, trying to get some kind of perspective on the situation. Jake picked that moment to go up to the enormous nose and *lick* it—several times!

"*Jake!*" I hissed. "Don't *do* that!"

Jake turned to look at me, and I made *move away* motions. He didn't seem to understand. I was just about run forward and grab my dog, when I saw the nose quiver visibly and, a moment later, there was a muffled explosion and a rush of warm air from the nose. The ground quivered slightly, too. It was just as if a very *large* someone, almost buried in this lawn, had sneezed.

I took several steps to the side, thinking that, during the first noise, I must have been standing right on the *chest* of the whatever-it-was.

The eyes again followed me as usual. They were still filled with that look of helpless appeal.

Jake, who had retreated during the explosion, moved forward again. Now, he stood right in front of the nose, wagging his tail. Then he gave several sharp barks, of the type he sometimes used to get me out of bed in the morning.

Somehow, that did it.

Against all reasonability I was suddenly convinced, stung into action.

"You wait here," I told the eyes. I got Jake's leash and, pulling him back to the sidewalk, began to trot back home. After several backward glances, he came willingly, though clearly, he was puzzled.

"It's okay, boy. We're just going home to get a shovel."

I WAS BACK, with a spade and a bucket containing a trowel and paintbrush, in less than fifteen minutes. I had been quite driven by excitement and the sense of urgency, but as we again approached those lawn ornaments, I was aware of a sense of doubt, and fear.

Jake, on the other hand, was all eagerness to return; he was at the end of his leash. This helped when I was again standing in the gaze of those eyes. I grinned and brandished my shovel in a heroic gesture. It seemed the eyes now registered something like gratitude, and I felt something of my earlier sense of intoxication return. Holding my rescue implements, I felt ready for anything—and, under the gaze of those eyes, I meant *anything*!

I put down the bucket and got to work. It was, I thought a bit giddily, like digging for treasure!

The task, now that I faced it, was not so very straightforward. For one thing, the lawn ran right up to each of the four protrusions, impossible as that seemed. I didn't worry about the last; the current situation was beyond the pale of "possible" things; I focused only on the job at hand.

I began just below the nose, driving my spade in just deep enough to cut through the sod. I cut the outline a long rectangle and rolled up the sod, placing it carefully to one side. So far so good!

I repeated the process until I had removed all the grass around the nose. This done, I got the trowel and began loosening the exposed earth, lifting it with my hands into the bucket. When the bucket was full, I dumped the earth next to the stack of rolled sod.

Jake, who had been watching me with great curiosity, now got into the act. He lowered his head and began to dig furiously with his forepaws, sending earth flying out between his back legs. I had to laugh.

"Good for you, Jake! Good dog!"

I—or, rather we, though Jake did take frequent breaks from his own efforts to go up and sniff the nose, the eyes and the forehead—continued to clear earth from around the nose. I quickly discovered the cheeks, for there was only a thin layer of dirt over them. I was momentarily reassured at this discovery. Part of me wondered what I would have experienced had there been no cheek, nothing—just a free-standing, partially buried, enormous nose; one that sneezed! The idea was so bizarre, so horrible, that I imagined, having unearthed it, I would just start screaming; screaming and screaming, and never able to stop.

Dismissing these disturbing thoughts, I worked at exposing more of the cheek, working away from the nose with hands and paintbrush to remove the final bits of earth. I encountered an upper lip and soon had fully exposed the entire mouth. Touching the large and rather full lips sent tingles of excitement through me. I wanted to lie down and kiss them.

Shaking my head to dispel this fantasy, I next worked upward from the nose to the eyes, which closed protectively meanwhile. I could see the closed lids trembling slightly and was struck by the beauty of those quivering eyelashes. I continued to work upward, brushing off the strong line of the brow and the curve of the forehead.

When I had done this and was standing up to stretch, those eyes opened again and looked at me with such a warmth of expression that I felt a shiver of pleasure run through me. I closed my eyes for several seconds to regain my center.

There's still work to be done, I remonstrated myself; and however pleasurable the task, it was still a task, and not a small one either.

I returned with increased impetus, clearing the dirt off right into the hairline and on either side, to where the ears began. Then I went back to the lower face and cleared the chin and jaw line. The intimate nature of the tactile experience, touching these magnified and beautiful male shapes had me almost shivering with excitement. The mouth in particular, being over half a foot in width, was especially distracting. Even looking at it made the heat between my legs become something closer to a distracting throb. *Much more of this*, I thought, *and I'll be coming in my pants*.

I shifted to the neck, and had gotten down to the Adam's apple, when I noticed the lips move and a large tongue peek out for a second. This stopped any progress for the moment as I just gaped at it appreciatively.

"Oh," came a voice as the lips moved. "*Thank* you!"

The voice was *very* deep, with a rumbly timbre that not only made the earth vibrate beneath me (I must be on the upper chest, I decided), but made my entire *body* vibrate. I had a rock-hard erection by now and had to shift it to make things more comfortable. My face was burning, too. All in all, what I was experiencing was a kind of symphony of disturbing sensations: excitement, Eros, adventure, and impropriety—even danger. Perhaps the last two were due to my upbringing—I had *chosen* to live in the suburbs, after all.

Still, I managed to look up at those eyes, which were still watching me, and reply, even though my voice sounded shaky.

"You're—you're welcome!"

There was no response to this, and I experienced a momentary disappointment. Then it occurred to me the giant's ears were still stopped with earth. Maybe he hadn't heard me.

So, I smiled and nodded, then got up and began work further around the sides of the head, exposing the full baroque curves of the insides of the ears at last. They were well-formed, and I experienced another definite thrill as I brushed these free of earth.

Somehow, neither of us spoke just then. I was eager to resume the excavation, heart pounding and still hard in my pants. I unearthed the line of the shoulders out to the massive shoulder muscles, which were not just round like cannonballs but fully as large as cannonballs. Brushing these off was a particular pleasure, though I thought I would rather have been spreading oil on that wonderful, soft-hard skin.

I paused, looking down at those broad, built shoulders in admiration and appreciation. Cannonballs *indeed*! I thought. And then some words from an old, folk song came to me. Something like: I had a man, long and tall, who moved his body like a cannonball.

A moment later I had to slap a hand over my mouth to stop a loud cry of appreciation and excitement as I realized this was the very type referred to in the song.

"Focus!" I murmured to myself. So, without further sightseeing episodes, I returned to the task at hand, putting the energy of my excitement, not to mention the other emotions that were moiling around inside me, into the excavation.

Another crisis moment came when working along the swell of a massive, jutting pectoral muscle that culminated in an enormous and disturbingly pert nipple! The urge to bite, albeit gently, to take it into my mouth, washed over me like a wave.

By then I had become more comfortable with my state of chronic arousal. It was beginning to feel like a kind of simple, joyful happiness, though with giddy overtones—and a rock-hard boner. I didn't adjust myself again. I thought if I took, as it were, the matter in hand, just one moment's grasp of the throbbing shaft would send me over the edge, and I would cum with a violence I could only imagine.

And how embarrassing would *that* be!

I focused my attention now on the *beauty* of the body I was gradually revealing. And not just that, but the sense of appreciation on how impressive every part was—the oversized and beautiful male human form. Every mass, every curve was indeed a work of art. And, not only that, but distinctly erotic art.

David! The thought came to me as I passed the form's waist and was just moving down over the regular undulations of the eight-pack of abdominal muscles. Michelangelo's statue! Wasn't it supposed to be oversized? I was pretty sure of that, and now even an image of it formed in my mind—the one hand holding the sling that had killed Goliath over his shoulder, the furrowed brow. I took a daring moment and gazed across the upper half of the form I had partially unearthed, and decided this body—torso, neck and shoulders especially—had that sculptor's effort hopelessly outclassed. This—whatever it was—was *built!*

So intense was my appreciation that again I had to put a hand over my mouth.

No screaming, please, sir! This is the suburbs after all.

I giggled helplessly and resumed my task.

Jake, by this point, was lying beside my work area, chin on his paws, watching.

"Hey, Jake!" I said to him. "Halfway through, eh?" He wagged his tail but otherwise didn't move.

I looked down at the leading edge of my diggings and for the moment quailed.

I had exposed, without my being consciously aware of it, the hip bones and the V of lines called the V of Adonis that led from the hips to the groin. Almost down to…

Dismissing this disturbing, tantalizing thought. I got shakily to my feet. I went to the figure's left shoulder, not looking at those eyes, but feeling them follow me as usual. Below the cannonball shoulder, I gradually exposed the bicep. This swelled impressively, to say the least. And then, on, to the forearm—another swelling that narrowed to the wrist, and finally the hand. The fingers, as I dug around them, were each the size of salamis, the middle finger about a foot long. Freed at last, they flexed, whereupon I almost cried out in intoxicated appreciation. They were just so *big*! But I kept my nerve and brushed away the residual earth—while fantasies of putting each digit in turn in my mouth and sucking and licking for all I was worth passed thru my mind. At one point this brought me almost to the brink of orgasm.

At last, the arm lifted majestically and flexed—which made the bicep bulge massively. When I had recovered from the effect *this* produced, I got to work on the other arm, and when both were freed, I felt the figure begin to stir. The head lifted up first, then the upper torso, arms on either side, until it rested on its elbows.

I watched this with a kind of stupefied awe, and a tiny amount of fear. But then, when I looked at those big eyes, which now regarded me with a twinkle added to the invariable interest—and saw the enormous mouth spread into a smile, I was utterly reassured, almost to the point of melting on the spot.

It was just then I saw something new, something *amazing*. The figure's face, and then its arms and torso, began to glow with a silvery light. I watched, open-mouthed in awe and only after a minute or so noticed the shrubs on either side were now visible, and had shadows. I turned. There, through a parting in the clouds, was the full moon.

I looked back at the figure, and saw it was gazing, not at me, but at the brilliant, silvery moon.

A moment later, the figure—or perhaps *giant* would be a better term— sat up fully, and reaching out with its enormous hands, began the work of excavating the lower half of its body, still covered with earth and lawn. I stood back and watched this with astonishment. The thought did hit me, to be grateful I didn't have to expose and brush off the massive private parts. And them, only a second or two later, this turned to disappointment.

It was amazing, watching those giant hands at work. For all their large size, they were curiously deft, each motion an act of care and precision, as they plunged into the soil and lifted the sod from below. In fact, there was something uncanny about how the strips of lawn parted when a large fingertip emerged, poking up through the soil. And it took very little time for the job to be completed.

And then!

Then, I watched in awe as the giant figure got slowly up, first to its knees, and then, at last, to its feet. And there it stood, fully revealed and totally naked, towering up above me.

I stared at the enormous, but beautifully shaped feet, pressing into the raw earth in which the figure had lain. The toes were as exquisite as the fingers had been. I then let my gaze travel slowly up the form, up the strong calf muscles, knobby knees, and the magnificent swell of massive thighs. My gaze leaped past the privates as if shied away, and I registered the vast, V-shaped torso, massive, jutting pectorals, up and out to those cannonball shoulders. The arms were out and down, fingers open and spread, and looking at the face I saw it was gazing again up at the moon.

And the silvery glow that now suffused that entire majestic form was so intensely beautiful that I turned to see if it was *only* the moon doing this.

The moon, which had fully emerged from the clouds now, looked more beautiful than I had ever seen it before. But it *was* just the moon, albeit a *full* moon.

I turned back to the colossus, which seemed *bathed* in silvery moonlight, giving off that silvery shine as if in some kind of sympathetic response. As I stared at this unearthly manifestation, I felt my jaw sag in abject, total appreciation. More than anything, what twisted my heart was the profound *beauty* I saw now in that enormous form.

With the giant gazing raptly up at the moon, I gathered my nerve and looked directly where I had *wanted* to look but had been too afraid.

And caught my breath, staring!

I swallowed painfully, but for several seconds I could not pull my eyes away. It was like looking directly at the sun, except it wasn't my *eyes* that were dazzled; *that* was going on all through the rest of my body! But at last, I found I couldn't sustain my gaze, and *did* look away.

What I retained, though, was almost too much to register. I recalled my previous thoughts about the beauty of the giant's form. *Form?* I thought now. *How wrong is that? This* wasn't a *thing*! It was—but again I caught myself—

No, I corrected myself. That simply wouldn't do.

The evidence, quite literally, was right in front of my face—or a foot or two higher than that. I could not even *dream* of referring to this giant as *it*. It wasn't just obviously, or even massively—no, it was *emphatically, breathtakingly* male—the very apotheosis of the masculine configuration that could only be referred by pronoun as—the most magnificent, most glorious manifestation of—*he*!

Chapter 3
By Moonlight

WITH THE GIANT gazing raptly up at the full moon, I felt free to continue my own rapt gazing. It wasn't, I soon discovered, easy to do. I found again and again that after about a dozen seconds of staring at that magnificent central manifestation of virility, I *had* to look away. Again, the idea of looking at the sun came to mind. But it wasn't *quite* like that. It wasn't painful—only overwhelming. And fun, too! For each time I looked away, at the right hip for example, or the navel, I did so with the delicious knowledge that in a little I would again be able to return to the well for another intoxicating sip of visual nectar.

And even if I didn't direct my gaze back at the Center of All Things, just looking at another part of the giant's physiology seemed, inexorably, to lead back by means of contiguous, topographical features, each of them massively and acutely male, to that most daunting and powerful center of action, the phallus.

And so, gradually, sip by sip, I acquired at least a heady sense of experience, of ready familiarity with that male member and its two majestic and adjacent masses that, large as coconuts, hung beneath.

I looked around then, at the stillness of the suburban street which I saw the moonlight made unusually beautiful too. I looked up at the moon, too. I had always felt there was something magical about that queen of the night, something about its light. Now, at full moon, seeing its effect on this male giant, it showed a strange, unearthly, yet festive feeling, by which I imagined night animals might celebrate.

All that from reflected sunlight!

But no! That rational approach would not work here. I looked up at the giant again and choked back a laugh. *Rationality*, I thought, *is not in the ascendency here and now.*

Looking away from the giant silvery form and back at the moon, I repeated the term, *queen of the night,* in my mind. *Queen? No.* That wasn't quite right. It wasn't enough. I sought the word, and finally murmured, "Goddess!"

Yes, that was it!

And then I remembered part of a line from a poem I had been forced to memorize by my sixth-grade teacher who, idiosyncratically had made us learn one poem a week all year. They were short poems, but still—writing them out from memory on Friday each week was a challenge. And now? I only remembered two of those poems in full. One was "Loveliest of Trees" by Housman, the other "Ozymandias" by Shelly. But this, one about the moon as a goddess. How did it go?

I stood there, staring up at the full moon, and opened myself up to its mysterious beauty, murmuring the word over and over: "Goddess." Nothing came for several minutes. It was only when I was about to give up, that the line came to me:

Goddess excellently bright!

Oh, yes! And it fit, too! *Those words!* That syncopation in the second word, breaking the rhythm of the meter, somehow perfectly. So *beautiful*! It fit the moon goddess—who was that? Diana? That sounded right. Repeating the phrase over in my mind, I gazed at the full moon, which was so bright, and at this wonderful giant it was illuminating, making him *excellently bright*, too!

A sense of magic seemed to permeate the very air of the night. Did it come from that full moon? I looked at the giant, struck again by his silvery glow, by his majestic form and his massive size. It wasn't the moon, I decided. The moon merely—what? Activated the magic in him? In any case, the magic now came from him. In fact, it seemed fairly to *pour* from him, into the still night air.

Into me.

Now, moved by wonder and beauty, I found I could look at the giant—all parts of him. Yes, he was magnificently masculine. Of that there was no doubt. He seemed to embody the masculine archetype, every part of him exquisitely formed, beautifully proportioned and massively muscled. And—again—everything was so *big*!

Looking at the giant's face again, I decided it wasn't exactly handsome. But it *was* virile, and in its own way quite beautiful. He was still gazing up at the moon too, eyes wide open, as if he was drinking *in* the moonlight.

It was at this point all this fixation on beauty and wonder was, at least possibly, a kind of deliberate distraction—from the object of central interest. But I was uncertain. So, I would have to test this theory. I looked right at the giant's genitals.

Oh!

The phallus curved massively out over a pair of coconut-sized testicles. Even semi-flaccid the shaft was as thick as my forearm and over a foot in length. The enormous head was proudly shaped, its curves majestic and seductive, its surface shiny smooth like a massively overgrown plum.

Taking all this in, I felt a flutter in my stomach. I became possessed of a desire to simply step forward and reach up—to where it hung like some tantalizing, forbidden fruit, higher than the top of my head—to touch it, to simply put my open palm under it and lift, to feel its warm spongy solidity, its heft—and even, perhaps, to caress it.

Dimly aware I was beginning to feel a bit silly, I stifled a giggle. It was then the suppressive part of me, having got my attention, said, *Well? What exactly could you* do *with it?*

Certainly, this was a point. But another part of me, the joyful (and horny) part, responded this was completely beside the *real* point—which was simple adoration, celebration in proximity and in touch—especially of the rubbing sort.

Certainly, it was far too large for any kind of penetration, but so what? Its *presence* was what counted. Its profoundly virile, intoxicating quality, nature and being, as the center of the giant's overall masculine quintessence, was what I wanted to luxuriate in. It was beyond mere horniness, any desire to simply get my rocks off. I had now been completely overwhelmed and had surrendered deliciously to a chronic wanton state of reveling in which touch alone was sufficient.

A line I had heard from a sit-com came to me—that whatever that massive phallus might be "saying," I only asked to be a part of the conversation.

All this was getting a bit overwhelming, so I forced myself to look away. A moment later, I was aware of a change in my state. I was feeling observed again.

I looked up, at the giant's face, and saw he was looking down at me. His expression was benign, his large, pale eyes were gentle even while their effect on me was quite strong. He was, I thought about fifteen feet tall, almost three times my own six-foot stature. It made me feel small, which was something I was definitely *not* used to. And I found I very much *liked* the feeling.

But *small*, I decided, wasn't exactly how I felt. I searched for the term and came up with a word that wasn't quite it either, but closer: *petite*. I felt like those slightly-built guys I had always envied. I had *attracted* that sort of men myself, and I had attempted relationships with them once or twice. Only it wasn't what I wanted. I wanted to *be* them, not be *with* them.

And it was now, for the first time in my life that, looking up at this giant and feeling the power of his regard as he gazed down at me, I felt a welcome sense of rightness, of fulfillment of a my long-sought-after romantic dream. And so, in that massive, masculine presence, I saw not just beauty and powerful virility. I saw—*possibilities*.

Our mutual stillness was broken at last when the giant leaned forward, looming slightly *over* me, in what I realized after a second or two must be a bow. The experience of having him loom thus was disturbing and exciting at the same time. Then he stood upright again and said, "I thank you, sir."

The sound of his wonderfully deep, resonant voice again plunged me into a sea of Eros. I had to struggle to make any sort of reply. I managed to choke out something at last, though my voice sounding to my own ears both shaky and squeaky.

"Uh—you're welcome."

The giant smiled in response. Then he turned and looked down at the depression his extraction had left in the yard. Looking back at me, he grinned. "Perhaps we had better tidy this up."

I nodded, grinning back.

So, we both got to work. I didn't do much, really. It was the giant's large hands scooping such enormous amounts of soil that made short work of the task. It was also very distracting whenever he moved, the enormous muscles stretching and bulging. I saw again how those hands were amazingly good at the work, including the smoothing out. I did help replacing the pieces of sod, however.

When we finished at last, there was a pronounced dip in the lawn where his bulk had been. This wasn't a surprise. What *did* strike me was that the depression seemed much less than I thought it would be, given the giant's size.

"That will fill in by morning," the giant said, as if as sensing my doubts. "It always does."

Always does? I wasn't sure what this meant, but in my current intoxicated state, I decided if this big guy understood it, then that was good enough for me.

We stood there, in the still complacency of a job well done. It was comfortable, even companionable. But I began to wonder what to say or do next. My thoughts raced along various channels, some of which caused my pulse to race. The important thing, I felt, was not to lose contact with this magnificent male. But how to proceed?

At last, looking up at him I said, awkwardly, "Would—would you like to come back to my place? For—uh—a coffee?"

Having said this, I felt totally stupid. For one thing, my voice had been choked again. For another, the invitation struck me as utterly inane and inappropriate. It was a terrible cliché too, that sort of invitation in the gay community. For, though it might *include* coffee, such offers of hospitality generally were understood to mean other, more intimate things as well.

But I forced myself to continue looking up at the enormous face, as the big eyes continued to look down at me. At last, slowly, a smile—a *knowing* smile, I thought—spread over that big face, causing my heart to flutter at the possibility of *interest* in that look. And, though I had no idea just *how* that interest might express itself, I decided in any case I was interested—whatever was involved.

"Thank you," he said in his deep voice. "I would like that." Then he added, "You have freed me."

"Oh, uh, I was glad to be of help," I said offhandedly, shrugging.

But those eyes, still looking down at me, made me a bit giddy with pleasure, both at this expression of gratitude and the simple sound of that deep voice. In that moment, it made me want to—well, just dance around.

"And," the giant added, "thank you to your friend."

I saw, somewhat to my surprise, that the giant's gaze now rested on Jake, who was standing beside me, looking up at the big creature. I saw his tail wag at these words, just as if he had understood the statement. I smiled inwardly and experienced both joy and relief.

Oh, good! He likes dogs.

A moment later, I was slightly unnerved as the giant bent down and reached out a big hand toward Jake, enormous fingers outstretched.

Gently now, I thought, clenching my teeth in a moment of fearful anticipation. But, a second later, I discovered I needn't have worried, for the hand was wonderfully gentle. The tip of the forefinger barely brushed the hair along Jake's back and then the top of his head.

I was impressed, too, at how well Jake took this. Ordinarily, he didn't like strangers petting him. Yet, with this enormous being there was no backing away, no raised hackles, and no growling. Indeed, he wagged his tail, albeit tentatively.

After that gentle touch, the giant held the finger in front of Jake to sniff, which offer was accepted, and the tail wagging became more pronounced.

Watching this, I felt something inside me melt, for I trusted Jake's judgment of people. I decided I liked this giant—quite apart from any sexual excitation or appreciation of his beauty. He was "good people."

The giant straightened up and looked down at me again. Placing his enormous hand against his own chest, he said in a solemn voice, "I am called—Grendel."

I started slightly at the name. Apparently, the giant noticed this, for he smiled again.

"Yes," he said. "I am named after that—character—of that story, written in another age."

"Oh!" I was confused, but still very keen to show politeness in my turn.

"I'm Ken," I said hastily. Then I pointed at Jake. "And this is Jake. He's my best friend." I reached down and petted him.

I saw the giant—Grendel, I guess—nod approvingly at this. "Yes," he said. "That is well." And now he raised a big hand, palm out, fingers spread in a kind of greeting. "Hello Ken. Hello Jake."

"Hello, Grendel!" I responded, making the same hand gesture.

This somehow made me feel more comfortable than I had been up to that point. So, when the obvious question arose in my mind, I took a chance.

"I'm sorry," I said, "but what *are* you?"

A low rumble came from the giant's chest, by which I decided he must be chuckling. (The vibration of that sound distracted me again with pleasurable physical sensations.)

"I," Grendel said, placing his hand on his chest again, "am a troll."

"Oh!"

I wasn't quite sure what to make of this. Thinking it over, it occurred to me that this wasn't altogether welcome news. Everything I had heard or read about trolls was pretty bad. The character Grendel in the classic Anglo-Saxon poem "Beowulf," after whom my present acquaintance was apparently named, for example.

I saw that Grendel noticed this reaction too. He said in a sad voice, "I see that our reputation has proceeded me."

"Oh," I said, feeling guilty, realizing that my experience with Grendel thus far was anything but negative. "I'm sorry," I said. "I guess I'm being prejudiced."

The big head tilted slightly and then nodded, showing a smile. "I really *am* a nice person once you get to know me."

I experienced a thrill at these words. Gazing up at this magnificent physical specimen, I told myself fervently, *Oh and I want to get to know you!*

It was this renewed appreciation of the troll's physicality that made me notice, for the first time, that there were small, irregular areas on his skin that were darker than the overall silvery sheen. I decided they were probably bits earth sticking to the troll's skin.

"I'll bet you could use a bath," I said.

"Am I dirty?"

I suppressed a grin, and the desire to say: I certainly *hope* so!

What I *did* say was, "Actually, I'm surprised there isn't *more* earth sticking to you."

The smile broadened, and at this moment I felt myself again *liking* the troll, quite apart from anything else. I realized I was beginning to think of him as a new friend—a friend with a beautiful smile (among other things).

"Oh," said Grendel, holding out his arms in front of him and looking at them with a frown. "We generally do not have that problem. It is just that—sometimes, it is something that the passage does."

"Oh," I said, not really understanding this. Faced with such beauty, I found that I really didn't care very much whether I understood the guy or not.

"Still," the troll said, his voice becoming even deeper (was that suggestiveness? I wondered), "a dip—would not go awry."

"Terrific!" I felt my heart leap. "I know just the place."

Chapter 4
Pool Party

AND SO, WE headed off down the deserted street. Jake, I noticed, had already accepted Grendel's inclusion in the "pack." He was sniffing here and there, exploring scents as usual. It was, I thought, an odd procession, me walking along the sidewalk, Jake exploring, and Grendel massively accompanying us both on the street itself.

Incredibly, we didn't encounter anyone—the trick-or-treaters had by now gone through their respective hoards of candy and were either in bed or, high on sugar, resisting parents' attempts at getting them there. And those who had gone to Halloween parties were still there. The adult and older teen gatherings would still be going on for some time, tomorrow being Sunday. What I was most concerned about were early teens who might be shooed out by the stricter parents. But we didn't have far to go, just to the end of the block and around the corner. There, two doors down, stood a house rather larger than those around it.

"They're friends of mine here," I explained as we walked up the driveway and around the side of the house. "I teach their kid sometimes—tutor him, you know. They've got a heated pool. They said I could use it anytime I want and bring a friend if I liked." I grinned. "So, I am."

I looked up and saw Grendel smiling down at me. "We are friends then?"

I felt my heart flutter and face heat up at this. Not only were his words encouraging, but his smile gave him such a definite air of gentle kindness that I felt myself melting again.

"I would like to think so," I said, after swallowing.

"Me too."

Oh, lord! For a few seconds I felt like I was floating an inch off the ground. *Me so happy! Me so happy!* In my mind I was skipping joyfully.

The backyard was completely dark, but I knew where the pool lights were. First, however, I checked to make sure no one was about. I was not surprised to see that there were no lights on in the house; the Philpot family was very active socially. I tried to imagine the sort of party they were at, and chuckled when I failed. It would involve cocktails and costumes, everything symptomatic of wealth, but I could picture no specifics.

Money had never been the point for me. I liked my work and was happy it had afforded me my present house, but for itself, for opulence—it just didn't attract. This was perhaps why I always felt a little uncomfortable with people like the Philpots—those who had a lot of money and for whom that was important. And, despite their friendliness to me—which seemed vaguely a policy rather than a sentiment—I always had the sense that they saw me as not their sort of people.

And there was another reason I didn't envy people with money. The Philpots' son, Bruce, the kid I had tutored for several years now, was rather messed up. He resented his parents' wealthy lifestyle, yet at the same time was fully dependent on its advantages—me as his tutor being a case in point. It seemed to twist him up inside. And, while I felt for the kid, I was careful to keep some distance with him.

I found the switch and turned on the overhead lights—which flooded the entire poolside patio. Then I flicked the adjacent switch, and the *pool* lights came on, their underwater illumination creating a beautiful, slightly eerie effect. Everything was luxurious and for once I was both very aware of this fact and happy about it. I wanted to impress my new friend.

The October night was just cool enough for there to be a hint of steam over the surface of the water. In another month, I knew, they would be closing the pool for winter. But right now, the warm water, with its clean, slightly chlorinated smell, was heavenly, and the low thrum of the cycling pump, which came on along with the pool lights, reminded me that any dirt coming off Grendel and myself would be removed by morning.

"Hop in!" I said, smiling up at my friend.

He didn't "hop" exactly. That probably would have sent about half the water out of the pool. In fact, he got in quite gingerly. In such a huge and virile person, I found this both amusing and strangely beautiful. Grendel began by literally dipping in a big toe. Then he looked at me and grinned.

"Go ahead!" I said, grinning back.

"It is warm."

I nodded and motioned for him to proceed. Keeping one foot on the fitted slate tiles that surrounded the pool, Grendel bent this leg so his other foot descended slowly into the pool. It stopped when the knee was just above the water surface. He looked at me and smiled, then carefully lifted the other leg and put this into the water, so he was standing in the pool.

I laughed delightedly.

"You make it look like a kiddy wading pool," I told him. What I didn't say was that the picture reminded me of my long-cherished conception of the ancient colossus of Rhodes that was said to have stood astride the entrance to their harbor. It had been an erotic fantasy, imagining sailing between those legs—

I was struck now with the idea that my fantasy now stood there, right before my eyes! To *swim* between Grendel's massively muscled legs!

Oh, my!

Grendel blinked his big eyes solemnly. "It feels—nice!" he commented.

I laughed again and motioned at him. "Well, go on! Sit down! Lie down, have a bit of a swim."

Grendel nodded. He slowly lowered himself into the pool, until finally he was seated *across* the width of the pool, his back against one side, his knees just at surface level. With his upper abdomen exposed, he just looked like someone sitting in a bath.

He began to splash water over his upper torso in a reflective manner. Where he was sitting, he was illuminated by the moonlight as well as by the patio lights, and so still had that silvery sheen. I watched the water run down over his massive contours—those cannonball shoulders, the jutting pectorals—where it fell in droplets it glittered like diamonds. I stood there, transfixed, feeling an ache in my heart more potent than the heat in my loins.

At last Grendel looked up and smiled.

"Will you join me?"

I thought you'd never ask! I thought, as I hurried to undress.

Jake, meanwhile, after sniffing around the yard, had by this time settled himself into one of the chaise lounges that were positioned next to the pool. He wasn't too keen on swimming even in summer, so I wasn't surprised in the coolness of this Halloween night he intended to give the pool a complete miss. He seemed content, however, just watching. As long as he was part of things, he was like that, content—and I generally made sure he was included in whatever I did, from the doggie beds positioned around the house, to his own special padded chair in my backyard.

When I was naked, I ran along the side of the pool and leaped into the deep end, holding my ankles in a cannonball dive.

When I surfaced, I heard Grendel's rumbly, deep laugh, which was wonderfully intoxicating, making me feel silly all over again. I swam toward him, feeling no fear at all. But, when a large hand rose from beneath me and lifted me gently into the air, I did experience a momentary thrill of terror. It was the sort one feels on a roller coaster, terror without any feeling of real danger. It was just unnerving, and I was startled by the action. But I was thrilled too. I lay there, securely enough, my ass cupped in the hollow formed by palm and fingers, holding onto the tip of his forefinger.

He lifted me up until his arm was extended straight up. And, looking down I saw below me his face, looking up at me, his mouth open in a wide grin.

For a split second, seeing those enormous, pearly teeth, I felt a spasm of real terror, for I had the sudden realization that parts of me would fit into that mouth very nicely—my leg, for instance; it would be about the size of a chicken leg. But I repressed a shudder and focused instead on those big pale eyes, which were regarding me with their usual intense interest—playful, I thought, but still—I realized I wasn't *entirely* sure what sort of interest it was.

The moment of fear and doubt passed, for my contact with Grendel's big hand communicated his gentleness, which was very reassuring. Besides, there was that intoxicating aspect not only in that touch, but in the very situation. A thought passed bizarrely through my mind that even if I *were* eaten by Grendel, that wouldn't be such a horrible thing.

Then, Grendel said, "Look out!" Whereupon he threw me up and toward the deep end of the pool. My passage arced up and then, after being poised high in the air for a second, I began my descent, finally hitting the water with an enormous splash.

I coughed as I rose to the surface, laughing as I swam back to my companion. There was still that erotic element to this game, and I was more or less fully hard at this point. Given my diminutive relative stature, however, this didn't seem important or embarrassing. The experience, more than anything else, was playful and fun.

I was ready for Grendel's hand coming up from below this time, and as such found it even more exciting (and erotic) than the first time. Instead of raising me above his head, however, he gently deposited me onto his massive chest, which was wet, and therefore slippery. When he let go, I slid and slithered down, onto his belly and into the water between his enormous thighs. He must have lifted his ass off the bottom of the pool, for I felt a passing contact with his enormous phallus. I was laughing as I climbed back up between those thighs. The terrain was a wonderland of masculine mass and shape, and I felt wonderfully intoxicated.

Grendel didn't help me this time, and the only way onto his torso was to grasp the large phallus—which offered me even greater thrills.

I rather took my time, delaying the point where I didn't have an excuse to continue holding it. And, during this interval, I quite definitely felt it swelling and hardening. At one point I was holding on with both hands—and squeezed, savoring the girth, as the skin tightened, growing to about six inches in diameter. And the head increased in size too, maybe eight inches in diameter, swollen into a wonderfully taut, majestic shape.

But at last, I reached Grendel's belly, with one foot pressing down against the upper side of the phallus root. I felt Grendel's hand gently push me upward, along the surface of his chest, until my head just below and to one side of his chin. My feet rested against the upper part of his thighs. All of this kept me hard as a rock and tingling with pleasure.

I tilted my head back and looked up at him. He had bent forward and was looking down at me. Close proximity to those big eyes caused another shiver. I saw in them a twinkle, and a second later he moved his knees apart so I lost my footing. I slid down the contoured slide of flesh, this time making a deliberate grab at the upward-curving phallus as I flew past but missing and ending up in the water.

I laughed giddily until my head went under, after which I swam under the surface, among those massive legs, in a blissful state of feeling enclosed and safe.

We continued this play for about an hour. I was in heaven, and Grendel seemed to be very much enjoying himself. And, as his phallus rose higher and higher above the water, I just felt my intoxicated delight rise right along with it.

WE HAD SETTLED at last into repose; I was resting against Grendel's chest, when I felt his body stiffen. A second or two later, I caught a sound, and tensed as well. It was a voice, someone singing. And it was getting closer.

As I listened, I decided there was just one voice, which was something of a relief. I sat up and looked round at Grendel, whose expression was concerned.

"I'll deal with this," I hissed, adding, "I think I know who it is."

Grendel nodded and, lifting me up carefully, deposited me beside the pool. I ran to the chair that held my clothing, and hastily put on my T-shirt, which hung low enough to cover my thankfully now-deflating hard-on. Then, gesturing for Jake to stay where he was—he had stood up in his chair but hadn't moved otherwise—I went around to the gate and through it— just in time to see Bruce Philpot approaching.

He was weaving slightly, and clearly drunk. When he saw me standing there, he stopped his singing and stared.

"Ken?" he said. He sounded confused, not surprisingly—and *very* drunk.

"Yeah," I said, walking forward. I was nervous, feeling the imperative of keeping him out of the pool area.

"Oh," he said, and looked me up and down. "You havin' a dip?"

"Yeah. You know your parents said I should come by any time for swim."

"My *parents*!" Bruce repeated, scornfully.

Oh, no! I thought. *He's in one of his I-hate-my-parents moods.*

But now he was looking past me, over my shoulder.

"The pool lights are on," he commented. "You havin' a pool party or something?"

"Uh—no—I just—" I floundered for a second or two, then caught myself. "Well, I didn't want to swim in the dark, Bruce!"

Bruce stared at me, then suddenly pushed past me, so before I could decide on a course of action, he was through the gate and into the backyard. I followed agonizingly—before realizing to my great relief that Grendel was not in sight.

Jake, on the other hand, jumped from his chair and ran up to Bruce, his tail wagging.

"Oh, hi Jake!" Bruce murmured, squatting down and petting my dog. "How 'r' you, boy?" He let Jake lick his face, and chuckled. Then, unexpectedly, he said in a bitter voice, "Dogs are so much better than people." And then I heard what I thought was a sob.

"You okay?" I asked as he stood up.

"What d' you think?" he replied, slurring and turning to glare at me. "What do you *fuckin'* think?"

I stepped forward and put my arms around him. He hugged me back, and then turned his head to nuzzle my neck. I gently extricated myself from the embrace and stepped back.

He was looking at me, his eyes bright with unshed tears, his expression resentful and miserable. He looked around at the pool area, then back at me.

"Why were you trying t' fool me?" he said angrily.

"What?"

"Like you were tryin' t' hide somebody." Then he added, "You know I had my birthday last month."

"Oh, did you? Right. Sorry! I didn't know—" I began to feel uncomfortable. I wasn't exactly part of the Philpot family, and birthdays were things they viewed as family events. They had probably gone to an expensive restaurant with him, along with cousins, aunts and uncles.

Bruce now shrugged. "Why should you?" His voice became markedly bitter. "I'm just the kid you're tutoring, righ'?"

I opened my mouth, but closed it again. I didn't know what to say.

"Anyway," Bruce continued, "I'm eighteen now." He paused and looked at me defiantly. He fumbled for his wallet and managed to drop it on the slates. "Damn!"

"I'll get it," I reassured him, and picked it up.

"Well?" he said. "Open it! Look! At my—driver's license!"

"That's okay," I said. "I believe you." I stuffed the wallet back into his pocket, and then, with a hand on his shoulder, said, "And—uh, congratulations!" I tried to sound like I meant it, but it felt false.

Bruce was again glared at me. He stepped forward and, putting an arm around me, leaned in and kissed me. I was so startled, I pushed him away without thinking. This made him angrier than ever, and as he staggered back, he growled, "That's righ'—that's fuckin' right'—push me away! Push me fuckin' away! All the time!"

His voice was loud, and I felt uneasy.

"Sorry," I said. "I was—just surprised."

He was silent, regarding me suspiciously.

"Bu' hey, 'm eighteen, righ'?" he said, and tapped his own chest.

"I know. And I said, congratulations."

He scowled. "So?"

"So," I repeated in a neutral voice.

"So!" he cried out. So, I'm no' jailbai' 'n'more—'kay!"

"Not so loud!" I hissed. "Yes. I hear you, Bruce." But I had a sinking sensation.

Bruce was now regarding me tensely. "I mean, tha's wha' you said, righ', when I—you know, 'trie' to start s'mething,' as you put i'? I was underage, righ'?"

"Yes, yes," I replied, feeling my gut tightening.

"Well?" Bruce stepped back and crossed his arms over his chest. "So—wha' 're you goin' t' do abou' i'?"

"I—uh—"

"Wha'?"

I lowered my head and breathed in deeply. And it took all my will to say what I had to say now.

"It's just—I'm sorry, Bruce."

"Wha'? You're no' int'rested?"

I shook my head.

"Why no'?" His voice was shrill with outrage and pain.

We regarded each other for a tense interval, until finally I sighed and said, "Because, you're—not my type."

Bruce stared, then moved forward suddenly and reached under my T-shirt, grasping the shaft of my cock. "Ha!" he said. "You're half hard! Don' tell me you—aren' attracted t' me." He put his face into mine. "'s no one else here. So?"

I lowered my gaze, further embarrassed. "I'm sorry," I said quietly.

Bruce was silent for a long time, but the bare honesty of my statement, the sadness in my voice, must have convinced, for he let go of me and stood back, turning away. He was, I reminded myself, a good kid at heart; just someone with parent issues, and the pain of the teenager.

"Well, 'sn't tha' peachy!" He went and dropped into one of the patio chairs. Then, leaning forward, he put his head in his hands, and began to weep.

I reminded myself that the kid was drunk, and I saw that as the determining factor. I went over and put my hand gently on Bruce's shoulder. The lad shook it off without looking up, which I expected—I thought I should offer the opportunity for him to do some rejecting of his own.

"You're a bit tight," I said, still gently.

After a pause, Bruce sat up defiantly, his enunciation clearer. "Well, why not? I mean 't's Halloween, right? Was at a party, right? I was *supposed* to have a good time!"

"I'm guessing you didn't," I offered.

He shook his head, then, quietly, "No. No' really."

"Well, you know, maybe that's not your thing. It's not mine either. I learned that years ago."

Bruce sat back and stared up at me. "But isn't tha'—?" He shrugged.

"What? Wrong? Expected?" I shook my head. "No and no." I sat down in the chair next to him. I summoned all my nearly-thirty-years-old wisdom and came up with, "One of the compensations of getting older is that you learn to accept yourself as you are. You learn that all the expectations of normal behavior are just that—norms. You should—"

"Learn t' be yoursel'!" Bruce interrupted bitterly. "Yeah, I know! You always sayin' tha'. You mus' 've said it thousand' times."

I bit my lip. "Sorry!"

There was another pause, and then Bruce leaned over and took hold of my arm, giving it a squeeze. "No," he said with a sigh. "Guess *I'm* sorry. Guess it *did* help, I mean, with the—you know—accepting being gay. It's just tha'—well, all the gay guys I know my own age, they love parties."

"So? So what? I mean, if you don't, you don't."

"I'm *trying* to mee' someone."

"You will."

He glared at me. "Says who?"

I nodded. "You're right. I can't predict the future. But I know you, and I think you're a really good guy, and I *believe* you'll find someone."

Bruce nodded dutifully, not looking at me. Then he did look at me, his face screwed up.

"You sure you're no' interested—" he gestured to himself, "in this?"

I shook my head. "Sorry."

"'m not your type."

"No."

He stood up a bit unsteadily and looked down at me. "Well, 'd sure like to mee' the guy who *is* your type!" And with that he turned and went to the patio door. There was a clink of keys, and he stepped through, into the house. I dimly heard him stumping up the stairs, and then saw a second-floor light go on behind curtains. Bruce's bedroom.

I sighed and turned to the pool, just in time to see a large head rise slowly out of the water at the deep end of the pool. For a moment I almost screamed in sheer surprise, *and* the image was frightening, archetypally so.

The motion stopped when the eyes were just above the surface. Smiling, I nodded, and the rising resumed, first the rest of the head, then the shoulders. It stopped when Grendel's pecs were fully exposed, the skin, especially the nipples, glistening. He was at the deep end of the pool, and I realized he was standing. What was the deep end? I looked at the number painted on the side, which said, *11*. Eleven feet deep.

The tableau was quite magical, and beautiful as well as erotic. I began to get hard again. But I mentally shook my head.

"We'd better leave," I said quietly.

Grendel nodded and began to walk forward, from the deep end, his giant form slowly rising up out of the water. This too was distracting. But I managed to wrench my gaze away long enough to grab my clothes. He climbed out of the shallow end in one step, and stood there, silvery in the moonlight, and so beautiful that I had to force myself to focus on the task at hand. I put on my trousers, shoes and socks, and went to turn off the pool and outside lights.

Then I grabbed Jake's leash and we went around the house and through the gate. The fact that we were headed back to my place, for "coffee," made my heart pound again. And I was fully hard under my clothing.

Chapter 5
Digger

IT WAS ONLY a two-minute walk to my house. After my encounter with Bruce, I was anxious not to meet any other party-goers returning home, so I encouraged a quick pace, which reduced Jake's sniffing enterprises. But he was sensitive to my mood, and knew something was up.

We were on my own street when my fears were realized: a group of three teen-agers, two girls and a guy, on the far sidewalk, heading toward us. I glanced at Grendel and suppressed a squeal of fear; I simply couldn't imagine them not spotting him—and reacting in a way that even contemplating made me shudder. The three were clearly on something—alcohol or some other drug—their exchanges mostly hushed giggles. As they approached, I saw that their intense self-focus had prevented them from looking over toward us—and I began to hope.

Just as they drew abreast, however, I caught a glimpse of the guy turning and glancing across. He turned back to his companions and there were loud sniggers, and the word "faggot." I had encountered that word before, living here in the suburbs, and had become inured to it—if not quite indifferent.

I employed my usual calming routine, reminding myself that such remarks were just ignorance. Sure, they knew or suspected I was gay. But so what?

It was only when they were well past that it suddenly hit me.

They hadn't reacted to Grendel, the fifteen-foot troll walking beside me—at all!

I nearly stopped to turn around and look at them but caught myself and continued to trot the remaining distance to my yard. *That* mystery was something I could worry about later.

We arrived and went around the side of my house and into the backyard, whereupon I collapsed in one of my own patio chairs and sighed with relief.

Grendel sat down on the patio slates and looked around.

"Nice," he said at last.

I frankly couldn't see anything that might be described that way. Most of the yard, from my modest patio to the rear fence, was largely untended—thanks my own preference for what I called "natural gardening," but which was really just a consequence of my not possessing a green thumb. The six-foot fence around my backyard was my single contribution, built so I could have Jake off-leash here. Reminded of this, I leaned over to where Jake was sitting next to my chair and unhooked his halter. He immediately took a drink from his water bowl, and then headed off to patrol the yard.

I got up and went inside, returning with towels. I handed a beach towel to Grendel. He thanked me and stood up to dry himself off with it, though in his hand it looked like a washcloth. It was entertaining to watch, however; he was very careful in wiping himself, besides which, it was hot, like one of those candid video clips of a straight guy in a change room (which I *never* watch).

It was during this that a penny dropped inside my head. I looked at his magnificence, and then at the back door to my house. I frowned. When he had finished and looked at me, I shook my head, pointing toward the house.

"You know—I don't think you're going to fit into my house."

The truth of this now seemed so self-evident that I began to laugh. Grendel looked at my house and back at me, and joined in, though only decorously.

When I had recovered, Grendel went over to my back door and peered inside. It was both comical and a bit disturbing, that image of a giant—sorry, *troll*—peering into my home. Undoubtedly, I thought, he could have gotten through the door, but only by lying on his side.

Turning back to me, he hesitated before saying in earnest tones, "May I stay with you?"

I stared in surprise at him. The question, coming after what I had just said, seemed incongruous. But I looked into those big, pale eyes and found myself saying, "Sure! Of course."

I meant it, too; there was simply no way I was turning away this—well, troll—he was too much a magnificent specimen, and sweet to boot.

My perfect man. The thought made me giggle at the juxtaposition of the undeniable truth and the outrageousness of the observation.

Clearly, Grendel would have to stay outside, then. I looked around my yard. There was the fence, but that wouldn't give much privacy for someone of Grendel's stature. There would be sightings by neighbors, who would then call the cops, and so on and so on—worse and worse.

I sighed and shook my head. *What to do?*

There was some thought I couldn't quite catch. But after pondering for some time, it came to me at last.

"Grendel," I said. "Those three teenagers on the street. They looked across and must have recognized me. Why didn't they notice you?"

Grendel nodded. "I suspect they were not looking for me."

I stared. "What does that have to do with it?"

"Well, noticing things, especially unexpected and new things, depends on being open open-minded. Those three were so much in their own world, with their own preconceptions and judgments, that they were not open to something as unusual as me."

"Judgments," I repeated. "Faggot."

"Please," Grendel reached out and touched my arm gently, "Do not use that word in such a way."

"What way?"

"The negative, hateful way it was used on you tonight."

I blinked and stared at him. "What other way *is* there?"

"Well, playful. And others. Words are powerful and wonderful things after all." He paused before going on. "For trolls," he said, "there are other words for us."

"Really?"

He looked at me challengingly. "Surely," he said, "you are aware of others."

Others, I thought, and tried to think of synonyms for *troll*.

"Oh!" I said after a little. "I guess—what? *Monster*? No, that's too generic. *Ogre*, I guess!"

Grendel nodded, raising his eyebrows as if to say, *And?*

"Uh—" I laughed. "*Orcs*, I guess."

"Yes. *Orcs*, from *orcus*—Latin for *hell*, and *orco*—Italian for *demon* or *monster*. It does suit. There is, however, another—"

I set myself the task, and at last came up with, "*Goblin!*"

"Yes!" he said, smiling. "That is considered a term of abuse by my people. And yet," he chuckled, "we play with it ourselves. For, it is not the word that matters, but the way the word is used, the attitude that lies beneath its utterance."

I was staring at Grendel now, open-mouthed.

"Wow!" I murmured. Then I added, "I guess it makes sense, the words used to describe your—uh, people." After a pause, I added, "Actually, I'm quite fond of words myself."

"That is, I think, a good thing. It is part of what keeps your mind open."

"Really?"

"Yes. I believe it is a symptom of that openness."

"Open. Open to what, though?"

Grendel chuckled deep in throat, which sent me shivers of pleasure through me.

"Well, you noticed me, for one thing. Even when I was—not that—apparent."

I nodded slowly, but then frowned.

"Actually, it was Jake who noticed you."

"Why not both?" he countered.

"Sure." I grinned and looked around, spotting Jake. He was sitting at the corner of the patio, keeping watch on the verdure at the back of the yard. This was necessary, I knew, to keep in check the occasional outrages such as visits from interloping raccoons.

"Anyway," I said. "You won't fit into my house. Do you have any suggestions?"

Grendel got to his feet and stood, looking around the yard for a minute or two before turning back to me.

"If it is alright, I might dig a cave."

"Oh!" I said, surprised, then added, "A cave? Really?"

"A hole, yes. I am good at digging."

I stared at him, then smiled. "Yes," I said. "I thought you might be. But sure, go right ahead."

Grendel got to his feet and wandered around the yard, evidently looking for a place to start digging. His enormous, naked figure was not as bright now, the moon having gone behind some clouds, but seeing him moving around my backyard was not only strange and beautiful, but something else too. Somehow, that felt *important*. It reminded me of a painting, perhaps by Goya, of a god, towering over a landscape, a dark shape: Uranus, the father of Kronos, himself the father of the Greek gods. The power of that image had always haunted me, and now here it was, literally in my own backyard. *Yes*, I thought. *Important. Profound.* I was pretty sure of that, for somehow, at some level deep in my spine, it felt true.

The word *archetype* hit me, then. One of Carl Jung's terms, wasn't it? I had worked hard at that single course in psychology I'd taken in college, and still retained bits and pieces of it. I wasn't really sure what an archetype was, except that I thought Uranus was one, and Grendel—he had something of that too, a kind of deep *oomph*. What he was in fact displaying as he moved about my dark yard. And I was certain that I would never forget this moment—watching him like this.

At last, he stopped. Evidently, he had discovered a good spot. He began to dig.

And could he *dig*!

I didn't interfere or offer my help, which I saw wasn't needed. But I stood by and watched as he used his big hands like backhoes, enormous fingers sinking into the soil with a strange ease, then lifting up an enormous volume of earth.

He worked steadily and efficiently, placing the excavated earth carefully to one side or the other. I noticed too that there were no back-slippages. The sight was worth watching. Just seeing his enormous muscles moving beneath his skin, it hit me how powerfully erotic such calm, efficient, and industrious activity in a male was. It made me understand why I had always been attracted to construction workers. The sight of a male in a hard-hat, provided he was not grotesquely obese, did it for me. Only this—this massive, magnificent and excellent worker, he was of a different order entirely! At last, I went and got a patio chair, and sat down to watch, as close as I could without getting in his way.

Jake, who had until then been watching Grendel work, now decided to get into the act. He trotted up to where the troll was working—on the surface now as he enlarged the hole he was making—and began to dig. Earth spouted from between his back legs as Jake dug industriously with his forepaws.

I laughed, and Grendel, looking up and seeing Jake, grinned and laughed too.

"Good work, cousin!" he said, and returned to his work.

Jake was a considerate dog, and only helped when he could do so usefully. That meant that when Grendel had enlarged the surface of the hole sufficiently and was digging further down, Jake returned to sit beside me, and watch.

In what seemed like a short time, Grendel's digging was so deep that he was completely below ground level. Only the loads of dirt that kept flying up from below betokened his continuing industry. This rhythmic action, the periodic flying dirt, was peaceful, almost hypnotic. I lay back in my chair and finally slipped into a kind of doze. And, although I don't think I fell asleep, my mind became peaceful and ceased its habitual turning things over.

Eventually, Grendel's head reappeared. I was immediately aware of his gaze and became fully awake. It was sometime later, for the moon was now in the west, near the horizon. When he saw me looking, he turned and moved to my left, rising with each step, as if he was ascending a set of stairs.

When he was standing above ground once more, he beckoned to me. "Come!"

I shook myself and got to my feet.

As it turned out, there *were* stairs—a set of wide, smooth, Grendel-sized stairs leading down into darkness. Grendel gestured and smiled. "Come see what I have done."

I looked down into the hole.

"It's dark."

"Oh! Yes. That is right. You cannot see in darkness."

I stared at him. "What? And you can?"

Grendel smiled and shrugged. "In a way."

"Oh." I felt a chill at these words, suddenly aware of possible hidden depths of strangeness. It was the first time, since we had been at the Philpot's pool, that I felt a distinct sense, quite apart from size, of Grendel being something other than human. But I dismissed these thoughts firmly, and said, "Well, I can get a flashlight."

I went into the house to retrieve it, and on impulse also got several blankets from the closet.

When I was standing once more at the head of the descending stairs, Grendel escorted me down, a sausage finger under my arm. Hesitant at first, remembering this was just newly-packed earth, I was surprised to discover how solid the stairs felt. There was no give at all, and there was no crumbling at our passage.

Down and down we went! It was the sheer extent of the excavation that really struck me mind. I didn't turn on the flashlight immediately; I didn't want to come across as distrusting, and Grendel's touch reassured as we continued down those stairs. After a descent of perhaps forty feet, the stairs ended and there was a floor. I felt it was time for the flashlight, so I turned it on and pointed it directly above me. Overhead was a broad archway. Then, turning the flashlight's beam forward, I saw an enormous chamber, just ahead.

I stared at Grendel. "How—how did you do that?"

In the light of my flashlight, Grendel smiled modestly. "I told you, I am good at digging."

"I'll say!"

We entered the chamber, and I directed the beam of my flashlight around, exploring its walls and ceiling. The floor was hard and about twenty feet square. Smooth, curved walls rose up on four sides. The corners were rounded as well. Moreover, as the walls rose, they began curving inward at the level just above my head, and finally came together at a maximum height of perhaps twenty-five feet, forming a smooth, shallow dome.

"Wow!" I murmured.

One thing I noticed, was that all the surfaces, with the exception of the floor and steps' horizontal surfaces, were curved. And even the lines of the steps curved in a convex shape across their width.

Most impressive, and inexplicable, was the ceiling, and I shone the flashlight lingeringly over it. Its height allowed Grendel free movement without bending to within a foot or two of the walls, and the highest part must be just out of reach for him, even standing on tiptoes. I shook my head in amazement.

"But how—?" I stopped, not quite sure how to put the question.

Grendel nodded and cleared his throat. "We—are able to—work with earth. We can—harden it when we wish."

"Ah." That explained the solidity of the stairs—and the ceiling. "But—how?"

Grendel Rising 39

"You would know?"

I hesitated, thinking about the strangeness that Grendel had already shared, but decided I did want to know. I nodded.

Grendel shrugged. "Spit. If we mix our saliva with earth, it forms a paste like clay, which rapidly hardens. It is a part of troll nature. We have a way among earth and stone."

"Huh!" was all I could say. I was impressed—and slightly disturbed.

Grendel sat down against one of the walls. Jake, who had followed us down, was happily sniffing around, exploring the room. I put down my blankets next to Grendel.

"I brought these."

"Thank you, but I have no need for them."

I laughed. "Yeah, but I thought that *I* might."

Grendel's eyes lit up with pleasure at this, and he laughed too.

I put the flashlight on the floor, standing on its end so it lit the ceiling, which cast light back, giving the entire room a gentle glow. I found the earth color comforting. When I next looked at Grendel, however, I saw that his skin was shiny with sweat.

"Oh!" I said. "Maybe you could use another bath."

"That is not necessary," Grendel said. "It will slough off, the sweat, when it dries."

But this was not something that appealed, and Grendel must have sensed that, for he looked at me questioningly.

"They should be asleep over at the Philpot's house," I said. "We could probably slip over and have another dip."

Grendel smiled and nodded and got to his feet.

WHEN WE ARRIVED at our destination, I saw that the house was completely dark, and the Philpot's car was in the driveway. Evidently, they were home, but in bed. It wasn't surprising, given how late it was.

We didn't turn on any lights, and when my eyes had adjusted, I found I could see well enough by the light of the westering moon.

We slipped quietly into the water, Jake again hopping up on a poolside chair.

Once in the pool, Grendel went to the deep end and lowered himself until he was completely submerged. I followed, and in the dim underwater light, could just make out his shadowy form. Apparently, he was *sitting* on the bottom of the pool.

I swam around on the surface, titillatingly aware of the massive presence below and wondered if he would at some point reach up and grab me. The prospect was a bit unnerving, but not really frightening. I felt safe with Grendel, I now realized, and that made a kind of glow in the center of my chest.

After some time, I dove down into the near-complete darkness. I reached out and touched Grendel's enormous form. When I did this, a low, deep sound began, a single deep note that seemed to fill the water. It was strangely comforting, and I swam several times around the unmoving form before having to resurface for air.

I repeated the dive several times, and the note just went on and on, so I began to wonder how long a troll could hold his breath underwater. Then I remembered how Grendel had submerged himself during my entire conversation with Bruce Philpot.

At last, Grendel got slowly to his feet—his head and upper chest out of the water. After taking a deep breath, he tilted his head back, closed his eyes, and resumed his humming. It wasn't loud and again I found it comforting. I swam lazy laps around Grendel, tingling with excitement each time I brushed past the solid masses of his form, particularly his swelling pecs and biceps.

Time seemed to have stopped and I felt utterly content.

But at last, the moon began to set and the sky in the east to lighten.

With a sigh I got out of the pool and began to dry myself. Grendel joined me, using the towels I had brought for him, one in each hand.

All over again, I found it enthralling to watch as he ran these pieces of fabric over the swelling shapes of his various body parts. I wasn't quite so sexually aroused now; the lateness of the hour had given me a kind of gentle calm in which the sense of my companion's beauty was predominant.

After drying off, we sat side by side on the pool's edge, feet dangling in the water. I pondered my intense reactions and concluded that partly it was the *size* of Grendel's every body part that caused them. The largeness seemed to heighten my awareness of their physicality, making it up close and personal.

Sighing, I surreptitiously adjusted the towel that I had draped over my lap. I could still get a boner, just being around him. I would just have to get used to it. Beside me, the troll looked very content, though I noticed he was examining his hands. I looked more closely and saw that there were blemishes on the pads of Grendel's fingers.

"What are those?" I asked.

Grendel closed his hands and shrugged. "It happens," he said, "from contact with the barrier."

"What barrier?"

"Oh, the geostatic barrier."

I shook my head. This answer made no sense, so I decided to back to my original question.

"But what *are* they? They look like blisters."

Grendel nodded. "They are, of a kind. As I said, they come from making contact with the barrier—the geostatic barrier."

"The *what* barrier?"

"Geostatic barrier. It is the barrier that lies just below ground level. It forms one of the defenses they put in place. Although it is basically a natural phenomenon, they have a way to enhance it—I do not know the technical means by which they do this, exactly—but they do it to stop us from coming up—like I did tonight. I thought I could make it through, though, you know—tonight."

My mind whirled. Each of Grendel's answers seemed only to produce more questions. Sorting through the words, however I seized on one point. "Tonight? Why tonight?"

"Oh! Well, because it is Halloween, of course."

"Of course." I paused. "*Come up*, you said. Come up from where?"

Grendel shrugged. "From the Underworld."

"Oh!" The word struck me so unpleasantly that I shuddered. I reminded myself, "Underworld" could just mean the world under the ground. But now I wasn't sure I wanted to ask any more questions, for I was experiencing a mixture of confusion and creepiness. Instead, I just looked up at my companion, who was now staring up at the lightening sky.

In the gray light, Grendel's form looked quite different now, not as magical as it had earlier in the moonlight. Its color appeared to be something between gray and tan; almost earth-colored in fact. But, as the magic diminished, something else replaced it, something still very pleasing.

"My God!" I murmured. "You are *so beautiful!*"

It was only when these words were out that I realized I had spoken the sentiment aloud. My cheeks began heating up as Grendel turned and looked down at me with those incredible eyes.

"Thank you," he said, and smiled.

I got to my feet, my face still burning. "We'd better go."

Grendel nodded. I dressed and called quietly to Jake.

Chapter 6
Magic and Numbers

We encountered no one on our way home. In Grendel's chamber he half-lay with his shoulders and head propped against one wall. I lay on one of the blankets next to him, and Jake made himself comfortable between us.

I didn't need to turn on my flashlight now, since the early-morning light filtering down the stairs provided sufficient illumination at least to see forms. We sat in companionable silence as the dawn light on the stairs slowly increased. At last, however, I asked the question that was uppermost in my mind.

"So," I began hesitantly. "Uh—*why* did you come up, then?"

"To the Overworld?" Grendel looked at me and then away. "Oh—I just wanted to see the sights. The sky for one thing." He sighed. "And the stars. They are as beautiful as I remember them."

Stars? I thought. The stars weren't very impressive here in the city, with the ambient light. I had the oddest sense that my friend was being evasive.

"What about the moon?" I asked him.

"*Oh!*" he replied, and in that sound, I felt all the reverence that he had shown, gazing up at the moon, and its effect on his skin, giving it a silvery, glowing quality.

I waited, but he didn't continue. Finally, remembering that line of poetry I had remembered, I spoke it now.

"Goddess excellently bright."

I cursed myself for not remembering more of that poem. But I noticed Grendel was gazing down at me, his shadowy eyes widening. Something in that, a sense that I had perhaps impressed him, acted as a stimulus to my memory, which had failed me earlier. It was like a spring being released.

"*Queen and huntress, chaste and fair,*
Now the sun is laid to sleep,
Seated in thy silver chair
State in wonted manner keep:
Hesperus entreats thy light,
Goddess excellently bright.

"Earth, let not thy envious shade
Dare itself to interpose;
Cynthia's shining orb was made
Heaven to clear when day did close:
Bless us then with wished sight,
Goddess excellently bright.

"Lay thy bow of pearl apart
And thy crystal-shining quiver;
Give unto the flying hart
Space to breathe, how short soever:
Thou that mak'st a day of night,
Goddess excellently bright."

Partway through my recitation, I had become aware of a low humming, which acted like an accompaniment, and when I finished, I realized it was Grendel humming.

He had his head tilted back against the wall his eyes closed. The humming slowly faded away into silence, and he murmured, "Oh, *yes!*"

I felt all fluttery inside. He lifted his head from the wall and looked down at me, smiling.

"*Goddess excellently bright,*" he repeated, his voice especially deep and heavy, filled with reverence. "That is it. That is it, exactly. Thank you!"

"Oh," I said. "I didn't write it. It was by, let me see—Ben Jonson, I think, in the sixteenth century, or the seventeenth. I forget which."

Grendel regarded me solemnly and shook his head.

"You did not write it, but you did remember it," he said. "There are three distinct goods in beauty: the creating, the having, and the sharing. I meant thank you for the sharing. I enjoyed it very much."

"Oh." I felt tickled. "My pleasure."

He continued to regard me with a new curious interest.

"You—understand," he said. "I think."

"Oh," I replied, not knowing what else to say, and not really knowing what he was talking about. But the idea that my friend thought I might understand anything that meant something to him—well, that was very welcome.

The silence returned, broken only by the sound of birds outside twittering their welcoming of the new day. I sat there, my shoulder touching Grendel's arm, savoring the warmth and tingling excitement of contact. My mind, meanwhile, meandered, and finally it came back to something Grendel had said.

Without moving, I said, "You've been up before."

"Yes. A long time ago." He added, after a pause, "It is not—easy."

"Huh."

Again, the conversation lapsed, until Grendel said, "You are cold."

"What?" I considered the point and realized, to my surprise, that he was right. I pulled the blanket higher, covering myself.

"Lean back against me," he said. "I am quite warm."

With that he raised his arm and I shifted, so I leaned back against him, my head resting on the side of his torso, his massive arm loosely around me. Jake explored the new configuration and settled in as before, between us.

This was much warmer, comfortable, and very pleasurable. I could feel Grendel's deep, slow breathing, and even the lub-dub of his heart. And his smell was pleasant, too. It reminded me of certain spices, mushrooms, and the good, earthy scent of the deep woods. All of these sensations combined to produce in me not just a sense of deep contentment, but a sense of gentle but insistent sexual arousal.

My thoughts meandered over everything Grendel had said and all that had happened tonight. Vaguely, I wondered why I wasn't more freaked out by all of it. Its impossibility, for one thing, representing a sudden and vast deviation from normal reality. It was, I decided, because I just felt so good. My heart, for the first time in—well, possibly, ever—was full. There was some anxiety, over what might or might not develop, but right now, in Grendel's incredibly powerful presence, touching him, I felt safe and—though I hesitated to even think this—for the first time in my life, *loved*.

I had one hand just resting on Jake now. He was curled up, apparently quite content. That was something too—Jake accepting this new friend of mine. I trusted my dog's instincts.

But now, I became aware of a change—of being watched again. After shifting my head slightly, I turned and looked up, and saw Grendel looking down at me, those big eyes filled with that interested quality. As our gazes locked, the ambient physical pleasure I had been feeling began to increase noticeably, becoming more sensual, and erotic.

I distracted myself from this by asking, "How do you do it, though? How do you come up through the earth?"

Grendel smiled. "We have—an affinity, with earth and rock. They are our natural habitat."

"Huh." I recalled the image of those salami-sized fingers sinking with apparent effortlessness into the dirt.

"And what is the—what did you call it—barrier?"

"The geostatic barrier. It is a layer, like the film on any liquid surface."

"Surface tension?"

"Yes. In a way."

"And you said you came up tonight, because it was Halloween. Is that right?"

Grendel nodded.

"But, why?"

Grendel's eyes widened as if in surprise. Then he smiled.

"Oh, yes," he said. "I forgot. You do not remember these things in modern times." He sighed and continued in a didactic fashion. "During Halloween, the barrier is weaker. Actually, during Halloween *all* barriers are weaker, but the one that counts for us, for me I mean, is the geostatic barrier. Anyway, it is weaker tonight. So, I thought I would try it."

"Oh," I said. "I didn't know that Halloween was anything but a silly holiday."

"Well, it *is* a holiday—that is, a holy day. That is what holiday means, and holy days are not arbitrary. They are special days, days when the rules change. But people in the Overworld, you have forgotten most of that."

"Okay," I repeated. "But—you seem to be saying that about Halloween in particular. What makes Halloween special—I mean is it? More than the other holidays? Or did I get that wrong?"

Grendel shook his head. "No. You are right." He gave me a quick smile. "And you are quick. Halloween *is* the one special holiday when the barriers are weakest of all the year."

"Okay. But why?"

He smiled at me as he searched my face. "You would really know?"

I nodded. "I always thought there was something—I don't know, behind the spookiness of Halloween. So, tell me!"

Grendel shrugged slightly.

"First of all," he said. "Fall is the dying time of the year, just as spring is the burgeoning time. In fall the various powers that act in the world are—quiescent, diminished somewhat."

I nodded.

"Yes. Well. I understand humans have set aside the study of numbers—"

"What? Math? No. Math is big, as far as I know—"

"I did not mean math, *per se*. I meant numbers as in numerology. Yes." Grendel smiled as he saw my incredulous look. "Numbers do matter. They are one of the principal modes of understanding the nature of things."

"Oh."

"Well, to begin with, four is the number of the universe: four points of the compass, the four seasons, four sides and corners to the most ubiquitous and stable shape used in human construction: the square or rectangle, and finally the four dimensions."

"Wait a minute! *Four* dimensions? Oh! You mean, Einstein's space-time, where time is the fourth dimension." I thought for a second or two. "Wait a minute!" I cried suddenly. "I took a course on modern physics in college—

there are four fundamental forces too, right?" I looked at my companion, thinking that perhaps trolls were not science oriented. But he was nodding.

"Yes. That is right: the strong and weak forces, electromagnetism, and gravitation. Anyway, the point is that four, being the number of all things, is essentially stable. But if you take from that a unity—"

"Three," I interjected.

"Yes. In that case you have a number that is, essentially, an incomplete four, in which the forces of the universe are *not* stable. It is this instability that makes three a magical number, a number associated with magic. Even in your myths you make especial use of that number: three wishes, three bowls of porridge, even 'three rings for elven kings.' Humans have understood the magical quality of three, which comes from the fact that—it may be put this way, at least: All things seek stability and, given that four is the number of stability; anything that is three will have associated with it certain forces—the magical element—at loose, free to act."

"But—quarks!" I burst out. "What about quarks?" I looked at Grendel. "You trolls know about quarks?"

"In a way. In fact, what humans call quantum mechanics is a kind of turning back toward the view that we have always had: things influencing other things across distance."

"Huh!" I had *heard* the term *quantum mechanics*, of course, but whatever I had been taught about it had pretty much gone in one ear and out the other—terms like *wave equations* and *eigenstates*. They made my head hurt. "Well, anyway," I said. "In that modern physics course, they said that, apparently quarks come in three—what are called *colors*—though the term has nothing to do with visual color—and that quarks form the fundamental particles by grouping in threes, so the colors add up and kind of cancel, like positive and negative charges cancel." I looked at Grendel. "What about that?"

"What about it?"

"Well, that's three, isn't it? In the fundamental nature of the world, or whatever? How is that possible?"

Grendel smiled broadly and nodded. "You have put your finger on something very important."

"And that is—?"

"Well, the property of quark *colors* is the singular manifestation of three in the fundamental structure of the universe. And, you say, how can that be? I say in response: what makes you think that the fundamental particles of nature should not have, in their very nature, an element of magic? Magic is a part of the world, after all, part of it rather than something outside of reality."

"Wow!" I murmured, then added, "Sorry! You were going to explain about Halloween?"

Grendel nodded "Yes, well. There are four seasons, four quarters of the year, and of these quarters, or seasons, it is in the third quarter, which ends with the autumnal equinox, that things are most unstable, and magic is more present. During the equinox as well—which means *equal night*, during which day and night are equal, the forces of light and dark are balanced. This is also a magical time, for it is in the twilight, sometimes called *the crack between the worlds* that elements otherwise constrained are set free. And so, in the evening of the autumnal equinox there is a weakening of the forces of stability; things get through."

My head was spinning a bit at all this, but that final statement made me object.

"But Halloween isn't at the autumnal equinox," I said. "That's September 21 or so, isn't it?"

Grendel nodded.

"This is where you might have difficulty following," he said.

"Numerology?"

"Yes."

"Okay," I said. "Fire ahead."

"Well, you were right about the equinox. But there is more. Once the fall equinox is past, darkness grows until the yule solstice in December—which is the *sun-stop*, at which point the darkness ceases to grow and the sun, and light, begin to wax once more."

I nodded slowly.

"In this final quarter of the year, there is a point in this darkening period, when one third of it has passed and then another third of that third—and note these are all elements of three. On this day, in the dying part of the year, in the evening twilight, the dying part of the day, all of the magical elements of the world become most potent. And all barriers are at their weakest."

"A third of the third of the last season," I repeated confusedly.

Grendel smiled. "Let me help. September 21, more or less, is the autumnal equinox. After that third quarter of the year, the darkness grows for the remainder of the year. But a third of that is roughly a month—thirty days, and a third of that third is ten days. So, you have the end of the third quarter of the year, the equinox, plus a third, plus a third-of-a-third—three threes, very powerful—on the fortieth day after the autumnal equinox. And that is October 31, Halloween, in which the *magic* associated with darkness, the darkening of the year, is at its very strongest."

I blinked. "Wow! It works!"

"And that is why," Grendel continued, "Halloween, at dusk, the darkening of the day, is most associated with *dark* magic. It is then that you have ghosts and ghouls, witches and dead corpses released from bondage and free to roam the earth." He smiled. "That, at least, is the myth. But in any case, these myths are appropriate, for it is at Halloween that the earth magic is most powerful, where stability is at its lowest, and the barriers between worlds, its realms, and various states of being, are weakest."

"Wow!" I said again but held up a hand. "If there's more then, that's enough for now."

Grendel grinned. "I warned you."

I chuckled and felt myself melt just looking at this wonderful person.

And it was on that night, I told myself, *that Grendel rose from the World Below to the World Above and surfaced—emerging through the front lawn of a house in my quiet suburban neighborhood.*

After we were both silent for a time, thinking about all that numerology and stuff about magic and barriers, I shook my head in wonder. "And we humans have forgotten all that! Wow!"

On impulse I reached up and gently stroked Grendel's chest, on which there were a number of surprisingly soft, pale hairs. "I'm glad you came up."

Grendel's eyes widened. "And I am glad that I met you—and that you—saved me."

I frowned. "You said that before. But I don't understand. You were just below the surface, part of you above the grass."

"But I was exhausted. I was—stuck. I thought I was stronger." He sighed. "I was wrong." He gave me another grateful smile, one that filled me with a warm glow. Then another thought came to me.

"But," I asked uneasily, "if I hadn't—uh, dug you up—I mean, what would have happened? Would you have descended again?"

Grendel shook his head sorrowfully. "No."

"Then—what?"

He closed his big eyes and said in a quiet voice, "If you had not rescued me, I would have been reabsorbed—back into the earth—I am a creature of earth after all."

"No!" I cried. I got to my feet and reaching out, threw myself onto his torso, my arms reaching as far around it as they would go. My head lay against a pectoral muscle, and through it I could hear the slow lub-dub of his heart, which right then seemed to me an infinitely precious sound.

Gently, very gently, I felt his large hand come down and rest upon me. This gentleness, juxtaposed with what he had just told me, brought me close to tears.

After a bit, I heard his humming again. It came through me from his skin, passing into my body, and this made it more intimate. I tightened my hold.

Eventually, however, I raised myself up and, after looking at him for a while, lay back down against him, feeling weary and sad and confused.

"You are very lucky," Grendel said at last.

"How so?"

To be able to see her whenever you like. You only have to raise your head and look up into the sky."

"Her?"

"Diana. Selene. Mistress of the Night. What you call—the moon."

There was something in the way he said *the moon*, that made me chuckle, registering as I did the disapproval of such a mundane name and concept for the mysterious and magical orb I had heard referred to as "queen of the night."

"Goddess excellently bright," I murmured.

"Goddess excellently bright, indeed," he repeated. "That is the first element of her."

"First *element*?"

"Indeed! And all great things have nearly infinite elements. They go, like the turtles, all the way down."

I laughed and turned to look at him.

"How is it you know all of these things—these mythological names, and the concept and joke about the turtles holding up the world?"

He raised his eyebrows. "How is it that I know and speak your language?"

"Indeed!" I said and laughed again.

I waited, but he only said, "Perhaps you take it for granted. That is indeed sad."

"It? Take what for granted?"

"Your proximity. Your ready ability to see her at any time, more or less."

"Oh. Yeah. I guess we do."

"That is too bad. I suppose, though, that that is in part the effect of the machine. It reduces true contact with the reality of your existence, your real contact with the world."

I said, looking at him with a new admiration. "Yes, I think that is true." Then, I added, "There still is some of the magic of the moon around, though. It comes out in romance—*under the moon*, that sort of thing."

"Yes," Grendel murmured, not moving his head. "Selene is a source of magic, deep and wonderful magic for all living beings—especially those in the two inner worlds."

"Inner worlds?"

"Yes. The world above and the world below, the Underworld and the Overworld, your world and mine. It is the light of fair Selene that works wonderful things for denizens of both worlds."

"Oh," I said. Then, considering, I asked, "Why moonlight, though? What about sunlight? I mean, moonlight is just reflected sunlight, right?"

Part of me was wondering that I was having this conversation of mundane physical facts with this improbable being while in his newly-built cave.

"Ah!" he said. "But that is the alchemical nature of it! The light of the sun is changed when it is reflected, as you call it, by our sister planet. Selene imbues this light with something of her own nature, transforming the sunlight, removing its harshness, imparting and revealing its inherent magical influence through the property of beauty—it might be said to be *cooled* by that contact—from almost intolerable brilliance into gentle beauty."

I nodded, but then was struck by something.

"You said *sister planet*," I pointed out. "But, I mean, that's not quite right, is it? The moon revolves around the earth. It's not a planet. Or do you mean that a moon *is* a planet?"

Grendel looked at me, his expression mysterious. At last, he shook his head.

"What? Do you mean the moon isn't a moon?"

He shrugged slightly. "Well, what is a moon?"

I felt a rising challenge now. "Something—a chunk of rock, or, uh celestial body—that orbits a planet."

"And a planet?"

"A chunk of matter that orbits the sun."

"Exactly!"

"I don't get it. Exactly—what?"

"Well, what you call the moon—Selene—does not orbit the earth. It too orbits the sun."

I thought about this. "Oh," I said at last. "I think I get it. The moon orbits the earth as the earth goes around the sun, so it orbits the sun too."

But Grendel shook his head at this.

"What? What's that?"

"Oh, I—" The big troll looked embarrassed.

"Tell!" I said before I could stop myself. Fortunately, the troll didn't seem upset.

"I was just wondering how it was that humans—who can *see* the moon—how they should know so little about it."

I felt my face grow hot. But I put aside any incipient indignation.

"Okay," I said. "But please, explain?"

Grendel nodded. "Selene and the earth both go round the sun, and they orbit each other as well. Therefore, both are planets."

I tried to make sense of this but couldn't. In fact, it took a while to formulate the problem I had with the statement.

"But that's true of the other moons in the solar system, too," I said. "You're saying they're all—sister planets?"

Grendel shook his head. "No. They *are* moons."

Grendel Rising 51

"What's the difference?" I could feel myself getting annoyed.

But the big troll merely nodded, as if I had asked the *right* question this time.

"The difference is that the attraction Selene experiences from the sun is greater than the attraction it experiences from the earth."

"You're *kidding*!"

"No. It is true."

"And that makes a difference?"

"In how Selene affects the denizens of earth? Of course! It has a profound effect on all earth's creatures, those on the surface and those below the surface."

"Trolls."

"Yes. And others." He paused, and then added, "And these influences, experienced in the nature of our being, are also present in the purely physical realm of mechanics. Selene stabilizes the earth, too."

I nodded. I thought I had heard of that.

"Brawn *and* brains," I murmured, feeling a rush of pleasure. In retrospect, I think that was the moment that I first felt myself truly falling for this big troll. Intoxicated not only by his presence, but by his very nature, who he was. I was filled with a powerful desire to get to know him better—in *every* sense of the word, including the Biblical.

Chapter 7
Carnality

AFTER ALL THIS intellectual stuff, I found myself brought back to an acute awareness of the here-and-now, the purely present and physical. I realized Jake had left the chamber and was probably on his chair up on the patio, keeping vigil against raccoons. I smiled at that, but my attention returned to the physical, which took both the form of actual touch and a kind of awareness of the massive masculine presence that was so near to me—something like the gravitational field of a mountain, which I had read was measurable—only stronger, and more wonderful.

The contact was reassuring and intensely pleasurable and I lay there, not wanting to move. I had closed my eyes and was feeling so content that when I felt one of Grendel's big fingers touch my cheek, I didn't start. It ran with great care along the side of my face. From there, it proceeded down my neck and the front of my shirt. I noticed how much better *direct* contact was, and so felt a strong desire to ditch my shirt.

Why not? I asked myself a moment later. Wasn't Grendel himself stark naked? And I had been naked around him too, at the pool—twice. So, I stood up and took of my shirt and, after only a moment of hesitancy, my pants, and underpants, until I was completely naked. It felt right. So, with virtually no shyness, I turned and faced the big troll.

He was looking at me with appreciation and approval and was smiling. I felt my heart melt as a sense of acceptance and safety washed over me. I climbed on top of him, then, and lay on my stomach. It felt closer, every inch of me that touched him, skin against skin, was alive with the balm of contact and the thrill of excitement. I felt his finger again, this time sliding slowly down from the back of my head, my neck, and down the length of my back. When it reached the curves of my ass—which felt especially pleasurable—it stopped and was joined by several other fingers. This delicious contact felt so right, so intimately provocative, that I became rock-hard as a result.

I wanted to do something myself, so I raised my head and, seeing one of his nipples just inches in front of me, I reached up and took it between thumb and forefinger—and squeezed. The fleshy solidity of it felt wonderful, but far more exciting was the deep rumble that began inside Grendel's chest when I did this. His moaning, or groaning—it was deep, and its vibration went through my entire body, exciting me further.

Turning my head, I saw that I could reach both nipples, and in another moment had both pert protrusions in hand. I squeezed them together, which caused Grendel's moaning to increase, so the entire chamber was filled with deep vibration.

Lifting my head, I saw his enormous face above me, his eyes closed. I reached up and slid my hands over the lines of his shoulder on either side of his neck and pulled myself further up his chest. At the same time, I shifted my feet so they rested in the spot where the top of the thigh met the abdomen and pushed.

In this way I moved upward until my mouth was level Grendel's. I did what I had been wanting to do for some time—I planted a kiss on Grendel's big, soft lips.

The sweetness of the kiss surprised me. It filled my world, stunning like an electric shock, but infinitely sweeter. And then his lips parted, and a gargantuan tongue slid out. I took its tip into my mouth and sucked on it. I had never been so turned on by another guy's tongue. Some of my excitement I decided was due to this tongue's size. But there was also the fact that it was Grendel's tongue. There was something of his gentleness in its movement and presence. He wasn't forceful at all, never pushed, though I wouldn't have minded that. Possibly due to our size difference, he was letting me take the lead, which was okay with me.

I raised myself onto my elbows, and then pushed down with my hands on either side of his broad neck, pulling my body up his chest. I felt my hard-on slide into the depression between his pecs, which was insanely exciting. I began to thrust slowly, forward and back, sliding my dick along his flesh, and was soon leaking pre-cum, which made the contact with his flesh deliciously slick.

I was close now, but I wanted to prolong the experience, and I wanted to feel *him*.

First, I shifted my hands, so they were pressed into the yielding hardness of his pectorals. Then, I moved my legs closer together, and was immediately aware of an impressive physical presence that thrust up to the level of my knees. I pressed my legs against either side of the shaft and could feel the hardness and heat of the enormous phallus. Though there seemed little I could *do* with it in terms of penetration, I had a powerful need to merge with it in any way I could. I wanted to *feel* every part of it, explore its shape, its size, as intimately as I could.

So, I spread my knees, frog fashion, to the sides and, pressed the bottoms of my feet against either side of the shaft. That was better. I could feel its shape better, and I shifted my feet up, exploring from its base right to the swollen, spongy head. The full realization was beyond intoxicating; it blew my mind and came close to blowing my load.

Why, the whole thing must be two feet long! And six inches thick!

I felt out the contours of the large mushroom head with my toes and decided its proud curves made it almost *eight* inches across! Even better, when I squeezed it with my feet and then felt the tip with a toe, I came in contact with the hot stickiness of Grendel's pre-cum.

This produced a rush of desire. I wanted—*needed*—a more intimate contact. So, I rolled over onto my back and slid down until I was astride the base of the enormous phallus, the phallus itself pressing up in front of me, the enormous head just over my solar plexus. This was shiny with slick pre-cum. I lifted my legs, pressing my thighs against either side of the shaft, crossing my ankles so I could increase the pressure. Right before my eyes I saw more of the pearly pre-cum ooze from the tip.

I gingerly reached down and encircled the shaft just below the head with both hands. With thumbs touching, I found that the middle fingers of each hand could just meet. *Amazing!* I put my arms around it and pulled it against me, so its heat ran right up my torso, from my groin to my chest; its presence communicated both massiveness and domination, the overall effect being almost akin to actual penetration.

My actions had Grendel moaning now. It was quieter than before, yet its deep vibration filled my body with a tingling pleasure on top of all other stimulations. *Almost there*, I told myself. *But not yet!* I wanted to bring off Grendel first, certain that the experience would take me over the edge.

I bent my head forward and down, until I was just able to touch the top surface of the phallus head with my lips. The scent was heavenly—deeply earthy—and when I reached out with my tongue and *licked* the top of the head, I discovered it tasted almost exactly like cream of mushroom soup.

And I *love* cream of mushroom soup!

So, I began simply to adore the tip of that huge head, rubbing my lips, my chin, and my cheeks against it—though this required really straining my neck—until the hot, sticky wetness covered my face. But mostly I *licked* the head, especially the tip, and sucked up the hot, oozing cum that was beginning to flow in greater amounts from it.

And this, I congratulated myself, *was only the pre-cum! What must the full ejaculation involve?* I felt giddy as I contemplated *that* deluge!

Now, Grendel began a slow thrust with his hips. I set my own movements in counterpoint, so the relative action was amplified. I clutched the shaft tightly in my arms and between my thighs, jerking down when he was thrusting up, and vice versa. The effect was that the shaft—*and the head*—stiffened and swelled. A flush went through me as I sensed he was close.

But I wanted—*needed* more!

Loosening my clutch and lifting my head, I said, "Could you roll over, big guy? I want you on top of me."

So, Grendel rolled over, holding me in place with an enormous hand on my back as he turned. Then I was lying on my back, against the floor, which was warm from Grendel's body heat, and with the massive shape of Grendel's body bearing down on top of me. He was, as I knew he would, holding most of his weight on his elbows and knees, so I wasn't made into jam.

The residual pressure was just right, considerable and dominating, but not uncomfortable.

I felt I was in heaven, completely encased in a world of male musk and hot flesh. And the most insistent pressure was Grendel's phallus. I no longer hugged it; I had no need to: it now pressed down, against me, insistent and exquisite. In the turn I had been shifted up slightly. And I had to lower my legs, but still I could feel the lower part of the phallus between my thighs—which was just where it was most welcome. It pushed against the side of my own engorged and tingling cock, and up my belly. Reaching down, I could squeeze the mushroom head from either side, the sensation of its swollen girth so wonderfully intoxicating that, with the sense of being physically dominated, I was on the brink of cumming.

I had been holding off deliberately. But, when Grendel began a slow thrusting of his hips, I knew that I would shortly reach the point of no return. Though I murmured to myself, "Never let this end—please, never let this end," I felt the heat of orgasm rising in me, and the increase in tautness of Grendel's phallus at the same time.

As an enormous groan echoed through the chamber, I felt my cock explode, my veins filling with butter as ecstasy overcame me. And thick wads of heavy cum shoot up from the head, in the narrow space between our two torsos, and literally into my face.

I cried out as my orgasm continued, in a euphoric ululation.

And Grendel's seed kept coming, until I began to think I might drown in the stuff. But all I could think was, *What a way to go!*

I surrendered even to that but needn't have worried. I turned my head—first one way, then the other, so as the spunk began to slow my entire face and neck were covered with the thick seed. I also had my mouth open and was imbibing as much of the stuff as I could.

Then I sank into a post-coital bliss in which I floated for some time. Grendel, though he did raise his body off mine entirely, seemed disinclined to roll away. I didn't mind this in the least, and found myself filled with a desire—indeed, almost a *need*—to take in more of his seed. I ran my hands over his skin and my own, gathering up the thick substance and licking it off my fingers and palms. The more I swallowed, it seemed, the more my desire increased. When I came to the end of what could be salvaged—which must have been half a cup at least—I began to feel something else: a lessening of desire and an increase in feeling, in some way, *filled*. For a little I had the startling idea that I might be experiencing a kind of pregnancy, but finally decided it was more just a feeling of being full—but with unusual attendant qualities.

Strange sensations moved through my body. Subtle but definite. They were not sexual, nor were they in any way unpleasant. Just odd. The idea of toxicity I quickly dismissed; it just didn't feel like that; it didn't feel bad. Quite the opposite. It felt—stimulating. I chuckled at the idea that if I *were* being poisoned by Grendel's cum, there were worse ways to go.

Aside from this, I felt completely contented. I didn't want to move, and Grendel apparently didn't want to move either. So, we remained like this for long, peaceful long minutes. It was only with an awareness that Grendel was must be getting tired of suspending himself on his elbows and knees, that I felt motivated to move.

I shifted slightly, stuck my head out one side of Grendel's torso, and said, "How about you get on your side, big guy? Be more comfortable."

So, Grendel rolled onto his side, and after some shifting, we lay together, spoon fashion, my back against Grendel's chest and belly, and with the enormous, semi-erect phallus trapped between my legs.

It *was* more comfortable, and I felt more content than ever. I relaxed completely and was starting to drift off when I heard a low rumbling. Grendel was snoring. It was a pleasant sound, comforting and just a little exciting—reminiscent of Grendel's earlier state of excitement, and of his deep, resonant voice.

I lay there, my thoughts wandering lazily. I had never had sex like this before, and it occurred to me that I had discovered my "type." While I had tended to attract smaller guys and had taken some kind of satisfaction in being their "big guy"—there *never* had been this sort of excitement and fulfillment. Given the limitations of human size, I had never seen a guy larger than me that I felt attracted in the sense of wanting to be physically dominated in this way. Now I realized how *much* bigger my type really was.

Incredible!

I thought of Grendel, his story and nature, and the current situation. I chuckled contentedly and began to sink blissfully toward sleep.

My very last thought as I drifted off was to wonder what a future with this wonderful giant male might be like.

Chapter 8
G-man

I WOKE TO see a warm glow on the earthy ceiling that arched high over me. Blinking through a moment of disorientation, I then rolled onto my side, and saw that sunshine was pouring down the entrance stairs of this chamber, onto the floor just in front of me. Lifting my head, I saw that I had been lying with my head resting on one of Grendel's arms. He was lying on his back, his enormous bulk peaceful and reassuring as his chest slowly rose and fell.

As I rolled back in my previous position, my shoulder brushed the curve of his hip. The touch was comfortingly warm, a pleasurable reminder of the excitement I had experienced the previous night.

I lay there, going over the events of that strange evening, and was aware, of the curious complete lack of freak-out over the practical impossibility of every part of it. Instead, I felt an almost smug level of contentedness. I looked over at the giant form again and smiled.

Perhaps, I thought, the ineluctable physical presence of the fifteen-foot hunk was what overwhelmed any consideration of "impossibility." He was simply too *big*, too warm, and too—too wonderful, to be anything but undeniably real. I breathed in deeply, took in his scent—and sighed. That too. Everything, really—everything that cried out his vast presence had a magic of its own, a magic that dominated all of my emotional and cognitive processes.

I chuckled at the thought and quietly got to my feet. Finding my discarded clothes, I dressed hurriedly, and then turned toward the stairs. Jake was standing at the top, wagging his tail. Turning, I took one last look at the sleeping troll, imbibed the dollop of joy and love this produced, and then ascended into my backyard.

"Sorry, boy!" I said, petting him. Judging by the sun, it was around noon, and that meant that Jake had not had his morning walk. On the other hand, I reflected, Jake didn't sleep outside either, so maybe I was not being too derelict in my actions.

I went inside, fed Jake, and then showered. Finally, putting on a bathrobe, I went to retrieve the paper from the front step—where I got an unwelcome surprise.

"Howdy, Ken!"

It was my neighbor, Mr. Henderson, who was trimming the shrubs in his front yard. He wasn't usually that friendly, and I had learned a sunny hello generally meant he wanted to air a grievance—at me, or another of our neighbors.

"You know," he said, his voice now almost *offensively* sunny, "that's quite an excavation you got in your backyard. Funny I never noticed it before. You going to install a pool or something?"

It felt like a brick hitting me in the face. Of *course*, that sort of thing would be noticed! I groaned inwardly and suppressed a stab of panic.

I nodded. "Yeah, something like that." I tried to sound dismissive.

"*Something* like that! Well, what *are* you doing? Do tell! You know, I didn't see a building permit in your front window. Funny, that."

I nodded and forced a kind of grin. "Actually, it's in the works. I got the go-ahead, but there's a foul-up with the permit at city hall. Anyway, so far, I've just been digging. No permit is needed for that."

"Okay," he nodded. "But what's it going to be?"

Still keeping my smile, I said, "You'll see." Then added, "It's a surprise."

The man frowned and shook his head. "Well, whatever it is, I hope it won't affect my property values." Then he turned away to start on another bush. I went back inside.

Back in my kitchen, I made coffee. Whatever else happened, I decided, I did owe Grendel a coffee. I had promised after all. But I was unsure of how large a coffee a fifteen-foot troll would want, so I just made the maximum my coffee maker would hold.

Jake had finished off his own breakfast and was now standing in the back door, looking through the screen door at the yard. I smiled, looking down at him. He had been so good, not getting in the way earlier. He didn't like being excluded, and I didn't like shutting him out, so I had taught him that he could be present when I played with someone, but he had to be quiet and not get onto the bed. Though admittedly there hadn't been more than a couple of those occasions.

I got my own coffee mug out and then, after some consideration, got a mixing bowl on a plate. All of these I put on a serving tray, along with cream and sugar. Pouring the coffee into both "cups," I carried the tray out into the back yard.

When I arrived in Grendel's chamber, he was just waking, blinking his large eyes, and looking sleepy, cuddly, and adorable.

"I brought coffee," I said. "Remember? I promised you coffee last night?"

"Yeah," he said, slowly nodding. "We kind of got side-tracked."

We both laughed at that, and I put the tray down on a blanket. "Cream and sugar?"

Grendel shook his head. I proffered the bowl, which he took from me gingerly.

"It is good," he said after taking a sip. "Thank you."

"Oh, you're welcome." I took a sip of my own coffee and sat down—against Grendel's side, again savoring the warmth and sense of contact with him.

"A neighbor was asking about the hole in my backyard," I said casually.

"Oh."

"I'm wondering what they'll do if they see you." I tried to keep my voice casual. "Call the cops, probably."

Grendel sipped carefully from his bowl before saying, "Actually, I am not that easy to see—here, above ground."

"What?" I stared at him. Then I remembered what he had said the previous night with those three teenagers on the street. "Is that what you meant, about people not noticing you?"

He looked uneasy and gave a guilty smile. "It is something of that, but something more than that."

"More. How?"

"I can—influence—suppress the noticing."

"Oh."

We sipped our coffees in silence, and when we had finished, I asked, "Would you like some breakfast?"

"Oh. Well. Thank you."

"What would you like?"

Grendel shrugged. "I am not fussy."

I considered this. "How about bacon and eggs?"

He hesitated but then smiled. "Oh yes, please—if you have enough to go around."

"No problem." I went back into the house, got dressed in sweatpants and shirt, and drove to the local Seven-Eleven. I had to guess at amounts but figuring ten times what a human would eat sounded about right. I bought three dozen eggs, three pounds of bacon, and two loaves of bread.

As I was driving home, I looked at these supplies and the thought crossed my mind that this could get expensive. Immediately, I felt annoyed with myself. Hadn't last night's experience been the best, the most wonderful time I'd ever had? And there were those feelings beginning, the hope for something more. Even thinking about him now was giving me a hard-on. And yet here I was, worrying about *money*? I shook my head and sighed. Then I chuckled. After all, there were plenty of *other* things to worry about in this potential relationship!

We ate breakfast in his chamber, and I was pleasantly surprised to discover my guest had impeccable manners. Grendel handled with amazing dexterity what must, for him, have been *very* tiny utensils. It was only afterwards, when we were having a second coffee, that I began to think it might be time to ask some questions.

I shifted my position so I could look at him but was distracted by a sense of how uncomfortable my clothes were. And now that I thought about it, I had been having the same sense ever since getting up today. Momentarily I toyed with the idea that Grendel's glorious nakedness was making me less tolerant of the constrictions of clothes in general, but upon reflection I discarded that. No. It was more than merely subjective.

I looked at myself, frowning. I held out an arm out, and then a leg. Surely both garments had shrunk by several inches in leg and sleeve.

I picked at the fabric, irritated.

"I don't know what's happened," I murmured, pulling down on the sleeves, "Could I have shrunk these in the wash?"

Grendel chuckled, and I turned to look at him.

"What?"

He was smiling albeit slightly nervously. "They have not shrunk. It is the effect of my—well—seed."

"*What!*"

"It changes the—physiognomy." He gave a sheepish grin. "And, if you—consume more, the effect will increase."

I stared at the troll. "Do you mean," I said, my voice hoarse, "that I'm turning into a—well—like you?"

"You mean, into a troll?"

I nodded.

Grendel shook his head. "It is not like that. You are being affected in the sense that your Underworld self—the seed of that which rests in all humans—is growing. And, if you continue to consume more of my seed, this growth will continue, until you are fully what might be called the *Underworld Ken*. A demi-troll, if you like. I am sorry, I should have warned you."

I stared at him, speechless. Then I got to my feet. "Wait here," I said, and ran up the stairs.

In the house, I stood against the wall and marked the spot with a pencil. Then I got out the tape measure. Six-foot-three! I had grown *three inches!*

"Wow!"

"I am sorry," Grendel said when I returned to the cavern and shared the news. "I really should have warned you. Only, I was not thinking very well last night."

I laughed and, stepping forward, stood on tiptoe to kiss Grendel tenderly. "Neither was I."

Having reseated myself comfortably against him, I said, "Do—uh, trolls come up very often?"

Grendel shook his head. "Not anymore. Not since they—the human authorities—strengthened the geostatic barrier."

"When was that?"

"About a hundred years ago. Michael Faraday, I think, was one of the humans involved in that. He discovered the geostatic field."

"What are you saying? That you came up before that?"

"Once, but that was long ago, when I was very young. And, it was never—easy."

By *you*, I had meant trolls in general, but I realized with a sudden shock that Grendel had referred to a visit *he* had done *before* Faraday's time.

"You're that old?" I murmured. Then I giggled and said, "Funny, you don't look a day over a hundred."

"I am not that old for a troll. We live—a long time." Surprisingly, when he said this, he looked sad and shook his head slowly.

"Is that a bad thing?"

"What?" Grendel started. "Oh—well, it is just that—living without love that long, well it seems a very long time indeed."

"I don't understand," I said. "What about other trolls?"

Grendel's face looked even sadder. He shook his head again. "I am, not quite like other trolls. I am a romantic, a dreamer. I have longed to find a mate among the Overworlders."

"You mean humans?"

When Grendel nodded, I felt a thrill of excitement.

"It is not common, either, to find a—human, who is, well, interested in my kind—in the *romantic* way. Someone who is—suitable for love."

Suitable. I stared at the big face and felt a thrill of hope combined with fear bursting inside me. It was like a case of severe butterflies. But maybe I wasn't "suitable." Maybe I was just a "trick" for Grendel. A casual encounter, something to cast away. I shook my head to dispel such negative thoughts.

"Well," I said, "it's lucky we found each other then." Immediately, aware that I had taken a very precarious step, possibly an overstep, I added hastily, "Because, I mean, I am interested in, uh your kind. You, I mean." I stopped. My face was burning, and I was barely able to restrain putting a hand over my mouth, so horrified was I at my babbling.

But Grendel just nodded, and I let out the breath I was holding. Then I noticed he did not meet my gaze. In fact, he looked embarrassed. Finally, after a prolonged silence, he said in a would-be casual voice, "What about you?"

"What about me?"

"How is your—love situation?"

I almost laughed out of surprise and nervousness.

Was Grendel really asking whether I was single?

Avoiding his gaze, I considered what I should say, but at last decided anything but the bare truth was an impossibility—the very *idea* of deceiving Grendel hurt me inside.

"Actually," I admitted, "my love life was never very successful." Reaching down, I scratched Jake's ear. "Jake here's been the only lasting love of my life."

I chanced to glance at Grendel and saw with joy that his expression was extraordinarily gentle now.

"Yes," he murmured, looking at Jake. "I see that love. It is—most kind." And he touched Jake with infinite care. Jake lifted his head in response, pushing against the big fingertip, and wagged his tail.

Grendel was still looking at Jake, when he said quietly, "Do you know why? Why you have not found love?"

Before I had met Grendel, I wouldn't have been able to answer this, but after my experiences of the previous night, I thought I knew.

"Yeah," I said. "I think so."

"May I ask?"

I laughed. "Well, it's kind of embarrassing, really. And I—well, just discovered it—last night, with you."

"Yes?"

"I think I wanted some guy who was—well, bigger than me. To really do it for me, sexually and—emotionally." And now I positively cringed at what I had said, how much I had exposed myself. I waited with hammering heart for Grendel's response.

He was silent for a while. Then he said quietly, "Do you mean guys my size?"

I giggled. "Do I have to say it? I mean, after last night?"

Grendel nodded solemnly. Yet, a moment later something in this, representing a kind of innocent openness—especially in someone so vast—well, it melted my heart all over again, and quieted my anxieties. If *he* was so open, how could I *not* respond in kind—no matter the dangers it might create for my own feelings.

Looking up at him, I smiled. "Man—last night you—uh," I searched for an over-the-top phrase, "fucking rocked my world!" And a moment later I added, suddenly and surprisingly mortified at my casual use of profanity, "Sorry!"

Grendel chuckled at this, but then tilted his head to one, and said, "It is a pity."

"A pity? About what?"

"Size," he said simply. "Of course, I do not know whether you mean size generally, or—specifically."

Specifically?

This puzzled me, but at last I *thought* I saw what he meant. My face started to burn. "Well, both, actually," I managed to get out. "Both are—well, wonderful." Then I frowned. "But what was that about it being a pity?"

"Oh." He hesitated and looked away.

"Your 'fucking rock your world,' as you put it,'" he said. "I would like that, to rock it in that particular way."

I frowned, confused. What was he talking about? And I cringed at his repeating the profanity I had used. He was looking at me again, and there was something uncertain in his eyes.

"But," I said, speaking slowly, "You did."

He shook his head. "No. I mean—*that*, that word."

Word? What word? Again, I felt at sea. I looked at him expectantly, not wanting to ask that question and convinced whatever I would say would just make things more confused, anyway.

He shrugged. "It is sad," he said quietly, "that I cannot—you know—fuck you." His use of the f-word was so delicate that I almost laughed. *What a refined sensibility for such an enormous physique!*

A moment later, it hit me. "*Oh!*" My mouth fell open and there was a tingling of mixed emotions passing through me, all intense and some of them physical—sexual, I mean.

I licked my lips and simply spoke the question that was uppermost in my mind. He had said so, but somehow, I wanted confirmation of this important point, "And you'd like to?"

He smiled and nodded. "It is the most profound form of physical bonding—actual penetration."

His use of that last word gave me a rush of sexual excitement.

"I—would like that too," I told him, throwing myself against him. His arms came around me and I felt the wonderful sense of closeness and protection, as well as love. *Yes*, I told myself firmly, *I can admit that now.*

But another part of me replied instantly, *But maybe you're not* suitable. And I had to admit that I still didn't know what that entailed and was too timorous to ask at this point.

And then, incongruously, the memory came back, of my neighbor's interest in this excavation. I murmured, "But what are we going to do?"

"There are other ways to make love," Grendel replied. "We proved that last night."

I laughed and ran my hand deliciously over his skin. "Yeah. But I meant, what to do about my neighbors?"

Grendel nodded. "I must stay hidden. There are limits to my ability to remain unnoticed."

I thought of this and nodded too. "Well, you can stay here as long as you want," I said in a determined voice.

But at this, Grendel shook his head. "No. There is a government agency that keeps track of ruptures in the geostatic field. They will have registered my coming up. They will send agents—G-men as I think you call them."

"Oh," I said, and then, with horror, "*Oh!*"

"I must leave here, soon. Not immediately. It will take at least three days to discover the location of the rupture. Then they will come."

"Leave?" I felt a knot form in my stomach as I felt my world come apart.

We looked at each other. Then Grendel reached out and took my hand gently in his. "You could come with me."

I blinked in surprise; the idea was so outrageous. Did I really want—was I *willing*, in fact—to leave my comfortable home and my successful business for a life on the run—with a troll? For a few desperate seconds the thought came that I might work from wherever I was, using a laptop. That would take some effort—gathering up all my records, back-ups; and then there was the issue of receiving cheques. This was done electronically, to my bank account. That could be done okay, but the G-men or whoever they were would soon gain access to my accounts, and possibly freeze my assets or track me to wherever I was.

Undeniably, that sort of lifestyle didn't sound attractive to me. Then I looked at Grendel, who was watching me uneasily, and *that* at last did it. My heart melted completely, and I hardened a bit too. Somehow, I thought, I would make it work.

I smiled at him, then said, "What about a wash? I had a shower inside."

He looked a little disappointed but nodded.

"You could bring me some water and a washcloth."

I went inside and brought Grendel several large towels and a tub, which I began to fill with water from the hose.

"I'll get hot water from the stove," I told him. "I put two pots on high. I'll bring them out when the water's boiling."

Grendel touched my shoulder.

"Cold water is fine," he said. "I have my own heat."

"Oh!" I said, and then grinned and, leaning over his torso, kissed him. "I know you do."

So, I continued to fill the tub and then, somewhat to my surprise, Grendel requested to be alone for these ablutions. Then, I remembered washrooms also contain toilets. So, I left him to it.

When I returned half an hour later, I was impressed at how well Grendel cleaned up. His hair was slicked back and his skin fairly gleamed. I found this very agreeable. *It's one thing*, I thought, *to like big guys, but quite another to tolerate slobs.*

Although Grendel didn't say anything about his actual toilet activities, I imagined something like the behavior of cats: digging a hole and then covering it over. I didn't want to ask, though.

I had brought out cream for Grendel's blisters now. But to my surprise, I saw that they were much less severe than they had appeared the previous night. He did allow me to anoint the spots, however, and when I had finished, said cryptically, "It helps."

It was now early afternoon, and I found I was quite hungry again. Grendel was open to lunch, so I went into the house and made an enormous tray of sandwiches. It occurred to me that my hunger might be related to my odd growth spurt.

As we ate, giving tidbits to an alert Jake, Grendel talked about his life and the history of trolls coming to the surface.

"We are still allowed to come up through special gates. There are several. But it involves an incredible amount of stonework."

"Stonework?"

"Oh. I suppose you would say—paperwork."

I nodded.

"Contracts and permits."

I nodded again. "So," I suggested, "what you did was—illegal?"

"To say the least. When *allowed* to come to the surface, we are highly limited in our movements, and forbidden to make contact with civilian humans."

I frowned. "Sounds kind of like—prison."

Grendel nodded. "Yes. It is like that."

"Wait a minute!" I said suddenly. "How come you know so much about human society? Prisons, paperwork, all that. The names of goddesses."

"We have ways," he said. "They are—not like your ways."

"Oh." I was surprised to discover that I wasn't sure I wanted to know these ways. It struck me that they would not involve technology—what Grendel referred to as *our ways*. Possibly, it was something I had never heard of, like his uncanny digging ability, the shine on his skin under the moon, and not being noticeable to humans above ground. I decided I probably wouldn't understand it.

And now Grendel began to tell me stories, little vignettes about life in the Underworld. The picture I got struck me as very normal, but simpler than modern human society. In fact, it sounded attractive.

The effect of Grendel's words, and the sound of his deep voice, was to make me feel more and more comfortable. And, with his presence, and the feel of Jake curled up against me, worries about the future seemed to recede.

I began to slip into a doze, and so never noticed when Grendel had stopped talking. I was only aware of his presence, his touch. And so, we both drifted off into sleep—sharing an afternoon nap.

WHEN I AWOKE, it was late afternoon. Grendel was still asleep, but I was made restless by a renewed appetite. So, I went up and into the house and made myself a snack, attended by Jake who, as usual, got some.

I was just finishing my meal, when the doorbell rang. I looked at the kitchen clock, and saw it was just after 5 P.M. Frowning and with an odd sense of foreboding, I went to the door and opened it.

A thin man with dark hair and pale skin was standing there. He was dressed impeccably, in a dark-gray suit and carrying a very thin attaché case in one hand. Unaccountably, the first thought that struck me was that the guy looked unaccountably small. His head only came up to the level of my chin. But so what?

Before I could figure out any of this, however, the man reached into his suit jacket and held out an identification badge.

"I am with the FBG."

"The FBG?" I repeated.

"The Federal Bureau of Geostasis," that man elaborated, then added, "I wonder if I might come in."

The words hit me like a kick to the stomach. My only coherent thought was that *Grendel had said he had at least three days!*

I almost said this to the man, but instead, partially numbed by shock, I simply stepped back and invited him inside.

Chapter 9
Troll Nature

ONCE INSIDE, THE man handed me his card. I invited him to take a seat in the living room. Before I had seated myself, however, the card fell from my nerveless fingers. I stared down at it where it lay, but I didn't bend down to pick it up. Instead, I looked at the man seated on my couch and—as if by automatic reflex, asked if he would like something, tea or coffee. I suppose I was simply too taken aback to think properly.

The man, for his part, was polite but silent; he merely shook his head at my offer and looked around—discretely but quite definitely. I suddenly wanted to shout at him, *If you're looking for Grendel, he's in a cave in the backyard!*

The blast of anger that accompanied this thought almost overwhelmed me, and I realized with a shock that my entire worldview had been changed; I felt hunted, simply by being someone protective of my friend, who really *was* being hunted. *By my own government!* It seemed impossible, and it was painful beyond anything I had ever felt before.

"*Get a grip, Ken! Get an effing grip!*" I tried, but a moment later I clutched at the doorway to the living room as a wave of dizziness made the room tilt.

The G-man immediately got up and came toward me. He even reached out and took hold of my arm at the elbow.

"Steady there!" he said. "You okay?"

I stared at him blankly, for the moment not even knowing who he was. I was about to reassure him that I was okay when, remembering the situation and why he was here, I pulled myself away from his grasp and stood, breathing hard and holding onto the doorway, glaring at the man.

He, to my surprise and outrage, looked at me pityingly. Shaking his head slowly, he murmured, "Man, you sure got it bad!"

Oddly, my indignation at this remark, and even more by its tone, acted as a restorative. Drawing myself up, I snapped at him, "What the hell does *that* mean?"

But the man only shook his head again. "Nothing," he said, then added, "Forget it. A purely a tangential remark. I apologize." And he bowed slightly.

I blinked at this. *What the hell?* If the man had been Asian, I might have understood the gesture, but this clearly Caucasian guy, bowing like that, came across like the actions of an affected marionette. And *this* thought made me feel just a little better.

The next moment, however, I recalled Grendel's bow when he had first introduced himself to me. The similarity struck me as darkly suspicious, like I had stumbled on a completely new world, one of subterfuge, brutality, and desperate deeds.

The man, seated again on my couch, now leaned forward and said in confidential tones, as though speaking off-record, "It's alright. It's a natural reaction. You mustn't blame yourself."

This communication struck me as so odd, that I laughed out loud. The man looked slightly hurt by my reaction, and a moment later I got a hold of myself. I still had no idea what this jerk was talking about, but now I really did not care. I sat down in my favorite chair and regarded my visitor with detached watchfulness. He looked back at me, and the result was that we sat in silence for several minutes.

After a while, I thought that if the guy didn't speak soon, I would be entirely within the bounds of politeness to see him out. I didn't really expect to get away with that, however, and I knew that I wasn't the sort that could deal aggressively with government agencies. I was simply a quintessential law-abiding citizen. I liked peace and quiet, had chosen my neighborhood with that in mind, and with that went a strong respect for, and deference defer to, authority. The old dictum: *You can't fight city hall*, was one of my basic beliefs. And the feds, well, they were just the city hall folks—on steroids.

At this realization I sighed, as hopelessness rose inside me. Just then, however, I caught the corners of the G-man's mouth curl up. *He was taking heart from my despair!*

That brought some strength back to me. I saw in my mind's eye the big, wonderful guy out back, cowering in a homemade underground chamber, and I thought about his probable fate at the hands of officials like this. And, in response, I felt something deep inside change, harden. It was like a totally new side of me had come awake, possibly the one that had I had felt stir when Grendel had stood before me, shining and beautiful in the moonlight.

In that moment I resolved to get involved, to figure things out, act effectively and without compromise. And the first part of that was to find out exactly what this man was up to—what he wanted, and then to talk the situation over with my beloved Grendel.

The man was still looking at me with a mild expression, so I guessed he had not noticed my change of heart. So, I felt I could take a little time to figure exactly what *had* changed inside me. It seemed important.

Clearly, I was in a state of some resolve. But resolve for what? I sat with the question until the answer came, and when it did, it fairly blew me away.

I was apparently willing, if not eager, to fight like hell to save Grendel—for the sake of what we had together, or for the possibility of that. And I was willing to *take it all the way*! The phrase, *till death do us part*, now seemed a battle cry.

Really?

It seemed so. For what was life, what was comfort and ease—without love?

And so, it hit me: I loved Grendel. And I was convinced I always *would* love him, despite my not being entirely sure about *his* feelings toward *me*!

Damn! I thought. If only I knew for certain about that. If only we had a little more time! It was *maddening*! Again, I thought about Grendel's saying we had at least three days. *Damn! This can't be happening!* But, of course, it was. I sniffed back some tears and clenched my jaw.

I wasn't going to give in to despair, and I wasn't going to give up that easily.

Frowning, I pushed aside further considerations, and decided to take the fight to the enemy. So, I leaned forward in my chair and said, "So. What is it can I do for you, Mr.—?" Momentarily I glanced toward the card I had dropped, but then returned my gaze firmly to the man.

"Benson," he said obligingly. "Agent Benson."

I nodded politely.

The man sighed and ran his hands along the thighs of his trousers. "Very well," he said, and took a deep breath. "Your neighbors have reported some activity in your backyard that they are concerned about. Do you have permit for what you are doing?"

The image of my neighbor came into my mind, but I pushed away the anger that came with the conviction that he was responsible for this—had at least started the wheels turning, ending up with this personal visit.

"A permit?"

"Yes—a building permit, perhaps?"

A rising sense of panic was making me angrier with every word this man said.

"Well, no," I said, with sarcastic emphasis, "I *don't* have a building permit. And that's because I'm not *building* anything."

The man's eyebrows shot up, but he said nothing.

"I'm digging!" I concluded forcefully, but then realized my words were ludicrously inadequate.

After hesitating for a moment, the man nodded. "Ah! And what are you digging for?"

My brain whirled for several seconds, and without foreknowledge, I heard myself say in an airy tone, "Well, I thought I might find oil—or maybe diamonds. Yes, that's it. I've been having some financial challenges lately, and I thought if I could only find some *buried treasure*—" My tone by this time had become heavily sarcastic.

But the man merely shook his head. "We have no record of you having financial troubles."

Utterly blindsided, I stared at the man, at the idea that this government representative had access to my personal information to that degree. I leaped to my feet, outraged.

"Oh?" I cried. "You don't? Well, excuse me! I guess I'm just a little *under-informed*. I had no idea I lived in a *police state*."

"Mr. Connelly, please!"

"And what about my teeth?" I continued to shout. "Do you have a record of how they are doing?"

"Mr. Connelly!"

"*Well, do you?*"

"Of course, we do!" the man snapped, suddenly impatient. "Your teeth are in fair shape, but there's a molar that's going to need looking at soon."

My mouth fell open at this. A wave of weakness overcame me and I collapsed into the chair. It now was appallingly evident this person, this Bureau that knew so much, was very, *very* dangerous.

It took me more than a minute to recover. During this time the man continued to regard me with polite attention. He had evidently recovered from his brief lack of self-control. I sensed that sort of thing didn't happen to him very often.

When I had more or less marshaled my thoughts, I frowned and asked, "I don't quite get it. Have I broken some kind of law?"

"That is what my job is—to find out." The man smiled ingratiatingly, and I found myself wanting to knock that smile off his face. *And* I was deeply rattled. I had never had much *direct* contact with officialdom; my house purchase had been done with the help of a lawyer friend. Now, I was finding my first taste being at odds with the powers-that-be *quite* disagreeable.

I thought of other law-abiding citizens, who probably shared this distaste for challenging "city hall." It was probably this that underlay their life choices, and *that* thought didn't sit comfortably with me at all. I had never seen myself as a complacent member of the "herd."

Yet, here I was, and all I could think of saying to that was, *Moo!*

I shook my head to dispel this deleterious train of thought. What I needed, what I *wanted*, was to focus on what I could do in the present circumstance. I set my mind to it, and was still deep in thought, when I was startled by the sound of a deep voice coming from the kitchen.

"You had better bring him out here, Ken."

I rose shakily and went into the hallway that led straight from the front door to the back door. The back door was open, and Grendel's big head was framed in the doorway.

My initial reaction was one of shock, unexpectedly seeing Grendel's head framed like this, his troll features looking strange and incongruous. Plus, his skin in daylight had a distinctly grayish hue. The result was that I felt a distinct stab of horror at my situation, this coming from a completely different direction than a moment before—from that of its sheer *impossibility*.

The thought struck me, then, that this sort of thing, repeated over a period of time, might make one go literally mad. In defense, I closed my eyes and shook my head rapidly, driving out the sensation and the image.

When I opened my eyes again, the first thing I saw was Grendel's face—his expression, and his *eyes*. Those large, pale orbs were looking at me with such a depth of grief, of lost dreams—dreams that I had up till now joyfully shared—that everything else about the situation, the strangeness and impossibilities, became merely the background to the tragic sense of communion I now felt with Grendel. It was painful, but somehow joyful too, and it was in that moment that perhaps for the first time I knew that whatever happened from here on, our connection included *love* at its heart. That is, it wasn't just me: it was both of us.

And the relief that realization gave me now became my source of strength and resolution, all that underlay my ability to face the current crisis.

I turned to the G-man and saw that he had risen and was now standing just to one side and a little behind me, craning his head to peer around me at the manifestation in the back door.

I noticed *he*, at any rate, did not look surprised; not surprised at all. In fact, there was a look of smug satisfaction on his face that for the second time made me want to hit the guy. But instead, I drew in my breath, swallowed and, stepping back, said, "Please come this way."

At that point, Jake, who had been out in the back yard, slipped past Grendel and ran inside, barking at the G-man.

"Jake!" I said sharply. "Stop that!"

Jake looked at me, whined, and came to stand beside me. From there, he stared at the G-man and growled quietly. *Good enough*, I decided. I didn't want to chastise my dog for doing what I wanted to do myself.

The G-man and I sat across each other at my kitchen table, which looked out over the back yard.

Grendel, then, shifted his position and with some work and by lying on his side, managed to get his upper half inside. From this position his face and shoulders were visible in the opening that led from the kitchen onto the hallway. In this position he looked bigger and more incongruous than ever. (As well as, I thought, more beautiful.)

I sat in the chair closest to Grendel, facing partly away from him. The

G-man faced me, and therefore Grendel. I watched the man take a number of papers from his briefcase and lay these on the table between us. Extracting a pen from inside his jacket, he clicked this several times as he riffled through the papers. I said nothing, but sat with my arms crossed, leaving the next move up to him.

From time to time, as he sorted his papers, the man glanced up at me and gave me a perfunctory smile as if to say, "bear with me, please." He also looked out the window several times, around the kitchen, and down at Jake, who was lying on the floor next to my chair, eyes glued to the G-man, the barest growl still coming from his throat.

Something about the man's behavior bothered me, but it was only after watching him for a while that I realized what this was. The man *never looked directly at Grendel!* This I found very disturbing. It wasn't, I thought, fear; rather, simply aversion. But was that because Grendel as a non-human was viewed by this man as *sub*-human and therefore of no account? This was the only explanation I could come up with. The problem was it didn't feel quite like that. What it *did* feel like, I had no answer. Despite this, I still felt offended on behalf of my friend.

At last, the man tapped the top paper with his pen and gave a small sigh. He looked at me and said, "I am sorry."

I blinked, not understanding, but refrained from asking him *why* he was sorry. I didn't want to make this easy for him.

He looked at me expectantly, shrugged and cleared his throat. When he spoke, his voice was just a little forced, possibly because of the hostility directed at him.

"As you might know, your, uh, guest's—" here the man's eyes flicked briefly toward Grendel before returning to me "—coming up to the *Overworld*—"

He paused, and I was given a moment to note how strange it was to hear this new word coming so matter-of-factly from a government official.

"Well," he continued. "It is, in fact, highly—problematic."

"Problematic?" I said before I could stop myself. I had never liked the word and, at the moment I found it quite objectionable. Why didn't the guy just say things outright?

"It's illegal," he elaborated. "It's against the law."

I said nothing, unsure of what I *could* say. Something in me wanted to tell him that it was no law I had ever heard about. But I knew from my lawyer friend the principle: *ignorance of the law is no excuse*. And then there was Grendel's enormous presence. He made that sort of disavowal seem irrelevant.

So much for that!

The G-man, after looking pointedly at me for several seconds, shook his head. This set me off. Glaring at him, I half-snarled, "*Why?*"

The man regarded me with the thinnest of smiles. "You are probably ignorant," he said, speaking quietly and in reasonable tones, "of the facts." He carefully shifted one of the papers on the table, then sighed and returned his gaze to me. "It's a modern phenomenon."

At this point, I happened to notice Jake. He was lying quietly, next to my chair. Thankfully, he knew enough to stay out of things when there was some kind of tension. But he was always there, and alert, ready to lend his weight if it came to a battle in defense of hearth and home. Now, seeing him watching me, I was reminded I hadn't given him his dinner.

Dinnertime for him was somewhat flexible—depending on my own schedule. He would only remind me, with small yips, if I was more than an hour late. I glanced at the clock and saw it wasn't much after his usual dinnertime, but still, given that I was annoyed generally at this man, I felt that I would be *damned* if I let this put my best friend's dinner off one more minute.

Getting to my feet, I said stiffly, "You'll have to excuse me. I've got to feed my dog."

The man said nothing. I got out Jake's dinner from the fridge in silence. I cut up a raw chicken wing, removing the largest bones, and added some ground beef. Then I placed the dish on the floor, and Jake got busy.

Watching him, I sighed and turned to the man.

"Uh, I'm getting myself a Coke," I told him. "Would you like one?" I didn't want to make him something like tea or coffee, but I felt I really couldn't *not* offer him a Coke.

For a second the man looked like he would refuse, but then he nodded. "Yes. A Coke would be fine, thank you."

I felt a spasm of irrational anger at this response, but I suppressed it. Turning to Grendel, I asked, "Would you like some?"

Grendel nodded and I got two large Coke bottles from the fridge, lifted down two glasses from the cupboard, and a large mixing bowl. I filled all three, and carried the bowl over to where Grendel lay, making a point of serving him first. As he reached to take it, we exchanged a look of commiseration that made my heart jump a little. I wanted to kiss him but wasn't going to do that in front of the G-man.

"Thank you," Grendel murmured. I kept my hand on the bowl a second or two longer than necessary, so our hands touched. It was almost as good as a kiss, and he smiled gently, which made my eyes fill with unexpected tears. Then I turned, squared my shoulders, and carried the two glasses over to the table. The G-man picked up his and took a sip—but said nothing.

I sat down, holding my own glass but not lifting it. As I looked at the man, I felt a new wash of irritation. I couldn't stop myself from making a disgusted noise.

At this, the man looked at me, startled and confused. Then, seeing me glaring at him meaningfully, he looked down at his glass, and said hastily, "Oh. Thank you!"

I sniffed and looked away, taking a sip of my Coke. When I looked back at him, I saw with some satisfaction that he had flushed at his minor failure of manners.

Good, I thought, and though I meant this as a celebration of the G-man's embarrassment, a moment later I had to admit that his reaction also did suggest a certain level of decency. Though, how much *that* mattered in the current circumstance, I had no idea.

Thrusting all that aside, I put my glass down on the table and looked at the man expectantly.

"So," I said. "You were saying this—legal question—is a modern—phenomenon?"

The man nodded.

"Would you care to elaborate?"

The G-man nodded again and looked out the window into the back yard.

"You have probably heard the legends, of trolls, from old fairy tales."

"I suppose so. But those are just fairy tales."

The G-man looked at me gravely. "Actually, there is much truth in such tales. The old term for such tales was not in fact 'fairy tales,' at all—"

"Yes, yes!" I said, interrupting him. "They were called *fire-side* tales, tales told around the fire, part of the heritage of the common folk back then. But really! Witches, gingerbread men, pots of gold—surely those are just fantasies."

The G-man pursed his lips and shifted in his seat. "Well, in a way. The information back then, was—" he hesitated, looking at me cautiously, after my challenging display of knowledge "—well, symbolic in many places, rather than explicitly literal."

I thought about this and had to admit that the point seemed quite reasonable—even when a real, live troll (who by his size might equally be termed a "giant")—was reclining just inside my back door, only a few feet away.

"Anyway, the folk tales of old, representing as they did the wisdom of the various peoples, handed down from generation to generation—some elements were less symbolic, closer to bald truth."

I said nothing, but merely shrugged.

"Not that all of the details were correct. But anyway—" The G-man paused and licked his lips nervously, then breathed in sharply through his nose, "Trolls, were depicted as coming up, to prey—"

I stared at the man. "Pray? You mean as in religion? They came up to go to church or something?" My tone was scornful in part because I was becoming frightened—at what this man might come out with, and what the consequences of that might be.

But the man now shook his head. "No. I meant, *prey*—P-R-E-Y—as in *feed*."

I felt ice go down my back. This was the sort of horror I had feared—and expected. I stared at the man, who said nothing but merely looked at me, a trifle coolly, I thought.

"To *feed*?" I repeated, my voice a whisper.

The G-man nodded gravely. "But not, perhaps in the literal, flesh-eating sense. At least—" he again shifted in his chair, "not as far as we are aware." He coughed, and then continued. "They—steal the young of humans."

I felt cold all through my body now. I leaned forward, across the table. "But that's—just the fairy tales though, right?"

The G-man regarded me levelly, and then shook his head slowly from side to side. I stared back at him, my mind numb with horror. I wanted to turn and look at Grendel, to get his word on this. But I couldn't bring myself to do this.

"You're kidding!" I whispered.

Again, the G-man shook his head.

There was silence in the kitchen for a considerable time after this, which was broken at last by an unnerving, low growl, which made me jump in my chair.

It was Grendel, of course! I looked quickly at the G-man, and saw that he was looking frightened, his face slightly gray in color. Then I looked at Grendel and was somewhat taken aback by the fierce expression on his face. I had to admit, on a face that large, such fierceness was quite frightening, even when it wasn't directed toward me.

"You have not told him all, *human*." Grendel said the last word as if it were something dirty. *That*, I found disturbing as well. I was human too, after all.

I looked at the G-man. "What's that?"

The G-man was sitting motionless. Clearly there were processes going on behind those eyes, but I had no idea what they might be.

"*Tell him!*" Grendel growled.

Chapter 10
Rock Fever

I STARED AT the G-man, who had turned pale, but he didn't respond at first. Finally, he shrugged a bit uncomfortably, and shook his head. His shoulders had sagged slightly, and it seemed something in the man had changed—or given way. And the result was, oddly, that he looked just a little less odious now. Less official; more human, as it were.

"They steal," he said at last, "Well, from the data we have compiled—though the research is, as you can imagine, far from exhaustive—"

"*Tell him!*" Grendel growled again, quiet but menacing.

The G-man nodded and licked his lips. "Our research suggests that they—I mean trolls—take the children of people who are—well, disagreeable."

"*What?*" My head was spinning, and all I could think was: *Too much information!* How was I supposed to process this? A whole new world, and a complicated and bizarre one, too!

"But they do steal them," the G-man said defensively. "And—" his voice recovered some of its force, "*We* don't know what they do with them." He licked his lips again and shrugged uneasily. "There is no evidence of—cannibalism, if I might use the word for between different species—and they *say* that doesn't happen."

This, at last, was something I could get ahold of.

"*What?*" I said, outraged "You're saying that you don't *believe* them?"

The man said stiffly, "Not exactly." Then he added, in what was an attempt at a reasonable-sounding tone, "Look, we just have no evidence, one way or the other. We cannot penetrate—that far—into their—uh, realm." The man swallowed and, picking up his glass, took several long sips of his Coke. "They have—defenses."

"As do you," Grendel growled.

I turned and looked at Grendel questioningly. He, after glaring at the G-man for another second or two, turned and looked back at me, giving me a smile and shrugged.

"You are familiar, perhaps," he continued, his voice quiet, "with our cousins—the maggots?"

"Familiar? With *maggots*? You mean the *worms*?"

He nodded, and I shrugged. "Yeah, I guess I know—uh, something about them."

"You know, then, what they consume?"

"They eat the flesh of corpses."

Grendel nodded. "Do you know that they are used in medicine, on live patients?"

I shook my head.

"They are used on burn and accident victims, for they consume only *dead* flesh. They thus get rid of the dead cells, and this allows the live cells space in which to grow, to recover from the trauma that killed that flesh in the first place."

"Oh!" I turned back to the G-man. I wasn't sure what I thought this man might know about what this meant, but when I raised my eyebrows at him questioningly, he nodded.

I turned back to Grendel. "But what does that have to do—?"

"I called them *cousins*, because we, in some ways, are like them. But rather than dead flesh, we consume dead *souls*."

The G-man made a sour noise but quickly stifled it.

"Your fellow human," Grendel said, looking at me, "I am guessing, does not believe in 'dead souls.' Let us say, then, diseased souls—though the distinction between dead and diseased in the case of souls depends on what level you are talking about."

I stared at him, feeling quite lost. He sighed and looked down at the floor. "We live in the darkness," he continued, "in the bosom of Mother Earth, in the emanations of the Earth-power. We hear the rumor—of waves, the waves of life, as they pass, here on the surface. We are the gardeners, in some ways—we come up and—remove the weeds, or perhaps better, the dying or dead plants—those with diseased or dead souls. In truth, Ken, we take away the unloved children, taken them away from non-loving environments. We rescue them—from lives of misery, you might say."

The G-man's small noise of disapprobation was suppressed more quickly this time. I ignored him, trying to make sense of what Grendel had said.

"But the children—!" I began. "I mean, why don't you take the parents, the ones responsible?"

Grendel shrugged. "Who is, at end, responsible? And besides, the parents, they pass away soon enough. You humans live such a short time. It is the *souls* we are interested in, that which they have passed to their children. It is said, 'The sins of the father are passed down to the sons, even unto the third and fourth generation.' Well, that is true, in fact—generally."

"And you—put a stop to that?"

"Yes. We weed the stock. We are the farmers of human souls."

I looked at the G-man, whose face was a mask of disapproval. I was puzzled. Surely, if what Grendel was saying was true, the people who treat with trolls must know about it. Or was there such a level of hostility on the part of the government agency that it refused to accept unwelcome facts? I had less trouble believing that, than that Grendel would deliberately tell lies.

Grendel looked pointedly at the G-man, who resolutely looked elsewhere. Grendel's face was stern, reproachful, but not frightening. It struck me that Grendel *did* look a bit like a farmer.

"Your G-men," Grendel said, speaking to me but still looking at the G-man, "do not—approve of this. They resolved to put a stop to it." He chuckled grimly. "And in part that was because many of those in the upper echelons in power were the very ones whose progeny were treated heartlessly. But they had power, and so, eventually, they succeeded. They learned about the geostatic barrier, thanks to your scientists, and in time how to *increase* it—to keep us out. And so, the poison of unloved human lives increased, from generation to generation." He sighed and murmured as if to himself, "Oh mankind, how well you protect yourself from that which would do you the most good!"

I was still trying to make sense of all of this, and I was quite shaken, and confused. Yet, when I considered what had been said on either side, it seemed obvious that Grendel's words spoke truth. In fact, the G-man wasn't really contradicting him; the difference was just one of perspective, and values. That seemed to make sense, for Grendel—possibly trolls generally, to some degree—were about emotion; that much seemed clear. And the government? Well, I was beginning to see them in a different light. They *served* the populace in a way, yes. But the FBG, these rules, seemed more about control than anything else.

I glanced at Grendel. He was still looking at the G-man, with a somewhat hostile expression. All in a moment, seeing his face large, in my hallway and moon-like, a new thought came to me. I opened my mouth, and said in something like a whisper, "*You! You're* the bogeyman! You're the one who comes to steal away the bad children, you're the one parents say will come if the children don't eat their vegetables."

Grendel frowned in response and switched his gaze to look at me.

"That is a distortion. But yes, your folk tales did address something of our general purpose—getting it more wrong than right, of course. We come in the night to spirit away those who have inherited gravely diseased or dying souls." He chuckled sadly. "Nowadays, these are often the children of what you call Wall Street. What we did was correct in another way too, for nothing punishes a parent more than losing a child, especially to a night terror—even if that child is not truly loved. It is worse than death itself."

"You prefer the children."

Grendel smiled, showing enormous teeth. "They are more tender, are they not?"

I shuddered and stared in horror at my friend. So did the G-man, before looking away again. It was then that I caught Grendel shake his head minutely and was reassured.

"How do you tell which ones are—the right ones?" I asked.

Grendel raised his hand and touched his nose with a big finger. "The nose knows," he said. "It is the original sense, the most fundamental one too. There are single-celled animals possessed only of smell, and they get along in the world alright. That is why we come out at night. When the world sleeps and the great golden eye is gone, then you, vision oriented, asleep or otherwise quiet, are at your weakest. It is then that smell is most powerful. We come, and steal away the rotten-souled babes, and even, on occasion the youth, or adult. We—remove the dead flesh from your metaphoric social body." He glared at the G-man. "Or at least we *did*, until the barrier was enhanced up by your people."

I wanted to jump to my feet and yell, "No more, no more!" It was all becoming too much to take in at once. And yet, at the same time I still wanted to hear more, to find out the full truth, from Grendel. For it was quite evident to me that there was much between his words that he had not explained. But he wasn't going to do this in the presence of the G-man.

I turned and looked at the man, who now was writing on one of his papers.

"So, what happens now?" I asked him.

Without looking up or interrupting his writing, the G-man said, "I am making my report."

"Saying what?"

"Just the facts of the case."

"About Grendel, you mean?" I said, my gut tightening.

The G-man looked up from his papers, first at me, and then for a darting glance at Grendel. I wondered at his odd expression as he did this, but then realized I hadn't used Grendel's name in front of this man before. As the man bent over his paperwork again, I felt a sick sensation at the realization I could very well have made Grendel's case worse by giving the government his name. Wasn't there something in old legends about knowing someone's name gave you power over them? And, since Grendel was quite literally the stuff of legends, wouldn't that mean I had put him under the power of this G-man?

I glared at the top of the man's head as he continued to fill in his report.

For a moment I considered assaulting him, tying him up so we could get away. I was still turning this over in my mind when the G-man stopped writing and looked at his watch.

"Oh," he murmured. "I should check in." He stood up. "Might I go into the living room to make my call?"

I shrugged. "Sure, I guess."

The man went out of the room, and we listened to the murmur of his side of the call. I looked at Grendel.

"Can you hear what he's saying?"

Grendel shook his head. "My senses are—sometimes overloaded here, on the surface."

"Oh," I said, and felt more hopeless than ever.

A minute later the G-man returned to the kitchen. Seating himself, he shuffled his papers for a moment. Then he turned to me.

"This sort of operation requires careful monitoring." He gave a darting glance at Grendel, before returning his gaze to me. "So no one goes missing."

I exchanged glances with Grendel as the man flipped rapidly through his papers. He appeared to be doing a final check of them.

He had just looked up and was about to speak, when Grendel forestalled him.

"Mr. Government Man," Grendel said, his voice ominous. "Why do you not ask *why* I came to the Overworld?"

The G-man stiffened and his face went quite red. I had the sense that he was *really* restraining himself from looking at Grendel now. He said nothing at first, but, licking his lips, which had apparently gone dry, he shrugged.

"The question of *why* is not relevant," he said shortly, adding, "I am following procedure. It is important to keep this professional."

Not quite understanding any of this but wanting to support Grendel and challenge this government official, I said, "But, aren't you curious?"

The man stared at me for several seconds, then closed his eyes and rubbed the bridge of his nose. At last, he took a deep breath, and said, "Okay. Why did—you—" I saw his hesitation in his use of personal pronoun. Probably, he would have preferred to say, "why did *he*," to avoid directly addressing Grendel. I felt a small sense of victory at his acknowledging Grendel to the point of seeking information from him—a person and not an object.

"Come up?" he concluded. His face was even redder now. He still pretty much avoided looking at Grendel, resolutely looking at me instead. Despite this, I thought that in some way he *was* attending Grendel—and this perception caused a new idea to form in my head. As if he was aware of what I was thinking, Grendel now said, "Mr. G-man, why will you not look at me when you address me?"

The G-man's face, which had been red, now went quite pale. *Fear?* It seemed the only possibility. But even that—

I watched as the G-man as he turned his head slowly, unwillingly, and shifted his gaze, to look directly at Grendel. Their gazes locked for perhaps a dozen heartbeats, after which the G-man made a strangled noise in his throat and managed to croak, "Okay?" he said. "I *did* ask you, right?"

"You appeared to be asking the *room*," Grendel replied, and I snorted, nodding my agreement.

The G-man, as if aware of his situation on this point, gave the smallest of nods and, after taking a deep breath, said, "Okay. Why *did* you come up?"

Grendel's eyes bored into the man as he said, "To find love."

I glanced at Grendel, feeling a surge inside my chest. *Was that really true?* I desperately wanted to believe that it was—and as far as I knew, Grendel didn't lie—and I wanted to believe that the love he was seeking involved me.

But Grendel continued to stare at the G-man intently, whose face had gone red again. "You know about love, human?"

The G-man opened his mouth, but closed it again. Then he took the handkerchief from his breast pocket and wiped his forehead. After this, he cleared his throat noisily and got to his feet. Facing me, he said quietly, "May I use your washroom?"

I stared at him for a second, then shrugged. "Sure." Nodding toward the hallway, I added, "Up the stairs, to the left."

The man left a bit hurriedly.

When he was gone, Grendel and I looked at each other.

"I make him uneasy," Grendel said.

I shook my head. "I don't think that's quite it."

"What then?"

"I think—he's fighting something. I think he's attracted to you, *strongly* attracted."

Grendel smiled. "A thing for trolls, you mean?"

I shrugged and then grinned. "It's been known to happen—among us humans!" I pointed to my own chest.

Grendel nodded, but still seemed puzzled. He shook his head. "If he is—so inclined, then—would he take such a job?"

I remembered having read about, and even seen, something of this sort. "Sometimes," I said, "those who have a desire—unadmitted and buried in their deepest souls—they become active in persecuting the very thing they desire. It's a way to stamp it out, in their own feelings." I grinned. "While at the same time maintain a link with their suppressed desires, I suspect."

"Could that be true?" Grendel shook his head again, slowly. "If so, then how sad!"

"Well, I think that's the case with some people. I mean, how many homophobes are there who are trying to eliminate their own hidden homoerotic needs? And I think it's general. I think it applies to all socially disapproved of activities."

Grendel regarded me in silence for a long time, then leaned forward and, reaching out, ran the tip of his forefinger lovingly along my cheek. "Yes," he said quietly. "I suppose we are even more disapproved of than many other things in the human psyche."

When I had recovered from this caress, I frowned and looked at him. "What? You mean because of the child-snatching thing?"

"Not only that, I think. We represent the final repose of your earthly shells—the earth, the soil, the very *ground* of your final defeat—your mortality. But yes, there is the myth of our stealing your children."

I frowned. "But you *do* do that. You said you did. So, it's not a myth, right?"

Grendel shrugged. "A myth is a story that is so powerful and so moving that it matters not whether it is true or false. And, better than saying that we indiscriminately steal your children, is to say that we remove the diseased or deadened souls among you."

I stared at him, not sure of what he was saying. But then I dismissed the issue. It was whatever it was.

Grendel's eyes, still regarding me, now softened. "You are young. Some of the most important truths are subtle, and subtlety often requires many years of contemplation to be fully—distinguished."

"I'm twenty-eight."

"That is still young. If you knew how old I was—"

I blinked. "How old *are* you?"

Grendel looked at me. Then he grinned and batted his eyelashes, looking coy. "How old do you *think* I am?"

I laughed and, went over to him—he was half-sitting, propped up by one arm, which put his head just at the level of mine—and kissed him. "You know," I said, "I really don't care."

Grendel laughed delightedly at this, a deep rumble that went on a full minute and got me heated up. Grendel gently pulled me close to him. "That," he murmured, "is the *right* answer!"

I looked toward the hall leading to the stairs, then back at Grendel. "You know, that guy said something at the beginning—that I *sure had the touch*. Any idea what he meant?"

Grendel chuckled. "Yes," he said. "It is the very thing you just referred to. By some it is called *rock fever*—analogous to what humans call *jungle fever*—a strong sexual interest in black people as sexual partners. *Rock fever* refers to a similar interest in trolls."

I laughed. "I guess he was right, anyway. Though I wonder how he could tell." Then I grimaced and laughed again. "But maybe I got the fever pretty bad, eh?"

Grendel grinned. "And there is only one cure. Not a cure actually. More a treatment."

I grinned. "And what's that?"

Grendel leaned forward, his huge face close to mine. "Repeated application of a healthy troll phallus."

A tingling went all through my body at this point. I laughed and leaned against him, placing my hands on either side of his head. "Well, sign me up!"

Grendel smiled. "Okay."

Looking into his large, pale eyes, so close, I felt I was melting into a pool of happiness. I kissed him on the tip of his nose, and said seriously, "For a life-time supply."

Grendel's face changed, though the smile remained, and I could see an enormous tear form in each eye. He sniffed. "Thank you," he said, his voice slightly choked.

"You're welcome! But what about this G-man? What are we going to do?"

The tears welled up in Grendel's eyes, and he shook his head. "I do not know."

I reached out and brushed away each tear. "Well," I said. "I did have the idea of knocking him out and tying him up or something. But that calling-in business, he probably has to do it regularly, so if he doesn't, they'll send someone, maybe more than one."

Grendel nodded, now looking unhappy. "I thought I would have more time," he murmured. "Apparently, I miscalculated—several times." He sighed. "I am sorry."

I put my hand on his lips. "*Don't!*" I told him fiercely. "Don't blame yourself! It's not you, okay?"

He nodded hesitantly, and I kissed him. Then, feeling my throat tighten, I said, "I'm just glad that you *did* come up. *More* than glad."

Grendel smiled at this. It was a smile so sweet that my chest hurt.

"Come on!" I said, now speaking to both of us. "Surely, we can come up with something!" I rapped the side of my head with my knuckles. "Think, Ken! Think! What is the salient factor, here?"

We were both silent for a minute or two, when Grendel's eyes widened. "Oh!" he said. "I have one. Perhaps it represents a possibility, though I am not sure—"

"Never mind that!" I said hurriedly. "What is the salient point?"

"His—*rock fever.*"

I considered. "Oh! You mean that his loyalties might be divided?"

Grendel nodded.

I shook my head slowly. "You know, I don't think so. From what I've heard about homophobes, they do a good job sublimating, if that's the word, their attraction into hate. It takes the urge from the feeling realm to the judgment realm, and the attraction energy stirs them into judgmental hatred and loathing—projecting their self-hatred onto the external manifestations that energy: gays."

"Curious," Grendel murmured. "But it seems very human, to suppress feelings and encourage judgment."

"Yes," I agreed unhappily.

"But," he said, his voice more hopeful, "Might there not be a way to reverse that suppression?"

"How?"

Grendel smiled mischievously. "By stimulating the attraction."

I laughed. "Seduction, you mean?"

"Yes."

"Actually, that might work—at least to the point where he is fighting against himself. But the problem with that is, how do we know what the result of that struggle would be?"

"It might make him more sympathetic."

"Get him on our side, you mean?" I shook my head. "I don't know. I suppose it's worth a try."

We both pondered, and Grendel finally nodded. "If that is not enough, then we must stimulate him beyond appreciation, to the point where the energy of his hidden desire—*overwhelms* him."

"Negates his judgment. Makes him act rashly?"

"Yes."

"Oh! I see!" Then I frowned and looked at Grendel uneasily. "You mean, get him to act, to compromise himself?"

Grendel nodded.

"Wow! It might work." Part of me was uncomfortable with the idea, but I pushed against this. This was no time for niceties, I told myself, for proprietary possessiveness.

I looked at Grendel, whose massive physical presence was in a sense all around me. It felt extraordinarily powerful. And my appreciation of it was not just admiration. There were very strong sexual and aesthetic elements in it. I began to think that Grendel's idea might work.

If he tried hard enough.

Again, I was assailed by a sense of aversion to what that might entail.

Being proprietary! I chided myself. I looked at my friend, and all the love I felt for him now swept aside the doubt and the selfish possessiveness. It was to *save him*. Of *course*, I would go along with it—whatever that might include!

I saw Grendel was looking at me, a slight questioning look in his eyes. He was concerned about my feelings! And that produced another wave of love for this gentle soul.

"I say: Go for it! Whatever it takes. I mean—" I laughed a bit uneasily, "give him what he wants."

He smiled tentatively but nodded.

"To be with you," he said quietly. "I will do this thing." He still looked uncomfortable. "Although it might be a problem, for one or both of us." He smiled. "You see, I am a faithful troll. I do not have sex with just anyone, anyhow."

I was reassured if a bit puzzled by this last, but I nodded. "Like you say, to save yourself. For us."

He nodded again, and I took a deep breath.

"Okay," I said. "How do we—implement this plan?"

After a silence, Grendel said, "I will go outside. Tell the G-man this—" And he told me what to say. Then he edged his way backward, out the door. I watched him go to his diggings and descend the stairs and wondered what the words he had entrusted me with meant. The sun was just setting, and its orange light reflecting pink against some clouds seemed to bring a sense of somber influence, of the imminence of change, which was somewhere between hope and despair, but steeped in magic.

Chapter 11
Buying Time

SEVERAL MINUTES LATER I heard the toilet upstairs flush, followed by the sound of running water, and footsteps coming downstairs. When the G-man arrived in the kitchen, I saw that his hair was wet and freshly combed, and he appeared to have washed his face as well. *Or cooled it*, I thought, sardonically.

The G-man looked quickly around. "Where is the troll?"

The troll? This sounded so cold, so—well, *species-ist*—that a black anger rose up in me. But I forced it down. He was only a cog, after all.

"I don't know," I said, doing my best to sound puzzled myself. "He went outside, into the backyard. I made a show of looking out the kitchen window and shook my head. Turning back to the G-man I said, "Can trolls disappear?"

"Of course not!" the G-man snapped. He paused, then added, "They can avoid being seen, but not by someone who knows they are there." He was looking out the window himself.

"Did he leave the yard?" he asked, more to himself than to me. Then, before I could respond, he added, as if to himself. "No, he couldn't have done that."

When he turned and looked at me again, I decided it was time to pass on Grendel's message.

"Actually," I said, as if coming clean, "he went down into a digging he did in my backyard."

The G-man nodded, as if that seemed logical, something a troll would do.

"And," I continued, "he said he had discovered something, something shiny down there, a silvery bit of surface."

The G-man's mouth fell open at this, and he stared at me for several seconds. At last, he closed his mouth, scowled and said in a fierce whisper, "There is *no way!*"

I shrugged my shoulders with a show of indifference, though I had no idea what any of this meant.

The man glared at me. "Where was that surface? On the wall or the floor?"

That took me aback. Grendel hadn't said anything about either. Then I caught myself. Why the hell was I worrying about answering this odious little cog, this instrument of governmental oppression?

"*Go see for yourself!*" I shouted at him. "I'm not going to rat on my friend. I hope he *did* get away. And I hope you get into serious trouble with your precious Bureau."

After this outburst I caught myself, feeling that I probably shouldn't have said any of this. The goal, after all, was to get the guy on our side. On the other hand, it *did* feel good just to plain vent.

The G-man regarded me belligerently, and for a moment I thought he was about to shout at me. But then he turned and headed for the back door.

"Make yourself at home!" I called after him. "Just go where you like!"

As I followed him out, leaving Jake inside, I saw the man silhouetted against the evening sky. He was standing at the top of Grendel's stairs. He seemed to be hesitating. Then, to my horror, he drew what looked like a pistol from his jacket. This seemed to restore his nerve. I was about to shout a warning to Grendel but decided there was no way a pistol bullet could do much to him. *And* I had faith in Grendel's words—just leave things to him—and in the idea that he knew what he was doing far better than this G-man.

I watched the man descend the stairs slowly, then I went to the top of the stairs. He was standing at the bottom. The evening light, reflecting off the side of the stairwell, illuminated the space to just beyond the bottom of the stairs. Then it seemed to cut off abruptly, the space beyond an inky darkness.

Curious! It hadn't been like that when I had been down there.

The gray shape of the G-man hesitated at the edge of the darkness. He held his pistol in both hands, pointing up, in what I could only assume, from watching cop shows, was the approved position prior to sighting the target.

"I have a field unit!" I heard him say, his voice that both fierce and shaky. "I am protected if you are here!"

There was a pregnant silence after this. Then, slowly, the inky darkness that had filled the chamber slowly melted away, and the dim, reflected glow of evening light spread throughout. At this point I was several steps from the bottom and could see Grendel clearly at the far side of the chamber, an enormous, shadowy figure, standing, his back against the wall. In spite of his size, the impression he gave was so much like a trapped animal that I felt a stab of pain mingled with anger. I leaped down the last few steps and, lunging forward, grabbed at the G-man's gun.

My action was impetuous and unexpected, with the result that I managed to wrench the weapon from the man's grasp without trouble. I was a bit surprised by my own action. Then I realized he hadn't even struggled at all to hold onto it. With the weapon safely in my own hands, I looked at him now, and saw that he hadn't even moved. He was staring at the shadowy figure of Grendel as if transfixed.

I stepped around him, until I was between him and Grendel. Then, pointing the gun at him, I made several upward motions with it. He seemed to come to himself, and looking at me vaguely, he slowly raised his arms. But then his gaze drifted back to where Grendel stood.

Stepping back, I turned and saw that Grendel too was standing motionless and still looking trapped. My eyes, having adjusted to the dim light now, I could just make out the G-man's face. His eyes were wide, and there was a look of something like astonishment on his face.

This puzzled me—until I remembered my first sight of Grendel's full form, when he had stood up, naked in the moonlight of the front lawn. I turned and this time really *looked* at Grendel, and again was assailed by a sense of reverential awe, the powerful and daunting physical presence, the majestic shape and masses of his body, its profound masculine beauty.

I was still doing this, when Grendel shifted his gaze and looked at me. I made a hand gesture to him, as if to say, *so now what?*

Grendel nodded and moved forward in slow steps, around me and up to the G-man. As he approached, the G-man's head slowly tilted up, but not *quite* enough to be looking at Grendel's face. I took several steps to the side and saw where the G-man's eyes *were* focused. I snorted quietly, with a sense of satisfaction. The man looked completely helpless, fascinated as he was.

Not that I blamed him. Even flaccid and hanging down, curving over the enormous scrotum, the phallus hung there, complete with the full roundness of the huge head, looking again like a ripe piece of forbidden fruit, just above the G-man's eye level.

I felt the pull of that manifestation myself and had to wrench my gaze away to regain my self-control. I saw that the G-man had no such strength of will. Or what he was experiencing was more powerful. Did Grendel have the power to *direct* his whatever-it-was, his physical pull?

I was still looking at the captured face of the G-man when, without any other movement, he said out of the corner of his mouth, "You—you're holding me prisoner?"

He hesitated, licked his lips, then added, his face strangely blank while his voice made a valiant, if less than fully successful, attempt at sounding stern, "If—if I don't report, there will be a swarm of agents here—" He stopped, but now there was a defiant smile on his face. "And I have already set up the barrier."

I looked up at Grendel, wondering what this meant. But Grendel was still gazing resolutely down at the G-man.

"Human," he said solemnly, in his deepest, most resonant voice, the sound of which made the chamber echo so I felt its vibration throughout my own body, making me feel slightly intimidated—and more than a little aroused.

"Human," Grendel repeated in the same tone. "You have brought a weapon into my home."

I saw the G-man lick his lips nervously at this. But he still seemed defiant.

"This isn't your home," he said—but his voice cracked as he spoke. Nevertheless, he didn't give up. "The current statute forbids overground habitation of denizens of the—"

"*My home!*" Grendel repeated, his voice louder, more menacing, so my own knees quivered. "This space I made, with the permission of my friend Ken, on *his* land. Your statutes do not overrule the law of hospitality, human!"

The G-man at this point took a step back and, though he licked his lips again, he didn't speak.

"Such weapons desecrate the law of hospitality. *Beware, human!*" The chamber really echoed with these final words, and I felt a sudden urge to pee.

The G-man, I saw, cowered, though he did manage to stammer desperately, "B-but he—t-took away m-my g-gun. I have n-nothing."

"So you say. But perhaps you have more weapons, hidden on your person," Grendel's tone was quieter, but still aggrieved and still menacing.

"N-no! I p-promise!"

But Grendel shook his head. "You must prove that. Show me!"

The man stared. "Show y-you?"

Grendel, without shifting his gaze, now said, "Ken. I would ask you to demonstrate for this man. Show him that you have no hidden weapons."

I blinked for a second or two, then I caught his meaning, and nodded. I stripped and then, laying my clothes down, went over and stood in front of Grendel, facing the G-man.

"*Ecce homo!*" Grendel murmured. "Behold the man!" I stood there, my arms held out, palms toward him, in a gesture of openness. Looking up, I saw that Grendel was matching my stance.

But the G-man only stared. His gaze shifted from Grendel to me and then back, but he seemed incapable of movement. So, I pointed at him and said, "Now you."

After nodding slowly, as if in a dream, the man disrobed, carefully folding his clothes and laying them on the floor of the chamber, staring at us the whole while, until he too was naked.

When the man was standing before us, naked as the day he was born, Grendel said, "That is well." Then, he pointed at the G-man, at me, at himself. "Are we not all of a single form? Are we not creations of the same Creator?" He gestured to the G-man. "Why must you persecute your fellow creatures?"

The G-man, whose mouth had slightly open, now closed it. He licked his lips.

"It's—it's not up to me—" he began, and then stopped, his expression suggesting that his own words sounded hollow even to himself.

"And if I speak of love," Grendel said. He gestured again down at me, and lowered his big hands to rest gently on my shoulders. "Who are you to deny this?"

"I don't—" the G-man said in a half-whisper.

"You do!" Grendel said. "You seek to come between two souls. You cite statutes. But such rules are for hollow creatures, not those who feel—those who *love*."

At the touch of Grendel's hands on me, I had stepped back, to be closer to him, until I could feel the warmth of his legs against the back of my shoulders. Feeling both protected and supported, and I tilted my head back, to look up at him, but saw only the curve of his phallus hanging majestically over his enormous testicles. They blocked my view, and so, without really thinking, I reached up and hefted the round phallus head in my hand. It felt so wonderful, warm and spongy and heavy, that I reached up with the other hand, and took it between my hands, feeling its surface, savoring the silky smoothness.

Wonderful!

In response to a rush of sexual excitement, I squeezed my hands together. It responded by swelling still larger, which sent another thrill through me. I squeezed again. And now I saw a pearl of pre-cum at the tip. Reaching up, I wiped it away with my fingers and then, lowering my hand, licked the wet stickiness off my fingers. I moaned quietly at the rich mushroom-like taste, finally licking each of my fingers in turn.

So content, so filled with the experience and the presence that loomed over me, I hardly registered the presence of the G-man. But when I happened to glance over, I saw him staring at me, his whole manner alive with a look of desperate longing. I saw he was fully erect, and, if I may say so, with a somewhat impressive size—for a human.

Nice dick, I thought.

Tilting my head back again, I repeated the "milking" process, even more languorously this time, making a show of every action. The product of semen this time was greater and this time I paused my hand inches from my lips and looked at the G-man.

I raised my eyebrows questioningly and reached out to him in an offering gesture.

He didn't move at first, but that was not entirely unexpected. I crooked my forefinger, slick with semen, and beckoned. After several seconds, he lifted one leg and took a slow, sleepwalker-like step forward. Then another. And another.

When he was close enough, I lifted my hand to his mouth—he was several inches shorter than me and looked in that moment unaccountably *small*. He touched quivering lips to my fingers—clearly hesitant but eager too. I felt all this in his touch. *My God*, I thought. *He's shaking!*

I felt some compassion but reassured myself that this would pass. And, as he, slowly at first but then with increasing eagerness, licked my hand and each finger clean of Grendel's seed, I saw a change in him. He seemed to take on a new energy, a stronger sense of being. I reached down, and felt not only his rock-hard erection, but considerable pre-cum as well.

He shivered at my touch, and I felt he would be easily brought to climax. But instead of helping him out with this, a new idea struck me. I squatted down, wrapped my arms around his legs and lifted him up. Tilting my head back, I saw him embrace Grendel's phallus.

The attention had its effect, and I watched in awe as the great thing slowly swelled in size and rise slowly from the testicles. Now, the G-man was grasping the shaft and rubbing his entire face over the semen-slick head, just like a cat with catnip.

He moaned quietly and, still holding onto the shaft, was slowly lifted from my grasp by the rising phallus. At last, the man was literally hanging from Grendel's phallus. I took several steps away and looked up at my friend. He was clearly enjoying himself—not in a spiteful way, I thought, but rather in simple amusement and the natural gratification at being so ardently appreciated. I noticed, however, that there was none of that love light I had seen when he and I had made love. And *that* was a good thing.

Now, Grendel stepped slowly backward, until he stood against the wall of the chamber. Then he gently slid down the wall until he was half-sitting, half-lying, and the man lay on top of his abdomen and muscular thighs, still adoring the phallus and seemingly oblivious to anything else.

Taking advantage of his position, the man removed one arm from around the phallus shaft and, continuing his act of devotion, began to caress the head with his free hand, occasionally forcing it up and against his face with eyes closed, so he was soon *covered* with Grendel's pre-cum.

All of this attention, simple physical stimulation, I saw was having its effect on the enormous phallus, which seemed to have grown tauter. Grendel had tilted his head, back against the wall, and half-closed his eyes.

He's getting close, I thought, and wondered what I might, or should do.

Looking again at the G-man, I thought of what Grendel and I had agreed: *Give him what he wants.*

Okay. But what was that?

Now, the pre-cum was really beginning to flow slowly from the tip of Grendel's phallus. I acted quickly.

The G-man was of average height and medium build. At the moment, however, because of my own increased size, and juxtaposed with Grendel's great mass, the man seemed more diminutive than ever. I seldom wanted to dominate smaller men sexually, but I experienced that now. I was turned on watching Grendel's arousal and possibly, sensing his physical pleasure with a small human, I wanted to participate, to get involved.

I climbed onto Grendel's thighs and, moved up them on hands and knees, until I was on top of the G-man. He turned his head, looking up at me, and when his eyes met mine, his expression quickly changed from surprise to welcome, to what was a truly pornographic look of surrender. It wasn't desire, I thought, but something more akin to actual *need*.

Fair enough! I thought. *Happy to oblige!*

I was poised above him now, my cock hard and hanging down, just touching the line where his ass-cheeks met. With one hand I reached up and ran my fingers along the tip of Grendel's phallus, collecting his semen. It took some strength of will *not* to put my fingers into my mouth, but I managed to rub it instead over my cock, especially the head.

The slickness was exquisite, and I was now hard as a rock myself. I lowered myself, savoring the sensation of my cock sliding between the cheeks, pushing them apart and then, wonderfully, press against and through the man's sphincter. He was tight, so the sensation of penetration was delicious, bringing me for a second or two close to climax. I shuddered, and remained quite still, until the sense of imminence passed.

Then I thrust slowly forward, the waves of pleasure passing from my cock throughout my body. And, when I was in, right to the hilt, my belly and thighs pressed against the curves of the G-man's cheeks, he responded by pushing back like he wanted more, and groaning.

This, I thought to myself, *is going to be a lot of fun.*

I looked up to see that Grendel was gazing at *me*. This caused a wash of warm pleasure that somehow combined the sexual with the love feeling. I grinned at him and lowered my head to begin some full-on thrusting action.

After that, I was so caught up in the experience that I only glanced periodically up at Grendel. Once, I thought I saw something like doubt or worry in Grendel's big, pale eyes, but at the time this didn't bother me. I was awash in my first threesome—and *what* a threesome!

Finally, the man's physical stimulation of Grendel's phallus worked itself up to where the big troll grunted and climaxed. I felt it moments before, a tightening of the massive thigh muscles beneath my knees, and then a thick geyser shot up, over the G-man's head.

The first jet of semen flew high and fell, splattering on the man's back. It ran down this, pooling in the hollow of the small of his back, followed by another gout of semen, and then another. The G-man had raised himself onto his knees, and I wrapped my arms around his torso while I continued to thrust into him. He had his arms wide in welcome to this rain of seed, even catching some in his mouth.

This was so exciting that I felt my own cock tighten and the heat between my legs boil up and overflow, and then I was cumming, deep inside the G-man. Perhaps it was his sensing this that did it, for a moment later he too was climaxing; I could feel his sphincter rhythmically clenching the shaft of my dick.

All of this was *very* gratifying, and as the G-man slumped forward, I did as well, resting on top of him, feeling his heart and mine racing in syncopation as our breathing slowed, and below and behind this the low bass of Grendel's breathing too. I was utterly exhausted, and at some point, without shifting further, I fell asleep.

I AWOKE TO see the light of morning streaming down the staircase and filling the chamber with a warm light. Lifting my head, I saw the G-man at the foot of the stairs, hastily getting dressed. Something in the way he moved told me that, if ever there was a person possessed of morning-after horror, it was this man.

I didn't move until he had disappeared up the stairs, shoes and socks in his hands. Then, I got up and, gathering my own clothes, dressed. Turning to look at Grendel, I saw Jake lying next to him. He was awake, however, and watching me. I made a gesture that he was to stay where he was, and he lowered his head again, onto his paws.

I went up the stairs, and when I entered the kitchen, saw the G-man sitting there, tying up his shoes. He didn't look up but completed the task. It was only when he stood up and had picked up his briefcase that he looked at me.

I was a bit nonplused, unsure of the situation. Should I offer the guy coffee? Or breakfast? I must have been partly asleep, for the deeper aspects of the situation didn't quite register at this point. In any case, the man seemed in a hurry to leave. He paused only long enough to point at the several sheets of paper on the table and say, "This is your record of the charge and action. I will be back tomorrow morning, early, with a van."

"A van?" I stared at him stupidly.

"To take your—friend—into custody." The G-man was frowning and did not meet my eyes.

I was still digesting this when the guy hurried from the room. I was sinking into a chair when I heard the sound of the front door open and close. It was only after this that the full horror of the situation began to dawn on me. I felt stunned.

After last night, what had happened—*this?* My face alternatively went hot and cold as washes of outrage and terror swept over me. I had been expecting at least that the guy would be amenable to *some* kind of compromise.

Apparently both Grendel and I had seriously miscalculated.

I picked up one of the papers without reading it and felt a sensation of utter defeat come over me—and settle in, to stay.

Chapter 12
Window of Opportunity

"Tomorrow?"

"Yes! He said they would come early in the morning, with a van." I was down in Grendel's cave, relating what the G-man had told me.

"But—*tomorrow?*"

I stared at my big friend.

"Yes," I repeated, not understanding. "Is that important? I mean, I guess they have to do some paperwork." With a sick feeling in my stomach, I added, "Maybe requisition the van or something—"

But Grendel placed a large fingertip over my mouth, both silencing me and distracting me as well. I took hold of it and kissed it, almost without thinking.

I felt something cold and wet touch my calf. Looking down, I saw Jake looking up at me expectantly.

"What? Oh! Breakfast! Sorry, Jake!" I turned Grendel. "I have to feed Jake. Is that okay?"

Grendel nodded absently. I wondered about that, but right now, I welcomed mundane things like meals as welcome diversions that could keep my mind off the disaster that had befallen us.

"C'mon, Jake!" We went up the stairs and inside. While he was eating with his usual gusto, I got busy making breakfast for Grendel and me. As I did this, I had the unpleasant thought that this was probably the last breakfast I would make for us both. I shook my head and focused on the job at hand.

Carpe diem, I told myself; seize the day.

Perhaps it was the freshness of the morning and the blue sky, but I found myself embracing something of that philosophy. I couldn't *quite* yield to despair.

I made French toast, using a dozen eggs and a loaf-and-a-half of bread. This took concentration, and it was only when I was standing with the laden tray at the top of the Grendel's stairs that my earlier thought came back, and I felt a twist in my chest and a lump in my throat.

No, no! I told myself, firmly. *Make the best of things, live in the moment!*

So, I pasted a smile on my face and descended the steps, Jake in tow, moving with a procession-like air.

When Grendel saw me, his worried face changed, and he smiled. Smile? It was more of a grin, actually. I stared at him and, though I could see *some* worry in that grin, I also saw a sense of excitement in his eyes. I wondered about this, but since he said nothing, I laid the plates out and we began our breakfast in companionable silence, attended by Jake, who always got some.

Whatever his silence was, mine was me savoring every moment of this repast together—and refusing to let negative thoughts ruin the experience.

It was only when we were lingering over our coffees that Grendel spoke.

"So nice," he murmured.

"What's that?"

"This. This coffee, this breakfast—with you."

I nodded. "Yes," and added, "Oh. Thanks!" I blinked back a sudden urge to tears and gave him the best smile I could manage. He smiled back at me, but his was a *real* smile—warm, loving, and joyful.

Wait a minute! Joyful?

I studied his face. There could be no mistake. And, when he saw my puzzlement, his smile broadened into a grin. That unnerved me enough that I put down my coffee. Getting to my feet, I went over, put my hand on his massive shoulder, and looked him in the eye.

"What gives?"

Still grinning, he shook his head. Then he blinked, and I saw tears in his eyes.

What? I thought. Was the love of my life losing his marbles? I looked at him expectantly, a hand on my hip.

"Well?"

He nodded. "I will explain. Please, sit down." He patted his thigh. "I would like you near me, touching."

So, I climbed onto his lap, my head resting in the hollow between his pectoral and bicep muscles. Jake jumped onto his ankle and ran up his leg and onto *my* lap. I chuckled at how comfortable all of this was, but then tilted my head back and looked up at him. He was smiling down at us.

"Yes," he said, as if marshaling his thoughts. "You said they would come back tomorrow—"

"Yes, early in the morning—"

Grendel shook his head. "That does not matter." He paused, and then said seriously, "You must understand this single point, Ken."

"Okay."

His gaze became earnest now as he said, in a half-whisper, "But, they *never* do that."

"Never do what?"

"They never—leave," he said. "The van, and the squad *with* the van, it comes *immediately*—while the primary agent is still present."

I frowned, unsure of what exactly this meant. "Are you sure?" I asked him. "You said you haven't been up since—a long time ago."

Grendel shook his head impatiently. "It is not me. It is what I always have been told, by others. It is known generally. We have ways of—knowing." He now seemed almost awed. "*Always, invariably!*"

"But—" I began, but stopped, unsure of what I wanted to say. Finally, I managed to clear my thoughts sufficiently. "But that means—" I stared at him, my heart beating fast with the birth of a new hope. "We have—time?"

He nodded slowly.

"But is it *enough* time?"

Slowly, he shook his head. "That, I do not know. Let me think. I did not imagine it would be like this—a brief reprieve."

I got up from his thigh and put Jake down. I felt restless, and began to pace up and down. Jake watched me carefully, while I, for the most part, watched Grendel.

At last, he nodded to himself, and looked at me—and gave me a slight smile.

"I suppose," he said, speaking slowly, "it is as good as might be expected. He has his job to think of, after all."

I frowned, less inclined to forgive the G-man for turning Grendel in, even with a one-day reprieve. It didn't seem like that much to me. I only hoped Grendel's reaction meant it represented a real chance.

"I think we got to him," he said in a pleased but tentative voice.

I snorted. "*We* nothing. It was *you*! *You* got to him, big guy! You gave him what he had always wanted." I laughed, tears filling my eyes. "You fulfilled his fantasy." I shook my head. "And that's—really nice." I went to him, leaned forward and, standing on tiptoe, kissed him on the lips, stroking the side of his face tenderly. In response, his free arm came around and pulled me against him.

Jake gave a bark. He had run up Grendel's leg again and was halfway up his chest. His tail was wagging furiously. I petted him and drew him up, so he was between us.

"He wants to be part of things," I explained to Grendel.

"Of course!" he said. "And he should be."

I grinned at that, but then became serious again. looked at my big friend and said, "What now?"

"Now," he said. "We have at least a chance."

My stomach tightened slightly at this—I had been hoping for better. "Well, I don't know, but we could probably get pretty far by tomorrow—"

To my dismay, Grendel shook his head. "Did you not hear what he said, yesterday in your kitchen?"

"He said a lot of things," I growled, remembering.

"He said, *This sort of operation requires careful monitoring,* so *no one goes missing.*"

I blinked. "But that was about his checking in, right? So, we couldn't bash him on the head."

Again, Grendel shook his head. "It is not only that. You are not familiar with this, so I will explain." He sighed. "Before the agent enters the location of the target—me, he or she lays down a kind of barrier around the place."

Barrier! I suddenly recalled the G-man saying something about that.

"You're kidding! Like the—geostatic barrier?"

"Oh, no. Nothing like that. They put down devices—" He shook his head. "I am not fully up on their technique, but they have certain crystals that do the trick."

"Crystals."

"Possibly."

"And they're for—what?"

"Preventing me from escaping." He smiled. "I could otherwise make quite a break for it, could I not?"

I nodded appreciatively, though my stomach sank.

"Say!" I added, remembering his earlier remark. "What was that you said about giving some hope? From what you're saying, it sounds like you're pretty much up the creek without a paddle."

"Yes," he said. "But that barrier is for me, not for you. You will be able to pass."

"What?" My mind whirled as I realized he was talking about my "escape," which meant that if I didn't leave—*my own home!*—somehow I would be in trouble too." My fear was swamped by outrage, and that by anger. I shook my head.

"Look," I said fiercely, looking him in the eyes. "I'm not going anywhere without you. And anyway, it's *you* they want. Right?"

"Oh. I think so," Grendel said, smiling gently. "But that is not what I mean."

"What, then?"

"Well, there is another way to escape—for me, I mean."

"What's that?"

Grendel lifted his hand and pointed a big forefinger directly down. "I can return."

I stared. "But—how? I mean, you said you couldn't make it *up*—quite. And didn't it, that experience weaken you? And it's not Halloween anymore, so won't it be more difficult?" A sudden thought struck me. "Or do you mean it's easier to descend than come up?"

Grendel shook his head. "It is the same both ways. No, I cannot return on my own, without help."

Grendel Rising 99

I felt puzzled. "Can I help?" It seemed improbable, but I was willing enough.

"There are—tools," Grendel said, "tools that can help. And you can purchase them for me—perhaps."

"Well," I felt panic rising inside me, unsure of what that meant. But I was resolved. "Anyway," I said. "We *can't* let him arrest you. Okay. So, tools. These tools can help get you past whatever barrier he set up—" I pointed toward the stairs, "up there? Couldn't we just—I don't know, leave the city—find a place—?"

I ran out of words as the prospect seemed improbable. And then I was annoyed all over again. Why was it that the literal light of day should make one's dreams of happiness, however unusual, seem so impossible? I looked helplessly at Grendel.

He nodded slightly. "That is possible."

"Okay then! I'll get those tools, and we can just get out of here, go on the run."

But Grendel looked at me sadly. "It is not that simple."

"What are you talking about?"

"Well, if you think about it, when you brought me home, and took me to the house with the pool, you always led the way. I can move about when you do that, but otherwise, my movements are somewhat—restricted."

"*What?*"

"There are—well, *fields*—what you would call *magic*. There are binding fields associated with homes—houses and their associated yards. They are difficult to penetrate. It depends on the families, the people that live there. I am a denizen of the deep, where the fields are different; the Overworld is not my world. I am limited here."

"What about where there are no people?"

Grendel nodded. "There, I am freer, almost as free as you."

"Then we'll go there, out to Arizona or New Mexico, or north to—I don't know, north to Canada."

"Yes," Grendel said, speaking slowly. "Those places, less well-peopled, would be better. But—you do not understand. Although I might be able to leave your yard—and I am not certain they would sell you tools even for that—there are other fields, other barriers. My progress through this part of your country would be very slow. And they will be after us then. And the more you get involved the more the charges against you there would be."

"I don't give a damn about that," I growled. "Now, what about these tools?"

Grendel now took my hands delicately in his. "First, we must decide. Will it be tools for going out or for going down? They will be different. I know little of the former. I can only be sure of the latter."

"Why not both? Maximize our options?" I said, frowning and staring at Grendel. "But where—who—what sort of shop, are we talking about here anyway?"

"I will need to look at your—directory. Do you have one?"

"You mean telephone? Or business?"

"Business with telephone."

WE WENT BACK to the house, Grendel again lying on his side in the hallway leading from the back door, looking into the kitchen. It took over an hour before I had the address of a store that apparently dealt in the sort of tools that Grendel needed. Searching for such a store wasn't straightforward, Grendel told me, because they wouldn't be obvious in their advertisement.

"Why not?"

"Because it is illegal."

"Oh!" I had to process that for a minute. "Well, I don't care," I said recklessly. "What do we look for?"

It took some time, numerous tries, and we had to use the Yellow Pages I had on a lower shelf in the kitchen, because I discovered I couldn't log on to the internet. Grendel consoled me in my outrage, kissing me gently and telling me that this was only to be expected.

I was really quite angry, and felt like the scales had been removed from my eyes; the society I had always found comfortable and reasonable was now starting to take on an entirely different cast.

I chuckled at last, and when Grendel asked me about this, I told him I supposed this was how revolutionaries were formed. To my slight surprise, he merely nodded.

I managed to calm down in the end, because this distraction wouldn't help our cause. So, we searched the Yellow Pages, and I was surprised at the number and complexity of the hidden clues, some of which could have been mistaken for mere typos or part of an illustration, that we had to parse before finding what we wanted.

I called the shop on my cell—only to discover it wasn't working. I looked at Grendel and he nodded.

"Try your connected telephone," he suggested.

Realizing he meant on my land line, I called on that, and was very relieved to discover it was working, and I got through to the shop.

Because Grendel had told me the phone line was probably tapped, the conversation I had with the man at the other end was necessarily elliptical. Fortunately, the guy seemed familiar with this sort of thing, and we had what was ostensibly a straightforward talk about his stock of gardening supplies, including the different kinds of fertilizer, grass seed and spreaders, all with Grendel coaching me *sotto voce* periodically, while I held down the Mute button.

The final words from the storekeeper were his store hours—which he had already repeated several times throughout the conversation.

When I thanked him and rang off, I mentioned this to Grendel. He nodded slowly.

"Well," he said at last. "Now we find out just how far our G-man was influenced."

"Really?"

"Yes. Of course! If he has not interfered with their regular functioning, then they will know everything more or less immediately, and will already be on their way."

We were both silent for a minute after that, but there was nothing to say on this.

"What about his repeating the hours?"

"I think—I think it means that those are *not* the hours."

"*What!*"

"Yes. And I think that means that you should go as soon as possible."

"Okay. I will. Is there anything I need to know?"

Grendel considered, then shook his head. "They are—helpful," he said. "But without direct contact, I cannot clarify things. Do you have paper and a writing pen?"

I got these. Grendel, holding the pen delicately, made marks on the page. Taking the pad, I saw a dozen lines of text, each line comprising letters constructed entirely of straight lines, what I thought were called runes. But I had no idea what any of it meant. Besides the text, there were two vertical brackets on the left that marked off the top five lines and the bottom ten—so three lines were within both brackets.

"What are these for?" I said, indicating the brackets.

"They are what is needed for going out—the top elements—and for going down—the bottom elements. Show it to them."

I nodded, removed the page from the pad and folding it, put it in my pocket.

"It will be enough information," he told me. "I think they will help—or not, if they cannot."

"Great!" I said, halfway between hope and sarcasm.

"It is the best we can hope."

I got my keys and wallet, went out the front door to where my car was parked in my driveway. As I got in my heart was pounding. I was thinking about the shop. Then, I discovered the car wouldn't start. After several tries, and pounding the steering wheel in my frustration, I decided I would just walk to the nearest main street and hail a cab. Somehow, I thought the idea of ordering a cab from home wasn't a good idea.

So, I got out and headed to the sidewalk.

When I was still two yards from it, however, I began to feel faint. This was accompanied with a slight sense of nausea, and a curious numbing sensation that rose up from my feet. I feared if it reached my head, I would pass out, so I turned and staggered back to my front steps, where I collapsed.

Chapter 13
Trapped

IT WAS SEVERAL minutes before I could even get myself into a sitting position. Then I sat, my head still swimming, holding onto the wrought iron railing, confused and devastated.

What the eff was going on here?

When I had recovered enough to pull myself to my feet, I stood on my front stoop, staring out at my front yard and the street scene in general. Everything was peaceful. Quiet. And *very* normal, completely benign. I closed my eyes and breathed deeply.

Okay, I told myself. *Let's just see.*

I took a cautious step down, holding onto the railing, and stopped on the next step for several seconds. I repeated the operation carefully, and again, so at last I was standing my front path: concrete slabs that ran straight to the sidewalk.

Simple enough!

Gingerly, letting go of the railing, I took a step forward, and stopped. Okay? Yes—

I took another step, feeling a little more confident this time, and stopped again. Again, I didn't feel anything wrong, anything bad. Shaking my head, I started to walk, slowly and carefully forward. It was on the third step that I thought I felt something—curious sensations, disturbing and— oppressive. I hesitated but took another step.

It got worse.

Huh.

Another, more cautious step—and *this* time there was that curious numbing sensation in my feet and partway up my calves, like they had gone to sleep. On top of that, yes, now there was the nausea—not strong, but noticeable.

What the eff?

I lifted my foot to take another step, at which point my head began seriously to swim, so I put my foot down again, and took a step backward, and then another.

The symptoms decreased—slowly but definitely—to the level I had felt *at that same spot*, going forwards.

Positional?

Carefully, I turned around and walked back to the house, into it and through it, to the backyard. When I descended the stairs into Grendel's chamber, he looked at me without speaking.

I shook my head.

"Couldn't make it to the street," I told him. "I'm guessing that's the barrier the G-man set up works on me too."

Grendel nodded, his face turning grayer than ever; he even clutched his head in his hands and groaned and murmured, "Yes. Yes, of course."

"I thought it wasn't supposed to affect me."

Grendel lowered his hands and looked at me. "I feared this."

I frowned. "Then why didn't you tell me?"

Grendel shook his head slowly. "It is difficult to explain. And, these things are subtle. They involve the mind—the soul actually—in addition to what you call the physical world. To tell you would have planted the seed of the barrier in your mind, your heart. I had to hope that, if the barrier they set up *did* affect you, your ignorance of the fact would keep the effect small enough that you might pass."

I blinked. "That sounds like a pretty poor barrier, if I could do that because of ignorance—not that I was able to, of course."

Again, Grendel shook his head. "Its effect on you—should not be very strong. I hoped that fact, and your obliviousness, your thinking of other things, might together facilitate passage. You would notice certain effects but would probably dismiss them."

"Not very strong," I repeated. "Why not?"

"Have you measured your height today?"

I stared, then cried, "Oh!"

Grendel nodded. "The transformation. Thus far, it is only partial. So, the action of the barrier on you is only partial—less strong, weaker. Evidently, I have made another mistake."

His tone was so wretched, I went forward and kissed him. "Don't," I said. "Don't beat yourself up." After a pause, I added, "*I* think you're wonderful, really."

He looked at me at that, and his grim expression softened.

"Thank you," he said. "That means—much."

"Good," I said, switching to a brisk tone. "So. What do we do now? I can't go through that again. I almost threw up."

"What?" Grendel said, his tone sharp.

"I had nausea, among other things. I almost tossed my cookies."

Grendel Rising 105

Grendel's eyes widened.

"Could you recount," he said, "exactly what you experienced in your front yard—with every detail?"

So, I did so, beginning with the car failing to start.

"Yes," he said. "That I expected."

Any other time I would have pursued this point, but now I just continued with the tale of my adventure and waited for his response.

"The nausea," he said at last. "It is puzzling. But perhaps things have changed. Our news of the tricks of your government are, possibly, not up to date. And, again, I am a little surprised at the strength of your reactions. You are still quite—small."

I said nothing, but experienced a rush of pleasure that had definite erotic overtones.

"It was almost as if—" he began, and then stopped.

"As if—what?"

He looked at me. "As if the barrier had been set for you specifically."

This idea brought an unpleasant rush of fear—one that was perhaps latent in every law-abiding citizen: of the State taking a personal interest in them. I shuddered.

"But how could he do that?" I asked. "And I thought it was for trolls only. It can't be for humans, too. I mean, *he* was able to leave."

I caught myself, realizing I was babbling. Grendel had said: *set for me specifically*.

Grendel sat there, silent, head lowered, eyes unseeing, as he thought. When he raised his head at last, he said, "I think I have it."

And now he turned to me, and put both hands—forefingers, really—lightly on my shoulders and looking at me intently. "Tell me, did he take a sample of your bodily fluid?"

"What?"

"He would have had to get something, saliva or blood, mucus, anything."

I laughed awkwardly. "Well, I did *cum* inside him. That would probably count, right?"

"Oh. Yes." He grinned. A moment later, he became serious, frowning. "Actually, that might not work. Your—semen—" he grinned again momentarily, "would be—changed, by his body chemistry."

Okay, Connelly, I told myself sternly. *You are now officially out of your depth.*

"He might have gotten some saliva from your glass—in the kitchen," Grendel said at last.

"You're kidding!" I cried. "Like DNA?"

"It is—mmm—like that. Amount is not as important as—purity. It is a subtle business."

"No *kidding*!" I murmured.

Grendel was again silent for several minutes. "That might be it," he said at last. "When he went to the washroom—he could have mixed your saliva into a solvent, possibly in a small vial in his pocket. And then, when he left, he could have added that, somehow—the details do not matter—to the crystals he had already set in place."

"Wait! What? What crystals? And how could he have already set them in place—whatever that means?"

"Oh." Grendel nodded. "The crystals are what sets the barrier. They look like small, blue stones—crystals or gems. Though they are not easily seen. It is only if you look for them that can you notice them at all."

"But he set them in place *before* he knocked on my door?"

Grendel blinked. "Of course! It is their standard practice, and necessary for their goal."

I stared. My mind was whirling. "What? So, he put the barrier down, and then, while he was here, *enjoying my hospitality*, he set about collecting a sample from me so now *I* wouldn't be able to leave either?"

Grendel sighed and shook his head despairingly.

"But this is outrageous!" I stormed. "We're *both* imprisoned here?" I felt a rising tide of panic and outrage. "But this is—"

"Ken," Grendel said gently, "they are your government."

"Well, damn our government, then!"

But Grendel shook his head. "They are not all bad." And then he sighed and added unhappily, "Probably not even mostly bad." And he pulled me to him and hugged me in the warm, gentle way I loved.

After a long silence, Grendel sighed and said in a weary voice, "Of course, there is another possibility."

"What?"

"Well, as I said, it is subtle. And your government people, they might have changed the properties of the crystals they use, so it might have nothing to do with a sample of your body. It might—" He shook his head and smiled sadly. "You see, I really do not know. It could act on anyone."

"But what about the G-man?"

"He might have triggered it as he left. Or any of a number of possibilities: he might have had a counter-crystal on his person. I have no knowledge of that sort of thing." He stopped again, and shrugged, before adding, "The— you might call it the bottom line—point is that we do not know fully how the barrier they set works. There could well be unexpected effects."

He nodded, as if satisfied with his description of the situation, and then sighed.

"Well," he said gently, looking at me tenderly, "it has been wonderful, this time with you."

I pulled away angrily. "You're not going to give up, are you?"

Grendel shrugged. "I thought I would have more time. It was a gamble. I did not think they would come the very next morning. There is something unusual in that, something—beyond me."

I shrank against Grendel, wanting to cry.

"What will they do with you?"

Grendel said nothing at first. Then he said in a quiet voice, "It is a capital offense, to come up like that."

"Capital offense! *What!* But that means—" I stopped, horrified. "But surely, you *don't* mean they'll—" I couldn't say the word.

"They might not. Who knows? They might." Grendel chuckled morosely. "But really, that would be better than the mines."

"Mines?"

Grendel laughed. "Salt mines—yes, they really exist—not salt exactly, we just called them that—for a hundred years, or more—perhaps a thousand."

"Where are these salt mines?"

Grendel shook his head. "Do not ask the details."

I shuddered. Then a new thought occurred to me, a new question.

"But what *about* mines?"

"I beg your pardon?"

"I said, what about mines? Don't mines run into that—that geo-something barrier or whatever it is?"

Grendel smiled and shook his head. Reaching out, he brushed back with infinite care a hair that had fallen into my face. "No," he said. "It is about contiguity—continuity. When humans dig a mine, that mine is connected with the surface, and so mine shaft becomes a part of the surface. The geostatic barrier is pushed down below it. And yes, that sometimes does interfere with some of our own passages. But we are practical. We simply fill those in and retreat."

I considered this. "But don't they find the filled-in passages?"

Grendel smiled again. "Oh, you cannot tell when trolls fill in a passage, that there ever was a passage there. We have, as I told you, a way with rock and earth. That is why we are so effective in your human mines."

"But," I struggled to understand, "how do your people tolerate that?"

Grendel shrugged. "Those who brave the ban and come up—they are criminals, are they not?"

"But I thought you said that was your ancient role, your prerogative or something?"

Grendel looked at me, his expression enigmatic, but he said nothing, and I decided to let the topic drop.

We remained like that for some time, and I felt love and despair battle with outrage and defiance inside me. At last, I pulled away from Grendel's enormous form.

"No," I said, quietly but firmly. "I'm not going to accept this."

Grendel looked at me with love in his eyes but said nothing. I walked pensively up and down. At last, I stopped and turned to him.

"I'm going to get those tools," I said.

"But you cannot leave your own yard," Grendel reminded me gently.

"We'll see about that." I felt an idea, vague but tantalizing, forming in my mind. "Those blue crystals, where are they? Do you know?"

Grendel shrugged. "They should be buried just below the surface of the lawn, on either side, at the front of your property line."

I nodded, then said, "Wait a minute! They only have them in front?"

Grendel nodded.

"Well, hell! What about escaping by the back, going over the fence?"

Grendel smiled but shook his head. "It is not like that. Your fences, they set up barriers of their own, of a sort. The crystals, in front, that will be enough to sustain a full cordon."

"Oh," I said, and added dejectedly, "Fuck."

"You see—" Grendel began.

"Yes!" I said, cutting him off. "The who knows factor! Well, I'm not going down that road, and I'm not going to give up! I'm going to work on the idea that those crystals are tuned for me, and that if I remove them, I *will* be able to leave."

I got up and said, "Wait here." And I went up to my backyard, and into my back shed. Picking up some tools, and silver duct tape, I went around to the front of the house.

Standing on my front stoop, I leaned over the railing, surveying the part of my front yard adjacent to the sidewalk. Wasn't that the property line? I wasn't sure. But still I was resolved and, after several minutes of looking and shifting my position, I thought I saw a glint of blue between several grass blades. It was situated at the left front corner of my yard, next to my driveway. Then, looking toward the other front corner of my yard, this time with more of a sense of what I was looking for, I spotted a second blue crystal.

I sat down on the front steps and, using duct tape, bound the top foot of my spade's handle to the top foot of my rake. The result was a tool that extended my reach by about nine feet, though I wasn't sure whether the spade or the rake end would be the most suitable.

"Okay," I murmured, and grinning at Jake, who had watched all this with interest, I went down the steps and walked slowly toward the left-hand stone. I was ready for the sensation, which came after several steps. Deciding that I could tolerate this level of unpleasantness, I slid the spade end forward, along the grass, toward where I had seen that blue crystal. I had to shift my head to one side to catch a glimpse of the stone again. From this distance, however, I saw that it appeared to be attached to a square peg driven into my lawn.

My reaching device came to within inches of the crystal, so I took another step forward, clenching my teeth as the wave of nausea hit me. I pushed the spade forward, face down, until it encountered the peg. Then, I pushed. For a second the resistance increased, but then the spade slid to the right.

Grunting in disappointment and leaving the implement where it was, I went back to the stoop and sat there, recovering and thinking. Jake sat beside me. He had been watching my efforts from there, and that struck me as odd. He was a smart and obedient dog, but curious too, and would have felt it his duty, not just to explore my front lawn, but to see what I was doing.

The crystals?

I got up and went through the house and into the backyard, where I found a largish rock that Grendel had unearthed. Taking this, I returned to where they rake-spade lay. I repositioned the spade so its tip pressed against the wooden spike, and then gave the rake end a sharp blow with the rock.

Nothing. The spade had slipped to the side again but there was no sense that the blow had affected the stake's position at all. Gritting my teeth, I repositioned the blade, and *this* time the blow seemed to produce some give. Heartened, I repeated the operation.

It was a tedious business, for I had to work with both precision and strength. It took perhaps twenty blows before I felt the resistance to the blow suddenly disappear. I went back to the stoop and leaned out over the railing, to assess things from a better angle.

Yes! The stake was now lying on the grass, the blue crystal glittering at its far end. I returned to the operation and this time gave the rake end so hard a blow with the rock that I almost lost hold of the handle.

But I saw the stake and its crystal, shoot away, across the sidewalk and over the curb, disappearing into the gutter.

I stood up shakily, and Jake, who had been watching from the front stoop, barked. I turned and grinned at him. Walking wearily back to the steps, I sat down and hugged Jake to me, while he wagged his tail furiously and licked my face.

"Jake," I said to him. "I think you know more than I ever thought possible." In that moment my life seemed enriched almost beyond credulity. With Jake and Grendel—and the prospect of escape—

That thought, unfortunately, brought me down again, but I set my jaw and said to myself: *I don't care. All the rest doesn't matter a hill of beans.*

After about maybe five minutes, I set to work in the same manner on the other crystal, and soon it too was off my lawn. It was even further away, in the gutter on the *far* side of the street, where I could see its blue light twinkling.

I carried my reaching tool back to the stoop, laid it against the railing and, squaring my shoulders, began to walk along the front path, straight toward the sidewalk. I got to where the symptoms had begun before with no problem, but when I was about a foot from the sidewalk, I was assailed with the nausea and dizziness. I almost fell and almost vomited.

With my senses reeling, I turned and made a giant leap back, vaguely in the direction of my house. I was a bit off in my assessment of this, luckily, for I fell onto the grass rather than the concrete of the path. I heard Jake's sharp barking and, looking toward the steps saw him coming toward me, slowly—almost crawling. He was now making some quiet, whimpering noises.

"Go back!" I gasped, gesturing him away. He still came on, however so, with a supreme effort, I got onto my hands and knees and began to crawl toward *him*.

We met at the halfway point, and he licked my face, while I hugged him and wept weakly. Just the physical contact helped, however, and knowing he was with me. I lay there for several minutes, wondering how I must look to anyone happening by. Then I sat up and petted Jake. Finally, I was able to get to my feet. I walked shakily up my front steps and turning, held onto the railing and looked out at my front yard.

I had shifted the position of those crystals, but it hadn't been enough. I could feel tears of weakness as I admitted defeat.

Chapter 14
Bruce to the Rescue

I DON'T KNOW how long I sat with my head bowed, quite unable to make a decision about any further action. I was completely out of initiative, caught in the jaws of failure and despair.

"*Hey!*" called a voice. It seemed to be addressed to me, but I didn't respond at first. What was the point? Also, I *really* didn't want to have to make conversation with anybody; I just wasn't in the mood.

"*Hey!*" called the voice again. And then added, "*Ken!*"

The moment I heard my name used I recognized the voice. I wearily raised my head, and saw Bruce Philpot sitting on his bicycle, foot on the curb, just where my front path met the sidewalk.

My first thought was, *How can he do that, sit there like that, so calm, casual and collected—oblivious to my nightmare situation?*

He was regarding me curiously, and when I slowly raised a hand in a vague wave, he said, "You okay?"

I shrugged and nodded listlessly.

After a few seconds, he shook his head. "Well, you don't *look* okay."

At this point, one of my neighbors came along, walking his dog—Clancy, a collie and friend of Jake's. Jake wriggled out of my arms and went down the steps but stopped halfway to the sidewalk. He gave a single sharp bark, at which Clancy stopped and wagged his tail, but wouldn't go further.

The man looked a little puzzled at this; usually Jake was all over his friends when they came by. Clancy, I saw, seemed inclined to stop. He seemed puzzled too by Jake's apparent reticence. The man, however, after waving at me and glancing at Bruce, gave Jake an odd look, and continued on his way.

Bruce watched the man and dog go. Then he looked at me and finally at Jake, who was now sitting where he had stopped, looking after the other dog.

Bruce frowned. "That was—odd."

I nodded.

Bruce looked at me again. I thought he going to say something, but then he seemed to change his mind. It occurred to me that in another minute he would be gone, and an idea struck me. I stood up.

"Bruce!"

He looked at me and nodded questioningly.

"Uh, do you have your cell phone on you?"

"Yeah!"

"Could you—call me on it—my landline?"

He looked surprised. "Sure!"

I watched as he extracted his phone. Several seconds later I heard the sound of my own phone inside the house through my open front door. I went in, to the kitchen, and picked up the phone.

"Hello?"

But there was only static on the line.

I felt a cold wash of horror at this. I had used this phone to contact the shop not that long ago. Which meant they were onto us. In a spasm of annoyance, I banged the phone on the table several times and spoke into it again.

"Hello?"

More static.

I went back out to the front stoop.

"Not working!" I called. A couple walking down the sidewalk across the street looked over, and I became aware of the odd spectacle Bruce and I were making, half shouting across the twenty-five-foot depth of my front yard.

Bruce now let down his bike's kickstand and got off. I stood up.

"Wait!" I cried, holding my hands out in a gesture of warding off. Bruce stopped and stared at me, his mouth slightly open.

"What?"

Feeling sick in my stomach, I shook my head. "Don't come closer. Please."

"Really? Why?"

"I—" I stopped, seeing my neighbor come out onto her front porch. She had a cup of coffee and was picking up her paper. Then she sat down in the porch chair. She was as close to me as was Bruce. I felt defeated. I couldn't have a shouted conversation—especially considering what I wanted to *say* to Bruce.

"Hold on!" I told him, and made a praying gesture.

He nodded, crossed his arms, and broadened his stance in a waiting posture.

I ran through the house and into the backyard. Grendel looked at me when I jumped the final steps into the chamber. I was a bit out of breath, but he calmly waited for me to speak.

"My land line's not working now. All I get is static. Is that—them?"

Grendel considered, then nodded.

"But—I mean, the phone worked earlier—"

Grendel Rising 113

"That was—earlier."

"Oh! They're tightening the screws?"

Grendel hesitated, nodded again.

A sick feeling came over me. *Okay*, I thought. It made a kind of grisly sense. They were preparing for the planned pick-up next morning, not wanting the bird to have flown meanwhile. My sense of dread and desperation rose sharply, threatening to choke me. But I took a deep, calming breath, and explained Bruce Philpot was out front, on his bike, just on the sidewalk.

I outlined my plan to have him do the shopping, but said I was uneasy about a shouted exchange on that issue. Grendel listened without comment until I had finished.

"I think it well," he said at last, "not to let him come to the house. He might become—trapped as well." He grimaced. "As I said—unexpected effects."

I nodded. "That's what I was thinking, too. As a possibility. We can't take that chance."

Grendel nodded. "I would err on the side of caution, not to bring into this someone else—an innocent bystander."

"Exactly! I mean—Jake, he won't go down the walk, even to greet a friend of his."

Grendel looked grim but said nothing.

"What do you suggest?" I asked, feeling put against it.

Grendel put his big hands together and, lowering his head, evidently thinking. After a minute, he raised his head and smiled.

"Technology," he said. "That is your enemy here. It is the poison of your modern human society. They—the government—use it as a means to control the citizenry."

If anyone had told me this before all this with Grendel had started, I would have called them a conspiracy nut. Now, sadder and wiser, I merely nodded.

"So," continued Grendel. "Avoid—technology."

I frowned. "But—I want to talk to Bruce—" I began, but Grendel held up a hand.

"Do you have empty cans? Soup cans?"

I stared. "Yeah—"

"And—something like—string?"

I blinked several times, and finally the penny dropped. I had experimented with that sort of primitive telephone as a kid. I remember having been surprised at how well it worked.

"Thanks!" I cried, and ran back up the steps and inside.

After telling Bruce to give me several minutes, I gathered the supplies:

cans, a pair of large scissors, and a ball of twine. Then I sat on the stoop, hard at work with my construction.

"Ever tried one of these?" I called to him when I had finished. I was holding up the two cans.

He shook his head.

"Here!" I cried, and tossed him the can. He caught it, and holding it, looked at me.

I saw that the twine had been several feet too long. Gesturing for him to wait, I reached into my can and pulled through the excess twine. Cutting this off, I knotted the end, and pulled the string taught.

"Hold it to your ear to listen, your mouth to speak. Okay?"

He shrugged. But he was grinning now. Evidently this manifestation of his tutor's more whacky side amused him.

We had, I noticed, gotten several puzzled glances from my neighbor. I knew she had good hearing and was thankful we had this way to communicate. Remembering the disastrous influence my neighbor on the other side, Mr. Henderson, had had on the situation, there was no way I wanted more neighborly interest.

"Okay!" I said, and pointed to my ear and then to him.

Bruce obediently put the can to his ear, and I stepped back to further tighten the string.

"Okay," I said into my can. "Nod your head if you can hear me."

He looked slightly astonished but gave me a thumbs-up. I nodded back, and took a deep breath. *And here goes!*

I told him how I was in a very odd situation, that I could explain, but not right now, and that time was of the essence. To do him credit, he listened without visible reaction, though I saw the expression on his face become puzzled, and possibly somewhat impatient.

"Did you get that?" I asked him.

He nodded, and then pointed to his ear and toward me. I nodded back and put my can to my ear. Bruce put his own can, open end to his mouth, and heard his voice in that strange, muffled way I remembered from my youth.

"Can you hear me?" he said.

I nodded and gave him a thumbs-up signal.

There was a pause, and then I heard his voice say, "Is this—something to do with the, uh, person I saw you with in the swimming pool the night before last?"

I lowered the can and stared at him. He was regarding me piercingly. Then, he motioned to his ear again. I raised the can to my ear and pulled the string taut.

"I saw you—through the curtains," he explained. "When you came back, just before dawn." Then, after another pause, "He was there with you, in the pool, when I came home, right? I didn't see him, but I'm guessing he was there anyway. Is that what's going on now? Something about him?"

I pointed to my ear and to him. He put his can to his ear, and I spoke.

"Can you—tell me, what you saw?"

He lowered the can and looked at me suspiciously. Finally, he nodded, pointing at his ear and at me.

"It was—I don't know. He was—hard to see, kind of." He paused and we both gazed at each other in silence. "But—I had the impression—that he was—really, *really* big." He grinned then. "So, tell me I'm crazy. But you knew that." He paused and added in a sad voice, "You always knew that."

I felt my chest tighten at his tone and what he had said. I smiled, pointed to my ear and to him.

"No," I said. "You're not crazy. It's the situation that's crazy. You have *no idea!*"

He nodded, pointed to his ear, and said through the cans, "Okay. But what do you want me to do?"

I felt like swooning in that moment—hope, so distant and small, seemed to rush toward me and all but overwhelm me.

"Thank you!" I called, without bothered with the cans. This got me a look from my neighbor, and a frown, but right then, it didn't bother me. I used the can to say, "Just wait here. Please!"

He smiled and nodded, and I, with butterflies and a pounding heart, sped through the house to get my secret cache of cash, which was in a shoebox in my bedroom closet. After hesitating, I took all of this, came back downstairs, put a rubber band around it. Sitting down at the kitchen table, I took out Grendel's note. I had written the shop's address on the back of this, and now I hesitated, wondering whether it would be a good thing to add the name of the shop as well.

I decided against this—you never knew. But looking at Grendel's rune list, I felt Bruce needed some assistance, so I wrote a brief explanation, drew some arrows. Then I made a few further marks, and wrapped the note around the cash, fixing it with another rubber band, so the address was showing.

Okay!

I went out my front door again, and saw that Bruce was now sitting on the curb, next to his bike—which meant, of course, that he was facing away from me. When he heard the front door close, however, he rose and turned. Descending the steps, I lifted my can and pointed to his.

With a curious sense of unreality, I described what I wanted him to do, told him about the list and the money I had enclosed in it, adding that if the cost was greater than what was there, I would pay him back. When I had finished, I asked if he understood.

He lowered the can and looked at me. Then, to my surprised delight, he grinned and gave me a thumbs-up signal. With a laugh, I threw the package to him, and he caught it.

Tucking this inside his shirt, he gave me a thumbs-up, tossed me his can, and rode away on his bike.

I HAD TO sit down to recover from the experience. I was shaking and almost crying, and I took great comfort in Jake sitting loyally beside me. I petted him and sniffed.

"Okay," I murmured at last. "So far, so good."

Then I got up and we went inside. I poured myself a glass of Coke and drank this before my brain began to work again. I looked at the clock. It was just before two P.M., and I was *starving*.

So, I got busy and made a huge tray of food. I unthawed and heated all of my frozen spaghetti sauce and cooked up all the pasta I had. To this I added ham-and-cheese sandwiches, ice cream, and several different types of snack food, including potato chips and cheezies—and, of course, Coke.

It took two trips to carry everything. When I descended into his chamber, I saw that Grendel was asleep. Then I noticed something else: there was a large tunnel dug out of the far side of the chamber. Next to it my wheelbarrow was parked.

Grendel had been busy!

I looked at his sleeping form for almost a minute, admiring his innocent beauty as he lay, eyes closed, hands resting on his chest, snoring gently. Then I returned for the rest of the meal, and when I had brought that, I saw that Grendel had awoken.

"The smell of good food," he said, smiling.

"I hope you're hungry," I said.

"I can always eat," he said, smiling.

As we ate, I told Grendel about sending Bruce off with the list, and some money. Grendel looked uneasy when I mentioned the latter, but said nothing, so I didn't ask.

And then, out of the blue, I began to sob. "Sorry!" I said through them. "Nerves, I guess."

I had been sitting, my shoulder against Grendel's side, and now he put his arm around me. It was very comforting, and gradually I recovered.

At last, I sniffed, and said, "I just can't believe Bruce is doing this for us." And I explained he had seen Grendel in his backyard.

"Yes," Grendel said. "I am not surprised." Then he added, "He is a good friend."

"Yes," I said, and sniffed. "But, funny. I didn't—know that."

"*Not* funny," Grendel corrected me. "It is in the crises of life that we discover who our true friends are."

I nodded. "I wonder whether he believes it—"

I felt more than heard Grendel's rumble of amusement.

"What?" I said, looking up at him.

"I am just wondering," he said, smiling down at me, "whether you do."

I blinked in surprise, then reached out and ran my hand along the smooth solidity of Grendel's enormous hand.

"I believe in you," I said.

Grendel nodded. "Yes," he said. "I am thinking that of your friend, that it does not matter whether he believes in what you told him, only that he believes in *you*."

"Oh!" I said, feeling a sudden lump in my throat. I took hold of Grendel's hand and kissed it. "I—feel kind of bad about him. I guess—I don't know. I kind of feel that I wasn't a good friend to *him*."

"But you said you were his tutor. Is that right?"

"Yes—"

"And were you a good tutor?"

"I think so," I said, slightly defensively. "But I don't think I was a good *friend*, Grendel! Surely that matters more?"

"You were a good tutor. You are becoming good friends. I see nothing bad in that."

I considered this, and chuckled.

"Boy!" I said. "You're right. I really do make heavy weather of things!"

"Yes. I would say, if you wonder about your being a good friend to Bruce, perhaps keep that in mind now and in the future, when you act."

I considered this. "Oh, I get it. A test?"

"Indeed."

"Oh! Good! Well, whatever happens, I won't let him down." I felt a little doubtful about this, however; I wasn't sure what might be required of me.

"And remember," Grendel added after a minute. "He saw me with you, in the pool."

I looked at him, puzzled. "That had some sort of—effect?"

Grendel's deep, rumbling chuckle gave me pleasurable goosebumps.

"No, no. You have it backward. It is his nature—the nature of his heart—that made him able to see me, or rather, left him open to seeing me. The hidden nature of each person's heart—that is the center of all wonder and magic in the world, and a true joy when the discovery of that heart is made through this sort of action."

I nodded, feeling an especially warm glow toward Grendel. I leaned against him, and he held me more tightly. This magical moment was only interrupted briefly by Jake insisting on climbing onto my lap and licking Grendel's thumb, his tail wagging furiously. I put my free arm around him and pulled him in, Grendel watching this with his great, mild eyes.

"They won't defeat us!" I said quietly to Grendel as I looked into his eyes. I felt not just determined. I felt undefeatable; what I felt, what Grendel and I shared, was too good, too real, and too *important* to be destroyed by petty politics and narrow bureaucratic thinking.

IT OCCURRED TO me that I really should be out front when Bruce returned. It wasn't as if he could phone me when he arrived. So, with reluctance, I left Grendel and went back into the house. He told me he would do some digging.

I opened the front door, only leaving the screen door closed, and told Jake to keep watch. It was something he understood and, in between watching what I was doing, he ensconced himself on the back of my couch, where he could look out the front window.

I cleaned up the lunch dishes and started prep on dinner. This included several capons from the freezer downstairs, potatoes in several pots, and mixed canned vegetables. I started each capon in my microwave, then shifted them to the oven—*ovens*, I *should* say; the previous owners had been observant Jews and had had two ovens to keep their cooking kosher. While I knew little of such things, I was grateful now for that second oven.

While I did all this, I listened for the sound of Bruce's return, and wondered how long it would take—if it was going to be successful at all!

It was just before five o'clock when I took coffee out to Grendel. This time I noticed how the piles of dirt and rock in my yard were much more considerable than they had been. I descended to the chamber and saw it was empty. I went to the opening to the tunnel and peered into it. It descended fairly steeply, the stray illumination from the top of the stairs rapidly fading into inky darkness. I shivered slightly; it would be a definite slog climbing up that slope for any distance. I wondered how long the tunnel was.

I called down, "*Hello!*"

"Yes?" Grendel's echoey voice came from what sounded like a considerable distance.

"Coffee!"

A pause. "Oh. Yes. Thank you! One minute."

Grendel appeared out of the darkness of the tunnel so suddenly that I

Grendel Rising 119

started. I saw that his skin was slick with sweat, which I found *very* attractive. *The hotness of the working man*, I thought to myself as he seated himself in the chamber. I held out his coffee, and as he took it, the movement of his muscles made them glisten in the dim light of the chamber.

We shared our coffee in silence while I looked at him, at the tunnel mouth, at Jake. I finished my coffee at last, stood up and stretched. Then I looked at him, taking in his beauty.

"You're very clean," I commented.

He looked down at himself, then at me. "Yes. Dirt tends to slough off—thankfully." He grinned at me, and I reached out and ran my hand over the slickness of his thigh muscle. It was warm and my fingertips tingled with the electricity of contact. Grendel was sitting with one leg bent, foot on the floor of the chamber, knee at roughly the height of my chin. With a small moan, I moved forward and wrapped my arms around the leg, placing my chin on the knee. The leg was wonderfully slick and I ran my hands over the skin in a state of sensual bliss.

I felt Grendel's hand come and gently touch my back, and I soaked up the sense of connection that touch added to my pleasure. When the hand was removed after a minute or two, I stepped back. I looked up at him.

"Back to work?"

He nodded, holding out the now-empty mixing bowl "coffee cup." I took it, and we exchanged smiles of understanding and commiseration before he turned and headed back down the tunnel.

With a sigh, I went up the stairs and inside. I poured myself a second cup of coffee and took this out onto the front stoop. Sitting there, Jake beside me, I sipped my coffee as we kept vigil. I noticed Jake was very alert, and he was keeping close to me. He didn't look worried, but he knew something was up. I petted him affectionately, thankful for his solidarity.

I had just finished my coffee, when a cab pulled up. Bruce got out, went to the trunk and lifted out a large canvas bag. When the cab drove off, he went to the far end of my walk and gestured: Could he approach? I shook my head vigorously. When he opened his mouth, I got up and threw him one of the cans.

I saw his shoulders sag at this, but he picked the can up and put it to his mouth. And when I had mine against my ear, he said, "Well, I got the stuff."

I nodded to him and gave him a thumbs-up. He saw this but still held the can to his mouth.

"You gonna tell me something about all this? Is there some kind of infection or something? The plague?"

I shook my head, then pointed to him and to my ear.

"No," I told him. "If you could toss the bag to me." Then, I added with all the assurance I could muster, "And I *will* explain later, I promise."

He scowled but nodded. Then he tossed me the can and picked up the canvas bag. He started to turn and, going round and round like an athlete in the hammer throw event, finally let go, so the bag and its contents soared up and over, right toward me. I leaped aside, and the bag landed with a muffled clang on the railing of my stoop and then fell onto the stoop itself.

"Good one!" I called to him. He nodded, but then gave me a disappointed look.

"Thanks!" I added, and then, "Later! Promise!"

He nodded again and then, putting his hands in his pockets, slowly mooched off. I took the bag inside, feeling like a kid at Christmas, about to open a present.

Now, I told myself, *we have at least a chance.*

AS I CARRIED the heavy canvas bag through the house to the back door, I had the definite sense that the clock of countdown had begun to tick. I took the bag straight down to Grendel's chamber. He was down the tunnel so I went to the tunnel mouth and called.

"*They're he-ere!*"

Grendel appeared after maybe twenty seconds. Evidently, he was now moving more quickly than before. I thought, he must have the same sense of the ticking down of the clock.

After smiling his thanks at me, he opened the bag and surveyed its contents. Then he lowered his head, as if in prayer and remained like that for a while. Finally, breathing in through his nose, he murmured, "*Yes!*"

He began to go through the contents of the bag, now and then removing items. He did this with a striking exactness, setting each down gently on the floor of the chamber. He was not emptying the bag; presumably extracting the items he wanted immediately.

His search of the bag's contents began to take on a different quality, and a puzzled expression formed on his face. At last, he stopped and, turning to look at me.

He said in a quiet but intense tone, "*What have you done?*"

Chapter 15
Barrier

THE WAVE OF hope and joy that had washed over me during this extraction process was quenched by a wash of icy fear.

"Uh—what?"

Grendel stared at me, then into the bag again. He frowned, and I could see he was restraining his emotions—which in itself was scary.

"There was something, a device," he said quietly. "It is for—short-circuiting their barrier crystals. It was the first item on the list I wrote, that you gave to Bruce." He paused, and his expression changed, anger gone. "Perhaps they did not have them. But still, it is curious."

I felt my face burning, and I swallowed. Every muscle in my body tensed in preparation for the moment he would look at me again. He was still searching the bag.

"And there is the other—" He stopped, and added, "And—"

He straightened up and looked at me. This time his expression was confused and hurt rather than angry. His gaze was almost shy, as if he found it difficult looking at me.

"It is strange—" he said.

"I crossed them off!" I blurted out. "Those first items—for going out rather than down."

His eyes widened and his mouth opened.

"I don't want you to go out," I continued, desperate to explain myself. "It sounded like a horrible life. I want you to be safe, to go back down."

He blinked but said nothing.

"And—" I began, choking slightly. "I was hoping—well, that I could go with you!"

It was only when I had said this last that I breathed a sigh of relief. At least I had gotten it all out. Now I only had to wait for whatever his response would be. Frankly, I didn't have a lot of hope that I could go down with him. But I was firm in not wanting him hiding and running, and possibly getting caught somewhere in the wastes of wilderness out west. And for that, well, I was willing to lose him altogether. If I knew he was safe, back in the Underworld, well, I figured I could cope with that. Maybe there was even some way to communicate—rock banging or something—

I had lowered my gaze during all of this, but when Grendel moved, I looked up again. He came toward me and took me gently into his arms and rocked me slowly side to side. I found this reassuring, and infinitely welcome. It was some time before I spoke.

"Do you understand?" I said, my voice muffled by his chest.

"Yes," he murmured, adding, "And, yes."

I blinked, wondering about this second *yes*. Then it hit me and I struggled out of his arms and stepped back, to stare at him.

"*You mean*—?" I gasped.

He was smiling his beatific smile. "Mean what?" he said, but from the smile I knew that he knew what I meant. With a sob I threw myself back into his arms and began to cry with happiness.

"Yes," he murmured, holding me close again, "Yes, and yes, and yes."

Again, we stood like this for some time, and it was not until Grendel spoke again that I felt myself capable of coherent thought.

"There is something," he said, "in this bag."

I stepped back and he went to the bag. Reaching in, he pulled out something that was cloth. Turning, he held it out to me.

"For you," he said.

I took it. It was a garment of some sort, gray in color and made of a fabric that was incredibly soft and supple. On impulse, I held it against my cheek.

"Nice!" I murmured.

There were two items—a pair of sweatpants and a sweatshirt. When I held them up, I saw they had a subtle gray-on-gray camouflage pattern. I held the pants against my waist.

"They fit!" I commented. "Though they'll be a bit loose."

Grendel smiled mischievously. "You will grow into them, I think."

His smile made me think, and a moment later his meaning hit me.

"Oh!" I grinned, thinking about the effect of troll semen on size. "I'll outgrow them, I guess." I looked at him questioningly.

"We'll see," he said, with a smile.

At that moment, I was reminded of our threesome the previous evening. "You know, that G-man is going to have that problem, too. I'm pretty sure he, uh, absorbed at lot of your—seed last night."

Grendel nodded, his smile becoming almost wicked. "It should be interesting," he said. "They will know why, at the Bureau, when that happens."

I had mixed feelings at this thought. The guy *had* helped us—at least by delaying things by twenty-four hours. But there was something satisfying, an appreciation of ironic justice, in the idea that he would probably be suffering

Grendel Rising

a career setback due to his one instance of indulgence with the *enemy*, so to speak. And, who knew? Maybe it would inspire others with deeply repressed cases of *rock fever*.

Coming back to the present moment, I shucked my too-small clothes and put on the new sweats. The feel of the fabric against my body—wonderful! I ran my hands over my chest and legs, experiencing a tingle of sensuous pleasure *and* a slight but delightful erotic heat as well.

"Wow!" I murmured. "Like cashmere!" I remembered once having felt a cashmere item on display in a department store and discovering why it was so expensive.

Grendel smiled in a pleased fashion, but then, as if remembering the ticking of the clock, he turned to the bag and extracted a spade. He held this out, pointing to the blade, which I saw was silvered.

"These tips are specially designed, for penetrating the barrier." Then he sighed. "It is no longer Halloween, so getting past will be more of a challenge. But with these tools, we will be able."

A thought that had been at the back of my mind now came to the fore.

"That barrier—the geostatic barrier. You said it's different from the barriers created by those crystals?"

Grendel nodded. "Yes. It is natural, for one thing—"

"But, I mean, is it—different, in its—I don't know, in its nature?"

He looked at me. "Well," he said. "I am no expert on that sort of thing. But if you *see* the geostatic barrier, perhaps you will form your own opinion—having already seen the other, those crystals."

"Okay." Then I realized what he was saying. "Oh!" I cried excitedly. "Can I help?"

Grendel looked at me solemnly. "The geostatic barrier, it is for separating the two worlds. It is the nature of trolls to pass through, however. Of humans, I know little. Certainly, the human authorities understand these things, and can—" He stopped and shook his head. Then he looked at me and spoke sternly.

"No doubt you can assist. I will say this, however. The geostatic barrier is dangerous. Very much so. I ask you one thing: You must not go near it. I mean, near enough for direct physical contact. Do you agree to this?"

I swallowed, wondering how I was going to get through, if I was to go with him beyond the barrier. But I nodded, and he smiled and nodded too, relieved. He put a fist to his chest and said, "Then you may—I mean, I would very much value and appreciate your assistance in the work to be done."

I laughed at his solemn formality, grabbing his hand and putting it against my cheek.

"Hadn't we better hurry?" I said. "Or is there much further to go?"

"Not much further, no. But there is the barrier. That—in itself is, well—if you come down to help me, you will see."

He was just reaching down for the tools, when I said, "Food!"

He stopped and looked at me.

"What about something to eat first? I've been cooking!"

He smiled and nodded. "Of course. Thank you!"

WE PICNICKED IN the backyard. I spread out the meal on a tablecloth set on the only grassy part of my overgrown yard. In addition to gallons of Coke, there was a green salad, a potato salad, the two roast chickens, with vegetables—all in large amounts. Jake sat on the edge of the tablecloth and received occasional tidbits from each of us.

It was a *feast*. I couldn't help thinking of it as a possible last supper together but pushed the thought away. Food was fuel; I knew that, and by hell, I resolved we would both be full of juice for whatever transpired in the next twelve hours.

Afterwards, Grendel lay down and seemed to drift into a dreamy state, though his eyes were open; he seemed to be looking up at the blue sky. I leaned back against him, thankful that neighbors, looking out of second-floor windows, would not notice the enormous male figure—*naked!*—that lay in my backyard.

I was brought out of my peaceful state by the sound of something like a motor, except more high-pitched. I had been vaguely aware of the sound before it had registered consciously. It had been increasing in volume, which suggested that, whatever the source of the sound, it was approaching.

I sat up and looked around, searching for the direction of the sound. I realized to my surprise that it was coming from somewhere *above*!

I scanned the rooftop of my neighbor's house and the sky above it, and saw at last *something* that was moving slowly, about fifty feet up and coming nearer. Finally, I was able to see that it was one of those small drones—comprised of four horizontal propellers, set in a square frame, with something in the middle.

Probably a camera, I thought with a stab of fear.

Grendel sat up on his elbows, and was looking at the object, too. Now it hovered over my neighbor's back patio and descended to a height of about twenty feet. It drifted away from the house, then came toward my yard—but stopped when it was directly over my backyard fence. It then retreated, drifted further along, then approached again. Again, it stopped when it reached the fence.

This pattern of movement was repeated several more times. It struck me that it was like an insect trying to get through a closed window. Something about that bothered me, but I was distracted by Grendel's low chuckle.

"I am impressed," he said when I looked at him.

"By what?"

"Well, with the crystals, no electronics should function at the boundary to your yard."

I stared at him. "What *should* happen?"

Grendel continued to watch the device. "It should," he said, "fall."

I stared at the drone, which continued to hover just on the far side of the fence, apparently considering another attempt at approaching again. A thought struck me.

"Is it them—the government, I mean, spying?"

Grendel shook his head without letting the drone out of his sight.

"No. Not them."

Momentarily, I wondered how he knew, but that really was beside the point.

"Who, then?"

"It is—a benevolent source. Curious rather than hostile."

"Oh!" I put my hand on Grendel's shoulder. "It might be Bruce," I said. "And, he's kind of electronically minded."

"The friend who brought the tools?" Grendel asked.

"Yeah. What do you think?"

"Possibly."

"What should we do, though? Could you bring it down?"

Grendel looked at me and smiled. "Certainly!"

"So?"

Grendel hesitated, then shook his head. "Do no harm, save against direct aggression or definite malevolence," he said. "That is the law—and a good law it is."

"So. What then?"

He shrugged. "We continue our work."

And, with that he got up and headed toward the stairs. I remained where I was, staring up at the drone. Finally, resisting the urge to raise a middle finger at it, I waved vaguely instead, and followed Grendel.

WHEN I ARRIVED at the entrance of the tunnel, I saw that Grendel had extracted two further items from the canvas bag. One was a lantern, the other a large metal can. He held the lamp out to me, saying, "Oil lamp."

I took this and shook it slightly. It was full.

"And a reserve of oil," he continued, indicating the can.

I examined the lamp. Fortunately, I had done enough camping to be familiar with this kind of lamp. It had a flat wick and, from the label on the oil can, apparently burned paraffin oil. I twiddled the knob to see the wick rise and descend, which would control the size of the flame.

"Should I light it?" I asked, before realizing I hadn't brought out any matches.

Grendel, who had been rummaging in the bag, lifted something out and, turning to smile at me, tossed me a package. I caught it and saw that it was a dozen boxes of matches in plastic wrap.

"Ha!" I cried. I extricated one of the matchboxes from the wrap and looked at him.

"Light it?" I asked again.

He nodded and, gently taking the remaining matchboxes from me, replaced them in the bag.

I squatted down and lit the lamp. When its tiny flame was burning steadily, I stood up and brandished the lamp, swinging it from side to side.

"Clang, clang, clang!" I cried. "Approaching points! Stop, then proceed with caution!"

Grendel laughed and I joined in. "Probably not correct," I admitted, then added, "Why not an electric—oh!"

Grendel nodded.

"Low-tech," I said. He nodded again.

Grendel bent and picked up an item that had been lying next to the canvas bag. It was a vinyl backpack.

"For you," he said.

I took it, putting the matchbox I had used into one of the outside pockets and the oil can in the main part. Then, hoisting it onto my back, I picked up the lantern. Grendel had replaced the tools in the canvas bag, and now slung the bag onto his shoulder. Thus encumbered, we headed down the tunnel.

I was struck how the play of that small light source on the magnificent form in front of me seemed to underscore the mythic aspect of what was going on here. The only problem, I thought, was that I didn't really see myself as belonging in any myth.

At the other end of the tunnel, which must have been at least several hundred feet in length, and fairly steep, though I found it manageable, was another chamber of sorts. Holding up the lamp, I looked around, and was startled to see how big the chamber was.

The roof was about as high as his first chamber, but it was oddly shaped, like a triangle, with slightly rounded corners. The tunnel opened at one of the corners, so the chamber widened out to left and right. In front, the far wall was perhaps twenty feet distant. I turned to look at Grendel.

He pointed to either side. "To put the detritus," he said. "From this point on, I do not want to expend the energy of carting material to the surface." For a second, I thought of suggesting I might, but then realized the steep slope of the tunnel would defeat me, even with a modest burden or earth or rock.

I nodded. Then, looking around again, I noticed in a far part of the chamber the dim shape of my wheelbarrow. I pointed to it and looked at him again. He nodded.

"It is not far, now. Though the—progress will be difficult."

"So, I cart the stuff away, to the far parts of the chamber. Is that right?" I asked just to be certain.

"If you will."

"Certainly!" I resisted the urge to hug him; this was a time for industry, not emotions.

I looked down, then, and noticed Jake was standing quite close to me, in fact between me and Grendel, as if he had decided that was the safest place for him in this troglodytic space. Reaching down, I petted him, and then, standing up, gave Grendel a "well, let's do it," look.

Grendel nodded and reached his arm out to the rough wall he was standing in front of.

"This," he said. "Is where the barrier lies. It is quite close." I noticed this wall of the chamber had a kind of rocky shelf in it, running the full width of the chamber. I looked at it, then at Grendel.

"Okay."

"I can," he said, indicating the shelf, "deal with this sort of thing—rock—manually. But it takes energy. These tools," he indicated them where they lay on the floor, "amplify my physical strength. I need not use my—troll faculties as much."

"Okay," I repeated, not sure I fully understood.

"So," he said, and picked up a pickaxe, "we begin."

I had dimly registered the fact that the tools Bruce had brought, scaled for humans, looked small when Grendel handled them. It was only now that I realized just how tiny a tool this was for him. It almost looked like a toy in his grasp. But he positioned himself feet apart, took hold of the haft with one hand over the other, and swung it in an arc, slowly, testing, with straight elbows. I noticed he didn't hold it two-handed in the way I imagined workers held pickaxes, one hand at the end of the handle, the other partway down the shaft, but rather like a golfer, one hand *over* the other, both near the end of the handle. Then, drawing it back, he paused, and with sudden, startling speed brought it forward.

When it struck the rock, there came an explosion of sound, steel on rock, which shot through my head and echoed like mad.

I blinked, shaking my head to rid my ears of the persistent ringing. It did no good, however; clearly the sound would take its own time to fade. I looked around for Jake and saw that he was gone.

Smart dog! I thought, chuckling. He'd probably headed up the tunnel the moment Grendel's swing had begun.

Grendel was looking at me, his eyebrows raised questioningly. I grinned and gave him a thumbs-up signal. He motioned that I should move further away, though there hadn't been much in the way of rock debris from his initial stroke. I saw that he had seemed to have opened a fissure between two rock masses, a crack that extended vertically maybe five feet, though it was only an inch wide at its widest point.

I did as he had indicated, more willing due to the sound level of the first blow, and I put my hands over my ears for the second strike. And so, it began. He made regular blows with the pickaxe at the rock shelf and I, moving back and forth with the wheelbarrow, picked up and carted away the bits that landed around him. I adapted to his rhythm, watching his actions, using my hands for each successive blow to protect my eardrums, and moving in to pick up rocks closer to him when he paused between blows.

We made steady progress, and I was impressed with how quickly he had pulverized that rocky shelf.

I had settled into a kind of regular work state, immersed in the rhythm of our joint action and feeling rather good about it while taking glances at Grendel's magnificent form now and then, which was shinier than ever with sweat from his exertions, appreciating how his muscles rippled as he worked. I was even starting to feel distinctly randy, when one blow produced a shriek quite different from the steel-on-stone sound. The sound seemed to go right *through* my hands, assaulting my eardrums. I leaped several inches into the air and landed, staggering, my hair standing on end.

"*What the hell?*" I shouted at him in the ringing silence. "What was that?"

But Grendel was examining the site of his blow and nodding to himself. Without responding to me, then, he pulled his arms back for another blow, and I cringed, hands on ears for a possible repetition of that unnerving shriek.

I clenched my teeth, closed my eyes and stiffened every muscle. The fact that I expected the sound this time helped, somewhat, though it did cause a shiver to pass through my body. *It sounded so—organic! Like something alive, something shrieking in pain.*

This time, after examining what the pickaxe had achieved, Grendel turned to look at me.

"What?" I said, removing my hands.

He beckoned to me, and I approached hesitantly. He was pointing at a small region, recessed within the current workface.

It was shining in a silvery, bluish fashion!

I stared at it for what seemed a long time. I even hazarded leaning in, so my face was within a foot or two of it, and was unpleasantly struck by a sense that this silvery surface was not just shining but also *buzzing*. Shifting my head slightly, I wasn't quite sure that this was an auditory phenomenon, or simply a subjective phenomenon arising from an instinctual sense of the surface's active, menacing nature.

Standing up again, I stepped away and turning, looked at Grendel. "*That's* the barrier?"

He nodded, his expression grim.

I looked again at the ragged opening in the surrounding rock that exposed the shining silvery surface and shook my head.

"You came up through *that*?" I murmured. When Grendel said nothing, I looked at him. He shrugged and nodded.

"It is—something—different," he said, "when it is just me and the earth and stone and the barrier, which as I told you is to some degree natural."

"Oh." I didn't say more, because I had an odd sense that perhaps I didn't want details of this.

Grendel's chest was still heaving, I noticed. He had the definite air of someone preparing himself for a further effort at a harrowing task. At one level, I registered the powerfully erotic quality of this—a rugged virility that was almost pornographic. But I didn't really respond to this, for there was another element, more potent, more powerful, a kind of gothic majesty: Grendel's primordial form, now lit as much by the glowing silver radiance as by the lantern, set against the rough stone and earth walls and ceiling of the chamber. It was breathtaking: beautiful and awe-inspiring. *Archetypal,* in fact!

I blinked, hardly knowing *what* to feel, confronted with all of this—and happily focused on my sense of connection, my feeling of love for this massive person, this majestic troll, and once more felt grounded in my own reality. This, I told myself, would keep me sane and functioning through—well, everything!

Grendel now dropped the pickaxe and picked up another of the tools, a silver-tipped spade, and held it out to me.

"This edge," he said, indicating the half-inch of silver that marked the lowest part of the blade, "is effective. It extends—" He hesitated then and shook his head. "Here," he said, pointing at the rock surface immediately to the right of the glowing exposed barrier. "Chip away with the edge of the spade only." He demonstrated and, with two sharp blows that seemed mere taps in comparison with his previous blows, caused that small piece the rock face to fall away, exposing more of the barrier.

I was struck by the increase in the buzzing sound, but Grendel picked up the large flake of rock and held it out to me. "Like this," he said. "But do not touch the barrier itself with the spade."

Then he demonstrated what I was not to do. The moment the silver blade made contact with the shining blue surface there was a kind of angry, sizzling sound that made me step back. Looking at Grendel, I saw him grimace for several seconds, as if in agony. Then he gave a quiet sigh, and recovered.

Handing me the spade, he said, "Remember. Around the edges. Chip the rock away." I nodded. He paused, and said, "If you *do* touch the barrier with your blade, let the energy go *through* you. And take a break when and for as long as you need to."

What? I thought. *To recover?*

But now Grendel had retrieved his pickaxe and was winding up for his next blow. I dropped the spade and put my hand to my ears just in time. Even so, that shriek was still very loud and still *very* disturbing.

It took me a few seconds to recover. I was about to move, to begin my own business, but froze as he drew back for another blow, covering my ears. I wondered how I was to contribute at all with this regular assault on my senses. For the moment, I decided just to watch, to wait until some opportunity presented itself. But it went on and on, a kind of pseudo-nightmare of nearly continuous noise as the series of blows against the barrier increased in pace.

And I saw at last how *hard* Grendel could work. Like a demon, really, and the sweat fairly poured off him. The sight of his Herculean efforts, his slick muscular form moving so purposefully, muscles straining, his skin glistening the in the strange silvery light of the barrier, was truly an awesome sight. It would, I thought, have made a really fine porn video all by itself; I had to remind myself repeatedly that I had a perfect right to look—well, stare, really, to be honest.

Why not look? For, as it turned out, I didn't quite have the nerve to contribute myself. Not only was there the endless series of shrieks, but any contribution I might make would have required my getting just a little too close to that industrial-level activity.

After some time, it occurred to me that Grendel could use some refreshment. So, I went back up the tunnel to my backyard, and brought the garden hose down into the first chamber, along with my two buckets, which I scrupulously cleaned beforehand. Then, thinking on it, I decided I could do a little better. So, I went into the house and squeezed all the lemons in my fridge. Jake, who was keeping away from even the stairs down into the chamber, accompanied me in the kitchen. But, when I was returning, he hopped onto a patio chair and watched me from there. I stopped to pet him, telling him how smart he was to stay away from that horrible noise, and that I didn't like it much either. He watched me as I began my descent of the stairs with the pitcher. I paused, reassuring him that he was a good dog, when a new thought struck me.

Jake, I thought. *Had Grendel said Jake could come with us, down there? That noise—*

But I shook my head. I told myself that he *had* intimated this, and I set my resolve on the idea, given that descent without Jake was simply not going to happen.

It was then, looking at Jake, reddened as he was by the sunlight, that I realized the sun was setting. Evening was falling and night was coming on.

The night before the morning!

I descended the stairs.

In the chamber I deposited the pitcher and, before going to the tunnel, inserted the earplugs I had brought with me from the kitchen. In my descent of the tunnel, I found these did help. The only problem was that, while they reduced the loudness of the noise, they in no way diminished the unnerving quality of the shrieks.

Grendel was just as hard at work as he had been, and I had to pound on his leg to get his attention. He paused and looked down at me.

"Refreshments!" I shouted, my ears still ringing. I pointed to the tunnel. "Up in your chamber!"

We headed up into the first chamber, carrying the lantern. Grendel seated himself while I removed my earplugs. I held up the pitcher of lemon juice.

"I thought I might add some of this," I pointed to the buckets, "to make lemon water."

He smiled and nodded but said nothing. It was only after he had quaffed a full bucket of this lemon water that he leaned back and gave a loud sigh.

"Thank you!" he said. "That was—wonderful!"

I melted all over again at his polite decency. Reaching out, I ran my hand along his thigh, which was slick and firm and *very* pleasant to the touch. I looked up at him. He grinned and flexed his arms in a bodybuilder pose. I stifled a cry of sheer admiration and appreciation. His chest was still heaving, those massive, shining pecs rising and falling, and now, as he flexed, virtually every other part of him bulging, I experienced the familiar intoxicating rush of sexual excitation. He smiled mischievously when he saw this, and my face burned not unpleasantly. I felt *very* silly and *very* happy.

But a moment later I waved my hand at him. "No time!"

His smile softened and he nodded, still looking at me with a tenderness with was almost as unmanning as his sexual teasing.

"How's it going?" I asked deliberately.

He shrugged and said that he needed to go up to ground level. I nodded and, feeling that he wanted to do some personal business, I headed down the tunnel to where he was working. I took the lantern, but discovered there was enough light coming from the barrier itself for me to see.

I looked at the glowing, buzzing of the exposed barrier, which was larger now, unsure of what I was looking for. At last I saw that there was an area near the center of it where the surface appeared to be somewhat chipped away, but that was all. I stared, astonished. I had been hoping for more.

Confused and a little disappointed, I picked up the spade, determined to do some work myself while Grendel was absent, and fortunately remembered to put my earplugs in again first.

I struck the rock around the exposed barrier with the blade of the spade. I did this cautiously at first, but gradually began to use more force. At last, a bit of the rock gave way and the tip of the spade glanced aside, coming into contact with the barrier. I felt a kind of shock in my hands, and dropped the spade, crying out in pain and surprise. But I gritted my teeth and breathed deeply, remembering what Grendel had told me: *Let it go through*, and trying to think what that involved.

All I managed was to stand it, to endure. Gradually, the shock passed up my arms and through my body, even to the hair on my head and down to my toes—and then, gradually it began to die away. The relief I experienced as this last was quite wonderful.

When there was only a slight residue of the initial sensation in me, I picked up the spade, gingerly this time, for my hands still stung. Somehow, the whatever-it-was had passed up from the blade, though the wooden shaft, and into my hands. The pads of my fingers were still stinging, but not too bad.

Shaking my head, I resumed work. I had made several further strikes at the stone when I was startled by a gentle touch on my shoulder. I dropped the spade in alarm, and heard, barely, through my ear plugs, a gentle chuckle. I turned to see Grendel standing there, nodding at me and smiling.

To my surprise, he gestured for me to continue. So, I picked up my spade and resumed my work.

This time, when I made contact with the barrier I managed not to scream and, possibly inspired by Grendel's presence, *did* manage a kind of letting go—that is, letting the pain pass into my body and through me. It was unnerving, but it seemed to help, and afterwards I was not as exhausted by the experience.

Pleased, I looked around for Grendel, and saw that he was collecting rock pieces, putting them in the wheelbarrow and carting them off to the far end of the chamber.

So, I continued, until I was totally exhausted. Then I stood, hands on my knees, gasping for breath, head hanging down. My hands were really throbbing, too. I felt another gentle touch on my shoulder and, looking up, saw Grendel, holding his pickaxe in a business-like way.

I nodded.

"Could you make more of that lemon water?" he said loudly, but distantly because of my earplugs. I nodded, and laying down the spade, made my way toward the exit tunnel.

The first chamber was lit only by the lantern now and it was by its light that I poured the rest of the lemon juice into a bucket of water. Carrying the lantern in one hand, I brought the lemon water down to where Grendel was working and waited while he refreshed himself. I was slightly daunted by the fierceness with which he attacked the barrier when he resumed his work. It seemed he was now working with greater determination than ever. Somehow, this made me more aware of my own exhaustion and, after watching him another minute, I left him to it, carrying the empty bucket back up the tunnel.

When I arrived in my backyard, I realized why the chamber had been dark: it was night outside now. Jake greeted me, and when I lay down on a chaise lounge, Jake jumped up onto my lap, settling down on my chest so I could scratch his ears.

When I tried this, however, I discovered the pads of my fingers really hurt. It was too dark to see anything, and I was exhausted, so I just lay back, relaxing in order to recharge my batteries.

And so, I fell asleep.

Chapter 16
Breakthrough

I AWOKE WITH a start, realized I was on my patio and, remembering what the situation was, hastily got to my feet. The neighboring houses were all dark, the only illumination being my own patio light.

When I stood at the top of stairs leading to Grendel's chamber, I could hear the shrieks of Grendel's pickaxe blows filtering up from far below. Thankfully, they were muted here; there would be no neighbors calling the cops. It struck me that the blows were coming at a much slower pace.

Once in the upper chamber, I lit the lantern and put in my earplugs before heading down the tunnel. As I approached the lower chamber, I thought I could smell wood burning. When I reached it, I saw Grendel standing before the glowing barrier, with the pickaxe, and there was smoke rising lazily from its handle.

Grendel himself looked like he was on his last legs. As I watched, he swayed slightly, as if drunk. I went to him and thumped his leg. He turned a bit clumsily and looked down at me. I saw that not only was he slick with sweat all over, but that there were grimy streaks down his cheeks, as if he had been weeping.

I hugged his leg and, as I held back my own tears, shouted at him that it was okay, that he was magnificent, and other encouraging statements—all true.

He dropped the pickaxe and walked back to a wall, where he collapsed, his back against the wall.

I took out my earplugs and went over to where Grendel sat. Standing beside him, I gently caressed his cheek and ran my fingers through his sopping hair.

"You need to take a break," I said, gently but firmly.

Then it struck me that he hadn't put his arm around me, which he *always* did when I stood like this. I stepped away and faced him.

"Let me look at your hands."

"I have the hornier touch," he muttered evasively.

"None of that," I said. "Show them!"

With reluctance he held both hands, palms up, to me.

Grendel Rising

I gasped when I saw that the fronts of his fingers and his palms were *covered* with blisters. And there was blood.

"Oh my God! Don't move!" I ran up and into the house to get salve.

When I returned, I saw that Grendel was in the first chamber, and was drinking from the hose. My heart was wrung at the sight of how gingerly he held the hose, which bespoke of considerable pain in his hands. *And*, on an entirely different issue, I was out of lemon juice.

I made him sit down and put salve on his fingers. When I had finished, I looked up and saw him regarding me with a melting gaze.

"Hopefully, that will help," I said, and his smile broadened. My heart twisted at that, but I added, "Just—don't pick up anything for a while. Let me do it for you." And I found I had to stifle back tears.

"It is not the salve," he said quietly. "It is your touch that heals, your loving touch."

Wondering in passing whether he meant this literally, I ordered him to take a rest.

"I'll get some food for you. Okay?" He nodded, and I went back up the stairs.

Inside the house, I hovered between several options. For some reason, my brain wasn't working; I couldn't decide. In the end I went back down to the chamber to ask Grendel to help me out.

He was already asleep.

I stared at his heavily shadowed form lit only by the oil lamp, and I felt great pain and desperation, as well as pity and—oddly—a kind of general sorrow for all living things.

Instead of returning to the house, I took the lantern down the tunnel. Standing in front of the exposed barrier, I felt a kind of personal animosity toward it grow inside me.

"Mysterious, beautiful—and terrible, too," I murmured. "The last obstacle to Grendel's escape." Glaring at the thing, my anger was so strong that I felt I simply could *not* resist having a try at the barrier itself—and *yes*, making *deliberate* contact with it!

Filled with determination and all fired up, I might shudder at the prospect, but was in no way dissuaded. I picked up the pickaxe, which was quite big and heavy for me, despite my physical growth—I figured I must have grown about half a foot by now.

I held the tool resolutely if a bit gingerly, because of the residual pain in my fingers from my earlier work.

"Just wait!" I told my fingers grimly. "You ain't felt nothing yet!"

I might have, so to speak, screwed myself to the sticking point, but I was still cautious. I took a closer look at the exposed barrier, to see where Grendel had been working at it. It was centered pretty much at my eye level, so I was able to examine it closely. My fear was that it would look the same, that there would be no progress, but there did seem to be some. The worked area was about the size of a dinner plate, in which there were roughly-shaped rings, something like those of a tree, of lighter and darker glow, and a region the size of a silver dollar right at the center.

I almost wept with despair in that moment as I thought of the ferocity of Grendel's attack, the massive movement of his bulging muscles, his obvious strength and determination. And just—*this* for a result!

I was still staring at the locus of attack, when I was startled to see several of the concentric bands shift—*inward*. I felt stunned, and continued to watch. Then, maybe a minute later, another inward shift in several other bands. Neither were big shifts, but the point, I realized, was that the shifts were *inward*.

What did that mean? I thought I knew, but couldn't quite put my finger on it.

Think! I told myself.

For maddening seconds my mind seemed frozen. Then, all at once, it hit me like a bolt of lightning: this was a kind of organic healing!

The barrier was healing itself!

For a few seconds, my mind reeled. Did Grendel know about this? He must! But this made it like trying to bail in a boat with a hole in it! Or the reverse, if that made sense.

I glared at the center of those rings. Its shape and size hadn't seemed to change. It was the outermost rings that were slowly closing in, with a kind of knock-on effect of the adjacent inner rings. I stared and thought. Amid the horror, there was part of me that remained defiant. I put in my earplugs and hefted the pickaxe. *No*, I told myself. It was just too hefty for me to use with the accuracy I would need. Then there was the spade further off. No, not that either. I needed something with a point. I saw a crowbar. *Yes!* I picked it up and went to stand in front of that central spot of greatest damage to the barrier.

I licked my lips. Dare I hit the barrier directly? If Grendel, with his massive strength had managed so little for all his effort, it seemed pointless for me to add my pathetic effort. Nevertheless, I brought the silvered tip of the crowbar to within an inch of the central region of that ringed area and, taking a deep breath, brought it back and then drove it forward with all my strength, against the surface.

I had expected a terrible shock, and *boy!* I was *not* disappointed! But perhaps because I was mentally prepared—and resolved, the effect wasn't *overwhelming*. I did not cry out. On the other hand, I *did* drop the crowbar and dance around, my limbs jerking with terrible spasms. But I stuck it out and made use of Grendel's advice, surrendering to the pain, letting it do its stuff in me, then go through—and out.

When the agony had subsided considerably and my mind began to work again, I was struck by the idea that the *sound* of that blow, while terrible even with my earplugs, was different than Grendel's previous blows. It hadn't been a shriek, exactly. More of a sharp, whistling kind of sound. Perhaps this was because the force I brought to bear was much smaller than Grendel's. What was interesting about it was that *this* sound didn't bother me nearly as much.

When I had recovered, I positioned myself, drew the bar back as far as I could, and drove it forward, again hitting the central region with all my might. I knew what was coming this time, so I endured the effects better, the sound and the jangling agony in my body, witnessing them but not resisting, simply shepherding them through—though this seemed to take an unbearably long time.

One thing I noticed was that, as I opened up to this terrible assault, I could feel my energy and resolve being drained. And yet, curiously, as if in response, there came, rising up from some inner well of my being, a replenishment of both; the result being that I became fiercer and more determined.

Possibly I had discovered the full extent of the experience now. In any case, I breathed through the pain and, after stamping my feet to facilitate its passage through and out, I lifted the crowbar and drove it home again.

The crowbar, I now noticed, was becoming distinctly warm. I thought of that smoking pick handle and groaned at the realization that I didn't have gloves! But I shook my head. It didn't matter. I was committed to the job. I drew the crowbar back again and drove it forward once more.

After several more blows, I had to take a break, shaking my head to clear it and breathing deeply as the residue of pain that had accumulated slowly abated. The crowbar was close to hot now.

Groaning quietly, I loosened my earplugs and listened. I could faintly hear Grendel's snoring filtering down from far up the tunnel. And that was magical, a balm to my spirit, just listening to his beautiful, gentle snoring. I thought of Grendel lying there, resting after his great efforts in the bosom of that greatest of restorers: slumber. Then, I thought of the few hours we had left before the G-men would arrive. And what would happen to Grendel then? I groaned aloud as a wave of emotional pain swept aside any consideration of my own physical pain and, with tears in my eyes, I felt myself filled with renewed energy and even greater resolve.

I was able to apply myself with a kind of controlled, maniacal single-mindedness, driving the crowbar viciously against the point of my attack over and over again. Each time, the juddering agony that coruscated through my body combined with an oppressive sense of disorientation, creating a rising level of overall suffering that reduced part of me to quivering, despairing helplessness. I had the image of myself as a kitten, clawing at a heavy, oak door. I felt I wanted to give up, to throw down the crowbar, collapse on the floor and perhaps just *die*. But I couldn't; another part of me just wouldn't let me. Wave upon wave of outrage rose up from somewhere deep within me and just kept me at it. And at the same time my thoughts repeated over and over again the mantra: *It isn't right! It just isn't fair!*

There was one thing I could do, I told myself. Hastily, I took off my sweatshirt and wrapped it around the painfully hot crowbar. It made holding the tool more difficult, but it helped with the pain. When I resumed my attack, after several blows I realized something in me had changed. The physical suffering had become almost unendurable; I had to cry out as I drove each blow home. It was a scream of both defiance and agony. At the same time, I had a disturbing sense that I was straining myself to the limit. This brought fear into the mix, but my resolve never faltered, and I drove harder than ever, with a desperation that produced a kind of frenzy in the attack.

At last, there came a blow that produced new kind of shock, a shock of so much power that I was knocked off my feet. I was thrown back and onto the stone floor and lay there in the dim illumination of the oil lamp and that terrible, glowing surface. The earth below me seemed to tilt, the pain my body echoing with such intensity that my teeth felt like they were floating. I was too weak to scream, but I made a kind of pathetic whimpering sound—at first. But gradually, I began to feel separate from the pain, from even my own thoughts, from everything.

Oh! I thought. *Is this dying?*

I was still pondering this, when blackness came over me.

I CAME TO myself with the sensation of a wet tongue on my face. It was Jake, come to see if I was okay. I tried to raise my hand to pet him, but found I could barely lift my arm, I was so weak. So, I lay there, feeling my life energy return very slowly and murmuring soft words to reassure Jake, while my torpor-filled mind sorted through my situation. After several minutes, I realized I must have passed out. I hadn't died after all.

It took deliberate effort to push away the feeling of disappointment at this.

And then it struck me that this was very funny, and I laughed weakly and reached up to gather my little dog into my arms—but shrieked with pain instead at the moment of touching him. Poor Jake! He skittered back in terror. But he soon returned and recommenced licking my face.

"Sorry, boy," I told him. I held up my hands into the air to look at them. It was then that I realized it was too dark to see my hands as anything but shapes. The lantern must have gone out, because the only light was that eerie silvery glow that came from the barrier. I shifted my hands so my palms were facing the light, and I examined them. The palms and pads of my fingers were covered with enormous blisters.

Groaning, I let my arms fall to my sides, palms up.

Setback was the word that echoed around my mind then, but I was still resolved. Lifting my arms, I gathered Jake to me, holding him gently while avoiding any touch with my blistered hands. He lay down on top of my chest, with my arms resting over him.

"It's okay," I said, repeating the words over and over again while tears of weakness and pain and frustration leaked from the corners of my eyes and ran down the sides of my face.

We lay together for a long time. The throbbing of pain from my hands kept me from falling asleep, but I felt very weary. My mind wandered vaguely, and I thought of the lamp. Had it run out of oil, or had Grendel quenched it?

I found that I couldn't sort through the logic of these possibilities. I had to give the question up. The point was, it was dark—except for that silvery glow. I turned my head in one direction, then in the other, and realized, no—there *was* other light. It took the form of a rough circle perhaps a dozen feet away. This must be the tunnel leading up to Grendel's chamber.

The light was *very* dim, and I had to look away and back several times, closing and opening my eyes, before I decided yes, I really *could* see light there. It must, I thought, be coming down the tunnel—

And then it hit me: *Morning!*

I stared at the tunnel entrance in horror. The light was the gray of pre-dawn, which might have been reassuring, but somehow wasn't. It wouldn't be long before the sun rose. And then—the G-men!

With something between a sob and a groan, I sat up, and then got to my feet. Automatically, I turned to the barrier. It shone and buzzed quietly, and it struck me oddly that the silvery color had a distinct bluish tinge. I wondered vaguely what that might mean, whether it might be important. It was as if my weary mind was running on without purpose.

Give it up! a voice inside me snarled.

This sudden, vicious attack almost floored me. It was daylight, after all, which meant the G-men were coming. So, it was *all over*!

The bitterness of this reality filled me, and my parting glance at the barrier was one of infinite resentment. I stepped toward it, for a closer, more hateful look.

What?

Getting even closer, I that there was a dark spot in the center-most region of the work area.

"That's new," I murmured. But what was it? After staring at it, I decided it must be a piece of covering rock that had somehow got stuck. That didn't quite make sense, but my mind wasn't working well enough to figure things out.

Anyway, I told myself with some relief—I was done with worrying about that.

Grendel and I were toast!

I stifled a sob as I made to turn away. Then I froze in position as a new idea came to me.

Wait a minute!

I turned back toward the exposed barrier, getting even closer at that dark spot—so close that the buzzing made the skin of my face tingle.

Funny!

I turned away and half-groped, half-peered for the crowbar. Spotting it, I picked it up awkwardly, using the backs of my hands and my forearms. I tried positioning the silvered end at the dark spot, but my hold was too poor for that. So, I lowered one end of the crowbar onto the floor and caught the shaft in the crook of my elbow. Shifting this to my armpit, I held it in place and lifted the shaft with the back of my hands. It worked; I had sufficient control now.

I stepped to the barrier, and was greeted by the menacing buzz. The bar's silver tip now shone with reflected light. I moved it closer and closer to the spot.

It went *through*!

At the same time, it touched the edge of what I realized was a hole, and the familiar jolting pain and sharp sound hit me. I leaped back, dropping the crowbar. I almost fell, but managed to keep my feet out of sheer buoyancy.

We had gotten through! That final blow had done it!

But I also had to endure the passage of the pain and resurgence of stinging in my hands, and this took some time—and in the end did not pass entirely. Perhaps the throbbing in my hands made me realize that my celebratory feelings were premature.

What? What?

From euphoria, I descended into despair, crushed by the dawning realization of the ineluctable fact that, even *if* that black spot *was* a rupture of the barrier, its *size* made it of no practical use. If the central area of greatest intrusion had been the size of a silver dollar, this hole was about the size of a penny. I thought of Grendel, lying asleep up there in his chamber while morning dawned and the G-men heading out, coming to catch him. *He* was played out. I knew it and he seemed to, as well. And however much or little it meant, so I was I.

We were toast!

I collapsed right where I was, my head falling forward, and felt Jake come to me and lick my face. I smiled through my tears, and gathered him into my lap, and then I lay down—so tired!

I MUST HAVE fallen asleep, for when I opened my eyes, I saw that Grendel was sitting beside me, looking down at me. I started, and looked at the tunnel. Thankfully, the light didn't seem much greater than before I had drifted off. But still, I groaned inwardly.

Grendel seemed strangely at peace, his expression as he gazed at me one of acceptance and love. Perhaps, I told myself, it was resignation. I found myself both envious of it and irritated by it. *Fight* was what was wanted, wasn't it?

Whatever state he was in, I had to admit, it made Grendel's big face startlingly beautiful.

"You were sleeping," he said quietly. "That is good."

From the background of my awareness, the throbbing pain in my hands thrust its way forward. I held up my hands. I winced. Somehow, just *seeing* the damage seemed to *increase* the pain.

"I tried working on the exposed barrier," I said and grimaced. "To not much effect, though."

Grendel nodded. He was looking at his own hands. "I myself cannot do more without starting to lose a lot of blood."

"We're both in a sorry state, I guess," I said, and Grendel nodded. "Well," I added with a bitter sigh, "we tried."

Again, Grendel nodded. Then he held out his hand, palm up.

"Place your hands on mine," he said. "I can do something for your pain."

I frowned. "What about yours?"

He shook his head, then nodded toward his hand. I placed my hands, one each on the tips of two of his fingers.

Raising his other hand to his face, he spat several times on his fingers. Then, after rubbing them with his thumb, he gently touched my hands with his fingers. I felt the wetness, and there was the tingling quality that his touch always had. It was not exciting or erotic this time, but warm and calming—a kind of balm. He moved his fingertips around on the surface of my hands with exquisite delicacy, before removing his hand.

I looked at my own hands and saw among the blisters evidence of healing: the irritated skin grew less so, and the actual blisters diminished slightly. Even more important, the pain was considerably reduced.

"Wow!" I said and looked gratefully up at him. "But still—what *about* you?"

Grendel smiled slightly. "The healing I gave you, do you imagine it is not at work in me even now?"

"Oh! Right." I felt sheepish, and relieved, but still concerned about him.

"Rest here," he told me. He got up and went over to examine the work face. He bent down slightly to examine the central work face, and once there, became completely still.

When he hadn't moved for some time, I asked, "What?"

He straightened up—with difficulty I noticed. His over-used muscles, I thought, must be stiff and aching. But now he turned and looked at me. I saw the expression on his face. It was puzzled and—something else.

"What?" I repeated.

He shook his head, frowning slightly and, still with that odd expression, said in a half-whisper, "You did not tell me you had gotten through."

I stared and then laughed dismissively. "Yeah! And we could probably push a pencil through the hole I made."

But Grendel's eyebrows rose in astonishment, and he shook his head again, a slight smile forming on his lips.

"You do not understand," he said, still quietly. "My friend! You have done it! Oh, my human love!" And he came over and, kneeling down, put his arms around me. Pulling me to him, he kissed me tenderly.

The experience was wonderful, and I was eager for good news, but I was still confused, and finally I pushed him away and got shakily to my feet. "I don't understand. At this rate, won't it take *weeks* to make a hole big enough? And, well, we're both a mess."

"You do not understand," he said again and, getting to his feet, he went over to the exposed barrier, leaned down and beckoned to me to approach. "Look!"

Taking a deep breath, he reached out and inserted a finger *into* the dark spot, grimacing and groaning with pain as he did so.

I gasped and moved forward to pull his hand away.

"I am alright," he gasped, motioning me back. "Now—look!"

He turned his hand, rotating at the wrist, counterclockwise, slowly. Nothing happened for several seconds. Then, the dark region expanded like an iris, until the exposed barrier surface had withdrawn, leaving a dark hole that was roughly circular and about four feet across.

"Friend," Grendel said, speaking solemnly. "We are through!"

Had we been feeling better than we were, we might have cheered. As it was, we merely hugged by way of celebration. It was enough, however, given that I was, and I suspected he was too, close to collapse.

However, in the midst of my joy and relief that the passage of escape was open at last, I remembered there remained one issue I needed to settle with Grendel.

I stepped out of his embrace and, reaching out, ran the back of my hand along his forearm. Looking up, I saw him looking at me questioningly. I smiled back at him, blinking back the tears that underlay the fear I had about the sole roadblock I was about to bring up.

"Look—" I began, then paused, unable to continue. So, I took a deep breath and started again, lowering my gaze before beginning. "I was just wondering—" But again I had to stop. I cleared my throat, shook my head, and just *forced* out the words. "You said I can come with you."

He nodded.

"What about—canines?"

I felt uncomfortable about my own doubt and fear. It was a terrible business, but I just could *not*, now that it was a reality, even *think* of abandoning Jake. But Grendel dispelled all of this with a single laugh.

"Of *course*, dogs can live in the Underworld! And they are not just accepted; they are revered. For are they not diggers, too? Our cousins, in fact, as I have told you."

With waves of relief and joy I hugged my friend, who bent down to lift Jake into my arms. Jake, sensing good news, was eager to lick everything he could reach.

We were still standing there, savoring a triumphal moment of respite, when a voice came from up the tunnel.

"Helloooooooo!"

Chapter 17
Flight

I STIFFENED AND glanced fearfully at Grendel.

"The G-men!" I hissed, but Grendel shook his head.

"Listen!"

"Helloooooooo!" the voice came again. This time I did listen and realized I recognized the voice.

"Bruce!"

I went to the tunnel opening and saw at the other end a head silhouetted against the filtered daylight of the upper chamber. A moment later there were *two* heads, Jake's silhouette appearing as well. I wasn't surprised to see them together, or that Jake had allowed Bruce entrance to my backyard without his warning bark, since Jake knew Bruce well.

Having greeted his friend, Jake now ran back down the tunnel to me.

"Can I come down?" Bruce called.

"No!" I replied. I bent to pick up Jake, and as he licked my face I turned to Grendel, making a gesture toward the tunnel with my free arm, raising my eyebrows questioningly. He nodded and I called to Bruce, "We'll come up."

I put Jake down and we ascended. When we arrived in the other chamber, Bruce grinned at me, but also *stared* at Grendel.

"Oh," I said. "Grendel, this is Bruce. His family owns the house whose pool we used."

Grendel bowed slightly, and Bruce hesitatingly held out his hand.

"Oh, no," I told him. "We've both got blisters from the work."

"Oh." Bruce was about to pull his hand back when, to my surprise Grendel reached out and gently took hold of Bruce's hand.

Bruce looked at me questioningly, and I held out my hands, palms up.

"Ouch!" he said. "Work? You mean digging?" He looked around the chamber in appreciative amazement.

I shook my head. "No. At the barrier." I nodded toward the tunnel. "Down there. We got through! Oh, and thanks for getting those tools, by the way."

"No problem," Bruce said. "I—uh, took the liberty—" he said and gestured back toward the stairs leading up.

"What? No problem. But—you got past the barrier out there, right? The one around my yard?"

Bruce stared at me. I saw him mouth the word: *barrier*. He looked completely lost. At last he said, "You—uh, left your front door unlocked, man," he said. "I mean, I knocked first. Several times. Then I opened the door and called. Jake came and greeted me." He looked at Jake, who was watching us. "I kind of—I don't know—just wanted to see how things were going with you—" He paused and looked up at Grendel, then added, "both."

I nodded, appreciative of his concern, but I also felt a bit impatient, for Bruce's arrival just now had complicated the situation. Perhaps he saw this in my face, for he held his hands up, palms out.

"Look!" he said. "I don't know exactly what's going on here. I mean, about 'barriers' and that. I kind of get that it's a secret or something, and that there are people—" He hesitated. "Who are after you or something—?"

He stopped and I stared at him. How did he know all this? Then I remembered that drone.

"That was your drone, wasn't it?" I asked him. "Yesterday?"

He nodded.

"Well, I—you know, after our—interaction, getting those tools—" He stopped and frowned. "You know," he said, "those people in that shop: *man* were they weird! It was worse than buying illegal drugs!" To this he added defensively, "I mean, well, I just went along—" He shrugged.

It took me a second or two to figure out what he was talking about. Apparently, he was referring to his experiences buying illegal drugs, that he had only been with the person buying the drugs. The segue was typical of him; as his tutor I had always found focus to be one of his challenges.

"Never mind," I said reassuringly, putting a hand on his shoulder. "But look. Did you have any trouble coming onto my property?"

He looked at me doubtfully. "No. Should I?"

I laughed suddenly. "No, I guess not. It's just—well, complicated."

"You *did* leave your door unlocked," he said defensively, "like I said."

"It's *okay*," I said, again trying to be reassuring. "Not a problem. I was talking about—something else."

"Right," he said confusedly. Clearly, he wanted to know more. I saw Grendel looking at me now, however, his expression meaningful. Time to leave.

"Okay," I replied, as if in answer. "Thanks for coming. As you can see, we're fine, more or less. But the thing is, we were just about to leave—"

At this he nodded. "Right," he said again, and grinned. "Flee, you mean?"

I grinned back. "Yeah. Sort of."

"Oh. Right," he said. "Well, I almost forgot, but—c'mon up!" He gestured to the stairs.

So, we all trooped up to my backyard where he led us to the patio.

I was, more than anything, struck by the beauty of the morning light. The sun was just rising and everything looked pristine and quite beautiful. It struck me suddenly what I would be giving up, following Grendel in his flight back down into his own realm. Thinking this, I looked up at him—and felt completely reassured, for it struck me that he represented a greater beauty. What was that line from that Arab poet, Someone Khayyam?

A jug of wine, a loaf of bread—and thou
Beside me singing in the wilderness—
Oh, wilderness were paradise enow!

Yes! I thought, studying Grendel's face as he looked around, also taking in the beauty of the early morning. For the first time I felt I truly understood the truth in those lines of poetry.

Then I turned to Bruce. He was pointing to several large packs sitting on my patio table.

"What's that?"

"Sustenance," he said. "It occurred to me that if you were going on the lam, you'd need snacks."

"Oh!" I said, aware I had taken no thought for breakfast and also I was hungry. I turned to Grendel. "Maybe we should have something before heading down?"

He looked interested in the packs, but he shook his head.

"We best be gone."

I looked at Bruce—and saw that he was staring at me, his mouth hanging open.

"You're going to *dig* your away out?" he asked. "I don't get it."

I looked at Grendel, who nodded. I turned to Bruce.

"That's where Grendel is from."

"Oh." Bruce blinked several times, looking stunned. Then, suddenly, he gestured to the table. "But I mean—you'll *take* the food, though, right?"

I nodded. "Sure! And thanks so much! I wish I could take time to explain—"

Bruce laughed. "So do I, but I think I understand—enough." He stopped, and looked me up and down, puzzled. "You know, I don't want to be personal, but aren't you about six inches taller than you should be? Or have I shrunk?"

I grinned. "You haven't shrunk."

He shook his head slowly, eyes wide. "Curiouser and curiouser!"

"Yes!" I agreed. "And I'll tell you about it the next time I see you."

"*If*—" corrected Bruce despondently.

"No!" I said emphatically. "*When!*" And when he looked at me incredulously, I grinned and shook my head. "Don't tell me how I know; I just do, in my gut."

Bruce's eyebrows shot up, but he said nothing.

"Anyway," I continued. "I wouldn't worry about it." I gave him a hug. "But—the important thing is—I want to thank you, for everything! You've been a great friend."

He smiled sardonically.

"I guess that's my consolation prize." He chuckled. Looking up at Grendel, he added, "I mean, I get it now. I don't think I could ever compete—"

And then I heard, just discernable, the sound of my front doorbell. I started, turned to Grendel.

"*It's them!*"

Grendel nodded.

"Did you lock the door?" I asked Bruce.

He shook his head unhappily.

"It does not matter!" Grendel said. "We must *hurry*! They will not hesitate to come through the house, or around it!"

I nodded. "You first!"

Bruce and I went to grab the packs while Grendel quickly descended the steps. When we were all gathered at the entrance of the tunnel, Bruce gave Grendel the pack he was holding. I saw that it had its straps extended, to fit Grendel's size—and was impressed.

Then, seeing Jake watching us intently, he asked, "Hey! Is Jake going, too?"

"Of course!"

But Grendel was now rolling a large boulder that had lain in a corner of the chamber. It was quite round and about seven feet in diameter. He must have brought it up from below, I decided, and shaped it too. He now positioned it near the tunnel entrance, and carefully placed several small stones at its base, to keep it steady.

Finally, he turned to us.

"This," he said, putting his hand gently on the boulder which, at his touch quivered slightly, "can be made to roll down—with minimal force." I saw he was looking at Bruce.

Bruce stared. "You're kidding!"

Grendel shook his head. "I assure you; I have poised it quite precariously. Just push, at this position," he indicated, "with all your strength. It *will move*."

"If you say so."

Grendel grinned. "Yes, I do. But wait until I call—from below."

Bruce nodded, then turned toward the stairs. There were voices above. "Hurry!" he hissed.

So, we went, Grendel leading the way, careful not to brush against the poised boulder, then me, and Jake close at my heels.

We descended the tunnel as quickly as possible, driven by fear. When we arrived in the lower chamber, Grendel ran to a pile of stones near the barrier work area and positioned them before the hole with startling rapidity while I watched dumbfounded. The lower edge of the hole was about four feet above the floor of the chamber, but while I thought that a simple step would have sufficed, Grendel appeared to be constructing a ramp. When this was done, put his hands, fingers spread on either side of it and became motionless. I saw the gaps between the stones change and disappear.

Grendel got to his feet and turned to me. "You go first!" he said. "Try not to touch the edges of the barrier—and remember if you do, let it—the energy—pass *through* you."

I nodded and, holding onto Grendel's hand, I carefully stepped through—without touching the barrier at all. I was holding the lantern for this and could see that the floor of the space beyond the barrier was only *two* feet below the bottom of the hole. Consequently, I almost stumbled, but Grendel's hand held me steady, and at last I was standing on the far side of the hole. I put the lantern down and turned so Grendel could hand Jake to me. Jake took all of this with an excited acceptance, and when I set him down beside me, he immediately started to sniff about.

Then, Grendel handed me my backpack, the packs holding Bruce's provisions, and the canvas bag. I set these to either side and then turned back, to see Grendel standing in front of the hole. The only part of him visible through the hole was from his knees to his waist. I glanced worriedly at the hole's silvery edges, which I could hear quietly humming, it wasn't obvious to me that Grendel would be able to get through at all.

"You next," I called to him.

He bent down so I could see his head and motioned me away. When I had, he grasped the sides of the hole with his hands—producing a sizzling sound and eliciting low groan from him—he thrust his head through. But his shoulders were too wide, so he contorted himself, one shoulder passing through first. All the time he was making grunts and small noises of pain, but with some effort he finally managed to get both shoulders through. After that the rest of him came without any problem, and he sort of fell forward through the hole, in summersault fashion.

He landed on his side, and as he lay there we exchanged commiserative glances, both smiling with relief. A moment later, he got onto his hands and knees and put his head to the hole.

"*Now!*" he shouted. "*Bruce! Push!*" And then, unable to sidestep manners, he added, "*And thank you!*"

As if in response, distant cries filtered down from the upper chamber. Someone shouted, "No you don't!" And then Bruce's voice, "Oh, yes, I will!"

A moment later a low rumbling began, which quickly grew louder. Then the gray outline of a boulder exploded from the tunnel mouth, rolling fast, straight at us, and I suddenly understood the need for that ramp. I jumped away instinctively when the boulder, having hit the ramp, seemed to lunge upward, coming straight at the hole. A moment later—*crash!* It hit.

In that moment of impact, I had the image of the boulder filling the hole perfectly, like a stopper in a bottle. I expected it to rebound, of course, but it didn't, because Grendel, who had *not* stepped aside but had held his hand out in readiness, at the instant of impact, with fingers spread, *grabbed* the boulder.

I wondered at this, since I thought even his two-foot hand span wouldn't be able to grip that smooth surface. But I was not accounting for troll faculties. Incredibly, his touch seemed to *freeze* the boulder in place. And, as he held his hand in place I had the odd impression—entirely without sensory support—that the rock comprising the boulder was *fusing* with the rock that surrounded the hole on the far side of the barrier.

I lifted the lamp to get a clearer view of Grendel's face, and saw it was tense with effort, eyes closed. I watched with concern, wanting to help, but with no idea what I could do. So, I just waited.

At last, Grendel removed his hand from the rock and slumped, his head falling forward. I tentatively put my hand on his shoulder, at which he nodded and smiled, but did not move for a minute or so.

"There!" he said at last, his voice quiet, and turned his head to look at me. "The barrier—it will reform itself. I have created a temporary covering though—a scab, as it were." He smiled at me, then—a smile of weariness, but also of gentle triumph.

When he tried to get to his feet, he sank back, and murmured, "That was—not easy. I think I must sit for a moment or two."

So, he shifted himself so his back was against the rock surface just beside the newly sealed barrier hole. After hesitating, I sat down too, against his side. I was surprised to discover that I too felt like a bit of rest. But what had I done? I asked myself. I decided it must be the stress of the past few minutes, followed by intense relief. Perhaps I just needed to reorient myself to the new situation.

That was part of it, but I also think that I was learning from Grendel how to enjoy moments in stillness. His presence always helping with that, of course—*and* Jake, who now curled up in the space between Grendel and me. Feeling Grendel's warmth and resting my hand on Jake, I was well content.

❖

I THINK I must have sunk into a kind of dreaming reverie, for when I came to myself and an awareness of my immediate surroundings, I had the distinct sense that some time had passed.

What had brought me back were two separate impressions.

The first was an awareness of the return of the pain in my hands. In the light of the lantern they still looked raw; Grendel's spit had done *some* healing, but the reduction in pain must have been some kind of anesthetic—whose influence was now passing.

However unwelcome this was, at least it was something I was familiar with. My second impression, on the other hand, though subtle, was quite strange—and quite unfamiliar to me. I wasn't even sure how to describe it, other than to say that I just *felt* different than I had before we had passed the barrier.

I remembered my conviction I would meet Bruce again at some point and wondered at all of this. Was I becoming more intuitively sensitive in some way? If so, I wasn't sure I welcomed the idea.

I looked at the rock floor we were sitting on. It disappeared into darkness after some twenty feet, but there was something about that fading the struck me as wrong. Carefully, I got to my feet and raised the lantern to better illuminate things. But first I looked at Grendel and saw that he was still resting; his were eyes closed, though he wasn't snoring.

Was that it?

I shook my head and told myself not to be silly. Yet, I *was* struck by the stillness that surrounded me. But first, the chamber or whatever it was we were in.

I lifted the lantern still higher, wincing slightly because of the blisters on my hand. But I adjusted my grip to minimize the pain and looked again at the floor in front of me. Raising the lantern had had an odd effect on the rock floor that was unsettling. The fading in the forward direction became less, the transition to utter blackness sharper, forming a distinct horizontal line now. A cliff, or drop-off! I realized. This made my stomach tighten; I was always more afraid of heights than of closed-in places. But now, I felt it my—for want of a better word—*duty* to explore this space. At least, a little.

So, I walked slowly forward, holding the lantern before me. After several paces, I noticed the surface began to tilt *down*. I had to stop at that point to allow my suddenly-pounding heart to slow. What was *interesting*, I told myself in a deliberate attempt at a change of focus, was how *smooth* the floor was. Not polished, not that. But still, very smooth—*organic*, almost.

Now, where had I used that term before? Oh, yes! The barrier—healing itself organically.

A shudder went through me; the idea that I was inside a place where surfaces were organic had the disturbing connotation of being swallowed.

I shook my head rapidly. *Stop it!* I told myself and, happily, the incipient horror faded.

I turned on the spot and looked at the wall against which Grendel still sat. (Jake was lying against his big friend but watching me.) The wall was completely smooth. And it *curved* too!

We had passed through the barrier to emerge in a kind of shallow bay. On either side the wall curved forward. To the right, the curve continued to where the light faded, but to the left, the wall curved away again. I noticed something else, too. The wall itself as it rose, curved *outward*, soaring up until it too disappeared. Having gotten all this stowed away, I turned around again, and faced the downward-sloping floor.

I took several more steps and discovered the slope increased further. My hackles were up at this point. But I kept my courage (if that was the word) and held the lantern up and out, and thought I could just make out a dim, gray vertical surface, maybe fifty or a hundred feet in front of me. Though it was hard to tell, I had the impression that this surface was curved too, in a convex fashion. The mental image that formed in my head of this hollow space we were in was that of the bowl of a spoon on end.

A moment later I caught sight of Jake out of the corner of my eye: he was standing slightly in front of me, a foot or so ahead of my position. Evidently, he had come to see what was up, for he was facing forward in an interested fashion. I had to bite my lip not to cry out.

Controlling myself, I managed to hiss, "Jake!" He looked at me curiously, but without anxiety. I licked my lips. "Jake," I repeated, "we're going back now, okay? Let's go!"

And he came with me, back to where Grendel was sitting.

When I was close to Grendel, I turned again and looked out at the space, in all directions. This was so unlike any conception I had of naturally-formed caves, with their stalactites and stalagmites, that my head still swam a little.

I thought again of that odd feeling, of things being different. Partly, I decided, this was probably due to the fact that here the oil lamp was the *only* source of illumination; there was no gray daylight filtering down. That, of course, would produce a more closed-in feeling, but I was convinced there was something more.

It was like—the line of connection to the outer, above ground world had been cut. *Wait a minute!* I remembered that was close to what Grendel had said about the barrier: it existed where the contiguity of spaces connected with the Overworld ended!

Okay, I thought, *but what did that mean?*

Well, for one thing, I was beyond the barrier, in the Underworld.

At that I did feel a slight shiver, but not an unpleasant one. It was just—I was somewhere *else* now.

I thought again about the sense of being closed in. What struck me was that this idea wasn't in any way associated with any negative sensation; there was nothing claustrophobic about it. If anything, it felt—reassuring. *Wow!* It was like I was being gently enfolded or swathed in some way.

How strange! But also, how wonderful!

Now I remembered a song by the Bee Gees that had always haunted me. It was on their *Children of the World* album, the final song, and the title song. In the song, along with the "we are children of the world" theme, there was that line that said something about: from your very first day to when the curtains were drawn.

That was basically it, though I might have got a word or two wrong. That line had been burned into my soul—both for how potent an effect it had on me, and the oddity of what it seemed to say.

That bit about the curtains being drawn. I had the image of the curtains, not of a window, but of a Victorian four-poster, being drawn when the person in the bed dies. What was so strange was the *feeling* the image gave me. It was *so attractive*—even now it almost brought tears to my eyes. And *why* was it attractive? Because it signaled a closing in with soft curtains, the self, being protecting from the cold harshness of the world—brutal objects and harsh colors, selfish and unkind humans, the very dreariness of the day upon day of mundane existence.

All of this struck me now as undeniably true. Yet it had lain beneath a surface contentment I'd felt about my life, a quiet force pressing down on me. I hadn't been consciously aware of it—until it was removed. For it *had* been removed, now, and the relief I felt was so strong that it brought tears to my eyes. But it wasn't *only* relief. I was now aware of a heart-felt sympathy for all those still living above ground who suffered from that oppressive weight.

A moment later, catching myself, I shook my head. *But this was nonsense!*

Certainly. Thus spoke the rational part of me. However, there was that other part, and it was ready with an immediate response: *Yes. Perhaps. But it feels true, it feels real, does it not?*

It certainly did, but I decided to shelve the concept for now.

But, before I could wrench my mind away altogether, I had a final thought: that my sense of feeling different arose, at least in part from a change in my awareness; a reduction in the predominance of my *mind*—thoughts and such—and a corresponding *increase* in what might be called the operations of the *heart*—feelings and the like.

Anyway.

I turned around to look again at the wonderful person who had brought me here and was surprised to see that he was looking at *me*. And his eyebrows were raised interrogatively.

"What?" I said automatically, then, "This is an interesting place." Feeling more was needed, I added, "I feel—different." And then, after a pause, "Or—well, this *place* is different—is that right?"

Grendel's smile broadened, but he said nothing. I smiled back and went to him. I reached out to take his hand, and at the contact felt a stinging pain.

"Ouch!" I grinned. "Still hurts a bit."

I frowned inwardly. That pain had not been a bit in any sense of the word. Now that my mind was available, it seemed, the pain in both hands had returned, with a vengeance. I lowered the lantern and gingerly let go of the handle. Then I thought of Grendel's hands. If the same healing technique had been used on his far worse blisters, then how much must it still be paining him?

Feeling pity and love, I touched his shoulder with the back of my hand, and kissed his ear, which was at just the right height. I noticed he was sitting relative to the lantern light in a way that highlighted the contours of his ear, among other things. I was struck with how beautiful it was, its perfect curves, both the outline and the convolutions within. I kissed it again, and then licked it, and felt a thrill going through me. This distracted from the pain in my hands so much that I kissed it some more, licked it and even took the fleshy, rounded edge between my teeth and gently bit it.

Grendel made a deep rumbling sound, which was his chuckle and, lifting his arm, he gently ran the back of his finger along the side of my neck, and from there all over my head. It was wonderful; the welcome physical touch was so very reassuring. I leaned my head down and rested my forehead on the strong muscle that ran from his neck to his shoulder—the trapezius, perhaps? I felt a peace and sense of connection with him that was balm, and I just stood there, leaning against him, totally inert.

"I guess we should go," Grendel murmured gently. I lifted my head and looked at him, feeling the touch of his gaze. There was part of me that wanted to do anything *but* move along, but I nodded.

After we had hoisted our various packs, Grendel pointed to the right, where the wall curved away. There, the floor descended gently. I just hoped there was no drop-off later on. But I was with Grendel, I reminded myself, and this was his backyard. At that the incipient fear receded. He led, keeping rather close to the wall, and I followed, Jake close at my heels.

❖

How long it was I don't know. My initial state of wonder and excitement gradually left me, and the walking, always downwards and on a gently sloping surface, nevertheless increasingly became nightmarish.

Not only was I tired, but the pain in my hands increased as well, at last to the point where I had to grit my teeth not to make a noise. I didn't want to be the reason we had to stop.

I was unpleasantly immersed in such maunderings when Grendel stopped and turned to look at me. The way he looked me up and down for some reason irritated me.

"What?" I asked, my voice sharp.

It was only a moment later, however, that mortification swept over me. I went forward and put my forehead against his thigh. I found myself wanting to cry.

I felt his hands gently on my shoulders and looking up I saw him gazing down at me, his face in the lantern light filled with gentle concern.

"You are in pain," he said.

"Yeah."

"Maybe I can help."

"I doubt it," I said, but then added, "Sorry!"

He shook his head. "It does not matter. Show me your hands."

He took the lantern from me, and I held my hands out, palms up. The blisters looked ugly.

"I didn't bring the salve," I said fretfully, but he shook his head and gently put one of his hands beneath each of mine. I let my hands rest, each on the tips of two of his enormous fingers.

When he said nothing further, I looked up and saw that his eyes were closed.

"Let it go!" he murmured. "The shock from your work on the barrier. You remember. You let it go, then. Do the same with this injury, the pain of it."

I was unsure what he meant by this and, because of the pain, felt a bit irritated too. But I made the effort, focusing my attention on my body—which quite apart from my hands, was *filled* with aches. And I became aware of tension, too, tension both in my body and in my mind; this too was unpleasant. Yet I was convinced it was the only thing holding me together, allowing me to cope, to function.

Did Grendel mean to let go of *that*?

I didn't know, but I focused on it. And, with a sense of the strange place I was in, its strange nature, I was struck with the odd impression that even my breathing in of this air was bringing something into my body, my very being. I even imagined I could feel that quality, whatever it was, move through my body. Wherever it went—when I let it—it seemed to draw off the stress, the weariness, even the pain—to simply leech it away. At least, that was the mental image. I wasn't quite opening myself to doing this.

Was *this* what Grendel meant—to open myself up, to invite those negative sensations in?

My last resistance to acting was manifest as a suppressed whimper. Then I opened, hesitantly, and felt the jangling pain in detail, which made it an actual horror of agony in its felt detail and the associated sense of the bodily damage it represented.

This was *very* hard to endure. And there were moments of real terror as well, for as bits of resistance and tension were melted, I experienced a loss of stability, the feeling as of a superstructure creaking under near-catastrophic stress. But nothing *did* collapse, and when each small terror passed it was replaced by relief.

After a while, I became aware that this process of drawing away these negative sensations was not merely natural, not merely the result of my "letting go." No, there was something—in fact, some*one*—helping, pulling it out of me. And I realized with a start that this *must* be Grendel.

"*Oh!*" I said at last, coming to myself and realizing that I felt distinctly better. The pain now more an irritant than actual torment. Grendel opened his eyes and looked at me. I looked back at him.

But we gazed at each other in silence for several minutes, well content. I was the one who finally spoke.

"But—where are we going?"

Grendel chuckled, smiling. "We are through the barrier," he said. "Now we must find—a gate."

Chapter 18
At the Gate

"OH!" IT WAS all I could think of to say to this bit of news. Grendel's therapy had not removed my bodily weariness, and now my troubled mind imagined a long series of barriers or gates that would tax our diminishing reserves.

Grendel, who was watching me, chuckled, as if he guessed my thoughts. "But first," he said, "a repast."

I nodded, realizing that I was very hungry. We hadn't had breakfast. Maybe part of my difficulty coping arose from a nutritional deficit.

"And for this," Grendel continued, "we must find a suitable spot."

My mind reeled slightly at the idea of what a "suitable spot" might be in our current environment. But it was only several minutes later that we discovered a place where the wall beside us opened out into an alcove. The walls were smooth, looking as if the stone had simply been scooped out. And there was enough room for us to sit comfortably.

We removed our packs, and I went through the food packets Bruce had provided.

"Wow," I murmured, impressed. "Bruce didn't stint."

"That is real friendship."

The packs were stuffed with pretty much everything. Sandwiches, bottles of pop and water, fruit, and a variety of energy bars, all in very generous quantities. I imagined Bruce purchasing the stuff, his mind filled with his estimates of Grendel's size, and getting more of everything.

In one of the packs there was a smallish cooler-type container with two fitted tubs inside, one containing potato salad, the other pasta salad.

"Wow!" I repeated, and for the first time noted the temperature of our surroundings. It wasn't warm, or cool. It was just—pleasant. Coolish? But still. I set the opened salad tubs on the floor. "We'll have to eat these first, I guess."

Grendel grinned. "Not a problem," he said, but added seriously, "I do not have to be full in any sense. Just enough to keep going."

I looked at him and nodded. I was uncomfortably aware that he could probably polish off literally everything we had at one sitting. But I didn't want to stint, either. So, I decided to take him at his word.

Beside the food, I was delighted to find Corelle plates, and metal utensils inside rolled up *cloth* napkins.

"Looks like it's going to be a real king's feast," I commented, to which Jake gave an anxious little yip.

I laughed and petted him. "Don't worry. You'll get your share."

While we were eating, my brain began to turn over. Several times I looked out of our hollow in the direction we had come.

"Do you think they'll follow?"

Grendel nodded. "That is likely. But it will take some time, I believe. Still, after we rest and eat, we must continue. We must get out of physical reach."

I considered this. "But they'll have guns—"

Grendel chuckled and shook his head. "No. They will not take such devices beyond the barrier."

"No? Why not?"

"Well, they would not—work properly. That is a part of the nature of the barrier."

"Oh." I chewed some more. "What is it made of?" I asked. "The barrier, I mean."

Grendel looked at me thoughtfully, then shook his head.

"The barrier is not a substance, I think," he said. "It is a—mmm—*configuration* might be the best description. I can think of no word that is better. Also, I do not know fully about it. I am not an expert."

"Okay. But—you said it's a natural phenomenon?"

"Yes, but on the other hand, it is a part of the world that is affected by human activity—the edge of it as it were, but still—affected. And so, every time you humans develop a new thing of the machine variety, especially when powered, the barrier is changed somewhat. In a way, I suppose, fed."

I thought back to our breaching of the barrier. "So, that was why we used pickaxe and spade?

"That is correct. The use of muscles is natural, and manual tools just slightly less so."

I nodded. "But then we—humans, I mean—invented devices that do the work for us: hydraulic drills, jackhammers, dynamite—that sort of thing. And that increased—fed, as you say—the barrier."

Grendel smiled. "Yes, you put that well. I am so pleased you understand!"

"I see that part of it, but I don't understand—I mean, how it's wrong, or bad."

Grendel ate in silence for a while before responding.

"By extending your ability and effectiveness," he said at last, "you are able to do things that you otherwise could not do, but you do not ask yourself whether that is right or wrong, good or bad—in short, the effect its use might have on you. You are intoxicated with your burgeoning sense of power."

I thought about this but couldn't quite get it. "Okay," I said. "I see how some of the things we invent are misused. Atomic bombs, that sort of thing. But so much good comes from our inventions as well, right?" I shrugged.

Grendel regarded me thoughtfully. Then he lowered his head and sat still, chin on his hand, thinking, for some time.

Finally, he said, "It is the nature of things to do or be—to *act*—according to that nature, for part of the nature of a thing is the space to which it belongs, where it functions best with other things that are acting in *their* own natures."

I thought this through. "I think I get it. I guess, with machines, we put ourselves *out* of our nature, *above* our nature."

"Yes. And think how much damage you produce. It is like the old saying that you humans sometimes use: In asking whether you *could* do something, you failed to consider whether you *should*. They are not the same."

I could see his point, but I did feel a little indignant. I mean, wasn't it our *job* to invent, explore and build?

But Grendel was now getting to his feet.

"We must be gone," he said.

And so, we resumed our journey.

I felt somewhat rejuvenated by the meal and decided not to ask any more questions for the moment. I didn't understand what the business of a "gate" might be, but I would rely on my trust in Grendel. Also, even *with* the food I was still in a precarious state, beset with a fatigue that was associated with the trauma of the pain I had experienced, and with the residual pain itself. This was no time to bother about things that I could do nothing about.

Our passage, illuminated by the lantern, was quite easy. Though the slope was always changing, so I had to walk carefully, as we encountered dips and rises, these were always gentle; the overall trend was downward.

After some time, the dark abyss to our left gave way to a wall, at first distant and only dimly perceived, being at the very edge of the lantern light, but then closing in, until at last we were walking along a passage maybe eight feet wide, with no visible roof. The passage itself, in addition to its slight undulations, also curved in a similarly gentle fashion, to one side or the other.

It struck me that there were only two rules about any of these surfaces: they were invariably smooth and curved. This brought me back to the sense of being inside something organic that had so bothered me before. Now, however, I was less disturbed by the idea, without really knowing *why*. All I knew was that the nature of these surfaces, the curves and the smoothness just *felt* right, they *fitted* here, in the Underworld.

With this realization, I began to feel content. I even smiled to myself and had to suppress the urge to hum. *That must be*, I thought, *the result of that weight I had felt while aboveground being removed.*

SEVERAL HOURS LATER we emerged into an open space so vast that the light of the lantern showed only the patch of floor around us. This appeared nearly horizontal, nearly flat, but with a slight concavity. Grendel stopped and looked around, so I was reminded of his being able to see in the dark. Then, he nodded, gave a grunt of satisfaction, and resumed his way.

After a minute or so of walking a gray wall loomed out of the darkness ahead of us. This surface, which had a slight backward slant, was curved in a gentle concave manner, the shape extending away to the edge of the pool of illumination produced by the lamp.

Once we came up to it, we turned and headed along it to the left, Grendel studying the surface as we went. After perhaps a dozen yards, he stopped. To my eyes, this part of the surface looked no different, but Grendel, putting down pack and bag, stepped up to it and ran his fingers over the surface, as if feeling for something. At last, he stopped and turned to me. He was grinning.

"Iron," he said. "This is it, the gate."

I nodded, though it didn't look like iron to me.

Grendel faced the rock surface again and spread his arms as far as possible to either side, fingertips pressed against the rock, as if he was trying to grab the entire rock face. He remained like this for some time. I had the sense that he was doing something but wasn't sure what. At last, however, I realized his fingers had actually penetrated *into* the rock.

Bracing his legs, he leaned back, and then *stepped* back. I saw to my amazement that in doing this he had pulled away some of the rock face! My mind boggled for a second or two, until he lifted his arms over his head so I could see he was holding was a great flake of rock that was perhaps a foot in thick.

He took several careful steps to the right, and laid his burden carefully down, against the rock wall. When I looked at the newly-exposed surface, I realized this was what he had meant when he referred to *iron*. It was dull black and slightly concave.

Grendel extracted the spade from his canvas bag and stepped up to the surface. Putting his ear against it, he tapped it with the tip of the spade several times in what was a definite pattern. The dull, metallic clangs echoed loudly, then gradually died away. And in the silence that followed, Grendel laid the spade down, stepped back and turned to me. He was grinning.

"I have rung the doorbell," he said, and seated himself against the rock wall next to the black surface. "Now, we wait," he added, and smiled at me, patting his thigh.

I didn't need more than a hint. I sat down on his lap and leaned back against him, savoring his comforting warmth and solidity. Jake jumped onto *my* lap, and so we all settled down to wait in relaxation. *On the doorstep*, I thought, and was aware of feeling quite content and, despite our bizarre location, and perhaps aided by the vast and peaceful silent stillness around us, was able just to let my mind shut off.

Due to my weariness, I quickly slipped into a doze, and was only awakened by the sound of dull metal tapping that broke the silence. We all got to our feet and Grendel took the spade and made a return set of taps on the metal—a different sequence this time. After this, there was a long pause, then a low scraping sound began. A thin line in the shape of a large circle appeared in the surface, and the area within this circle began to rotate. After perhaps a minute, the entire disk of metal was pulled back, and a large face peered at out of it at us. It blinked in the light of our lantern.

It was clearly a troll. But I was struck at how much less human this face looked than Grendel's. It wasn't just non-human, either. It was downright *ugly*.

"My dear Grendel," the troll said, grinning. "You have returned most unexpectedly." Then the eyes shifted and looked at me. "And—how thoughtful! You have brought a snack!"

I was taken aback by this and looked up at Grendel. He was frowning and I sensed his anger.

"This one is not for eating," he growled.

"No?" The large eyes leered at me, and an enormous tongue slid out between the lips, licking them obscenely. I endured this with difficulty; part of me wanted to flee, or scream—or possibly both. Then, the eyes shifted and searched Grendel's face. They widened, and the mouth made an 'o' shape. "And—what is this?" he said, his mouth looking even larger. "Could this—could this be—*love?*"

"You shut up Ugluk! I *will* report you," Grendel almost snarled. "You know it is not your business to make such inquiries."

After a slight hesitation, the big face changed, adopting what seemed like a caricature of an abashed expression. "Just making conversation, Grendel. Good to see you again—and your—friend." Again, the face leered at me. Clenching my teeth, I shuddered.

I felt Grendel's big, gentle hand touch my back. "Do not be afraid, Ken," he told me quietly. "Nothing will happen to you."

"Nothing?" said the troll, grinning. He guffawed, but then withdrew. "Well," said his voice from beyond the circular door, "Come in, both of you!"

It was then that Jake, who had been hiding behind Grendel's leg, barked. A moment later the face returned, the enormous eyes now fixated on Jake.

"Oho! You have brought a canine friend!" And, as he said this, for the first time I heard warmth in his voice. Clearly, Ugluk approved of Jake, whatever he thought of me. This, in turn, improved my estimation of him—at least somewhat. We had one thing in common, for I approved of Jake—more than I did of any human being.

Grendel gestured for me to climb through. I hesitated and pulled Grendel away from the gate.

"That bit about me being a snack," I whispered. "Was that a joke?"

Grendel turned away, glaring at the big face, which still leered at us in the open gate.

"It *was* a joke!" he called to the other troll. "*Right?*"

The other troll laughed but appeared uncomfortable.

"Of course, Big G—just a little *hazing* joke." The eyes shifted to me. "Welcome, sir! And what be your name? Mine is Ugluk."

"Ken," I said, my voice shaky; I still felt unnerved.

Grendel was watching me and apparently observed this. He gave Ugluk an especially dirty look. "*You!*" he growled. "You mean your name is You-Jerk, right?"

Ugluk laughed. "If you say so, Big G." He turned to me again. "I am sorry," he said, and this time it sounded genuine. "I did not register. I did not realize that this was love." He grinned. "Thought it was just another—mmm—I will not say—" Ugluk sighed and shrugged, then murmured sadly, "We get so few."

I wasn't sure I wanted to know what this meant, so I said nothing. The troll continued.

"And please—do not judge Grendel by me. We door-wardens, well, we have to be a bit rough around the edges. Now Grendel here, he is a real gentle-troll. I can tell you about—"

"Alright! Enough!" Grendel said firmly. "Now that you have scared my friend. I do not know if he is even fully willing to come through."

Ugluk pursed his lips. "Well, I feel like a jerk!"

"Like I said: You-Jerk."

Ugluk rolled his eyes, and for the first time in the present situation I laughed. This seemed to lessen the tension between the two trolls. Then I noticed Jake was sitting there, observing all of this with interest, but no fear. That did it. Jake, being the wise dog he is, would *know* if there was any malicious intent.

So, I turned to Grendel and stood on my tiptoes. He leaned down and we kissed. Ugluk made a quiet *oooooo* sound.

"Let's do it," I said, and saw relief, and joy, blossom on Grendel's broad, kindly face.

"Watch yer step, gentlemen," Ugluk said, stepping back from the hole. Grendel entered first. I handed him the lantern and the packs, then lifted Jake into his arms. Finally, Grendel held out a hand to help me through.

Behind us the gate clanged shut and I saw that we were in a long passage, softly lit by luminous patches spaced periodically along its length, where the walls on either side met the ceiling. What struck me especially was that the passage was very *large*; it was about twenty-five feet wide and of similar height. Even for Grendel's kind, I thought, the proportions were large. There was more than enough room for trolls to pass.

The words came to me: *Twenty-five feet high and three may walk abreast.*

This was true enough, but I had an impression that I had read something like it somewhere. I immediately dismissed this as a distraction. The important thing was, we were *here* now, at last! *But where* is *here, exactly?* In the sense of the difference between the space outside the gate and inside this passage.

I noticed Grendel was watching me. I smiled up at him.

"Shall we go?" he said.

I nodded and, reaching up, took his hand. At my current height this was at the level of my face, and I felt a bit like a child holding a parent's hand. But I wanted the contact right now.

Just that touch caused a great wash of joy to flow over me. But along with this came an excited appreciation of Grendel's physical presence, both sensual and sexual. I grinned up at him.

"Maybe there's a place where we can—you know?"

Grendel started and then beamed. "Oh, you bet I do!"

As we headed off, I heard the voice of Ugluk behind us mutter, "Some trolls got all the luck."

We did not hurry, and I savored the experience, especially enjoying the sight of Jake sniffing around, trotting a little ahead at times to follow a scent. I wondered what scents there might be here. It just another question to heap onto the growing pile. I smiled to myself. It felt *good* not to know these things and, more importantly, having no *need* to know. We had passed the barrier and were in Grendel's own country now. And that meant a lot. Most especially, it meant that we were safe.

I took in the smooth regularity of the passage with approval. It looked very—civilized. There were no swooping curves here; all the surfaces and lines here were close to being flat and straight—but not quite. Whenever I looked closely at any aspect of the passage, I could always discern just a *slight* curve: the walls and ceiling concave, the floor convex, and ahead the passage itself curved to the right; I could only see about a hundred yards.

We had gone maybe three hundred yards when from far behind came an odd sizzling sound that was abruptly broken off and followed by a dull thud. We turned to look, but the gate was out of sight, around the curve of the passage.

Grendel turned to me as we heard the sound again. He put his hands on my shoulders.

"You stay here," he said. "There is some trouble." He paused, and added in an incredulous, outraged tone, as if to himself, "They have followed us! They are here already!" Then he added, "I must go to help Ugluk secure the gate."

I clung onto his hand. "I want to help too! Isn't there something I can do?"

"Yes!" Grendel said. "There is something. Get the local guard."

I looked down the tunnel in the direction we had been heading. "Where's that?"

Grendel thought for a second. "Forty-two," he muttered. "Okay. Go directly down this passage until you come to an intersection. Then, turn right and continue along that passage. You will come to the door of the guard house, again on the right."

I nodded and called, "Jake!" But he was right at my feet, alert to the sudden sense of danger. "C'mon!" I said, but then realized Grendel hadn't moved. I understood and reached up as he bent down. We kissed.

"Good luck!" I said.

"You too."

And with that we headed off rapidly on our separate errands.

DIRECTIONS, ALMOST BY definition, seem to contain problems. I had turned right at the first intersection, but having gone down that for several hundred yards, I came to another intersection: a meeting of three ways. I had not seen any door on my right, and now I had no idea which of the two passages I should continue on.

I became aware of how different I felt in this region of enormous passages without Grendel. I no longer felt secure or safe. And *right* now I was feeling—almost—lost. But I shook my head and forced myself to think. In the end, I decided on the right-hand passage, reasoning that if I failed to find the door after maybe twenty minutes going, I would retrace my steps and try the other passage.

After running along this new passage for about fifteen minutes, I saw a reddish-yellow light ahead. Coming up to it, I discovered a round doorway set into the right-hand wall. The door itself was ajar, through which light streamed.

Taking several deep breaths, I peered cautiously around the door. Two trolls in leather gear were sitting in enormous chairs near a fireplace whose burning coals gave the only light.

Summoning my courage, I pushed open the door and stepped into the room. One of the guards saw me and cried out, leaping to his feet. In another moment, both trolls were staring down at me.

In their uniforms they looked surprisingly like enormous versions of the Roman soldiers I had seen in history books. Though they wore nothing in the way of a tunic, the leather collars lying on their shoulders and around their wrists looked Roman. They had on leather harnesses, too, and below the broad leather belts hung strips of leather in the fashion of Roman soldiers. And they were wearing leather sandals, with straps running up to just below their knees.

I had to admit, they looked hot. I also noticed they were looking at me now in what was closer to leers than anything else. It was a little disconcerting, but I took hold of myself.

"They need you at the portal," I said. "There's, uh—an attack, a human incursion."

The guards looked at each other, then back at me.

"Why?"

"*Why?*" I echoed, incredulous at the question. Then I realized perhaps I needed to give them some context. "Oh," I said. "They followed Grendel and me, I guess. From the barrier, I mean."

If I had expected them to leap into action, I was sorely disappointed. They merely exchanged glances briefly and then turned their gazes back to me. I felt desperate and confused.

"Will you help?" I asked.

The one guard shook his head. "They are within their rights. Grendel broke the law. If he makes it back, then that is okay. But he must do it without the help of the Underworld."

What? The coldness of this policy struck me as incredible. And my head was starting to spin.

"But Ugluk," I said, "the door warden is helping him."

"But they are friends," the other troll said. "He is helping him out of friendship. There is no *reason* for us to help Grendel." He sniffed. "Nothing in the law."

Something in the emphasis of the word *reason* caused a light bulb to go off in my head, though this was facilitated by what I now noticed: The strips

Grendel Rising 165

on the front of the trolls' leather skirts were pushing forward. I blinked, trying to get a sense of what the hell was going on here.

They were—*extorting sex* from me? At this moment of crisis?

I looked up at the two leering faces without any sense of fear, despite their size. Perhaps the sexual energy they were generating was affecting me. For sex, when it is participated in freely, *is* play of a sort, and *that* obviated any sense of danger. Looking at the two trolls, I saw only horny teenage males so desperate to get their rocks off that they will bend the rules to do so at the first opportunity.

So, I squared my shoulders, nodded, and said, "Okay. Who wants to go first?"

To say the trolls were up for it was to understate the case. They hurriedly undid their belts, from which the strips of the leather skirt hung. And when these were tossed aside, I saw that both were fully erect. One of them even had a shiny pearl of pre-cum at the tip.

Both trolls were over a foot shorter than Grendel, which made their genitals pretty much at eye level for me. *Well*, I thought sardonically, *at least I won't have to kneel.*

The first troll was definitely not as well-endowed as Grendel, but still his phallus was at least fourteen inches, so there was no way I was going to get that head into my mouth, even at my slightly increased size.

The guy wasn't pushy, I had to admit. He stopped when the tip of his phallus was still a foot in front of me. I reached out and took the shaft in both hands and slid them back toward me—which caused more pre-cum to ooze from the tip. I opened my mouth as wide as possible and pressed my lips against the spongy flesh while with my tongue I licked up the pre-cum.

A rush of intoxicated pleasure passed through me, and my attitude became less dutiful and more appreciative—even enthusiastic. I had been horned up at our arrival here, and though that had been directed toward Grendel, the chemical stimulants remained and were still operational, in a more general way.

If you can't be with the one you love, I repeated a vaguely remembered lyric to myself, *love the one you're with*.

The fact that I was doing this specifically to *help* Grendel, pretty much dispersed any residual feeling of guilt. *Guilty pleasure*, I repeated to myself, *with an emphasis on the pleasure*.

In short, I went to *town* on that phallus head.

I licked it, rubbed it and even *nipped* it—a provocative act, but something I discovered this fellow liked. I had him close to orgasm in a very short time. But then, out of a sense of wanting to give them their *money's worth*, as it were, I stopped what I was doing, and turned my attention to the other—which brought a groan of sexual frustration from the first troll. It made me smile. I wanted to give them a good time, and part of that was to tease them, repeatedly, until they fairly *exploded*.

If they were to go help Grendel, I reasoned, the last thing I wanted was them to feel disappointed with my treatment of them. Grendel needed and *deserved* their full, enthusiastic participation, and if that meant I needed to spend just a little extra time to give these two a really good "ride," well, so be it.

The second troll was better endowed, always a pleasure, and I used the same fulsome adoration method on him as I had on his fellow. The first troll, evidently watching this, impatiently demanded attention, by shoving his phallus head against the side of my head. I turned, so I had them on either side, fleshy heads pushing slickly against either cheek.

The sense of being caught between the two phalluses was quite exciting, giving me the sense of being dominated. My own interest increased considerably, and I felt a taut throbbing between my legs. It was delightful to feel them both *push* so, jostling for principal position and thus the lion's share of physical attention.

There was something so innocent about their insistent need, their eagerness, their *desperation*, in fact, that charmed. I held onto both shafts, one with either hand, while I moved my head back and forth and all around, tonguing, kissing, nipping the spongy heads. I glanced up at them and saw them gazing down at me hungrily. And, at the same time, I felt both phalluses swell.

Oh! I thought. *They like this sort of thing!*

So, interleaved between my direct action, I gave them a deliberate, provocative look, each time fine tuning which expression worked best. I found that that was a kind of helpless but coy, beseeching look.

I soon had both trolls were groaning, phalluses hyper-erect, skin taut and trembling on the brink. At which point I sat back, and lowered my hands, removing all physical contact. This time there were *two* groans of frustrated need.

Music to my ears! But I was getting so excited myself that I found it difficult to pull away. And when I resumed, I resolved *not* to stop this time. But I took my time, replacing energy with languid sensuousness. It did the trick: they came violently, their spurts of semen shooting out in syncopation, so by shifting my head in time with this I could catch most of both loads in my open and eager mouth.

And *this* I found so hot that I almost came myself.

There was so much cum that I gagged, while the phallus heads slid their slickness all over my cum-covered face.

The first troll repeated as he did so, "Eat it! Eat it, human!" while the other murmured, "Swallow!"

These words seemed ironic, given how eager they were to cover my *face*, as opposed to cumming *inside* my mouth. I did my best to follow their injunctions, caught up as I was in my own, overpowering need—for their seed.

A minute or two later I was wiping my mouth and the two trolls were putting their skirts and belts back on.

"Okay?" I said, staring at them pointedly. The two trolls looked at each other. They were grinning, and both nodded. Then one of them looked past me and cried out.

"Hey! There is a little dog here!"

Jake, showing his usual discretion in the presence of my carnal activity, was lying in front of the fire, watching us. I called him to me, and he came forward, jumped into my arms, and started licking my face.

The one troll laughed excitedly. "Hey! He loves our seed!"

The other was more serious. "He is your friend, then?"

"Yes." I replied with the same seriousness, knowing how important this was.

"Oh, hey, well—let us help this dog and his friend's friend then!" The two trolls collected their weapons and put on helmets—one of them thrusting into my hand what must have been a dagger for them but was an enormous sword for me. Then they paused to bow respectfully to Jake, putting their faces down close to his—at which I was pleased to see he showed no fear—and ran out the door.

I followed after them, holding the enormous dagger. Trolls run more quickly than humans, however, and I was soon left behind. Fearful of becoming lost, I kept my mind focused, recounting the turns I had taken. But I slipped up somewhere and had a rather unpleasant time of attempting to retrace my steps.

My salvation came through my sense of hearing.

I heard loud shouts far ahead down the passage I was in. There were deep roars, the clash of metal, and the strange sizzling sound.

Into a brief pause in this noise, a human voice yelled, "Give back the escapee! You are breaking the law!"

"Sucks to the law!" Grendel's voice snarled.

"It is your law anyway," came the voice of Ugluk. "Not our law."

The clanks and sizzling sounds started again, louder and nastier than before. I found that, as I approached the location of the battle, I was going slower and slower.

I NEVER DID see the battle. Those final, several hundred yards of curving tunnel, while they transmitted the sound horribly, kept me from seeing what was going on. And, before I had gone close enough that I could see, I stopped stock still, doubtful about how I could help. I had images of fifteen-foot trolls battling some sort of military G-men, humans with weapons, including a weapon that—*sizzled*. And then there was the mere volume of that *noise*!

I never *quite* gave up, however, and managed to continue, step by step making my way toward the action. But, before I had come round that final curve, it all simply—ended.

There was a deafening clang, followed by the murmur of troll voices, talking. I heard bits of this: "That was close," "touch and go," and some other, less-than-charitable words about the humans they had been battling.

I felt such relief that I sank to the ground, and remained there, sitting with my back against the wall, when Grendel came round that curve and up to me.

He was beaming, though he appeared to be limping, and finally pulled me into gentle embrace. There came the sound of approaching voices, and we stepped apart.

"Ah," said one of the guards. "That was a good battle, reminded me of old times."

The trolls stopped when they saw me. Jake, who was standing next to me, wagged his greeting, and Grendel stepped forward, saying to his companions. "Gentlemen, I want you to meet my human friend, Ken—and *his* canine friend, Jake."

I smiled and nodded, even shaking hands with the other trolls, though the guards couldn't keep their smirks entirely off their faces.

Grendel shook the others' hands in turn, thanking them for coming to his assistance.

"Oh, it was our *pleasure!*" one of the guards said, laughing. The trolls departed, Ugluk with them, leaving me and Jake alone with Grendel.

Grendel had frowned in puzzlement at their departing backs, but apparently was too relieved at the moment to give this further thought. He took my hand gently in his and said, "Now we go home, beloved. I want you to meet my mother." He reached out and very gently touched Jake's head with a fingertip, at which Jake's tail wagged furiously.

But as he moved forward to take my hand, his expression changed from one of joy to one of confusion. He leaned in close and sniffed me. Then his face became truly terrible.

"How?" he asked in a menacing voice. "How could you—*betray* me, and so soon?"

For a second, I thought the big troll was going to strike me—which would be the end of me. I froze in terror, and before I could say anything Grendel gave me a rough push on the shoulders that sent me flying back, against the wall.

I came out of my stunned state sometime later. Grendel was gone, and Jake and I were alone. He was next to me, shaking and licking my face. I had slumped down the wall, and half-sat, half-lay on the floor. I shifted my position to a more comfortable sitting one and gathered Jake into my arms. At that point I still hadn't recovered myself physically, and I didn't feel like moving. My mind was a pit of darkness and my heart an aching void.

I was in the Underworld alone.

Chapter 19
Alone in the Underworld

I AWOKE SOMETIME later to find myself lying on my side, my back against the wall of the passage, Jake lying against my chest, his head resting in the crook of my arm. He appeared to be asleep, and he looked so innocent and so adorable curled up against me that, though my heart still ached, I was comforted by his presence and the knowledge of his unshakable loyalty. At least *he* wouldn't desert me!

When I thought about our current situation, part of my concern was for *him*, for *his* status in a predicament he had had no part in creating. He was in his way so helpless, and in response I fiercely resolved to protect him no matter what, even to the death if it came to that! And then I was sobbing, and Jake stirred, tilted his head back and licked my chin with concern. I pulled him against me.

"I-it's okay, Jake," I whispered between sobs. "Everything's going to be okay."

And, curiously, when I had said that I experienced a sense of equipoise, between two opposing convictions. The first was that I had misunderstood Grendel and was in the soup, pure and simple, that I had been deserted and was a helpless stranger in a very strange land. But the other was the *feeling* that, somehow, everything would be okay, as I had said. The words of—who was it? Oh yes—Juliana of Norwich, came to me.

It behooved that there should be sin; but all shall be well, and all shall be well, and all manner of things shall be well.

A friend had casually repeated the latter part of this, at a party of all places, and the words had hit me so profoundly that I had looked it up later. And, ever since, the phrase had remained like a balm to my soul, albeit transitory; once I had recited the words, the ecstatic hope and joy I felt would fade as doubts returned.

Only *this* time, things were different! As I lay there, having repeated the words to myself, amazement rose in me. For that balm did *not* fade; doubt didn't quench it; for *this* time, in *this* situation, I *believed* them!

And, with this feeling, I blinked away my tears, wiped my face, and sat up. Jake seemed to register my change in mood, for after looking at me for a few seconds, he did his languorous stretch, complete with a wide yawn. It was so wonderful, watching this, that my heart now filled with love for my little friend, and I felt considerably better, not just with the hope I had felt after repeating the quote, but with an odd sense of the—what was it? For want of a better word, the *rightness* of the current moment.

I sat there, petting Jake who, after climbing into my lap promptly rolled upside down, soliciting a belly rub. I chuckled and complied, attending to the practical while I considered my situation. I was still hurt and confused about Grendel's reaction to my infidelity; and I felt exposed and lonely being here, on my own, in this new place. It simply amazed me that I could feel all of these things and yet *still* be convinced things would turn out well, and that my current predicament could feel somehow *right*.

Jake was certainly enjoying the moment. I had paused, distracted by my thoughts, in my attentions to him, and now he opened his eyes, which had been blissfully closed for the belly rub, and nudged my hand with his nose.

I laughed and, leaning down, kissed the tip of his nose—and resumed my attentions.

"Hi, Jake," I said as he continued to gaze up at me.

At last, feeling a need to move, I said, "C'mon, boy. Let's get up."

He was on his feet while I was still getting a foot under me. I managed to stand up straight, despite the ache in my upper back where I had hit the wall, and slowly I stretched, arms over my head. Jake emulated this, in a repeat of his earlier stretch.

Okay, I thought. *Now we're both officially up.* I looked in both directions and listened. Nothing. No one.

Besides Jake and me, the only things in the passage were my backpack, the lantern, and Bruce's food pack. Fortunately, I had put these things down during Grendel's introduction—and before his shove. At the moment, the important part of these items was the food pack.

I looked at Jake, who was watching me expectantly. I picked up the food pack.

"How about it, boy," I said to him. "You like some breakfast?"

Bark! Bark, bark, bark!

"I see!" I said. "Well, let's find out what we have."

I sat down again and began to go through the pack. There was plenty of food left. I don't know who made the sandwiches, but they were certainly first-class and delicious. I got out an egg salad and a ham-and-cheese.

Of the bottles of drink in the pack, I chose iced tea for me and water for Jake, which I set out for him in a small bowl that was part of the pack's contents. As I watched Jake slake his thirst, I thought of Bruce and murmured, "Thanks, man! Thank you so much!"

This made me wonder what would happen to Bruce. Would he be charged with something? His father had the resources to fight for his son's rights, if so. That made me feel a *little* better. Then I thought about my own house, all my possessions. What would become of them—now that I had "disappeared"? Oh, right. The government knew all about where I was; they would certainly take care of that—in whatever way they chose.

A wave of anger came and went. I didn't really care that much about material goods, especially since I had met—

But now I had to stifle a sob. I shook my head, trying to push away the memory of that last painful scene with Grendel. But whether I wanted to or not, I saw again that look on his beautiful face, and his words—

"*How could you?*" I said, repeating them, and then felt anger boil up in me.

"How could *I?*" I said, my voice choked with outrage. For a little I struggled for articulation. "Because—it was almost *an exact parallel! You* had sex with the G-man to get him to let you slide, and I did *just the same thing* with those guards—to *help you, for heaven's sake!*"

I was almost shouting now, but I caught myself. I had to walk around now—I was so upset. I got up and began pacing up and down the passage. Jake followed me for several repetitions, but finally sat down to watch me concernedly. I sobbed with hurt, frustration, and simply feeling lost.

I continued for some time to walk and weep, instinctively working out my energy and letting out all my emotions. When I had finally tired myself, I sat down and put my head in my hands. The tears still flowed, but less stormily now. And after a time, they too had exhausted themselves. I felt better, then, peaceful in an exhausted way. I sat up and opened my eyes.

Jake was sitting close beside me, quiet and still, showing canine solidarity. This smote my heart and I leaned over and, putting an arm gently around him, kissed the top of his head.

Okay, I thought. *Now at least I can think.*

I contemplated returning to the gate, asking to be let out. But, no, that wouldn't work. There was the barrier further up, and the G-men—and possibly even soldiers of some kind. Wouldn't that be going from the proverbial frying pan into the fire?

I sighed and looked around, taking in the smooth regularity of the passage, and staring up at those odd lights that lined the ceiling. I stood up to look at them more closely. I couldn't reach them, but I thought they looked like a kind of moss. What was that called? Bioluminescence. *Huh!* Though I had heard the term, I didn't know how that kind of thing worked. I was only thankful for them.

Standing there, in the middle of the passage, I felt myself to be in a somewhat civilized area, unlike that strange place of ledges and curving chasms between the gate and the barrier. I tried to take comfort from this realization, but somehow, I couldn't. It wasn't *my* civilization, after all. There was a sense of alienness.

But, to avoid getting into a negative mental spiral I decided to continue along the passage—further in, just to see what I might find.

So, I hoisted my pack, and we struck out.

I soon discovered that activity did help my mental state. Now that I was walking along, I could turn over various observations and feelings. One of these was an awareness of the qualities that underlay my impression of the strangeness of my environment. These included an appreciation of the marvelousness of this passageway itself, and an abiding sense of mystery. And when I inhaled, I had the impression that even the *air* was different. I couldn't put my finger on what that might be—though it did tease and tantalize me.

I wasn't consciously aware I was avoiding thinking about Grendel, until a different emotion exploded over me. I was simply amazed at how *hypocritical* Grendel had turned out to be! And part of that amazement was my conviction that this didn't seem consistent with Grendel as I had come to know and love him! It *didn't fit!*

"He's a *troll*, you idiot!" the cynical part of me chided. "You expect sensitivity and fine behavior?"

Tears threatened then, for the truth was, I *did* expect those very things. No, that wasn't right. I had *seen* those things—in him!

I sighed and shook my head. Was it that simple? Had I taken his best behavior as his normal behavior? Phrases like "rose-colored glasses," and "the honeymoon is over," percolated through my consciousness. Yet, try as I might, I simply could not convince something deep inside me, in my heart, of this harsh "reality." Wasn't there something about the heart knowing things the head doesn't? I shook my head. My store of poetry had failed me here.

I came to a place where a second passage crossed mine. I stopped, and suddenly realized I hadn't been noticing where I was going. I had passed several crossings, hadn't I?

I felt a coldness go down my back. I thought I had been heading for that guard room, to talk with them, get directions or something. At least I knew them, and had given them some reason for being positively disposed to me—

I turned on the spot and realized I quite literally had *no idea* where I was.

With this realization a kind of terror began to settle on my mind as I imagined myself trapped in an enormous maze.

"No, no," I told myself severely. "Do *not* panic!"

I breathed slowly until I began to feel calmer. Then, slowly, I resumed my walking. My thought was, *I will eventually meet someone.*

After what must have been over an hour of walking along various interconnecting passages—all without encountering anyone, or any*thing* for that matter—the passage I was in ended at a what I thought at first was a cross passage. But when I came to it, I saw that the space opened into a large chamber. It was circular in shape and appeared to have an enormous well at its center. The only floor was a broad, circular path that went round, against the outer wall of the chamber, and the disturbing thing about this path was that it had no barrier along its inside edge, so the path formed a ledge, over the central abyss.

And then I saw, to my horror, that Jake had gone forward, right up to the drop-off, and was looking down into the well. Stifling a cry, I called him back while backing against the outer wall of the chamber and squatting down. Jake turned his head and looked at me, puzzled, where I crouched. After a second or two, however, he came to me, and I hugged him tightly, trying to calm my nerves.

After a bit, I told Jake to *stay*, unslung my pack and crept slowly to the edge. Below me, the well descended into darkness. And spiraling round its circular perimeter, was a stone staircase. I studied this and saw, directly across from where I was, a landing that led from the circular ledge I was on to the staircase. Following the staircase down—it was like the ledge, having no railing whatsoever—I saw another landing and the suggestion of a second surrounding ledge. They were about fifty feet down and in deep shadow, for there seemed to be no lighting down there. I looked up and saw, high above me, a dome ceiling with numerous glowing patches. It was this light, and the diffused light from the outer wall on my level, that was the only illumination in this chamber.

It was then that I noticed Jake. He was standing right next to me, looking out on the central well again. I clenched my teeth on a cry of alarm, and slowly backed away from the edge, gently calling to Jake. When we were back at where my pack was, I hugged my little dog. The image of Jake standing right at the edge over that terrible abyss put my heart into my mouth and it was sometime before I was in a state where I could do anything.

The curious thing was, part of my fear now came from an awareness of how easily I had lost my nerve. In this situation, alone in the Underworld, I decided that simply would not do. It was Jake, I realized; I could face stuff myself, but not the prospect of danger to Jake. I chided myself for not bringing Jake's leash. It just hadn't occurred to me—Jake was a very obedient dog, generally.

Without a clear sense of what I should do next, I decided we had both earned a meal. So, I got out sandwiches and a drink, and we shared a quiet repast. And, as I chewed, I looked across at what I could see of the chamber. It wasn't just that horrible drop, I decided. There was something else here that gave me the willies.

Focusing on this, the realization slowly came that what I felt was a sense of something rising up from below; not just warm air, though that might be true as well: I knew that warm air rises. The other was a quality, an essence, the only thing tangible that came to mind was a subtle smell of spice, though I couldn't say what kind of spice.

When we had finished our meal, I got some cord out of my pack, and tied Jake's collar to the pack.

"Now, stay here," I told him firmly. He just looked at me. I petted him, then picked up my lantern, lit it, and walked carefully round the ledge until I reached the landing. Crossing this, I began to descend the stairs, keeping my free hand on the circular wall of the well.

I made it as far as that first level below. It was quite dark here, the only light being that coming from above.

A moment later I was shot out of my skin by Jake's sudden questioning bark. It echoed through the chamber, and I cringed at this for some reason. Knowing he would bark again if I didn't respond, I gathered my nerve and, looking up, cried, "It's okay, Jake! You stay there! I'll be up in a minute!"

That, I thought, should do it—for now.

Holding up my lantern, I crossed the landing and walked around the circular ledge, pausing before each passage opening. There were five of these, each radiating out from the well. I saw nothing, however, and as the darkness was beginning to press in on me, when I reached the landing again, I climbed the stairs more quickly than I had descended them.

Jake gave a welcoming bark when he saw me, and I hurried my careful way around to him, hugging him to reassure us both.

"I am," I whispered to him, "completely out of my league here."

And, with that I untied him, and we left that place, heading down the passage immediately to the right of the one I had initially emerged from.

THE EFFECT OF that encounter was to make the regular, lit passages seem homier. Even so, the experience haunted me. For one thing, seeing those different levels, I realized now that I was in a maze of passages that was three- rather than two-dimensional. This deepened my uneasy sense of being completely lost, and at one point I stopped and, blinking back tears of hurt and anger, stomped my foot at the thought that Grendel had deserted me like this.

I caught myself, however, and pushed down these deleterious emotions. I would have to be strong—or at least tough—if I was going to get anywhere here. I looked down at Jake, and saw he was looking up at me. He wagged his tail tentatively, and I reached down and petted him.

"I've still got you, right Jake?"

After this I turned my mind back to that odd well and its curious qualities. I had vaguely noticed the walls and ceiling had been different there. All other passages were pristine, well-proportioned, smooth and regular, and they had had no ornamentation, other than horizontal channels running along the walls near the ceiling, and some symbols at the places where passages met. The well, on the other hand, had had walls that were quite decorated—in a way that reminded me of the pictures I had seen of various architectural works by Gaudi: shapes beautifully proportioned and vaguely organic. What did that mean?

I had to admit I had no idea. But pondering this at length had served its purpose; I was in control of myself again. I was even beginning to feel a fatigue that suggested a sleep. From this point, I began to look for a likely spot for this.

At last, I came upon a small alcove that suited my purpose excellently. I sat down in it, leaned against the wall, and opened my pack for some water. When we had both drunk, I closed the pack and lay my head on it, settling down for a snooze. Jake curled up against me. I sighed and put my arm around him, whereupon he sighed, which made me smile. My last thought as I drifted off to sleep was how much better everything was having Jake with me.

I WAS AWAKENED by the sound of Jake's warning barks. Sitting up quickly, I saw there were two trolls standing about five yards away. Jake was standing defiantly between them and me, and barking his head off, the sound echoing and somehow amplified in the passage. I reached for the dagger and got to my feet, trying to clear my mind of sleep.

Judging by their leather outfits, I decided they were guards, but not the two I had encountered previously in the guard room. They were looking, not a me, but at Jake, and their expressions were abashed, their mouths slightly open, their arms were held out in front of them in a defensive posture.

Jake, apparently, was *holding them off!*

I walked forward, next to Jake, holding out the dagger. Jake turned his head to look at me, and then resumed his barking, if anything louder, more defiant than ever.

The trolls' hands came up and covered their ears, their expressions somewhere between daunted and horrified.

It's almost comical, I thought. *They have no idea what to do.*

"*Jake!*" I shouted, and Jake shut up. He looked at me and I held my hand out toward him to keep him from resuming. I brandished my dagger at the trolls and shouted, "What do you want?"

One of the trolls, glancing at me, but without removing his hands from his ears, made an agonized face and, nodding toward Jake, shouted back, "Call him off, *please*!"

I backed up to my pack, got the piece of cord I had used earlier and attached it to his collar, Jake growling at the trolls the entire time. Holding onto this firmly, I again brandished the dagger.

Slowly, cautiously, the two trolls lowered their hands. One of them shook his head as if to get rid of a ringing noise. "Thank you," he murmured, shaking himself. "*Brrr!* That was *horrible*!"

I stared at the big creatures, amazed, but said in what I hoped was a tough voice, "I asked you—what do you want?"

The second troll looked at me and frowned. "*We* are the patrol here, human, and we will ask the questions! And so: What art *thou* doing here?"

After being distracted momentarily by the troll's mode of speech, I nodded. "Fair enough. I guess I'm a refugee—from the Overworld."

The first troll snorted, but the second one said, "That much is obvious. But how camest thou to be here? Explain!"

"I accompanied a—friend, someone who was fleeing the Overworld authorities."

"Did that friend have a name? Was he human too?"

"No. He was a troll. His name was—Grendel."

The two trolls exchanged glances. The first troll shook his head and murmured to his companion, "I knew that would happen. The dreamer has gotten himself in trouble." The other troll nodded, then shook his head too.

"But how," said the second troll, addressing me again, "camest thou to be alone here?"

I was not enjoying this inquisition at all. So, I let some of my irritation out by replying, "I'm *not* alone here. I'm with Jake." I gestured to him.

This remark had simply been a random retort. To my surprise, however, the trolls appeared taken aback.

"Of course!" the first troll said, exchanging a worried look with his companion. "We apologize! Of course, you are here—with your friend." They both made slight bows to Jake, who now seemed to decide things were going sufficiently well that he could sit down, though he was still vigilant, staring at the trolls.

The troll's use of the word *friend* made me conscious of Jake's leash. I squatted down and, disconnecting it, petted Jake to reassure him. The trolls watched this without comment, then turned to each other and began to confer in what supposed must be native troll-speak. It was mostly grunts, snorts and clicks. After a little they turned back to me.

"We would like to extend you the hospitality of our barracks," the first troll said in respectful tones. "Our captain is out on patrol; there has been some unrest along the barrier. But you are welcome to stay as our guests until he returns. Then he will—converse with you about your situation, and perhaps confer with you on what you would do."

The second troll smiled in an obsequious manner. "There are—extra beds, most comfortable, even for a human—if thou wouldst sleep alone."

I thought I saw a glint in the troll's eyes at this, and I sighed inwardly. Were all trolls this lecherous?

"We have food, too, if you are hungry," the first troll said, stepping back as if making the way open for me. He even gestured with an arm. "It is this way."

I considered this and then shrugged. What choice did I have?

At least, I reflected, *I'm no longer lost*. I felt I knew something about trolls now, even from my limited experience, so I wasn't as frightened as I might have been. What I knew wasn't perhaps all that nice, but it was something. For it appeared that in many situations a troll's first interest in a human was to have sex with him, which was certainly better than wanting to eat him: the door warden's "playful" first greeting still haunting me.

The trolls led us down passage after passage, and I was soon quite confused. I wouldn't have been able to retrace the journey from our place of encounter for the life of me, let alone to the gate. Our guides, however, did not hesitate even once.

As we went along, I thought about my situation. Part of me was still numb from Grendel's sudden change in attitude. As I thought about this, I became quite angry again at the apparent injustice of Grendel's outrage.

"What's good for the troll has got to be equally good for the human," I muttered angrily to myself.

"I beg your pardon?" one of the trolls asked, looking around.

I shook my head. "Nothing." And we continued on in silence.

At last, we arrived at an enormous, reddish-pink, metal door set about a foot into the rock surface of the side wall of the passage. The door was quite round, about twenty feet in diameter, and I decided must be made of copper. Its surface was covered with ornate scroll work, forming a complex and exquisitely beautiful design that was completely unlike the strange ornamentation I had seen in that well place.

The one troll struck the rock wall on the left side of the door several times in a complex rhythm, and the door, after several seconds, opened by rolling to one side, right *into* the rock, like a pocket door. The process was smooth and completely noiseless. I was impressed! It was the first sign of actual technology I had seen in this new world.

My two guides did not pass through the doorway, however. They went to either side of the door and, turning to face each other, put their right fists on their chests, coming to attention. Apparently, I was to enter first.

Chapter 20
In the Barracks

I HESITATED, HEARING the sound of troll voices coming from somewhere beyond the doorway. Jake on the other hand, after glancing up at me, simply walked forward, his tail wagging slightly. I smiled at how reassuring this was and followed him.

We were at one end of an enormous room, almost a hanger. It was about fifty feet wide and extended away in front of me for several hundred feet. The nearer part of the room had lockers and stores, swords and pikes and things like that, but beyond this there two lines of troll-sized bunkbeds, set against either wall. No one was in sight and the sound of troll voices was coming through a broad archway to my right.

One of my guides went to a locker and began to remove his uniform. The other walked toward the archway and, turning, gestured I should follow him. We passed through into another room that, while enormous, was not as long as the first room. It appeared to be a kind of lounge.

There were chairs, couches and tables, and an enormous fireplace in which coals were burning. There were about two dozen trolls here, talking and laughing. But when one of them caught sight of me it was like a signal. Conversation died away, and I was being stared at by more than a score of trolls.

My guide, facing the group, said in a carrying voice, "These are two refugees. They were discovered in tunnel 702 in the Isotok section. They will stay with us until the captain returns from patrol." A silence greeted this speech, and my troll guide turned to me. "Would you care for food, human—for your friend?" He bowed to Jake.

"His name is Jake," I said. And on impulse I added, "And mine is Ken."

The troll bowed again. "Pleased to meet you, Jake, and you, Ken." He put his hand on his chest. "And my name is Gog."

I had noted with amused indignation how he addressed Jake first. But it reassured me. And Jake showed no sign of fear looking up at this troll. He even wagged his tail once or twice at this greeting.

Though Jake was silent, my stomach had its own ideas, and growled in response to the troll's invitation. "Yes," I said, grinning sheepishly. "Food would, uh, be, appreciated."

Gog nodded and led us back through the archway. As I followed, I was aware of the gazes of the *all* the trolls following me, so intently and appreciatively that my face was burning by the time I passed from the room. We went across the entrance area and through an archway in the opposite wall. This led to a room that was in its proportions the twin of the lounge. But it was filled with long tables lined with benches, and in the far wall there were several openings that looked like serving hatches. At the sight of these my stomach growled again.

I was a little intimidated by size of the tables, whose tops were level with my eyes. They reminded me of my diminutive stature in this world. My guide gestured to the nearest bench, which was almost at the level of my waist. I lifted Jake up and then climbed up myself, trying my best to make it look easy and natural.

Our host went to one of the serving hatches while I sat, swinging my legs, hands on the table-top in front of me. It was the height of my chest, and I couldn't help feeling like a little kid. Jake was sitting contentedly enough, though his nose was twitching. I petted him, and felt my mood improve sympathetically. Jake wasn't worried or disoriented, I reminded myself; he just accepted the situation, living in the moment, which meant, as his nose told him: *food!*

Gog returned with two plates of what looked like stew, a large plate for me and a smaller one for Jake. Mine came with a spoon which, while oversized for me, must have been a teaspoon for trolls. Jake set to as the plate was deposited next to him on the bench, but I found myself distracted even as I set my own plate on my lap and picked up the spoon, by the presence of the trolls who had begun drifting in. Some sat, some stood or leaned against the table ends, in groups of two or more, all with an air of hanging out, doing their best to appear as though they were *not* there because of me. After intercepting several turning away glances, my face warm, I concentrated on eating, not looking up. I could feel their eyes on me all the same.

I wondered whether this was how a pretty girl or handsome boy must feel at a new high school. It was strange. Somehow, I had always imagined that sort of attention as feeling wonderful, but what I experienced now was sheer discomfort, to the point of feeling nearly choked. And the fact that the sensation was tinged with Eros didn't seem to help. I began to feel sympathy for those I had envied.

My guide seemed to take a proprietary interest in me, which I decided was a good thing, for the moment at least. He had gotten a plate of stew for himself and seated himself across the table from me. Jake, displaying the best in canine manners, had gotten through the food on his plate in short order and was now engaged in the ritual of licking the now-empty plate for any stray molecules. My companion, seeing this, asked if my friend would like more. I shook my head.

"No. That's enough for him." I scratched Jake's head as he regarded me hopefully. "I don't want him to get fat."

Gog took this as serious information. On the topic of the food, I had noticed it had been the same kind for both Jake and me. I pointed with my spoon at my plate.

"This is good," I said.

The troll smiled, and there was a murmur of pleased noises from the other trolls. Evidently, I was showing good manners. For my own part, I took my first really good look at my guide. He was dark-haired, with dark eyes, and his head was almost perfectly circular—not a great look, but decent, like pretty much every troll I had met—even Ugluk of the disturbing jokes.

When I had finished and, refusing a refill, set my plate down for Jake to lick, there was another collective murmur of approval. Then Gog suggested I might like to rest, so I got up and lifted Jake down.

Jake, who had certainly registered the attention of the other trolls, now went up to several in turn, and I was pleased to see how each troll bent down and held out a hand for him to sniff. One even reached out a forefinger and gently petted him. I was surprised Jake allowed this; ordinarily, he wasn't that welcoming of being petted by strangers. But the touch was gentle, and Jake preened at this attention.

Gog led us back into the main barracks room and between the rows of bunkbeds. He stopped when we came to one that was apparently free—for our use.

When I had deposited my packs on the lower cot Gog led me to the far end of the room, where a short passage opened into a washroom. There were several enormous toilet stalls that I decided I could just manage to use, if I was careful. Though the toilets themselves were made out of stone—polished marble, in fact—they appeared to be actual flush toilets. Beside this, in a corner was a square patch of dirt for Jake's use. Maybe there was a residual smell to this, for Jake went straight to it and, after sniffing around, promptly peed on it.

My guide, who had gone into another part of the washroom, returned with a cube about 18 inches square, made of wood. He placed it on the floor in front of one of the toilets and gestured in such a way that I understood it was for my own use. Then he discretely withdrew.

I did my business and used the cube to reach a washbasin. There was a further passage, which I discovered led into a group shower. I hesitated, but decided I wanted to lie down for a bit. So, I returned to my cot and, lifting Jake up, climbed onto it and promptly dozed off.

I WOKE UP sometime later, feeling very lonely. The big room was very dark now, with only the occasional ceiling spot glowing. Jake was not far—I could dimly hear his nails on the stone floor: click-click here—pause, click-click-click there—pause. The familiar sound was vastly comforting and as I lay there, I smiled to myself.

I could hear troll voices further away, talking quietly, probably in the lounge. I lay back, sighed, trying my best to relax into acceptance of my situation. My thoughts wandered all over the map, in part because I didn't want to brood on my situation with Grendel. Fortunately, there was enough that was new and strange here to hold my attention. For one thing, the discovery that trolls had their own language. Somehow, Grendel's mastery of English had convinced me that it was his first language. Now that seemed absurd. And then there were the differences in how trolls spoke English. The use of antiquated words like *thou* that the second of the pair of trolls who had found me. What could that indicate?

A friend of mine, Olga had done graduate work at college in European languages. She had laughed at the fact that her German was better than that of her husband, who *was* of German stock. *I just treat it as if it's Old English*, she told me. And from there she had launched into description of how Old English, also known as Anglo-Saxon, had melded with French after the Norman Conquest to form Middle English, which then, through something called the Great Vowel Shift, became modern English. And then she had told me, to my astonishment, that the English of Shakespeare was modern English—though, she had added with another of her laughs, *early* modern English.

What occurred to me now was the idea that the differences in spoken English in the trolls might reflect these changes, though how that might be I didn't have a clear idea. Interesting, though! There were other questions too—almost an endless number.

I shifted my position on the cot, put my hands behind my head and, staring up into the near-darkness, sighed again.

A second later I froze when, as if in answer to my sigh, there came the sound of a large body shifting on a bed close by. Momentarily, the sound reminded me painfully of Grendel.

Where am I? I found myself wondering. *Where is he? And is there any hope of reconciliation?*

I sighed again and heard the sound of a body shifting again. I turned onto my side, facing toward the sound. I could just make out the shadowy form of a troll in the next cot, rising into a sitting position. Once in this position, he became still, and I had the impression that the troll was looking at me.

As I continued to look back, I discovered I could just make out the whites of the troll's eyes. It helped "humanize" the situation. The eyes definitely *did* seem to be looking straight at me; I could see them blink from time to time. There was no further action, however, and after a while I thought I could *feel* the troll's gaze. Curiously, it didn't seem to be *too* attentive. I got the impression of shyness, along with something else I couldn't get, but which made me feel kindly toward the troll.

The fact that there was nothing assertive or aggressive in that admittedly interested gaze, made me sympathetic. It must be difficult, I thought, to have the object of interest so close and yet unavailable, as I certainly considered myself, despite the recent rupture with Grendel. I wondered whether there was something I could do to make myself *less* attractive to trolls—without disfiguring myself of course—

I caught myself with a shake of astonishment. Was I that accommodating? Why couldn't I just be myself, even here? The wash of irritation passed into a surprising revelation: I didn't *want* to be less attractive to trolls, quite apart from a resistance to accommodating others, I realized I *liked* being attractive to these trolls. It made me feel—what? Well, nice, warm—

I began to feel the heat of my body, a definite tingle of physical pleasure. I studied the troll's shadowy form a little more—and smiled.

The troll sat up straighter. "Art thou lonely, human?" he said, his voice a whisper. "Wouldst thou like a friend?"

It sounded like Gog's partner!

I considered the question. Undoubtedly, it was an advance. It reminded me of the German phrase Olga had taught me: "*Hast du lust?*" which meant "Are you interested?" I found the use of the more direct word, "lust," appealing. It was more honest, somehow, more direct. And now, here, looking at this troll, I found myself admiring the directness of this troll.

"I have a lover," I said.

"Yes," the troll nodded, and his shape slumped slightly. "Grendel."

I was taken aback by this and wondered how much was known about my current situation. When the silence that had followed the troll's remark had lasted a considerable time, it struck me that the troll did not ask why I was not *with* Grendel. Surely, he must suspect some interpersonal trouble. The mere fact that he *hadn't* asked about this, touched me.

"You seem to be having trouble sleeping," I observed.

The troll nodded. "It is difficult—" the troll began, then stopped.

I found myself wanting to laugh. A playful side of me took over.

"Do you mean *difficult*," I offered, "or *hard*?"

I waited for the troll's response, wondering whether he would be able to work through the double entendre. After about a minute, the troll rose slowly to his feet, and stepped forward hesitantly.

I rolled onto my back and put my arms behind my head. "Anything you want to do," I said helpfully, "that involves looking—is not a problem."

"Thou wouldst not mind then?"

I shook my head. This seemed to be enough encouragement, for the troll moved closer in small, hesitant steps, until he was standing next to my cot, near my head. I could feel the intensity of his gaze more clearly now. It was more intense, more openly interested. And, after a little, I could make out the shadowy shape of the troll's enormous phallus hanging over me. It was being stroked, slowly, by a huge thick-fingered hand.

After several minutes of this, the troll began to breathe hard. I looked directly up into the dimly silhouetted face and smiled in a friendly way. *This is okay*, I told myself. *It's the least I can do.*

The troll grunted once, twice. I was feeling aroused by the troll's sexual tension, and my sexual playfulness rose up in me. Trolls could see in the dark, I knew, so I put my head back and opened my mouth, touching the tip of my tongue to my upper lip in a coquettish manner.

The response was immediate. The troll gave a loud grunt, and a moment later I felt hot, thick gobs of sticky semen hit me in the face. My mouth had been open slightly, and some of the semen got into it.

The taste was slightly different than Grendel's, but still very delicious—and intoxicating. I swallowed and licked my lips almost without thinking, then reached up and grabbed the troll's phallus in both hands. I pulled it forward and down until, raising my head slightly, I could press its silky slickness against my tingling skin.

Taking this as an invitation, the troll leaned forward and with his large hand pushed the fat phallus head slowly over my whole face, something that I found intensely erotic. I was hard in my pants and it took all my will not to reach down and free my own cock, and grasp *it*.

No, I thought. I was treading a difficult line here, accommodating the need of this troll without engaging in sex myself, for that would be a betrayal. So, I controlled myself, though it was hard—pun most definitely intended.

At last, the troll stepped back, shy once more. "I thank you."

"You're welcome," I replied, feeling both euphoric and frustrated. I was very turned on and, my own need still unsatisfied by any climax, wanted badly—*more*.

As the troll turned and moved away, I turned my head, cum-covered as it was, to the other side, and saw several other large forms that had gathered in the near-darkness. One of these stepped forward. Not too close, I was amused to see. *By heaven*, I thought. *They're a polite bunch of horny buggers!* I couldn't imagine a group of human men in a comparable situation behaving so well—not in a hundred years!

With this realization I felt my heart open up. I laughed giddily and said in a loud, clear voice. "Come on, all of you! There's plenty of room! Let's see if you can completely *cover* me with your seed."

In two seconds, it seemed, my bed was surrounded on both sides by enormous, shadowy figures, with a veritable *forest* of troll phalluses hanging over me, making a kind of fleshy roof. Fists slid along these, some rapidly, others slowly. I decided, since everything was up to me, I should offer some encouragement, entertainment.

I reached up languidly and just brushed my fingers of either hand over this or that fat phallus head, or along as much of the associated phallus shaft I could reach. Once or twice I even grabbed at a set of heavy, hanging balls. It was all very enjoyable *and* exciting. The urge to pull down my sweatpants became almost painful in its intensity, but I resisted, feeling oddly virtuous. I would not, I told myself, cross that line into actual infidelity.

It wasn't long before one of the trolls came with a low groan. I felt spunk hit me in the neck and on the sleeve of my top. Then other trolls began cumming with grunts and groans. They seemed to aim for my face. Pretty soon I had to close my eyes, and once or twice I had to clear the spunk away from my nostrils so I could breathe—for I was keeping my mouth firmly closed, in that same vague determination to be faithful.

Still, there was so *much* hot, sticky cum hitting my face that I was close to the brink a couple of times. And, as I struggled *not* to climax, I got the distinct impression that this in itself was a turn-on for the remaining trolls. There were more loud grunts and groans, and more loads hitting my face with exquisite explosions that sent shocks through my entire body.

When these had stopped, I sighed and smiled to myself. I had done a good service for these trolls, and without betraying my own virtue, without climaxing myself. This thought made me feel so elated that I couldn't resist opening my mouth and tasting the semen that covered my lips.

Exquisite!

As the thick semen flowed slowly into my mouth I shivered and even whimpered. The sense of surrender I felt now made me feel so *filthy* that I moaned and thrashed my head about in an ecstasy of need. My eyes were glued shut, being covered with semen, so I didn't notice there was still one troll who hadn't made his deposit. The first knowledge of this was the touch of the fleshy mass of his phallus tip pushing against my lips, and a second later the eruption of semen directly into my mouth.

I gasped, but instead of closing my mouth, I opened it in a desperate effort to take in the entire head—which of course I couldn't do. But I did swallow every drop of that troll's load, and at the same time felt the molten heat in my loins rise up and overflow in my own climax.

Perhaps it was the sense of transgression, of being a total cum-dump for all troll comers, a surrender of the most debased kind, being fully dominated, *used* in fact, but I came in the most violent, most intense, even *bizarre* orgasm I had ever experienced. And, as I lay there, my climax ebbing, I became starkly aware that an essential part of this was due to the knowledge that I had betrayed my resolution of being faithful to Grendel.

Immediately after the climax, I became aware of a desperate need for air. My head was swimming. But I managed to snort through my nose hard enough to clear my nostrils for breathing. Then I lay back and gave myself up to the post-coital floating sensation.

I MUST HAVE drifted off, because I didn't hear the trolls moving about after that. When I awoke, everything was still. I was *covered* in semen, some of it starting to dry. I found I could not move my eyelids or even open my lips. And it was only with an effort that I was able to shift even slightly on the cot. It made me chuckle.

That was when I heard a slight cough from nearby.

"Wouldst thou care for a shower?" It was the first troll again.

I had to struggle for a few seconds before I managed to pull my lips apart.

"Yes," I said. "Um, could you help me?"

I heard a cot shift and several seconds later gentle hands lifted me up. I heard a bark from Jake.

"It's okay, Jake. You wait here, boy."

The troll carried me into where there was the sound of spraying water and placed me gently on my feet under a jet of warm water. As I stood there, feeling the semen begin to sluice very slowly down my face, I was shaken with a fit of the giggles. After several minutes, I became acutely aware of my sodden sweatpants and top. I removed these and then lifted my face, directly into the warm spray.

I was in this blissful state when I was startled to feel the troll gently put an enormous bar of soap into my hands.

"Thanks," I said, and began to wash myself thoroughly.

At last, I wiped hair out of my eyes and looked around. I was alone.

Across the shower room from me was a bench with a clean towel. I saw my clothes lying on the floor of the shower, and with deliberation I held these up to the spray, squeezing them until they were thoroughly rinsed.

Then I sighed and looked for the controls to the shower. There was a single tap that I could just reach, standing on tiptoes, and soon I had turned the spray off. Then, holding my dripping clothes, I looked around in a vaguely searching way.

A little distance away, I saw some large sinks. And, among other puzzling items I saw several large, smooth rocks. Going to these, I could feel their heat when several yards away. I looked at them, frowning, and then decided—unsure of how I had come to this conclusion—that they were *drying rocks*. I held my hand, palm out, an inch from them, and felt the heat. Would they scorch the fabric? Somehow, I didn't think so.

So, I laid my sweatpants and top carefully on two of the stones and stood back. The garments soon began to steam.

Good, I thought, and turned to look back to the bench with the towel. Picking up the towel, I went back to the drying rocks, and watched as my clothes continued to steam.

It wasn't long before this stopped and, nimbly picking up the top, I discovered it was more or less dry. It turned out the sweatpants were too, and now that I was dry myself, I dressed.

Going back into the near-darkness of the barracks room. I found my cot, on which the dim form of Jake was standing, wagging his tail. I sat down beside him, saw the shadowy form lying in the next bed and sighed. There was no response. I didn't want to wake the troll just to thank him.

Instead, I lay down in the enormous bed—noticing that someone had changed the sheets in my absence—and cuddled with Jake. The issue remained in the back of my head, of course, whether I had betrayed Grendel or not, but I was too content and tired to worry about that just now.

Grendel Rising

Chapter 21
Captain of the Guards

I awoke, immediately aware of my situation: in the troll barracks. I could see well enough, for the glowing spots on the ceiling were bright again. Best of all, I could feel the lump of warmth against me that was Jake. Petting him and rubbing his belly when he rolled onto his back invitingly, I reflected on the increased lighting. Another day shift, I supposed. I could hear the murmur of distant activity. I sat up and looked around. There were no trolls in my immediate vicinity, but when I got up and went into the dining room, I saw, seated at the benches what must have been fifty or sixty trolls. Evidently the captain's patrol had returned.

I felt shy but as we stood in the doorway, one of the trolls caught sight of me, then another, and soon *all* the trolls were looking at me. The sounds of eating died away; I felt embarrassed, feeling my face heat up. But one of the trolls rose to his feet and gestured, offering me a seat. I smiled and accepted his offer. By this point a number of trolls were on their feet too, but I ignored these and took the proffered seat, lifting Jake up beforehand.

Immediately, I saw another troll coming toward me with two plates of stew. I thanked him, put Jake's plate down for him, and set to. I was hungry!

While Jake and I ate, nothing was said directly to us, though conversation between the trolls resumed. It was subdued, however, and I had the sense that they were all very aware of my presence—and of Jake, too, of course. I had just finished my food, when a uniformed troll stepped up to me and asked me if I would attend the captain, in his office.

I stared at the troll in surprise. He looked very Roman in his manner of dress, much more than any of the other trolls—not just leather, but metal as well, which shone as if just polished. He was even holding a crested helmet cradled in one arm. He looked *very* official and military—in the spit-and-polish sense. I was impressed—to the point where I felt my loins stir in response.

Gulping, I nodded, and stepped quickly down from my seat. A moment later, to my chagrin, I was startled to hear Jake's preemptory bark. I turned to him.

"Oh! Sorry!" I apologized, lowering him to the floor. He could have jumped down from that height, but that wasn't the point. I petted him reassuringly for a little—in part to mortify my unwonted response to the uniformed presence. Then we followed the troll out of the dining room—by which time *all* the trolls were standing, though whether to honor me, Jake, or the messenger I had no idea.

After going through a smaller archway and down a hallway we came to a doorway, where the messenger took up a position beside it, came to attention, and barked out, "Sir!"

Through the doorway I saw a troll-sized office in which a blond-haired troll was sitting behind an enormous desk. He rose politely, gesturing me forward, toward a chair that sat before the desk. I saw a kind of stepstool in front of this, for my convenience, presumably. Beside the chair was a large cushion. I sat down in the chair, and Jake, having examined the cushion, settled down onto it.

The captain was blond-haired, but not at all attractive. Though his expression was formal, I had a niggling sense that he was aware of this. It made me feel embarrassed, as if, without any words or actions, I was rejecting any overture he might make. On the other hand, he *was* efficient and civil, starting off by asking me if we were comfortable and whether there was anything he could get me. After looking at Jake, who had his nose on his front paws, his eyes swiveled up to watch me, I assured the troll we were quite comfortable, thanks, and we had been treated with utmost courtesy.

At the same time, it occurred to me how easily I had climbed into this chair. A wash of mortification came then at the idea that I had grown in my sleep. I thought of all that troll semen I had ingested and groaned inwardly. I closed my eyes momentarily to dismiss these distractions, and then looked at the captain, who was regarding me politely.

"You were—found," he looked at something on his desk, "in sector I-702."

There was something in the way he said this that made it a kind of question.

"Would you like to hear my story?" I asked. "I mean, how I came to be there?"

He smiled and nodded, so I began. The captain turned out to be a good listener and seemed not just interested but genuinely sympathetic. I didn't mention my painful parting with Grendel for the moment, however. The captain nodded, got to his feet and went to the door.

After speaking with the guard outside, he returned to his desk and sat down. "You can sleep here," he said with a slight smile. "No need to tempt my boys more than necessary."

I felt myself redden. I hadn't told him about my encounter in the barracks. For a moment I wanted to ask, to disperse my embarrassment with a joke, "But what about you?" But I held this back. Not only would it possibly be a form of rudeness, but from somewhere the thought came that it is never wise not to offer pertness when one is completely in the power of another.

The captain seemed to like talking with me. He began to ask me about various things happening in the Overworld—odd little things. I couldn't figure out any theme in them at first, but after a while began to see that they had to do with ecology, things involving technology and the earth. For example, the rise of fracking in the extraction of oil.

I had a slight qualm at first, wondering about the idea that I might be giving away important information. I dismissed this without much effort, though. Humans, if I thought about it, had been callous about anything but their own affluence. I decided, if anything, I was helping to balance things out. But of course, that was absurd. I knew nothing in particular about technology, and the captain's questions themselves showed a considerable knowledge base on his part. So much so, that I wondered about how he had come by that knowledge.

Gradually, the captain's speech began to turn to relating stories about the Underworld, about its history and traditions. Some were amusing, but among them were occasional veiled references to conflicts with the human authorities of the Overworld—of which the attack on Grendel and Ugluk at the gate was only the latest skirmish.

We ate a meal in a kind of private dining room adjoining the office. There was a kind of drink that tasted something between beer and wine, with a not unpleasant bitterness to it. I asked what it was made from.

"It is what you would call mushrooms, mostly. Do you like it?"

I said that I did, and the captain topped up my glass. It was only sometime later that I became aware of the effects of inebriation. I began to alternate sips of the wine with those from the water glass that stood beside it on the table.

The captain became a little jolly himself and began to allow his interest in me to show more. Yet he was still charming about it. It became apparent that he was trying to woo me, something I realized didn't bother me at all. After several minutes, however, through a haze of alcohol I decided to fill the troll in on where I stood with Grendel—at least partially.

I spoke about our love, alluded vaguely to a misunderstanding that resulted in Grendel shoving me against the wall, and him leaving. I became quite emotional in the telling, but what surprised me was that the captain did so as well. And he appeared totally captivated by the tale, as if it was something quite alien to his experience or knowledge.

At one point he eyed me sidelong, and said slyly, "You know, I kind of thought that one troll was pretty much just like another for you humans." He lowered his eyes and added quietly and sadly, "It has always been that way."

"Always been that way?" I replied, stung by the other's words. "What are you talking about?"

"Well, those human children we brought below in ages past. They had their pick of lovers, and from what I understand, they had a fun time about it, going from troll to troll. The few who chose to take a lover over the long term, well, they tried out many before—settling down, as it were."

"They didn't all settle down?"

The troll looked at me curiously. "Human," he said. "Do you not find me hideous?"

I looked at the troll. I had to admit, he wasn't attractive, not like Grendel—but Grendel was different; I had come to appreciate that. But hideous? I shook my head.

The troll cocked his big head. "Then why do you resist me?"

I leaned back in my chair, surprised. "Because, like I told you, I love Grendel. Because I don't want to cheat on him."

"But—from what you said just now—after all, he left you. And in the barracks—"

"Oh!" I said, my face heating up. I didn't want to talk about the barracks incident, but the other I could explain. "I guess, only—I think it was because he didn't understand." Then, to my surprise, tears began to leak from my eyes. When the captain still looked puzzled, I explained about the two guards, who had required I fellate them before they would help save Grendel.

Then I related the threesome we had had with the G-man. We began to talk about the nuances of, and ideas behind, Grendel's attitude to our group sex versus my own episode of infidelity. And somehow, as we talked, I found myself becoming more and more appreciative of this troll, to the point of becoming attracted to him, and not just sexually. He was strong, decent, and kind. *Indeed*, I admitted, *this troll would make a wonderful lover.*

But, having thought that, my heart only ached in response. This troll's principal failing was that he was not Grendel. The connection, the feeling of not just having something in common, but of experiencing an innate sympathy of being—in some sense forming one complete *being* when together, was at the base of my feelings for Grendel. And just now, looking at this troll, I got the impression that he sensed that too, which was probably the reason for the forlorn expression in his big eyes.

Still, from what this troll had said, I felt a bit rankled at what seemed to be his view that Grendel's "infidelity" with the G-man was different than my own with the guards. I decided to challenge this idea directly.

"It should be equal," I said firmly.

"Equality," the captain said, "is a dangerous concept. Generally, trolls do not use it. For no one is exactly equal, everyone being different."

"What?" I asked, incredulous. "So, what, you have? A hierarchy? Oligarchy? Monarchy?"

The troll winced slightly at these last words and shook his head when I had finished.

"No, no," he said. "It is not like that. Situations are generally somewhat different, as are people, and each must be evaluated and responded to in an appropriate way."

"So, you don't have *any* equality?"

"Well," said the troll, "we do, I suppose. But a better word for it is 'fairness.' We treat each other fairly. But that is not based on equality."

"I don't understand."

The troll nodded. "An example. Consider, at the market, several trolls come to a table where certain fruits are being sold. Each is treated fairly, in that no one is given preference. The troll served is the troll who arrived at the table first, and so on. But—and this is important—prices are negotiated, dickered, and that involves the interplay of the seller and purchaser. A good friend might be given a special price—usually is, in fact."

"So, someone you don't like, you charge more as well?"

He considered. "No. Not exactly. It would be more a reticence to give a deal, a harder line in terms of price. But in the first place, not liking someone—that is not generally a consideration."

"What? Trolls never dislike other trolls?"

The troll winced again. "That word—'never'—it is not a good word, generally. There are—instances. But there is another principle at work. Dislike might be resentment for a past injustice, but those are few—we are careful to deal with injustices, a meeting is called. If there is, say, a lack of sympathy, based on a difference in opinions, that would be perhaps close to dislike. But, as I said, there is another principle that governs interactions. Respect. Provided only that a troll does nothing shameful—without making amends for it, that troll is given full respect by others. That is the—mmm—baseline, you might say, of our interactions."

I considered this. "It sounds like trolls are better than humans."

"I would say—different."

I looked at him and smiled. "Yeah, you would, I guess. But that's partly because you are a troll. By *our* standards, my impression is that you trolls sound *better* than us."

The captain looked uncomfortable, but finally shrugged.

"Anyway," I said after another silence. "What does that have to do with Grendel's hypocrisy—*one rule for me, another for thee*, that sort of thing?"

"Well, it *is* different for trolls and humans."

I blinked. "You're kidding!"

The troll smiled. "Would you like to take back your *trolls are better* judgment?"

I laughed. "*Touché!*"

"It is like I said, trolls are different in nature. So, the—mmm—evaluation of an action is different for a troll than for a human. It—means different things."

That got me thinking.

I thought I could see something in it. But I knew what most of my friends would have called it: privilege. I might have too, had I not met Grendel. Since meeting him, the experiences, changes in my feelings, had caused my values to undergo a kind of deepening. I wasn't so quick to judge, or label or dismiss. And, realizing this, it struck me that living like this was a lot more fun, and more *alive*, too.

"It is such a pity, this holding a grudge," the troll said.

"What?" I asked, brought back from my wandering mind.

"What you said about it being unfair, you and your troll lover's misbehaviors not being treated equally."

"Well, it is. But what was that about a grudge?"

The troll blinked at me in surprise.

"You object to being treated unequally. So, you must be holding a grudge against your troll friend."

"Oh!" I had to think that one over. When I had, I shook my head. "No. I don't. I don't hold a grudge."

The captain looked even more surprised.

"So, you would be willing to accept him back, even after what happened?"

I frowned at him. "Of course!" Then, with a sob in my throat, I added, slightly surprised at my own realization, "I would forgive Grendel *anything*." I paused, considered the words again, then nodded. "Yes. Anything."

"Oho!" the captain cried, clapping his hands. He looked at me with a piercing gaze for a time in silence. Then he put his hands on his thighs and said, "That is a different story." He got to his feet. "You wait here, human."

He went into his office. I heard a door open, then voices, and finally, after a little, the captain returned. I wanted to ask him what was going on, but somehow didn't feel I had a right to. The captain had another bottle in his hand, which he now proceeded to open.

"Oh," I said, holding up a hand. "No more, please."

But the captain looked at me and shook his head. "That is not for you to say. This is mead. It is for—special moments. You need only take a sip, but you must drink."

The troll filled two glasses and handed me one.

I looked at it and said, "Are you trying to get me drunk so you can take advantage of me?" But I took a sip, hiccupped. "You know—" I said, taking another sip. But I never finished the thought. This was *good!*

"Oh my," I said, taking yet another sip.

In no time, it seemed, my glass was empty—and it had not been a small glass.

The room began to spin slowly, and I found himself giggling. "And I don't know if I really care anymore."

But the captain looked at me solemnly and shook his head. "No," he said. "You *do* care."

He gave me no more mead after that and told me to drink the water instead. He talked about his previous human lovers. "I became spoiled for my own kind," he said, chuckling. "And they were—so beautiful." He sniffed. "Like you."

I began to feel sorry for this big troll and was also finding him distinctly attractive now. *Of course*, I reflected, *that could be the drink.*

Time seemed to slow down. I slipped into a stupor, after which I felt gentle hands lifting me and finally lowering me onto a cot. I murmured thanks. Then felt Jake's nose and tongue in my face. I petted him awkwardly and fell asleep.

I AWOKE WITH a pounding headache. I was alone in the captain's office—completely alone. There was no murmur of voices. With a sudden feeling of panic, I sat up and, despite the pain this caused, called out, "Jake!"

There was a distant bark, then the sound of Jake's nails getting closer. Finally, he appeared in the doorway, squeezing through the door that was slightly ajar. He jumped up on the cot and licked my face.

I hugged him close. "Don't *do* that, boy," I said, almost sobbing. "Don't leave me. I can't lose you, too." Then, relieved from my anxiety, I became aware of my headache again, and groaned aloud.

"You want to take that medicine," a voice said.

I opened my eyes and looked up. The captain was now standing in the doorway. He was pointing at a glass sitting on a small table next to my cot. He made a drinking gesture, then turned and left me.

After hesitating, I leaned over and shakily picked up the glass. I lifted it to my lips and, after another moment's hesitation, downed its contents and smacked my lips at the flavor. *For medicine*, I thought, *this is delicious.* It seemed, I decided, to taste of cherry tart.

Then I lay back again and lay with Jake's front paws on my chest, waiting and hoping that the pain would go away. At some point, the captain came back into the office, went to his desk and began to do things of a vaguely administrative kind, though from the sound of it, it involved stones rather than papers.

I was alone again, when I realized the cordial had done its work. The pain was completely gone, and I was lying in a pleasant state of simple physical contentment. There came a knock at the door.

I sat up and looked around. At last, I said, "Come in."

The door opened, and there, standing in the doorway, stood Grendel.

Chapter 22
Reconciliation

JAKE WAS THE first to react. Seeing his big friend, he gave a yelp of joy and ran forward, wagging his tail furiously and jumping up at Grendel. But Grendel, after reaching down and dutifully stroking Jake with a fingertip, only had eyes for me. He stepped forward into the room, approached my cot, and got down on his knees, bending his head.

I stared at this and when, after a pause, he said in a quiet voice, "I have been a fool. Please forgive me," my mouth fell open.

Licking my lips with unease, I said, "What do you mean?"

He did not raise his head, but said, "I did not know—I did not ask—why you did what you did with those—two guards. You saved me—again, and you sacrificed your virtue for me, and I—I turned away from you." And with that the big troll began to sob quietly, his shoulders heaving.

I got to my feet and went to him. Standing in front of him, I placed my hands gently on his shoulders, experiencing the familiar tingle of excitement at the physical contact. What struck me now was not just the beauty, the magnificence of this kneeling colossus, but the *importance* of those things.

This troll, the massive curves of whose flesh I felt with my hands, might have been made of marble; it—or, rather: *he*, Grendel—archetypal manifestation of masculine essence, felt in the moment so solidly *present* that everything else was rendered filmy, ephemeral in comparison.

His lowered head was just above the level of mine, and I had to stand on tiptoe to kiss him on the forehead. The touch again was electric, and after this, still on tiptoe, I let my head fall forward until we were touching foreheads. The connection I felt then, with its sense of reassurance and joy, was almost overwhelming.

When my arches began to ache, I pulled back my head and came down onto my heels, standing with my arms loosely around his neck. He lifted his head and gazed at me; the gentle light of his eyes, so near, were pools into which I felt myself sink. Refreshed and rejuvenated, I took a happy, deep breath, let it out, and smiled at him in sheer love and adoration.

But Grendel's eyes were troubled as he searched my face; they held love, yes, but concern too.

Still smiling, I shook my head. "Don't worry. It was a misunderstanding."

Slowly I saw the concern leech away from those eyes, and a tentative smile spread over his face.

I stroked his big cheek with a hand. "C'mon," I said. "How about you take me home?"

His smile became one of joyful relief, and now I *felt* the love that poured from him. He stood up and took my hands gently into his. And, we stood there, me looking up at him, him looking down at me, his expression as gentle and tender as I had first known it.

We both stepped forward and embraced in the fashion demanded by our size difference: my arms delightfully wrapped around his muscular thighs, his hands on my shoulders. But those hands pressed me gently but firmly against him, and that was everything.

Momentarily, however, I was reminded I had grown when I discovered I was face to face with his hanging phallus. I used to have to look up at it. Now, it brushed my face, the fat head pressing like a large, warm plum, gently against my lower cheek and chin. In the moment, this registered only as joy—it was simply a part of him; and the tingling heat of special excitement I associated with that most male part of him was now only a pleasurable background buzz.

All this was touch, and I realized I had closed my eyes for this embrace only when I opened them—and saw that there was something between that phallus and me: a smooth, almost filmy fabric. I blinked. The local clothing?

When we stepped back, I took a better look at the garment. It was something between a loin cloth and shorts, in a color close to that of Grendel's own skin. It looked supple, and I found myself wanting to reach out and caress it, drawn perhaps by the curves where it covered Grendel's phallus, which it did only barely, the flesh behind pushing forward in a provocative way. He was also wearing, I noticed, a metal-studded leather harness.

I looked up at him now and saw that his big eyes were full of tears, but he was still smiling. He seemed to want to touch as well, for he placed his hands again, gently, on my shoulders—whereupon I saw his smile flicker and fade, and a troubled look pass over his face.

"You have grown," he said quietly.

The memory of my experience in the barracks came back to me, and with it a wave of guilt. I felt my face heat up, but I said nothing, and in another moment Grendel's serious expression softened, his broad shoulders dropping slightly. And his smiled returned.

Pulling me gently to him, he rested one big hand on the back of my head, running his big fingers with surprising delicately through my hair, while his other hand slid down from between my shoulder-blades to the small of my back—that most intimate non-erogenous zone of my body, so I shivered slightly and experienced a wonderful melting sensation.

"I am sorry, Ken," he murmured. "I am very sorry." And a moment later I felt a big drop of liquid land on the hair on top of my head, and knew he was crying. I found that I wanted to cry too, just for the tragedy of misunderstanding and for the suffering of Grendel's tender heart, which now seemed so much bigger than mine—in the figurative as sense as well as the physical.

We stood there like that for some time, and I savored the tearful relief of just being with him again. The strength of our connection surrounded me. I was no longer lost, no longer afraid—of anything.

"Let us go," he said quietly, and I nodded.

We left the captain's office and headed back down the hallway into the main barracks room. The captain was there, with his personal guard. They were doing something with the contents of one of the lockers. Sounds of troll voices came from both the refectory and lounge.

Grendel and I both thanked the captain, and he courteously escorted us to the main door. It rolled aside, and we stepped through. Standing just outside, I noticed the slight melancholy expression in the captain's face. So, stepping forward and looking up, smiling, I crooked a finger at him. He leaned forward and I stood on tiptoes, kissing him on the cheek.

As I stood there an idea suddenly hit to me.

"I'm sorry," I said. "I don't know your name."

The captain blinked in surprise.

"I'm Ken," I said. "And this is—"

But the captain smiled and looked at Jake. "Yes," he said. "This is Jake. You are well known in our unit. Both of you."

"Oh," I said, nonplused. "But—your name—"

The captain nodded. "I have been remiss," he said and, putting a big hand on his chest, added, "My name is Dokkaebi, or Dok for short."

I smiled up at him. "Thanks," I said, adding in a whisper, "I think you are very beautiful, Dok."

When he stood up again, I saw he was looking confused and surprised, but he was also smiling, and that made me feel very good.

WE HEADED OFF, Grendel and I walking hand-in-hand, Jake happily trotting forward and back again, sniffing. We walked in silence for a long time, and gradually I became aware of a curious difference in my experience of these passages, having Grendel beside me. Jake, too, I thought, was aware, and felt this difference; for one thing, when he and I had been alone, he had kept closer.

At one point, after an unusually prolonged expedition ahead, Jake returned with something in his mouth. His tail was wagging happily as he looked up at us.

I stared at the thing, but Grendel chuckled. I looked at him.

"You see," he said. "It *is* a good place for dogs of the digger breed."

"But what is it?"

Grendel shrugged. "A kenylite. A kind of root or fungus, you would say."

"Oh. Is it—okay for him?"

Grendel chuckled again. "Trust the canine's instincts."

"So—yes."

Grendel looked down at me and smiled, giving my hand a gentle squeeze. "Yes."

I sighed and felt just a little silly. But no matter. We were together.

The passages were as empty as they had been before I had been found by the patrol. Now that I had met more trolls, however, I began to wonder where all the other trolls were. Perhaps we were in some kind of outskirts. A borderland, perhaps: defended but not lived in?

We passed numerous junctions and spiral ramps, and few staircases; and I began to realize just how vastly extensive these passages were. There were halls, too, from the fairly to the very large. I noticed that, while some of these had sufficient tufts of the luminous growth to light up their full extent, others had little, and in some few cases, no illumination whatsoever. I still had my lantern, but I didn't light it; even in the darkest of these caverns the luminance of the exit passages was always visible, and the floors were uniformly smooth and flat. Besides, I was with Grendel, and *he* could see in the dark.

At one point we came to a large circular chamber with an opening in its center. I thought we had stumbled across the well I had encountered earlier, but no. This one had no spiral staircase. Rather, it had a barrier around the central well about eight feet tall. I found that, if I stood on tiptoe, I could just peer over it. It descended into darkness just like the other well. And, looking up, I saw the same sort of domed ceiling, about fifty feet above, with its patches of glowing stuff. I turned to Grendel, who was standing next to me, looking over the barrier too.

"I encountered another chamber like this," I said. "It was a bit different though."

Grendel did not look at me or respond. It was only when I took hold of his hand that he seemed to come to himself. He looked at me, nodded.

"There are—a number of these places," he said, but did not explain.

"What are they, though?"

He looked down the central well again before replying.

"We call them *omphaloi*. They are—they lead down to the—ancient places." I was struck by the obvious pain and reluctance in his voice, and so said nothing.

"We left there ages ago," he added after a silence.

The sadness in this utterance was even more striking, so I didn't ask why. Instead, I asked, "And below that—is there anything below that?"

Grendel turned and looked at me solemnly, finally nodding his head slowly.

"Further below is the Deep Realm. It is a place—" he smiled winsomely, "that is as unlike the Underworld as the Underworld is unlike the Overworld—your world. It is said that there the Earth-power *flows*—like fiery liquid."

"Oh," I said, then, "Earth-power? What's that?"

"It is the source of all life, the planetary heart that beats all of the peoples into existence."

"Peoples?"

"Yours—and mine. The trolls of the world below and the humans of the world above, the two-fold symmetry that is—or was—the engine of both worlds."

"Was? It isn't anymore?"

Grendel shrugged. "There are differing opinions, but it does not work now as it did in the ages past."

I looked at him, his solemn, sad eyes that seemed to look into the far distance. I took hold of his big hand and squeezed it. He looked at me then and gave me a grateful and reassuring smile—and I knew he was back in connection with me, focusing on what we shared and what we produced in our love.

But I was curious, so I asked, "Why, Grendel? Why did it change?"

He frowned and shook his head slightly. But I wanted to know, feeling somehow that this was important—and relevant. He said nothing for a long time.

At last, unexpectedly, he said, "Let us go. This place—" He stopped and shook his head.

He seemed so distracted, possibly disturbed, that I had to lead him to the nearest of the passages that led from different positions on the outer circular path. When we approached this, he caught himself.

"Oh. No. This is not the way." And with that he led me to another of the passages, and from there we resumed our walk and gradually I saw Grendel's mood recover itself.

Seeing this, I thought to resume our conversation.

"Why did it change?" I said, repeating my earlier question.

"Uh—" He blinked. "It was humans. Humans changed."

"Oh." I thought about this for a while. "You mean industrialization?"

Grendel nodded. "And the so-called Enlightenment—the triumph of rationalism in the human mind just as machines triumphed in human society."

"Rationalism—you mean reason?"

He nodded.

"Reason," I repeated to myself, then looked at him, puzzled. "But—is reason that bad?"

"No," he said slowly. "It is not bad in and of itself. As a part of the human world view it is very useful—a tool for figuring things out, making things work well. But I did not say reason alone. I referred to the *triumph* of reason—rationalism. When reason triumphs, it pushes out the deeper part of the human mind and nature, it stultifies the richness of the human heart—what might be termed the soul."

I nodded agreement. "Yes," I said. "It has done that, I suppose. I think that's what I always felt was missing—a sense of living through my heart."

We continued in silence for a while.

"It's comfort too," I added. "Comfort and—functionality. Everything convenient and available." I gave a low chuckle. "And yet, it's what I wanted. It's why I moved to my house in the suburbs. I wanted peace, and comfort. And yet—it was in the end a little sterile. I felt that, and yearned for more—I don't know—more *life*, more heart-driven action." I laughed. "Yet I didn't want to give up my comfort or peace."

Grendel nodded. "Comfort and peace are good things, good things to strive for. But life—life, and joy, come from the striving, not from the success—after the first moments of it, anyway."

AFTER A CONSIDERABLE time of walking together in silence I brought up the issue I thought had not been fully laid to rest. It took me some time to come up with a starting point, however.

"I talked with the captain of the guards," I said, my tone deliberately casual.

"Oh?"

"Yes." But now I had the distinct feeling that I might just be picking at a scab over a wound not fully healed. I found it intimidating and was again unsure of just how to begin. It was that business of fairness versus equality, of each case being different. Then I had a bolt of inspiration.

"Spenser!" I cried.

Grendel stopped and turned to face me. "I beg your pardon?"

"Have you ever heard of the poem—and epic, I think—by Edmund Spenser?"

"Do you mean 'The Fairie Queene'?"

"Yes!" I cried and looked at him in surprise. "Oh! Do you know it?"

Grendel nodded. Then he looked down the passage and pointed.

"There is another way station a little way up there. We can rest—and talk, if you like."

"Yes!" I cried, grabbing his hand and swinging his arm. "I do like!"

This way station was a room reached by an opening like many we had passed. It was perhaps fifty feet square, and had cots on one side, benches and tables on the other. And in one corner there was a well of sorts.

Grendel got two mugs that were hanging on the wall next to the well, and scooped water into them. Setting these on one of the tables, he went to another place on the wall, where some large, brown growths were. He extricated two of these and brought them back for us. They looked like a cross between mushrooms and loaves of bread. I tried a piece and discovered the taste reflected the look rather well. Not unpleasant, though. I took a sip from my mug and discovered the water had a distinct flavor to it.

"Oh, it *is* water," Grendel assured me. "A kind of water. It is natural, and healthy, I assure you."

I took another sip and decided I rather liked the flavor of the water. I had lifted Jake up on the bench beside me and now discovered he too liked both the water and mushroom bread. So, we began a leisurely meal. At some point during this I remembered the food supplies I had brought with me and realized I felt no desire to get out sandwiches from my pack.

"About what I was saying," I began uneasily.

"Spenser." Grendel nodded.

I licked my lips and began, a bit uneasily, "Yes. Uh, that business, with the two guards," I said.

Grendel, I noticed, stiffened just slightly. "Yes?"

"Well," I paused and then forced myself to continue. "I was really upset at your reaction."

Grendel nodded and bowed his head. But I wasn't going to be distracted. I plowed on.

"Well, you apologized. You said you didn't know. So, okay." I paused before continuing.

"Well, that captain of the guards," I said. "He told me that such things were different for trolls. He said that humans and trolls have different natures, and therefore are rightly judged on different standards; the same behavior *means* different things to each."

Again, Grendel nodded. I plunged on.

"Well," I said, with an uneasy laugh. "It sounded like just troll privilege to me. But I thought about it. I thought a lot, and then I remembered what I had taken in college: Spenser, 'The Fairie Queene'."

Grendel looked puzzled now. I regarded him.

"And, you know something about 'The Fairie Queene,' yes?"

Grendel nodded, but still looked puzzled.

"The giant!" I cried. "I don't remember what book, but I do remember the story. It was about a giant, seeking to make all things equal or something."

Grendel's eyes widened and his eyebrows went up.

"Oh. Yes." He closed his eyes for a second, then said, "Book Five, Canto Two. Arthegal and the giant, yes."

I was impressed. "You *remember* that?"

Grendel said in even tones, "I remember—much."

"Do you remember how it goes, that story?"

Grendel closed his eyes, and at length he began to speak, at first with his eyes still closed.

"The giant—it has a pair of enormous scales, and proposes to make all things equal, raising the valley and casting down the hill, to fix the world. And the knight, Arthegal, shows the giant how he's wrong." Then he paused for a second or two, and began to recite:

"He said that he would all the earth uptake,
And all the sea, divided each from either:
So would he of the fire one balance make,
And one of th' air, without or wind, or weather:
Then would he balance heaven and hell together,
And all that did within them all contain."

"Balance heaven and hell!" I commented.

Grendel smiled slightly. "Well, it is an allegory."

"Oh. Okay."

"And he finds he cannot do it. It does not work."

"Oh." I nodded. "Why not? I don't remember exactly."

Grendel nodded and resumed his recitation.

"For why, he said they all unequal were,
And had encroached upon others share
All which he undertook for to repair,
In sort as they were formed anciently;
And all things would reduce unto equality."

I listened to this, distracted somewhat by an awareness of how pleasant it was listening to Grendel recite poetry; his voice seemed perfectly suited to it: calm, flowing, and sonorous. I wanted him to go on, but realized he had stopped, and caught myself.

"Oh, yeah," I said hastily. "Equality. That's right. The captain of the guards said that trolls are interested in fairness rather than equality. But, in the poem, the people were impressed by the giant. They wanted to profit from his equalizing everything." I frowned. "I can see that in people. What about trolls?"

"In trolls, too, I suppose. At times. We are not better than humans, only different. We have our own sins, but I think that we are more sensitive to the rightness of things."

"The rightness of things," I murmured, and shook my head.

After regarding me for a few seconds, Grendel held up his forefinger. "Listen!

"*All in the power of their great Maker lie:*
All creatures must obey the voice of the most high.
They live, they die, like as he doth ordain,
Not ever any asks the reason why.
The hills do not the lowly dales disdain;
The dales do not the lofty hills envy."

I considered this. "Yes. That's what made me think the captain was right—and that you were—well, I shouldn't judge you the same way. It's the idea that different types of things have different—what? Places?"

"Yes." Grendel nodded, smiling.

"So, apples and oranges."

Grendel winced but then nodded.

"What?" I asked, but I thought I knew why Grendel had reacted that way. "Apples and oranges—too—" I considered again. "Too much like a quip?"

Grendel shrugged, then nodded again.

"And," I said, continuing, "to prove that the giant is wrong, the knight tells the giant to try it out, to weight different things. But, go on, please."

Grendel smiled. "Yes," he said. "The giant tries to weight the true against the false." And then he resumed:

"*First in one balance set the true aside.*

"That means he put the *true* in one side of the balance, one of the two scales. Then,

"*He did so first; and then the false he laid*
In th' other scale; but still it down did slide,

And by no mean could in the weight be stayed.
For by no means the false will with the truth be weighed.

"And then, he tried it with right and wrong:

"Now take the right likewise, said Arthegal,
And counterpoise the same with so much wrong.
So first the right he put into one scale;
And then the Giant strove with puissance strong
To fill the other scale with so much wrong.
But all the wrongs that he therein could lay,
Might not it weight; yet did he labor long,
And swat, and chaffed, and tested every way:
Yet all the wrongs could not a little right down lay.

"Which when he saw, he greatly grew in rage,
And almost would his balances have broken:
But Arthegal him fairly began assuage,
And said; Be not upon thy balance wroken—

"*Wroken*, that means, revenged," Grendel commented.

"So, don't take it out on the scales," I suggested, and Grendel nodded.

We were both silent for a time, and I thought about what Grendel had recited.

"Wasn't there something about putting the *right* in the middle of the scales or something?"

"At the balance point, yes."

"Huh."

"It is an idea," Grendel said, "put forward by a Greek Philosopher, from some time ago. Aristotle. Perhaps you have heard of him?"

I flushed and then laughed in embarrassment. I *had* heard of Aristotle, but to be honest, I didn't know much about him or his writings; so *why* had I reacted as if Grendel had insulted me? Perhaps I was envious of how much Grendel knew about *human* writers—my own people, as it were. I grimaced as I felt the truth of this.

"Yes," I said at last.

"Aristotle defined the moral right as lying between two extremes. The middle way, so to speak."

"Oh." Then I saw his expression. "Why are you grinning?"

Grendel shook his head. "It is just at our own arrogance. We call our Underworld the Middle Kingdom sometimes. I suppose some of us see us as possessing the moral right from this."

"Middle? What's middle about it?"

"Oh, because we have the Overworld above us, and the Deep Realm below us."

I considered. "It makes sense, I guess. It's a kind of troll-centered viewpoint."

"Of course."

"Okay. But about that balance. I guess it says you can't balance—compare—things that are different, like right and wrong."

"Yes."

I shrugged and laughed. "Apples and oranges, then."

This time, Grendel smiled. "If you like."

"So, different rules for trolls and humans. Which means you get to whore around, and I don't."

Grendel bit his lip, which like almost everything he did, I found distractingly sensual.

"If you wish to put it like that," he said in a constrained voice.

I laughed and clapped my hands. Then, standing up, I leaned across the table and kissed him.

"Just teasing," I said. But then added, "Maybe you can tell me your way of putting it—the difference, I mean. Of standards." There was, I thought, a little bitchiness in me still, so couldn't help putting in that little dig. Grendel gave me a look, but then nodded.

"Really," he said after a pause, "it is just that I was wrong. As I told you."

I stared and then laughed. "You're kidding! Is that all you've got? No quoting Chaucer or somebody?"

Grendel looked at me seriously and shook his head.

It was then that it sunk in that I was being given the seriously abridged—Go Directly to Jail, Do Not Pass Go—version, and that Grendel was simply not ready to tell me more. So, I nodded and let it go at that.

Chapter 23
Grendel's Mother

WE SLEPT FOR a bit after that and, after another meal, left the way station. I felt somewhat better for our little talk, but I was also convinced I had not gotten to the bottom of where Grendel and I stood about this whole infidelity thing. It didn't feel resolved.

We were about halfway there, Grendel told me, which surprised me; it seemed so far. But still, I was in no hurry, and walking with Grendel, I discovered, was in itself pleasurable.

Finally, after another rest at a way station and more hours of walking, we arrived at the door of Grendel's abode.

Here the big troll paused and showed a curious hesitation. I asked what the problem was. Could it be something to do with Grendel being embarrassed to present a human mate to his family?

"Oh—uh—I—well."

I had been feeling just slightly giddy with relief and love during the final stage of our journey, so I felt comfortable enough to simply ask, with a laugh, "Out with it, troll!" At which we both laughed.

"It is just that—well—I had wanted to—um—carry you—you know—over the threshold."

I frowned. "Well, why can't you then?"

Grendel looked shyly at me. "Perhaps you do not know what that signifies?"

"I don't know. Among humans it's a tradition. The groom carries the bride over the threshold—oh, you mean—?"

Grendel nodded, looking uneasy.

"You want to get married?"

Grendel shook his head. "No. Here it is not like that. Here, when I carry my mate over the threshold—then we *are* married."

I felt a sudden, moiling confusion bubble up and resolve itself into simple, blissful joy. Then, without so much as thinking, I leaped as high as I could, and right into Grendel's arms.

"Let's do it then, big guy," I said, and planted a kiss on the troll's enormous lips.

Grendel now looked confused for his part. "You do not mind then?"

I stared. "How could I mind?"

Grendel put me down gently. "Well, you spent time alone in the Underworld. I deserted you—my very love."

"Look," I reached up and embraced Grendel as far as I could. "Like I said, it was a misunderstanding, that's all. Anyway, I survived and—besides that, well, it was rather sweet in its way. It tells me how you feel about me, how true your nature is."

Grendel, however, was not so easily reassured and I, filled with love for the big guy, nevertheless found myself wanting to laugh again with delight at the wonderful shyness of my lover. I pointed at the door.

"The important question is this," I said, speaking seriously. "Can you tell me the following?" Grendel nodded and waited for me to continue. "Is your own bedroom, with your own bed, on the other side of that door?"

Grendel nodded again, still solemn. "Well, it is down a short hallway—"

"Well, then," I said, holding up a hand and smiling up into the big face, "let's make speed." Then I stood on tiptoe and kissed the bottom curve of the big chin as Grendel leaned down. "I feel the need," I said, and giggled, "the need for your seed."

Grendel grinned and laughed as he picked me up again. He paused to kiss me, then pushed open the door and carried me across the threshold.

"Mother!" he called, "I have brought him home."

"Well, thank darkness for that!" came a gravelly voice from another room. Several seconds later an elderly female troll, her white hair tied into a bun, shuffled in through a doorway. She was slightly bent over and shorter than Grendel, maybe twelve or thirteen feet tall. But she was obviously very hale and energetic. She wore a loincloth similar to what Grendel sported, with nothing above the waist. Her breasts, I saw, were quite modest, mere bulges in the her chest. This sight made me wonder if she were typical for trolls, and whether heterosexual male trolls appreciated the fuller mammary gifts of human women.

Anyway, she came up to us and allowed Grendel to plant a kiss on her cheek. Then she looked at me, where I still lay in Grendel's arms.

"Well?" she said, frowning up at her son. "Are you going to put him down, or what?"

Grendel, smiling sheepishly, placed me gently down.

The old troll looked searchingly into my face, then shook her head briefly. A moment later, perhaps aware of how this might have looked, she caught herself and smiled at both of us.

"Mother, this is Ken," Grendel said, adding, gesturing to his mother, "Ken, this is my mother, Aeglec-wif."

"Good to meet you, Ken. You can call me Aeglec, or Mere if you like."

At this, both Grendel and his mother smiled, as if she had said something funny. Seeing my puzzlement, Grendel explained, "Mere is short for Mere-wif: *water woman*. It was a nickname given her."

"Oh," I said, feeling a bit lost. They seemed to be waiting for a reply, so I added, "Thanks—Aeglec." At this she smiled and nodded.

"Well, anyway," she said in a formal voice. "Welcome home to you my son and to you my son-of-love." To me she added, "This is your home now too."

And when we had both thanked her, she nodded briefly. Then she pointedly looked down at Jake, who was sitting there looking up at her without the least sign of fear.

"This is Jake," I said hastily. "My dog—my friend."

The old troll bent down and proffered a finger for Jake to sniff, which he did. Then, looking up at her and wagging his tail, he gave one satisfied bark.

Aeglec gave a grunt of satisfaction at this and looked at us.

"Okay," she said. "So, I have food on the table. You wash and come to eat." She turned away but said, "That is, if you two can keep your hands off each other long enough to eat."

Grendel and I grinned sheepishly at each other, and he led me down a hallway into a washroom. The washroom was curious. It had an enormous bath, comprised of a hollow in the floor. There was also a washstand, made of carved marble. The ornateness of the decoration surprised and impressed me. Both washstand and tub were fed by simple holes, appropriately positioned, in the wall.

Jake walked down into the tub, and Grendel touched the wall tile next to the wall hole twice in rapid succession. Water poured from the hole for a second and then stopped. Jake nosed the water as it formed a small pool in the center of the tub and started lapping.

We both chuckled at this, then turned our attention to the sink. "You turn it on like this." Grendel touched the wall tile immediately to the right of the hole over the sink. Water came out in a steady stream. There was something like soap, though very gritty, and we washed our hands. Grendel also washed his face and neck, and I followed suit. There were towels, not too rough, and very clean.

In the hallway we hugged, and then kissed. In fact, we kissed so long that there was a gravelly clearing of throat in the other room, and we had to break off.

The room we entered was a large kitchen-and-dining room. Aeglec was ladling something that looked like stew from a large black cauldron that sat on the stove. I began to wonder whether trolls ate nothing but stew.

There were four chairs at the table. Aeglec seated herself and looked at me, gesturing toward Jake and the fourth chair. I lifted him up onto this and seated myself. Grendel served the meal. When he came to the table carrying a serving dish, I saw for a second an odd expression in his eye—a troubled look, some kind of doubt, possibly even suspicion. A second later the big troll's expression cleared. But for the rest of the meal, it struck me that Grendel was more silent than usual.

The food was particularly excellent, quite a different taste from what I'd had at the barracks, though I wondered what the bits in it were. I complimented my hostess, who accepted my praise solemnly. And when she thought I wasn't looking I caught out of the corner of my eye her giving Grendel an approving nod.

The conversation drifted casually into Aeglec asking about my life in the Overworld. She nodded at many of my answers, as though what I told her confirmed what she already suspected. For my part, I was struck by her physiognomy. She seemed not to possess much resemblance with her son. She was certainly more troll-like. In fact, from what I had seen, Grendel seemed to be an unusually human-looking troll. Briefly, I wondered whether Grendel's father might have been human. In the face of my own contentment, however, I decided this was unimportant, and I let the question go for the time being.

When I watched Jake polish off his plate of food, I turned to Grendel and said, "I was wondering—"

Grendel raised his eyebrows and nodded expectantly.

"When—um—I was in the passages, I fell asleep, and I woke up with Jake barking at two troll guards. And—um—they were covering their ears while he was barking. I don't get it. Are troll's ears so sensitive?"

Grendel exchanged a look with his mother, and they both laughed. Then he leaned down and scratched Jake's head with gentle care.

"It is not the noise," Grendel said. "It is what he was no doubt saying."

I stared at him. "What are you talking about?"

Grendel grinned and then laughed again, so long this time that I had to slap the big guy's big arm to get him to stop.

"I am sorry," Grendel said. "But it is amusing. You are best friends with a dog, and yet you do not understand them as we do."

"Okay," I said, deciding to go along with the idea. "But do you want to explain that?"

Grendel with an effort mastered his amusement. For a few seconds he appeared to be marshaling his thoughts. "Jake's barking, you know, it is an historical act of protection of his species. It is a part of the relationship between dogs and man. Trolls have a language that is in principle similar to that of dogs, a language of sounds, tones—noises if you will."

I nodded, remembering the conversation between the two guards in the passage.

"Though that is our ancient tongue. Most also speak your language nowadays, though each speaks in the way that suits them best."

I nodded again. "I noticed that."

Grendel paused, distracted, and for a moment that expression of doubt returned. Then he took a breath and continued, "Trolls are creatures of morality. Perhaps that seems strange, and yet it is true. We live in the ground, and the ground—Mother Earth you know—is the source of all morality, even as she is the source for all life. Earth-power that is, what you experienced when we had passed the barrier."

He shook his head sadly.

Humans, in their development, have often stepped away from that earth-morality. And here is the thing: dogs have not. Dogs are direct reminders to humans of the roots of their own human morality, principles such as loyalty, honesty, openness, lovingness, gentleness, and fierceness in defense of the pack. All of these are part of the canine creed—their truth and their gift to humanity."

As I listened to this, I felt the truth in the words. I looked down at Jake and tears began in my eyes. All of this I had known, I realized, at some level. It was why I loved dogs.

"So," Grendel continued, "when Jake was protecting you against the two guards, he was hurling at them, what you might call an invective of challenge, his defense of his 'pack'—in other words, you." Grendel grinned. "And I am sure his message was painful to hear: defiance, accusation of aggression, strong warning, the outrage of a menaced pack, and so on. No troll could hear that without suffering. Hence the covering of their ears."

I thought this over. "I guess it's lucky that I had Jake with me then."

Grendel shook his head. "It was no luck. Your earth-soul, your kindness and your attractive humanity, all of these are echoed and evoked by Jake."

I was at first confused by these words. "Wait a minute," I said at last. "Are you saying that if I hadn't had Jake, you wouldn't have been attracted to me?"

Grendel looked embarrassed, but then shook his head, and shrugged. "It is not that simple. You keep trying to make things simple in that horrible way: cause and effect. Life—everything, really—is much more complex than that: ebbs and flows, cycles of interaction, influences and counterinfluences. Jake helped you see me—in my odd circumstance. You remember that? And you approached me on his behalf, to convince him I was something he knew I was not. And so on. But, yes, part of his effect on you is to evoke your kindness. Had he not been there to do this, I might not have seen your good earth qualities."

"Oh."

My head was spinning slightly, but I got down from my chair and hugged my little dog. "I knew there were a lot of reasons I loved you, boy," I murmured. "Now I've got another one."

After dinner Grendel led me into our bedroom. It was at this point that I noticed more clearly that Grendel's manner had changed. He was definitely bothered by something.

I didn't say anything but watched as my new troll husband showed me the features of the room.

One of these was a small, recessed shelf, on which half a dozen books sat. *Books!* I looked at them without touching. They definitely seemed to be actual books. Somehow, I hadn't expected that.

Surveying their spines, my eye was caught by what looked like a *very* old book. Bending closer, I saw written on the spine: *Chaucer First Edition*, printed by W. Caxton about 1477.

I turned to Grendel, who was watching. "May I?"

He smiled. "This is your bedroom, too."

So, I carefully pulled out this book and opened the front cover.

"*The Canterbury Tales!*" I cried, surprised. "But Chaucer didn't write it in 1477. Wasn't it more like—I don't know—1200 or 1300?"

"It was published in 1400."

"*Oh!*" I grinned sheepishly. "Only a century off!" I was puzzled at what the First Edition bit meant when it was printed *about* 1477, but then another thought struck me. I turned to Grendel. "Where," I asked, "do these come from?"

Grendel looked puzzled. "From your world, of course."

I nodded. "But—how?"

"There is traffic. We have—friends on the surface. Remember that shop where the special equipment came from."

"Oh. Right!" I looked at the book, its beauty, and ran my fingers gently over the front cover. "Do a lot of—uh, trolls have books?"

Grendel shook his head. "These are from the central archives. They are duplicates, borrowed. What we have only one copy of are not allowed out of the archives itself."

"Archives."

"Yes. The archives for artifacts of human culture. Books are a part of those artifacts. Histories, such as those by Winston S. Churchill, stories—what you call *fiction*, and some poetry."

I stared. "You say *this*, this volume, is a *duplicate?*"

Grendel nodded.

"So, you—here in the Underworld—have more than one copy?" I felt I was being stupid, but still, I couldn't quite believe it.

"Two copies were bought at the time."

At the time, I thought, and shivered at a sudden sense of the telescoping of time, something like awe.

I looked at the text. "Old English lettering," I muttered, and then grinned. "Well, I guess it would be!" Some of the initial capital letters, those beginning a new section, were larger and printed in red. The effect was stark, but beautiful, too—though thinking about it I felt a bit disappointed these capitals were not fully illuminated. No. That was only in the hand-written medieval manuscripts. I looked at the text more closely.

"*Some tyme ther was duellynge*...Wow! I guess that's the original—uh language—he wrote in."

"It is Middle English."

I nodded and looked up at Grendel. "And you can read this?"

Grendel nodded in embarrassment. "It is a part of my—interests. What I do."

I wasn't quite sure what he meant. Was that a position? A job? But I closed the book gently and replaced it on the shelf.

Next, I saw a book that had Chinese characters on its spine. Taking it out, I stared at the cover for a few seconds, then opened it up. It was written in Chinese. I looked at Grendel.

"Are you telling me you can read this?"

Grendel smiled, shrugged, and then shook his head. "Only a little." He pointed to the shelf, "I have the collected works of Li Po, in English, and also a primer on Mandarin. I have been—learning it."

"Mandarin?"

"A little."

"Okay," I said and made a *show me* gesture.

He grinned and said, "*Ni hao. Ni hao ma*. That means, *Hello*, and: *How are you?*"

I laughed. "Interesting!" I looked at the book again. "Do you have a favorite in here?"

He considered. "There is: 'Letter of a River-Merchant's Wife'." He said, smiling gently. "It is, perhaps the most beautiful love poem I have ever read."

I was surprised to hear a catch in the big guy's voice as he said this. He continued.

"In English I have read the translation by Ezra Pound. It is very beautiful, but I have discovered it is not a very *good* translation—from what I have learned of the original. But translating poetry is very difficult."

I nodded, and put this book away. After searching the remaining few spines, I laughed, pointing at a very thick volume.

"Spenser's 'Faerie Queen'!" I grinned at him. "Little did I know," I said in mock serious tones, "what depths I was entering when I quoted it to you from that august work!"

"You quoted it well," Grendel said. "I heard no mistakes."

"Oh! Well, thanks!"

Grendel was looking at me now with indulgent affection. I stepped up to him where he sat on the edge of the bed, stood between his spread knees and leaned forward, my head against his chest. I felt his hand gently touch the back of my head, and sighed.

We remained like this, silent and content for a long while, until at last Grendel removed his hand and sat back "We need more space, he said."

I stepped back and he looked at me. I shrugged. "If you say so." I thought I saw the return of his odd mood. And, when he saw me looking at him searchingly, I thought he seemed to be avoiding my gaze somewhat.

"Okay," I said.

And so, without ceremony Grendel set to work. He went to the far side of the room and, reaching for the wall, slowly pushed his fingers *into* the solid rock. I watched as he then appeared to pull rock *out* of the wall, and then in some fashion that bewildered my eyes, push the same rock to the *side*, leaving a large hole in the wall. It was like watching someone knead dough in slow motion, with the observer on a certain amount of psychedelics—for I thought I saw things, what I might call the fabric of space itself: dimension or distance, whatever, do things that I can't even describe.

We have a way with rock and earth, I remembered Grendel's words, and felt slightly dizzy; so much so I had to sit down on the bed and turn my gaze away from his working.

And it went on, and on! I noticed that, while Grendel was sweating, he was not sweating as much as when he had been attacking the barrier. It occurred to me that this might be a different *kind* of work; not just muscle work but involving the troll facility for such activity. I ended up lying down, my head on a pillow, with Jake lying next to me.

It must have been more than an hour of work. But finally, Grendel stepped back, and I saw that he had almost doubled the size of the room.

"Wow!" I said, getting up. I walked to him, looking at what he had done, and put my arm out, resting my hand on the curve of his hip bone. I did this without thinking, but a moment later, I turned to look at what I had done and was amazed. My eyes, I realized, were now slightly higher than the head of Grendel's hanging phallus!

"Wow!" I said again. I looked up at him, half-ashamed. It was those guards in the barracks of course. I was relieved he did not look annoyed—he probably didn't even know what my remark was about, for he looked quite weary.

"C'mon," I said. "Let's sit down on the bed."

I led him to the bed, where he sat down gratefully.

"Why don't you lie down?" I asked him.

He smiled and nodded but pulled me down onto him—something I minded not at all.

We lay like that, him lying on his back, me half draped over him, head on his massive shoulder, his arm behind me, fingers just touching my ass.

"I'm impressed," I said, nodding toward the extension. Then, a thought occurred to me.

"If you're able to do this," I said, "in solid rock, why were you caught in the soil of the front lawn? I don't get it."

"What?" Grendel stared at me distractedly for a second, and I saw again just how tired he was. "Oh, that. I thought I told you. I was drained by the geostatic barrier."

"Oh!" I said, thinking about that horrible, burning surface. "Drained."

Grendel nodded. "Of Earth-power, of my very life-force."

I remembered what Grendel had said that first evening we were together, about how if I had not rescued him, he would have been reabsorbed into the earth. I shuddered. It seemed so cruel.

Part of me wanted to ask how long that process took, but that was just a kind of ghoulish curiosity. Then, I remembered him saying to the G-man, that he had come up—*to find love.*

And he had found it, with *me*!

My heart swelled with the joy and the terror of the risk Grendel had taken, and how we together had struggled to escape the nets of narrow-minded officialdom. It made me feel very small, and very lucky!

I was about to say something else, when I heard Grendel's gentle snore. And that too swelled my heart. I was happy, just plain happy—now!

How wonderful!

And with that thought, I too fell asleep.

Chapter 24
Goblin Market

I AWOKE ALONE on Grendel's big bed. The room was almost completely dark, with only one glow spot next to the bed, near the floor. It was so much like a night-light that at first, I was convinced it *was* night. But this idea didn't sit well in my sleep-addled mind, and at last I recalled my situation. I experienced a moment of horrible claustrophobia at the realization of where I was: far below ground. This passed, however, when I thought of Grendel, and the fact that I was lying in *his* bed.

I reached out for him, but of course he wasn't there. I had known that, by the flatness of the mattress and the absence of his sleep noises and his wonderful body heat. But his earthy scent was there, and I stretched languorously, running my hand along the sheets, savoring the sense of his having been there, beside me. Then I looked again at the glow spot and realized sunrises and sunsets were simply not germane anymore. This had the effect of unsettling me and, seeking reassurance, I called quietly into the darkened room, "Jake!"

After several seconds, there came the click-click-click of toenails approaching—in fact coming down the hall and into the room. Then Jake jumped up onto the bed and I hugged him while he licked my face. I sat up, still hugging him, and looked over the side of the bed. Yes—there was a stool, placed there by Grendel for Jake's use. I smiled at this latest evidence of the tender thoughtfulness of my lover.

Or *husband*, I reminded myself, and felt a wash of heady pleasure pass through me. I lay back down and Jake settled in beside me, his warmth against me, and I felt quite content.

At last, however, I had to get up to go to the bathroom. I managed to use the oversized toilet and, after some exploration, discovered how the water for the bath was controlled. It was more of a shower, really, water coming out of the walls *and* ceiling, from virtually all directions, in misty sprays. It was refreshing, and afterwards when I dried myself off, I was feeling a different person.

Having dressed, I went to the kitchen, where I saw Grendel's mother—

no! *Aeglec*, I corrected myself, repeating the odd name to lodge it inside my head—sitting at kitchen table, drinking something out of a cup. It might have been tea, I thought, but thought it probably wasn't.

"Hello," I said feeling awkward.

Aeglec nodded. I stood there, hesitating, and then asked, "Uh, forgive me, ma'am, but may I ask, how should I address you?"

She looked at me, her expression blank.

"I mean—your name, or, if I'm Grendel's—husband—" the word sounded odd in my mouth "—and you're his mother—" I let the question hang there.

"Oh," she said, and thought for a minute. "Well," she said at last. "I suppose either my name or Mother. Whichever you like."

Oh, I thought, wishing she had been more direct. While I stood there, feeling awkward, she got to her feet. "Grendel is out. Have a seat."

She went over to the stove and returned with a bowl of what might have been oatmeal from its look but tasted different. "And Jake has eaten," she told me, smiling down at Jake.

Well, I thought looking between her and Jake, *you two seem to have made friends quickly enough.*

Aeglec reseated herself and I ate my meal methodically. I was about to offer the obligatory statement of praise of the dish, but when I opened my mouth to do so, I caught Aeglec's eye. Her face was expressionless, but she shook her head minutely and I nodded, feeling my face heat up with embarrassment. I was taken also with the odd conviction I had that she had *known* what I was going to say. I resumed eating

"Could I ask what this is?" I asked a little later.

Aeglec grunted amusedly. "You can, but I would not recommend it. It is from a plant you will never have heard of."

"Fair enough," I said, and we left it at that.

When I had finished the dish, Aeglec took away the bowl and brought a kettle from the stove. She poured steaming water into a kind of teapot sitting in the middle of the table. After returning the kettle to the stove, she poured liquid from the teapot into both of our cups and looked at me, eyebrows raised. I took a sip and considered the taste. It was nutty and, though odd, not unpleasant. I nodded and smiled at her, whereupon she topped me up and sat down.

I suppose I felt this as a kind of invitation, because for the first time I felt free to speak about Grendel's journey aboveground and our subsequent adventures together. Something told me that even among trolls a mother would not reject an opportunity to hear and talk about her son and what he got up to. Besides, she had said I was family now.

❖

THE CONVERSATION WAS pleasant enough. I did most of the talking. Grendel's mother smiled and nodded from time to time at the good bits, and she looked a grim and shook her head when I recounted the actions of the G-men. She didn't say anything about them, however. The only thing she commented on were the actions of her son and me. It was clear that she had not only great affection for him, but respect as well, though there was an element of tolerant disapproval of some of his actions. All in all, I decided she understood and sympathized with what both her son and I had done.

I was just finishing the tale when Aeglec stood up decidedly and told me she was going out shopping. On impulse, I asked if I might accompany her. After a hesitating, she agreed, but after looking steadily at Jake, told me that he could not come.

I was taken aback by this and had to remind myself both that this was a new situation whose rules I needed to learn and respect, and that trolls had shown nothing but an unwavering respect and appreciation of dogs. Still, it struck me as odd that trolls would be finicky about the presence of dogs, whom they revered, in a shop. But who knew?

I was relieved when Jake appeared to take the news with a minimum of disappointment. When we were leaving, he trotted off toward the bedroom, presumably to the bed.

"ALL OF THIS," I told Aeglec as we descended the third staircase and headed along another passage, "is rather confusing."

She chuckled. "You will get used to it in time. But I suppose, yes, it *is* confusing right now."

I was impressed with some of the passages, or "roads" as Aeglec called them. While most were of the simple, squared corridor type I had first seen after passing through the gate—impressive enough in their own way, due to size and exact simplicity—there were regions that had wall and ceiling ornamentation. This varied from region to region, some fairly simple, others quite ornate. The latter reminded me of the well I had seen. I asked my companion about these.

"They are commemorations," she told me laconically. When I asked what for, she dismissed this, saying, "Oh, various things—historical events, and personal histories too. Everything really."

I almost asked about the well, but we had arrived at a widening of the passage, along which several trolls were passing. They were the first trolls I had seen, I realized, which I thought puzzling. After another hundred yards we entered the first of several halls that comprised the market.

There were dozens, perhaps scores, of trolls here, and the space was about as large as a school gymnasium scaled up to troll dimensions—essentially a modest hanger by human standards. There were tables and stalls set in no particular order, yet something about the setup struck me as "right" rather than chaotic. The trolls were both male and female, some shoppers, other sellers.

"Wow!" I murmured and turned to look at Aeglec.

She smiled at me. "Welcome to Goblin Market!" she said and gave a brief chuckle.

"*Goblin*?" I said, staring at her.

She was still smiling, sardonically I thought. But she only shrugged.

"It is a name for trolls," she explained, "though not a nice one."

I nodded, but something was tingling at the back of my mind, though I couldn't quite ahold of it.

Accompanying her, I quickly discovered Aeglec was an efficient shopper, even though there was no sense of rush about her actions. She moved from stall to stall, looking, pausing now and then to examine goods, always with a sense of purpose. There were five or six stalls at which she purchased foodstuffs, some of which were wrapped in what looked like brown paper. She put each item in a string mesh bag that stretched to accommodate her purchase. I wondered what the bag was made of, and then dismissed the question: the same question could be applied to virtually everything here.

But I was struck by two things. The first was the fact that every purchase involved a certain amount of haggling over price. The second was my own palpable sense of being *noticed*—and more. Studied, perhaps. I told myself this was to be expected; I was an oddity after all. The troll women were curious but neutral in their interest. The males, however, seemed one and all to regard me with definite *interested* interest.

It was very distracting.

At one point I caught Aeglec looking at me out of the corner of her eye. She seemed slightly amused, but slightly something else, too—though what that was I had no idea.

I was doing some of my own looking, too. It wasn't easy, though. Every time I directed my gaze at a troll, I caught them just looking away. Still, I gathered a sense of the diversity of trolls, confirming my previous observation that most of trolls were less good-looking than my Grendel. I found that interesting. And they were of different sizes, varying from about twelve to seventeen feet tall. The troll women were no smaller than the males, but they tended to dress more fully, though breasts were generally exposed.

I discovered too that, while some of the male trolls here would be considered ugly, they all exuded a masculine energy that was distinctly diverting. I decided it was a combination of build and sheer size—both of which impressed and even daunted.

Once I made eye contact with a particularly impressive specimen, only to see him smile knowingly and, looking away. No, not just that. I gasped, realizing that he was *preening*! He raised his arm and ran the fingers of one hand through his hair, which was bluish black, but in such a deliberate way that I felt the troll's masculine pride in himself, the display aspect. It was *very* compelling *and* erotic, and I found that it took all my willpower to tear my gaze away.

After that, I avoided looking at anyone for a while, keeping my eyes on the tables and wares for sale. I thought I caught Aeglec glancing at me once or twice—which made my face heat up with mortification. Did she know? Could she tell how attracted I was to the male trolls? Certainly, she knew about *their* interest, which was pretty obvious.

At last, I settled into a kind of coping state. I unfocused my eyes and did not look directly at anyone or indeed anything. This caused me to stumble against one or two stalls, but there were no serious accidents. And all the while my face burned continuously with low-grade mortification.

To distract myself, I thought about what I knew of the Anglo-Saxon poem "Beowulf," in which the monster Grendel and his mother were featured. They had lived underneath a bog. It struck me how different the reality was. There was nothing dank or disgusting about the troll world. It was, if one set aside the strangeness of these places, *pleasant*, even homey. It was surprising how, being this far underground and a society of nonhumans, the feel was very much what I imagined a country fair in medieval England might have been like.

Goblin Market. I repeated Aeglec's words to myself. Now, where had I heard that before?

One effect of having given up on looking, I found myself paying more attention to the sounds around me. There was the combination of voices, some speaking in English, some not. But, among the other sounds and words, I noticed at various times sellers would cry something that sounded like: *Koombaah!*

Wondering what the word meant, the next time Aeglec happened to look at me, I pointed to my ear, and repeated the word: *"Koombaah?"*

She smiled at this and raised an eyebrow, saying as clearly as if she had spoken: *You figure it out!*

I took the challenge, and as I followed Aeglec from stall to stall I thought about that word or sound and Aeglec's term for this place and event. At last, with an *oh!* of surprise, words from a poem came to me:

"*'Come buy,' call the goblins*
Hobbling down the glen."

I blinked, forcing myself to remember. It was from a poem, by Christina Rossetti, titled "Goblin Market!" And, after some more effort, I managed to recall an entire stanza:

"*We must not look at goblin men,*
We must not buy their fruits:
Who knows upon what soil they fed
Their hungry thirsty roots?"

I remembered these words because I had always found them unsettling. But now, the feelings they evoked were more of the exciting variety, delight at a sense of the exotic and, beyond this, an organic sense of *earthiness—and* distinct arousal. I looked at Aeglec, who was at that moment looking at me.

"Come buy?" I suggested, grinning.

Her only reaction was an amused glint that came into her eye. She turned away, continuing her shopping, but I felt sure that she had been impressed.

Not bad, I thought, *making points with my mother-in-law.*

But the connection I had made between Rossetti's odd poem and my current situation was unsettling. Strange. Not that everything *wasn't* truly strange lately. But this was—*what?* I struggled, trying to understand the deep, unsettled feeling I had now, to get a basic sense of it—and failed.

At the same time, the attention I was getting from the male trolls pressed upon me like a wave. Combined with my own internal feelings, it was becoming oppressive—like an oddly erotic and disturbing headache—which in itself made no sense. I stood there blinking, feeling like an owl in daylight, and saw that Aeglec was looking at me again, her expression questioning.

"I'm sorry," I said in something of a choked voice. "I—think I need to leave, go for a walk—"

To my surprise, she nodded as if she understood. But what she said was, "Do you know your way? Will you not get lost?"

I shook my head. "I have a good sense of direction."

"Ah." Her eyebrows raised at this, but she said nothing further, so I turned and made my hasty way out of that hall.

AFTER MAKING THIS claim, I suppose it was inevitable that I should soon find myself quite lost. I *do* have a good sense of direction, and never got lost on the surface. But trying to navigate the complex three-dimensional configuration of troll passages was something like going from playing checkers to chess.

I didn't panic, in part due to the sense of exploration and wonder that came over me, but also because of something else. Being on my own again, it struck me that I was more aware of the impressions I was getting from my surroundings. That had been true when I had first been in the Underworld alone, but then I had been oppressed by a sense of abandonment. Now, I found I could better appreciate the sensations I was getting.

I continued on, choosing direction and passage by feel, or randomly, I didn't know which. But sometime later I entered a region where the passages were highly ornamented. Something in the beauty of this caught at my heart. I felt like I was walking through a magnificent palace, or a first-class art gallery: haunting and breathtaking.

In fact, I began to feel, looking at each ornate element of decoration, that I could *almost* understand what it meant—not in words, but in the sense of how it fit into the whole.

Studying this beauty, I continued, lost in the experience. At last, however, I found myself getting quite tired. I realized I had no idea how long I had been walking—let alone any conception of my location, and was about to stop to rest, when the passage I was in suddenly ended at another of those circular wells.

As on the first occasion, when I was alone, I had the sense of something rising up from below, and was aware of that odd, spicy scent. But now, as I lingered—indeed, sat down with my back against the wall surrounding the well out of simple fatigue—I was more aware of subtle nuances in this whatever-it-was that was coming up this well.

There was something intoxicating about it. Was it making me drowsy? *Curious!*

This was the last thing I remember thinking before I lost consciousness.

I WAS AWAKENED by the sound of Jake's bark. It was coming from some distance away. I blinked, opened my eyes and immediately felt a concern about Jake's safety. I waited for a second bark, wondering whether I had imagined, or dreamed, that first bark. Hearing nothing, I got to my feet and called out, "Jake!"

Immediately there came another bark, closer now. My heart leaped in glad anticipation as further barks announced Jake's approach. At last, he rocketed out of one of the passages, ran to me and leaped into my arms.

"Oh, Jake!" I murmured, rubbing my head over him while he licked me.

"Ken?" The deep voice came from a distance, but I had no trouble recognizing it, and felt an enormous wave of relief and joy.

"*Here!*" I called.

Now there was the sound of large feet running, and seconds later Grendel emerged from a passage. The concerned expression on his face changed to joy when he saw me, but he stopped for a while, his big chest heaving, before approaching. I put down Jake, and Grendel lifted me into a tender, yet bone-cracking hug.

The sense of contact with his physical massiveness, his warmth and his very being, was infinitely reassuring and something I found I needed.

When he had put me down, I nodded toward the well.

"I found another one," I said, smiling. "What did you call them?"

"Omphaloi," he replied. "Singular: Omphalos." He looked at it only momentarily, then, reaching out took my hand.

"Come on," he said. "Let us go home."

Chapter 25
Developments

I LAUGHED. "BUT a kiss first."

It was a wonderful kiss, in which I lingered, savoring all of the wonderful sense of completeness that Grendel gave me. These strange surroundings were rendered secondary now, in his presence. And so, without a backward glance, we headed off, hand-in-hand, while Jake happily trotted at our heels or explored ahead.

After a couple of minutes, Grendel commented in a deliberately casual tone, "You went to the market with Mother."

"Yeah."

"I, uh—she said, it got a bit—intense?"

I felt my face heating up at this, and I stiffened defensively, though I didn't quite understand why.

"Yeah."

There followed a long silence, during which I wondered where Grendel was going with this. It was only after many minutes that it struck me: Grendel wasn't going to come out with whatever was quite evidently bothering him. So, after struggling with my own reluctance, I initiated things myself.

"The male trolls," I said, "were kind of intense. Staring at me."

Grendel nodded but said nothing.

After another long silence I added in what I hoped was a steady voice, "I guess they were—interested. At least that was my impression."

Grendel nodded again. "Oh, yes," he said. "No doubt they were." His spoke quietly, and there was a slight bitter edge to his voice.

Just then we came to one of those way stations and, as it was unoccupied, I suggested we stop, take a break. Grendel nodded but didn't look at me. We both drank from the cistern and then seated ourselves in the chairs that were in the outer room of the station. I lifted Jake onto my lap, and sat there, petting him, feeling the unease that seemed to exist between me and Grendel.

After some time, I leaned toward him and thumped his knee with my fist.

"Hey!" I said sternly, and when he at last turned to look at me, added, "Something's bothering you. And I want to know what it is."

Grendel looked down and nodded. When he looked at me again, I saw pain in his eyes.

"You cheated," he said in an unhappy, quiet voice.

I was slightly taken aback by this. Hadn't we already sorted that out?

"Well, yeah," I said. "You brought me underground and then deserted *me*! Remember?"

"A misunderstanding." He was avoiding looking at me again.

I stared at the big troll, frowning. "Well, surprise, surprise!" I murmured, then added fiercely, "And now—guess what? We have *another* one!"

Grendel looked at me then. "What?"

"I'm guessing that you think I cheated on you again, after those two guards."

Grendel nodded unhappily. "Your size."

I felt a pang in my gut at that. I *was* larger; somehow, I had become sensitive to that. All those trolls, all that semen, in the barracks. I looked at Grendel, seeing his unhappiness. Part of me wanted to comfort him, but another part was just plain angry.

"How could I cheat on you when *you* left *me*? Is that what you're wondering?"

He turned and glared at me for several seconds, then looked away and let his head fell forward. "It is not your fault," he said almost inaudibly. "I know that."

"What isn't?"

Grendel shook his head and said, without raising his head, "Trolls are polyamorous."

"Oh." *That word!* I thought. I'd always hated the term, for it seemed to me merely a euphemism for unfaithfulness, a pseudoscientific word to remove personal responsibility. But what, I wondered, did it mean in this context? Then an idea occurred to me. I felt my face heat up.

"Does that mean," I said slowly, "that you want an open relationship?"

Grendel, I noticed, became very, very still—so much so I became concerned and, putting Jake down, slid forward on my seat and touched Grendel gently on the arm. He looked at me and then looked away.

"Is that what you want?" I asked again.

Grendel's voice came at last, very low and through lips that barely moved. "Is that what *you* want?"

I felt confused then. I wanted to get past this but didn't know what answer I was supposed to give here.

"Truth," Grendel said, his voice a little louder, with an imperative edge.

I quailed momentarily at the demand, but then nodded. *Of course!* I thought. I felt a rush of relief at this point. There had to be nothing but truth between us; it was the only way. So, I sighed and then suddenly laughed. Grendel looked at me in surprise. I felt embarrassed.

"Sorry," I said. "It's just—well—I just—" I paused and had to force the last words out, which gave my voice a gravelly quality. "I love you so much."

Grendel looked at me with a mixture of affection and puzzlement. I felt I had to clarify for him exactly where I was coming from.

"Okay," I said, after taking a deep breath. "It's like this: I love you so much that if you want an open relationship, well, I'll try to be okay with that. But, speaking for myself, what I would prefer, well—I don't really want to share you with anyone. And I don't want anyone else—not if I have you." I paused, and then added quietly, "I don't *need* anyone else either."

Grendel's big face twisted in an odd way, and he turned his face away. I wondered what this meant, but then noticed the big troll's shoulders shake. He was crying!

Immediately, all concerned, I climbed onto Grendel's lap and put my arms around his neck, leaning my own head on his cannonball shoulder.

"Sweetie, what's wrong?" I asked gently. "I—I'm sorry if I said anything wrong. I'll do anything you want—*anything*."

But the shaking just got worse, so I could only hang on for the duration, holding my lover close to me as well as I could. With one hand I stroked Grendel's hair, with the other I stroked his upper arm and part of his chest—and was distracted briefly, both annoyed and amused with myself that, even in such a crisis moment I experienced distinct arousal by physical contact with Grendel's wonderfully massive body. I even had the sudden urge to shift my physical ministrations further down his form but pushed the temptation away—I didn't want to be the kind of person who saw sex as a way to end interpersonal crises. Okay, maybe *some*, but not generally.

After many minutes, the troll's sobbing subsided, and some minutes after that Grendel turned his head to look at me. Putting his arms around me, he pulled me close with even more than his usual tenderness, and I gave myself up to surrendering, melting in fact, into the embrace of my husband's enormous arms, savoring the sense of complete protection, complete love they gave. It was only after several more minutes that I pulled back slightly and looked up into those enormous eyes that now regarded me so intently.

"I love you, Ken," Grendel said.

I smiled—I almost wanted to laugh, it was so strange—wonderful, yes, but strange too. It was, I thought, the first time Grendel had said this. Sighing, I ran my hand down Grendel's chest. "Can we get to the bottom of this, big guy?"

"You are tired?"

I smiled up into his face. "No. It's just that I'm feeling a little—warm." I smiled and looked coy, so after a little, Grendel understood at last, and smiled back. Then he sniffed, and finally nodded.

"Okay," he said. "It is just this: Like I said, I know that trolls are polyamorous." He hesitated. "But the thing is, I am not."

"Oh." I felt a great sense of relief, and grinned. "Let me get this straight: *you* prefer monogamy too?"

Grendel smiled slightly and nodded.

It was with something of a wash of great relief that I threw myself against the big guy's massive torso, positively snuggling against him, feeling blissfully happy. I think my brain stopped entirely; I was just living the blissful moment. We remained like that for some time.

When at last we separated, Grendel I saw was smiling his most beatific smile. "Whatever happened," he said firmly, "I mean, when I had left you. I—well, I do not care. That is behind us."

I sat back, leaning against his supporting arm, and looked into his face. "Good," I said, and we kissed. It was a romantic kiss that slowly became passionate. But even as I felt myself hardening, I pulled back.

"And now," I said, "now that you're okay with it, I'll tell you what *did* happen."

And so, I told him about the jerk-off session in the troll barracks.

Grendel stared. Then he laughed. "Oh, was *that* all?"

"That was all." I shrugged. "I felt sorry for the guys. They looked so—desperate."

Grendel's expression clouded again. He shook his head. "I know it should not bother me. I know they cannot help it, but still—it does bother me. I do not *like* it!"

We caught each other's gaze, and both burst out laughing.

When we had stopped, Grendel said, still somewhat seriously, "Well, I do not."

I blinked at him, then asked in an affectation of innocence, "Why is that?"

Grendel shook his big head, his eyes smoldering. "Because you are *mine!*"

"I don't know," I said, shaking my head doubtfully. "I've been here several nights already, and I *think* I'm beginning to feel my virginity starting to grow back."

Grendel snorted. He got to his feet, lifting me in his arms.

"Come on," he said. "Let us go home."

Jake, who had been watching us with attentive concern, now leaped up, barking.

WE ARRIVED AT Grendel's home in a shorter time than I had expected, although I did recognize our location just before arriving. I was learning!

Grendel Rising

"So, you found him!" Aeglec said when we entered.

"Yes. Um, we are going to lie down."

"Suit yourself."

Inside the bedroom, Grendel closed the door and carried me to the bed, laying me down gently.

"Now," he said. "We will *see* who you belong to."

I wanted to play along a little longer, but something in his words made that impossible.

With tears in my eyes, I looked directly up into his big eyes. "Ken belongs to Grendel," I said in a voice choked with emotion. "And that's forever, for as long as we both shall live."

He was silent and still then, and as we gazed at each other, the entire room seemed positively *filled* with love.

But Grendel's intense gaze was bringing heat into me, too. I smiled mischievously and shook my head with affectation of confusion. "So, then," I asked casually, "what's the problem with those other trolls being interested? I mean, exactly."

Grendel seemed taken aback by that. He had to think about it.

"I think," he said at last, "it is because I know what they would like to do with you."

I had to suppress a giggle of triumph as I asked, with an even greater affection of innocence, "And what's that?"

Grendel laughed and laid down beside me on the bed. He plucked at the fabric of my sweatshirt.

"It still fits," I said. "Despite my growth."

"Yes. It is—made for that."

I nodded and then looked at him coyly. He began with his large but clever fingers to undress me, while I ran a finger over his massive chest.

"You know," I said. "There is one positive thing about my getting larger."

Grendel gave a suddenly guarded look. "What is that?"

"Well, I was just thinking—you know—that maybe, well, maybe now I'm—you know, large enough."

"Large enough—" Grendel repeated the words in a confused voice. Then his eyes widened. "Oh!" A grin spread on his face, but after a few seconds this was replaced with doubt. "I am not sure you are. I would not want to hurt you." He was over me now, on his hands and knees.

I smiled and stroked the line of my husband's big face. "Don't worry. If it's—too—big, well, I'll let you know."

Grendel looked at me in silence for perhaps half a minute, while I looked up at him, feeling more and more the sense of his massive, reassuring presence change into something else: domination. Just from our respective positions, and his nature, and size, the sense of welcome, intoxicating dominance radiated from him, until with a sense of surrender, I turned slowly onto my stomach.

And oh! The delicious sense of warm touch when he lowered himself ever-so-gently down on top of me. He began to nuzzle the back of my neck, causing thrills of pleasure to race down my spine. Though I was pressed into the mattress, I knew Grendel was supporting most of his own weight. The weight I *did* feel was just right, and the realization of his care and consideration doing this, along with the sheer mass of solid, fleshy presence on top of me gave me further shivers or delight.

I pushed up with my ass, against him, but with his greater size, it was his solar plexus I touched. Still, the invitation was there, and I continued to push up, rocking my hips so my ass-cheeks slid along his skin, communicating my need.

The response was the feel of the enormous presence of Grendel's phallus swelling and hardening—but between my calves and knees. I pressed my legs together, trapping the massive shaft, squeezing it.

Grendel gave a quiet, deep groan, and began to shift his position, upwards. Slowly, slowly, I felt the heat of that shaft slide up, between my knees, then my thighs and finally come to rest, at last, with the spongy swelling curve of the head pressing insistently against the base of my ass.

It was intoxicating. And when he slid further up, so the phallus slipped along between my ass-cheeks, spreading them, I shivered again. I *loved* that massive thing!

Having slid up, it was his pectorals that pressed against the back of my head. I smiled at the mismatch, but he raised himself up and gently repositioned my arms so they were over my head, like a diver. When I lay down again, my hands were now at the level of his chin. By moving his head, he could take one hand or other between his lips, into his mouth.

He nuzzled my fingers very gently, an experience that was slightly unnerving, but very erotic. I moaned and writhed beneath him, pressing my ass up again, against the roundness of his phallus head, which I realized was now in perfect position.

I felt the head slide downwards, to the base of my ass, then then, ever so slowly, back up, now pressing in between my cheeks deeply, so I shivered again. Then, down the head moved again, and this time when it began to push up, I thrust my ass upwards, bending at the knees, so the upward motion of the phallus head this time was directly between my cheeks, toward my sphincter.

By this point, Grendel's phallus was leaking thick, viscous pre-cum so copiously that the touch of skin-on-skin was characterized by a sensuous slickness that was so warm as to be almost hot. I felt the imminence of penetration acutely, awaiting the forward thrust that would drive that massive head inside me at last.

It moved up and inward with maddening slowness, found my sphincter, and began to press against it, causing it to open slightly.

"*Oh!*" I gave a gasp and pushed back, enjoying the slight sting of pain as the sphincter spread further. I closed my eyes, concentrating on relaxing, and willing myself to surrender, aching for need of his being inside me at last.

Take me, man! I repeated mentally. *Take me, damn it!*

But, for all my willing it, the situation remained at a standstill, the insistent pressing of the fat phallus head holding my sphincter open, but not far enough. After a time, the head was removed. I felt the angle of the phallus change, and then, once more the enormous, fleshy mass pressed forward and inward. Again, I willed my own surrender, relaxing into the pain that became greater now—yet still intensely pleasurable as it was connected with my sense of being taken by Grendel, and something I would not have given up for all the world. It was like I was finally giving expression to a full and complete consummation with Grendel. So, I pushed up harder and back until, there came a stab of pain so intense that I had to bite my lip not to scream. I wanted to cry now, not just from the pain, but from the sense of failure: stretched as I was, the head of Grendel's *enormous* phallus was simply too big penetrate my sphincter.

After a time, he withdrew his head, slid the phallus down my ass, then up along the crevice between my cheeks. It was wonderful, but just slightly disappointing. I resolved to accept this, and was not in the end disappointed when, after repeated passes of this sort, he pressed the head against my stretched sphincter to ejaculate. For I felt the thick load of his seed spurt again and again inside my ass. This sensation, the sense of him effectively *cumming* inside me, caused my sexual excitement to erupt in me, so I came violently too.

And then we fell asleep together.

I DISCOVERED WHEN I awoke that I had grown again, at least an inch or two. And I grew each time we made love, each time that I accepted his troll semen into my body. It was a process, and one that both of us enjoyed: making me large enough for him to finally penetrate me. It turned out, however, that after a while I grew less each time, until when I was roughly eleven feet tall growth stopped completely.

"What gives?" I asked Grendel. "You're shtupping me like crazy, but I don't get any bigger."

He smiled. "You have reached your natural size, I guess. You are not a troll after all."

"No?"

He shrugged. "You are what is termed a demi-troll: someone who grew up as a human first."

"Oh," I said. I felt a little cheated, but then told myself that this meant that Grendel would always be larger than me—which was something I, upon reflection, *really* cherished. After that first attempt, we had forgone trying the penetration thing, but now that it seemed this was as good as it was going to get, relative-size-wise, I resolved to give it my best the next time we made love.

When I told Grendel of my resolution, he looked both happy and concerned at the same time.

"I do not wish to hurt you," he said.

I smiled and kissed him, fully determined to ensure it *did* happen.

So, when we were immersed in our act of physical consummation and I felt his massive phallus head pressing hard against me in that most private place, I focused like a laser on the sense of my surrendering to him, relaxing, and at the same time pushed back and up, harder and harder, with something of the desperate knowledge that there would be no further increase in my size, and if it didn't work now, then the future would be one of second best. I think that made me a little savage, because, although Grendel had been keeping himself still during my efforts, now as if sensing something of my situation he decided to help. So, he thrust forward, and it was enough.

A stab of pain made me bite my lip to stop myself from crying out—and then, magically, the round fleshy mass slid through, and the head was inside me!

And now there really *was* some intense pain. I groaned and writhed for a few moments while Grendel remained frozen and silent. There was a quality of the pain, however, the sense of its connection with the erotic, the emotional, that helped. And, as I breathed into the pain, it began to subside. The sensation of being impaled, physically ruptured by that awesome phallus, by *his* phallus, I found delightful.

Moreover, as the pain subsided and the sense of his being inside me increased, there came a new realization: I wanted more.

But I wasn't going to rush it.

After a minute or so, I began to ease myself back, felt myself sliding down the shaft of the enormous phallus, slowly, slowly. This brought back some of the pain, but not a lot; and it increased the sense of being penetrated, deliciously. And there I paused—provocatively, I hoped.

I thought I could sense Grendel's puzzlement, deference. I mentally shook my head. *No, no, my good troll; the ball is in your court now; it's entirely up to you.*

I almost felt his hesitation, until finally—oh bliss! He began to push, to thrust forward, slowly, down and in, on his own. The sense of him taking me, and *taking control* period, made me moan, as I was almost beside myself with pleasure both physical and emotional.

This, I told myself blissfully, *was being fucked!*

Both of us were now making similar moans of gratified desire. Grendel's was several octaves deeper, however, and produced a vibration inside me that sent further shivers of delight all through my body.

In this way, gradually, gently but thoroughly, Grendel began to fuck me. His strokes were slow and short to begin with, as though he was feeling out my tolerance for speed and depth. I was reassured by the noises he was making, however, which told me that the big troll was enjoying himself even while holding back like this. What his full-on rut-fucking might be like I fairly boggled to imagine (but quietly hoped to experience one day).

Meanwhile, during this first tentative fuck I focused on opening to him, for I wanted to take as much of the giant phallus as possible. And, as he continued, his massive tool pressed in ever-so-slightly deeper with each slow thrust. As new moments of pain were encountered, I relaxed my way through them, and gradually they desisted altogether, while Grendel's strokes became longer and deeper—though still slow. I began to gasp with fulfillment.

Gradually, the strokes began to feel less constrained, and each forward thrust was completed with a low grunt that seemed to say: *There!* It was as though Grendel were marking his territory. Not only did I not mind this. I found it more than a turn-on, an actual fulfillment of my desire, as though he was finally manning—or rather trolling—up to the position as my husband, now in the physical as well as the emotional sense.

I felt my entire body tingle with sexual heat that built with each stroke, and at last, not far into this new, serious fucking I came—violently, too, precisely because I was trying *not* to cum. I didn't want it to end this soon, but when I accepted the inevitability of the orgasm, I experienced a delicious sense of losing control such orgasms bring.

And, surprisingly, afterward I *didn't* experience a significant diminishment of arousal. The sense of Grendel's presence over me, on me, around me, and *inside* me, was just so damn wonderful that there was barely a pause in my interest, which immediately began to build again. He was still there, all around me, almost part of me, and I still welcomed the wonderful sense of being dominated it gave. I still wanted it. Wanted it? Hell, I *needed* it!

Grendel, meanwhile, had slowed his thrusts after my climax, but when I indicated my continuing interest by pressing back and squeezing hard on his phallus shaft, he got the message, and picked up the pace again.

It was odd, but somehow my climax seemed to have freed me; I now felt far more lascivious, playful, naughty. I gasped and moaned, pushed up against his torso, shoved back against his thrusting phallus—anything to increase the sense of contact and connection. Penetration was perhaps not all the way yet, but enough for the swollen head to rub up against my prostate—as I recognized that exquisite, dangerous tingle such contact always produced.

And then, as if sensing this, Grendel changed the direction of thrust slightly, and with his next thrust I felt the full explosion of dead-on, prostate-stimulation orgasm. I cried out in ecstasy, reared back, and felt his phallus begin to pulse as he pulled it back only to thrust forward one last time and holding it in place while he shot his seed deep inside me.

When this had ended, everything began to slow down, and a feeling of blissful peace stole over me. Grendel still lay on top of me. He had been increasingly allowing more and more of his weight to bear down on me as I grew in size, and now, judging by the fact that I could hardly breathe, I figured he had completely let go at last and that it was his full weight I was experiencing. The idea of this was the capstone on my happiness; he was letting go. We were together, were one, and it all worked beautifully.

It was considerably later that Grendel at last rolled off me and we lay, facing each other, looking shyly into each other's eyes, smiling contentedly. At eleven feet, I was smaller than him, but it was not a difference that seemed insane anymore; it was—just right, in fact, like Goldilocks' third bowl of porridge.

"It was—good for you?" Grendel asked.

I laughed. "How to put it?" I thought and laughed again. I felt, I realized, wonderfully silly. "It's like I never before felt totally *fucked*."

To my surprise, Grendel continued to look at me closely. "And that is a good thing?"

I laughed again, throwing my arms above my head. "Oh, *honey!*"

Then at last Grendel got it. He gave another growl, that of gratified masculine conquest, and pulled me against him, so hard that I thought one of my ribs might crack. But at the same time, I melted utterly.

I WAS AWAKENED sometime later by the sound of Jake's excited barking. I was on the point of yelling at him to shut up, when it struck me what I was hearing was Jake's *welcome* bark.

Odd, I thought. *Had Grendel gone out and was now returning?*

I hesitated between rolling over and getting up to see what was going on, when I heard a laugh. *That* got me awake, for surely, that was a *human* laugh! And even more than that, I thought I recognized that laugh.

I got up and pulled on my clothes. Then, yawning and stretching I headed out into the hallway.

There was a group standing just inside the front door: Grendel, another troll, and a human. *Other humans in the Underworld?* I realized I had no idea about that. Maybe there *were* some.

Jake caught sight of me and came running up to me, giving another happy bark before running back to frisk around the legs of the human. I was struck by the sense, as I approached the group, of how *small* the human looked.

The human was facing partially away from me, but now he turned and looked in my direction. I cried out in stunned surprise.

"*Bruce!*"

Chapter 26
The Return of Bruce

BRUCE'S MOUTH AND eyes opened wide when he saw me. Then he looked me up and down and finally cried out, "*Wow!*"

I was taken aback. "What?"

He came forward, grinning but still goggling at me. "What happened to *you?*"

"What? Oh." As he made his final approach he seemed strangely to diminish in size. He had always been small and was still shorter than me when he reached the age of consent at eighteen—about five-foot eight. Now, however, he looked *puny*.

It was a strange sensation, and brought home to me my own growth, my sense of size. I had been large for my age as a kid, and even in adulthood, at just over six feet tall I had been taller than most other men. But *now*—!

I felt momentarily embarrassed *and* confused. I didn't quite know what to say at the moment, or perhaps how *much* to say. I grinned sheepishly. "I guess I've been—transformed. Apparently, I'm a demi-troll now."

"Wow!" Bruce repeated, still staring at me. His expression slowly changed to puzzlement. "But how—?" he began.

"Wait a minute!" I said, interrupting him. "Let's deal with first things first. What are *you* doing here?"

Bruce caught himself, then turned and nodded toward the strange troll. "Better ask *him*."

I looked at the troll. He was a foot taller than Grendel, and broader as well. And, looking at him, all I found myself classifying him as *rough trade*. The troll not only looked tough, but there was an actual air of danger about him as well. He looked at me, his gray eyes scanning me up and down, and I felt a disturbing thrill that had, I realized with relief, awe and simple fear as its major components (as opposed to the erotic, though that was there too).

"Hello," I said, frowning slightly and trying to regain my mental footing by reminding myself that this was *my* home after all. I walked forward to stand beside Grendel but did not offer my hand.

"Greetings." The troll spoke with a voice so deep it was almost sepulchral. "My name is Crang. I am charged with—" He paused and looked around. "Is there some place we might talk?"

He was looking at Grendel as he spoke. Grendel nodded. "In the kitchen. Mother is asleep."

We trouped into the large kitchen and sat down around the table. Bruce was helped onto his chair by Crang, and it struck me that there was something in the interaction I didn't understand. But, when he was seated, Bruce turned to me in his old way and grinned as if to say, *Isn't this all exciting?*

I was still stunned by his appearance and was in the process of blinking away the last wisps of sleep. I had no idea what was going on. Who *was* this Crang person, anyway?

For several minutes no one spoke or moved, and at last Grendel got to his feet and went over to the stove. He set the kettle on and procured four mugs, which he set around the table. No one said anything during this, until Grendel had poured the tea and reseated himself.

Then, Crang broke the silence.

"As I was saying," he said. "I am charged with the task of determining the status of this human."

"Oh," was all I could think to say.

"I would like to ask you several questions," the troll continued, looking at me.

"Oh. Okay."

"How do you know this human?"

"Bruce," I corrected, frowning. "His name is Bruce."

"That is what he *says*." Crang spoke this with an ominous emphasis. I began to get an uneasy feeling about the situation. I looked toward Grendel, but he didn't look at me, and was keeping a poker face—which made me even more uneasy.

"Okay," I said, and added, "Yes, I know him." Then I gave a brief description of our relationship as tutor and student, of Grendel and I using Bruce's pool, and of Bruce assisting us in our escape. I finished with asking a question.

"Has he done something wrong?"

Crang remained still and silent for a while, but finally said, "He was discovered in the open, not far from the gate. He said he—" But at this point, he paused and gestured toward Bruce.

Bruce cleared his throat. "I followed those G-men or whatever they were—though they seemed more like military than anything—"

"They were agents," Crang interjected. "Agents of the Federal Bureau of Geostasis, but yes, they can be viewed as a type of military."

"No kidding!" Bruce replied. "I mean, those weapons they used—" But here he caught himself, cleared his throat again, and resumed his narrative.

"Anyway, I told them I was staying with you, Ken, at your house. One of them wanted to tie me up, but in the end, they just told me to get back into the house and stay there, keep out of the way."

I nodded, and Bruce grinned.

"So, I followed them," he said, with a shrug. "Through that—opening, whatever it was. And then," he grinned sheepishly, "I kind of got lost. I didn't have a lantern."

"Oh!" I felt some concern and increased respect for him now, imagining how it must have been like in that darkness, those strange paths, all alone.

"Those G-men, they had lanterns—rather than flashlights. I remember thinking that was odd. Anyway, I trailed them, at first. But they backtracked and split up for a while. I had to dodge their lights, keep out of sight. I'm not sure they knew I was there.

"Eventually, I got split up from them. *Man!* That was scary! But—" he tilted his head, "somehow, it—wasn't. I mean, not as much as I figured it would be.

"Anyway, I started to hear things—sounds like a kind of fight, or battle. I couldn't see anything, but I followed the sound, because, you know, I wanted to help—you and Grendel, I mean. But when I closed in on the action, saw it, smelled it—all that ozone—and that sizzling sound—it kind of freaked me out." He shrugged again. "So, I kept my distance. Then someone came running in my direction. I ran, thinking they were after me. I could see a little in the light of the guy's lantern, and I took a side turning. After that, I kept going and, well—at some point I realized I was completely lost. I couldn't see anything, or hear anything, and I had no idea where I was."

Incredibly, Bruce was grinning as he said this.

"What did you do?" I asked.

"Well, I guess I just sat down, where I was. To rest." He looked at Crang. "It was hours later that they found me."

He signaled that he was finished by picking up the mug in front of him with both hands and taking a long sip.

"Mm," he said. "Good!" He looked at each of us in turn over the top of the mug. I thought he looked—what? Perhaps unsure of himself, but if so, it was clear he was also excited by the bizarre nature of his situation, too. And when he looked at Crang—

I glanced at Grendel who was looking at Crang uneasily. Who *was* Crang in this? It occurred to me that I knew nothing about troll societal organization. Maybe it was a police state! But a moment later I dismissed the idea. Everything Grendel had said suggested trolls were a kindly, decent people. And my experience at the market. But still—maybe? *No!* Whatever the truth was, I decided, I wasn't going to indulge in dark fantasies. It served no purpose.

Grendel Rising 239

Crang, for his part, seemed to be deep in thought. There was silence around the table for several minutes. At last, Crang looked up and breathed in sharply through his nose.

"Very well," he said. "But we must keep this—Bruce, in custody for the time being." He looked at Grendel. "You understand that after what happened—"

Grendel nodded, looking unhappy. Crang studied Grendel's face, and added in more accommodating tones, "We do not know what will happen. This could be—quite unfortunate."

Grendel nodded again.

"Very well." Crang stood up and nodded to Bruce, who slipped off his chair. Crang headed for the front hallway, Bruce following. But I ran after them, and I caught Bruce by the shoulder and pulled him to one side. Bending down, I said in a whisper, "Are you okay?"

He looked at me, surprised. "Yeah. Of course!"

I shook my head. "No. I was studying you in the kitchen—you're covered in bruises, man! And there are plasters on your arms and one on your forehead. You look like you were *beaten*!"

He bit his lip at this and nodded.

"Who was it? Those G-men?"

He shook his head, looked at me, and shrugged. "When the troll scout found me, well, I guess I was difficult." He grimaced. "I mean, I didn't come along quietly."

"What? Who? Crang?"

Bruce studied my face then nodded, but at the same time grinned broadly.

Leaning close, he whispered, "Isn't he *hot*?"

"What?" I hissed back. "He beat you into submission and now you say he's hot?"

Bruce appeared to consider this, then he looked at me and nodded, still smiling.

"I think he thinks I need *discipline*."

"He does," said a deep voice. I looked up and saw Crang standing in the doorway of the kitchen, frowning at us. I felt my body go cold then, but Bruce only looked at me with a *you see?* expression of excitement on his face. I stared at him and shook my head.

"Okay," I said. "Each to his own."

"Exactly!" Bruce said. "I never knew how hot that sort of thing—" But then he looked at me again. "And you and Grendel! Is *that* why you're so big now?"

I rolled my eyes, but nodded, and Bruce almost jumped up and down. "I can hardly wait!" he said, half looking over his shoulder to where Crang stood. Crang was looking impatient.

"Coming!" he said and, giving me a mischievous look, turned and followed Crang to the front door.

When they were standing in the doorway, Bruce looked at me, his expression still excited but a bit worried too. Jake was watching all this, his tail wagging tentatively. I was gratified when Bruce knelt down and fussed over Jake a little. I knew he and Jake were friends, and this was reassuring—an element of the before-time that had survived and was present here.

At last, however, Bruce got to his feet and looked at Crang, who gestured for him to lead the way out the door. But Bruce turned back and came toward me, his arms out. I got down on my knees, and even then, his head came up only to the level of my chest. As I hugged him gently, I was acutely aware of not just how tiny this human was, but how fragile too. It made me feel very odd.

WHEN THEY HAD gone and we had closed the door behind them, Grendel nodded in the direction of the kitchen. In the door of the kitchen, however, I saw Aeglec moving about in that quiet, efficient way of hers. She looked at Grendel.

"Gone, is he?"

Grendel nodded, and we both sat down at the table. I took a sip of tea, which I saw had been topped up and was steaming. There was also a stronger spice flavor to it. Aeglec put down plates in front of us, each laden with what looked like French fries and poached eggs. I found myself thinking, *Green eggs and ham*, but really I had no idea what these were.

"Something to give you strength," she said, patting her son's shoulder and regarding him affectionately. Looking at me, she tapped the side of her head. "Protein, to help you think."

"Oh. Thanks," I replied. She then put a container of something that looked, and tasted, a lot like ketchup, which I saw Grendel pour over his fries.

"Mm!" I murmured after I had tasted my first bite. This was *good*!

When we had finished eating and were lingering over our teas, I looked at Grendel.

"What's going to happen with Bruce?"

Grendel shrugged, but then smiled. "Nothing bad."

"Okay, but what?"

Aeglec chuckled at this, seating herself at the table with a tea of her own. "No one can tell you that, dear. At least, no one in this room." She shook her head. "I heard Crang's name mentioned." She looked at her son. "You know what *that* means!"

I looked at Grendel, then at his mother.

"It means," she said, turning to me, "that this is high level stuff." She looked at her son, lowering her eyelids slightly. "Well. I hope *you* at least are happy!"

Grendel looked at her sideways, and they both started chuckling.

Aeglec looked at me. "There is no going against nature," she said.

There was a silence, after which Grendel said, "I will speak to the council." Then he got to his feet, muttering, "I thought I had done with all this."

He leaned down and kissed me, then turned and left the kitchen. When the front door closed again, I sat there, feeling completely confused. *High level stuff?* I looked at Aeglec and saw she was looking at me. When I raised my eyebrows questioningly, she only shook her head.

I was beginning to recognize Aeglec's ways. She would speak when she wanted to. So, I helped her clear the table, wash the dishes and put them away, after which Aeglec sat down at the table, with two fresh mugs of tea. We sat together in silence for some time, but at last I looked at her.

"Tell me about Grendel?" I asked tentatively.

Aeglec looked at me in silence for a while, then nodded.

"My son is an odd troll," she said. "He is too much ruled by his heart."

I blinked, unsure what to think. Then I asked, "Is there a reason for that?"

Aeglec looked at me sharply, and then nodded, as if to herself. "A quick one," she murmured. "Yes, there *is* a reason for that." She paused, but I didn't want to ask. "It is because he was—well 'born' if one can say that—on a full moon that was also the vernal equinox."

I stared. "The moon? But how—?"

Aeglec nodded. "It is an ancient troll tradition, to go above ground for the birth of a child. That was before the change, of course; before modern times. It was my husband's idea. But the timing—" She shook her head.

Timing? Oh. The vernal equinox, the full moon.

Aeglec stared at me. "You do not understand troll nature," she said. "I told my husband, but he would not listen. Imagine, boy, the silvery light of the full moon. Have you never seen it? Everything is made magical then. And that magic is very real. The vernal equinox, that too is special—magical—the equal position of night and day in the year, the harbinger of spring." She sighed and shook her head. "So, what could we expect?"

"Oh."

"That is why," she murmured to herself, "that is why he went to the above-world for love—because of the magic of spring in his blood, and of the full moon."

I stared at Aeglec. "You mean he went up looking for a husband?"

She looked at me sharply again and shook her head.

"Looking?" she said. "Oh no! He was not *looking*. He knew what he wanted. He went up only to *get* what he wanted."

"You mean a human."

"Not 'a human,'" she said impatiently. "Did he not tell you? Not just any human. He made his choice before that, from down here."

"But—" I felt my face heat up, my mind whirling. It was as if my whole conception of the world as I knew it had changed. It made me cringe inwardly while at the same time I felt a kind of gasping sense of incredulity. Perhaps it was to seek some kind of stability that I told myself that I wasn't really certain of what I had heard. And besides that, my rational mind told me, it didn't seem possible. My mouth had gone dry, but I managed finally to speak.

"How?" I got out finally. "I mean—how could he do that?"

"Oh, there are ways."

"Magic ways?" I asked. "Or technology?"

"I suppose you would call it magic. We do not have the sort of mechanisms that you humans seem to love so much. In the Underworld things do not work like that."

"Oh," I said, thinking of the geostatic barrier, and of how things had felt different when we had passed it.

At this point, however, I lapsed into silence, for the full impact of the main point in what Aeglec had told me sank in.

Grendel had chosen me! He had *risked his life for me!*

Part of me cringed at the magnitude of the idea of this, but this feeling was swamped by a wave of amazement and incredulous joy, that joined in a kind of swirling gush of intoxicated euphoria, filling my whole being. The idea that *I mattered that much* to *anyone*—and especially to that wonderful, gentle, good-hearted nature that I had come to see in Grendel!

It so overwhelmed me so I found myself blinking back tears. I also had to restrain myself from running out of the room and throwing myself on our bed and just—well, melting into a puddle or something.

Instead, I remained where I was, and outwardly composed—I hoped.

Now, Aeglec got up and fetched something from the cupboard. It was a small vial. From this she poured a dozen drops into my mug of tea. "This will help you sleep. Better sleep than worry. Grendel will be gone a while."

I looked at her. "Wait a minute! Didn't he report to the—uh, authorities, when he first came here? Before he and I—reconnected?"

"Yes. He did. But this—this is—well, with your friend there—Bruce, is it?—things appear to have become more—involved." She sighed again, but still smiled gently. "It is all a part of his nature."

This last statement almost overwhelmed me. It was as if I had reached the tipping point in my mental stability. So, I decided not to think about what it meant for now. I drank the rest of my tea, with those drops of sleeping potion or whatever. It tasted different, having a slight bitter flavor in addition to the usual mélange of mushrooms. But it wasn't unpleasant. Then I got up, thanked Aeglec, and went to bed. Jake was just snuggling in beside me when I slipped off into sleep.

Chapter 27
Rumors of War

I AWOKE IN the darkness of our bedroom, as something very large shifted its position next to me. Reaching out, I touched Grendel's shoulder. The contact, as usual, was very reassuring and very pleasurable, but I pushed that aside, feeling something was wrong.

"You okay?" I said quietly.

He sighed. The sigh, though not heavy, was nonetheless massive, and in the spirit of such reminders of his physical size, I felt a frisson of joy and warmth. I turned toward him and pressed myself against his back, running my hand along the curve of his torso, from his hip, up the curve that rose from his waist to where his chest broadened hugely, and finally to the massive cannonball shoulder.

The tracing out my lover's shape had been exquisitely sensuous, so much so by this point I was rock-hard. A rumble of amusement told me that Grendel was aware of this. Then he shifted his position, upwards along the bed, so my hard-on slid down from the small of his back, between his wonderfully full ass-cheeks, and finally between his upper thighs. He lifted the upper leg momentarily lowered it again, trapping my erection in between his warm thighs. The tightness and heat of this sent a wash of erotic pleasure through me, so I had to bite my lip to keep from groaning.

As if he sensed this, he murmured in an amused voice, "*You* okay?"

My head was now level with his shoulder-blades, and I pressed my face in the hollow between them, kissing the warm, musk-scented skin and turning my head to rub against him in a sea of pleasure that was reassurance, reverence, love, and the simple enjoyment of physical touch.

"Yes," I murmured.

I understood his invitation, but I didn't want to avail myself of it right now. So, I pulled back at the hips, slowly extricating my cock from its thigh trap. And, though the process itself produced a fresh wash of erotic heat that almost undermined my determination, I resisted the powerful urge to thrust forward again and rolled onto my back, my erection still throbbing.

I lay there, breathing slowly as the physical sensations clouding my mind passed. Sometimes there are things more important than making love, and I wanted to know how Grendel was doing and what was up with the council.

After a little, he slowly shifted his position until he was lying on his side, facing me, his eyes level with mine. I smiled at him, but his answering smile was more troubled than happy, at the sight of which a wash of love came over me, along with a powerful sense of how precious this enormous mountain of flesh was to me: the troll who had gone to the world above, braved the barrier, to find *me*.

"What's up, big guy?" I asked. I reached down to grasp his phallus, which was always at least semi-hard when we were in bed. I could just make contact with the head with my fingertips. "This?" It was a tantalizing situation, the object of my interest being just out of my reach. It made Grendel chuckle amusedly.

"That's better," I said, seeing the worried expression on his face soften.

He grunted and ran a big forefinger gently down the side of my face, which made me close my eyes with pleasure and the slow tide of happiness that came from the consciousness of being truly loved. He then moved his fingertip to my mouth so I could kiss it, which I did, and finally withdrew it entirely, after which he sighed.

"Okay," I said, and added, smiling to soften my words, "Spill it, big guy!"

He nodded, closed his eyes and took in a deep breath. I could feel the warmth as his massive chest expanded, the pecs pressing up against me. It made my head swim for a few seconds, but I was not to be diverted. I looked resolutely at his face.

"C'mon," I added. "What did the council say?"

He shrugged. "It is not the council *per se*."

I blinked. "What, then?"

"It is—" He paused and looked darkly at me for a second. "Your people."

I held a hand up between us, palm out. "No, no!" I said, shaking my head. "Not *my* people! They might be the government, but I never voted for them, or that. And I *don't* support them."

At this Grendel did his apologetic thing: he looked sheepish and touched his forehead with his fingertips. "I am sorry. You are correct. I mean—" He paused again and chuckled wryly. "It is not easy. You see, it is your species—humans, their representatives."

I nodded, feeling a deep shame for my own people. "Okay," I said. "But I don't support that, please just keep that in mind."

"I will." He drew a deep breath. "Anyway. The Federal Bureau of Geostasis, they have launched a grievance against the troll high council."

"Oh!" I blinked in surprise, realizing that I didn't know what to say, or even to ask.

"There will be a meeting of the general assembly. We are to attend."

We! I felt a sudden stab of joy at the joint pronoun that appeared to include Grendel and myself. But then, as I thought about it, I was suddenly unsure. "You mean, me too?"

He nodded, and I felt reassured.

"Okay." Then I looked at him suspiciously. "Is that what's bothering you? That I will have to attend this meeting?"

Grendel frowned and shook his head slightly. "Not exactly."

I feverishly wanted to ask, *Then what are you worried about? What is there to worry about?*

But the more I thought about it the more I realized that perhaps I *didn't* want to know.

"Well," I said briskly. "We'll just have to go, then. Is there anything I need to know? I mean, to prepare myself?"

He shook his head again but looked so somber that I couldn't keep from reaching up and stroking his cheek. He reacted to this the way a cat reacts to petting, pushing his head against my hand—something that always delighted me. I felt enormous relief at his reaction. And with that relief, a joy born of fresh feelings of love for him. I pushed at his shoulder, and he rolled onto his back. I climbed on top—and proceeded to seriously distract him from his concerns, pausing only once, to ask when the meeting was.

Turns out, it was in seven hours. We had plenty of time.

I intended we make the most of that time.

And we did. And, after our play, filled with a renewed sense of communion, we lay together for a time. Then we had a leisurely shower together and lay down again, with Jake lying between us, before getting ready.

I WAS STILL largely ignorant of Underworld geography with its three-dimensional maze of passages. I did, however, notice that we were headed into more populated regions. We passed numerous trolls, more than I had seen anywhere outside the market. Jake, I noticed, though showing no anxiety at the increased number of trolls, kept closer to our heels.

I noticed Grendel hadn't taken my hand. Wondering about this, I asked him about it, knowing that he generally enjoyed the contact, holding hands while we walked. Was there something improper about hand holding in public? He shook his head and smiled.

"I just do not want to rub it in."

That made me feel quite buoyant, as it added to the interested looks that

I got from the male trolls we passed.

At last, we arrived at last at a curving passage that was larger than usual. It had, I noticed, large entrances regularly spaced along its inner wall, about twenty yards apart. I was puzzled by this. It was a bit like the wells I had encountered, though the topography here was—what? In some way *inverted*? I tried to think what this meant, but just thinking about it made my head hurt and I soon gave up.

Then it hit me. It was like being outside of a large stadium: all those spaced entrances.

Numerous trolls were moving in both directions, some stood in groups of two or three near the wall opposite the entrances. I was struck by the ease with which everyone moved; there was no sense of bustle and no collisions. Each troll seemed to know their business and calmly went about it. It reminded me, in fact, of the market. And of course, there were the stares.

Grendel took hold of my arm, pointing toward the closest of the entrances.

"You see up there?" he said. "That sign?" I looked. Above the entrance was a large rune carved into the stone. "Well," he said, "that one is not it, but just keep going until you see a G-rune. You know the rune for G, yes? A vertical stroke with two diagonal strokes connecting to the right."

I had been about to shake my head but nodded after his description.

"Well, the seating area for you is G-9. You go up the stairs and then look for that. Okay?"

I nodded again. "No problem." I tried to sound confident.

Grendel hesitated, and I could see he wanted to hug me, but seemed averse to doing so with trolls moving past us. So, I squeezed his hand and turned away, walking along the curve of the passage.

"I will—see you afterwards," he called after me. I turned and saw him standing there. He looked worried.

That unnerved me a little. But I took my courage in hand and followed Grendel's directions. I passed several openings, until I saw the rune that Grendel had described. I chuckled. It was the rune that Tolkien had used for G in *The Lord of the Rings*.

"C'mon, Jake," I said. We passed the big archway and climbed the set of stairs that began just beyond it. These were troll-sized steps, of course, which took a bit of an effort for me. Jake, on the other hand, was quite undisturbed. He jumped up each step with a sense of excited satisfaction that made me look at him with admiration. I smiled to myself, blessing him and his wonderful presence.

We came out onto a landing in a great circular bowl that presumably was the troll general meeting hall. It was *vast*. There were tiers of benches rising on all sides, and high overhead was a great domed ceiling, jet black, with numerous luminous spots on it. At first, I thought they were a representation of stars in the night sky, but I soon discovered the constellations, if that was what they were, were not those I was familiar with. In addition to these there were torches burning in wall sconces high on the outside wall of the chamber. I wondered at this. They couldn't have given much illumination. After some consideration, I decided they must be more symbolic than functional.

The chamber, lit by these artificial stars and torches was quite dim, the effect being something like dusk. I could see, but not in too much detail. I thought about this. It wasn't surprising, given that troll eyes could see in the dark. (I had asked Grendel about my own sight, the fact that I still could *not* see in the dark. He had only laughed and told me it would come with time). I did feel a little disappointed, though. Given the evident importance of the meeting, I would have liked to be able to see better.

There were many trolls seated on benches, and more coming in at the other entrances. I decided I needed to find my spot. I wandered up the aisle that went up along the rows of benches next to the entrance where I stood. There were barriers between sections, each section had that G-rune and a number—of sorts. Perhaps I had expected the usual numerals, but these digits had no curves; they were made of short lines set in different configurations.

I thought I recognized several: a one, four and even eight, which was represented by two diamond shapes, one on top of the other. But the others, not so much. But I deduced what they must be, given the fact that they were probably ordered in an ascending series. Also, there was the fact that each digit was represented by the corresponding number of short lines, the two as a simple corner, the three as a lightning-bolt, and so on.

Thus, I finally came to my goal, section, G-9 (the nine being a two-diamond eight with a single line at the bottom like a tail). The section was completely empty, containing two benches, each about fifteen feet long and slightly curving, one behind the other. The benches were separated by a step, and around the section was a waist-high barrier, with an opening onto the adjacent radial aisle that climbed up from level to level.

I lifted Jake on the lower bench and sat down beside him. Finally settled in position, I looked around me with interest. The first thing I noticed was that all tiers of seating were broken into similar sections, some larger, some smaller, by low walls. It reminded me of what I had read about, the box pews that had been common in old Protestant churches, where each family had its own seating area.

As to the trolls themselves, I noticed they tended to sit in groups, and pretty much every group was busy talking together quietly. It made me uneasy to be alone in my section, but then I remembered Jake and almost

Grendel Rising

laughed aloud. He was, I decided, probably of higher status than I was! I put my arm around him, hugging him and enjoying the feel of his warmth against me.

It struck me, as it had from time to time recently, how Jake had become comparatively smaller as I grew in size. I had noticed that had not seemed to affect him at all, but my own sense of *him* was to increase my care in protecting him. Not that he needed much protection, other than from potential accidents involving large bodies. Now, as I pressed him against me, I felt the great love I had experienced from the moment I had picked him up at the breeders; for a small dog, whether as a puppy or fully grown, he had had immense confidence and immense curiosity. Irresistible then and now.

I was still enjoying this sense of connection with my pup, when I became aware that a group of five trolls close to me had turned and were standing *staring* at me. This took me aback, but I rose and gave them the standard troll greeting—or rather a combination of two: putting my left fist against the center of my chest and nodding to them. When I got no response, my face began to burn. I sat down again and decided to ignore them.

But a little later I noticed *more* groups had apparently caught on and were staring at me too. I began to feel about as welcome as an ant at a picnic.

Clenching my teeth, I focused my attention on the central area of the hall. Here there was a raised dais with two ornate chairs in the center and long benches on either side. It struck me that this part of the hall was better lit than the surrounding tiers, though I couldn't see how. I was scanning for possible extra luminous patches on the lowest ring of boxes, when I was startled almost out of my skin by a sudden bout of fierce barking from Jake. He was standing with his front paws on the back of our bench and was giving the hall at large a volley of his most challenging barks.

He must be reacting to the growing hostility, I thought, and I was mortified by the intensity of his challenge even while I was impressed at his courage and loyalty.

In that enormous chamber, somehow the sound was startlingly loud. And even when I had grabbed him, taken him into my arms and told him fiercely and quietly to shut up, the noise echoed for almost a minute before dying away.

The silence that followed was palpable. The trolls, I saw, had been, as it were, frozen in place, their miens utterly changed. Aggressively raised chins were lowered, fierce gazes lowered. From angry, resentful and hostile, they had become almost like small children: abashed and ashamed.

The silence continued, broken only by the quiet sound of shuffling feet as the entire troll presence reseated themselves, and Jake's low growl near at hand as he glared out, hackles up, over my shoulder. I could feel the tension—different than before, but still tension—that filled the hall.

And then, from across the far side of the hall, a troll got to his feet and, after bowing toward the dais, turned toward Jake and me, and bowed again. Now *this* bow was deeper than the usual troll bow, and after the bow the troll lifted his hand over his head, palm out, and spoke several words that, because he hadn't raised his voice, I couldn't quite get.

I *thought* he said something like, "We beg your pardon."

Another troll not far from the first, stood up. He spoke more clearly, and after his bow and hand gesture, said, "We have lapsed in our—courtesy to *guests* in our realm. We stand corrected."

After this, gradually the entire assembly of trolls rose to their feet, faced us, and made the same gesture with their raised hands. The gesture puzzled me. What did it mean? Clearly, it expressed goodwill. A benediction? No. That was a blessing from someone higher up. Then I had it: it was a gesture of obeisance.

Wow! I thought. Yet when I considered it, it did seem the correct interpretation. But it wasn't, I realized, directed primarily at me. It was directed at Jake, only indirectly at me.

"Thank heaven I brought you, boy," I said under my breath. Jake didn't look around, but at the sound of my voice he wagged his tail. I put him gently down beside me on the bench. I was feeling immensely grateful to him, but a little shaken by what had happened. Was I supposed to respond? And if so, how?

I chanced to look at the dais now and was rescued from my conundrum by the sight of my beloved Grendel just entering from one of the three archways behind it. He went along the dais and up several steps to an adjacent, raised area I hadn't noticed before. It had a single bench on it, and Grendel sat down on this bench, appearing to notice nothing of his surroundings. I felt something clutch at my heart. His solitary position as well as his behavior suggested someone about to undergo judgment.

At this point a number of trolls entered through those three archways. They were dressed oddly for trolls, in what looked like Roman togas. Two wore purple, and they sat down in the two chairs at the center of the dais. The others, in white, went to benches on either side.

The two purple-clad "chair-trolls" as I mentally christened them—and idly wondered whether this might be a pun—carried themselves with rather more of a sense of importance than the others. It was pretty clear that they were the bosses, but I was puzzled as to why there were *two* of them. Then, I looked at Grendel again, seated near the dais but isolated on his raised platform, and it struck me uncomfortably that he looked not just like a peasant in comparison to the finery displayed by the others, but a peasant on trial.

The chair-troll on the left, who was slightly shorter than the other, and had lighter hair—stood up, and a profound silence settled on the hall.

"This assembly," he began, speaking slowly and clearly in a voice that was deep and resonant, clearly that of someone used to speaking in public, "has been called to address a crisis that now faces us."

Murmurs greeted this, but these were quickly stilled as the figure raised a hand.

"The witness," he said, and gestured toward Grendel, "will recount the tale."

I felt a stab of desperate hope at this. *Witness!* I thought. And I hung onto the idea that Grendel was *only* a witness, that he wasn't being charged with anything.

The chair-troll sat down, and Grendel stood up—looking, I thought, unusually nervous. He told the story of which I knew much: his going up to the surface, his failure at this, being caught in the final feet of earth, my rescuing him—with Jake's help—and of our subsequent getting to know each other. He did not go into detail, but he did not appear to be trying to hide anything either, for he even mentioned the way he had compromised the G-man—which I noticed brought some rough growls of amusement from the trolls in the benches all around the hall.

He told about there being barriers set up around my yard, of our being trapped, of Bruce's coming to the rescue. And then our escape through the barrier and the gate and the attack by the FBG agents, and the battle at the gate. I hadn't known the details of that battle, since I hadn't been within sight of it, and Grendel had never talked about it after we reconnected. But the trolls had driven the human forces back, and they had returned victorious through the gate.

At this, Grendel stopped and turned to look at the chair-trolls. They both nodded and the light-haired one turned and gestured to a troll sitting in the front circle of benches. This troll stood up, and I thought I recognized Crang. When I heard him speak, I was certain. He related how, shortly after the battle, he had led a small patrol through the gate, to check the perimeter. They had discovered Bruce in the chasm not far from the gate and had brought him in. He said that, since Bruce's story had matched that told by Grendel, Bruce was cleared of any charge of spying. Crang ended by saluting the chair-trolls before sitting down.

There was another silence, and the chair-troll with the darker hair rose to his feet.

"And now," he said, his voice even deeper than the first chair-troll, positively grim, I thought, "we have received a demand from the humans."

A low, unnerving growl greeted this. I felt chagrin at the use of this word, specifically at my membership in the species. The chair-troll allowed the growls to continue, but when they began to die away, one of the trolls in the lower tiers shouted out.

"What are the demands?"

I was startled by this but decided by the response that such an utterance wasn't out of order here. In fact, the chair-troll bowed his head briefly before replying.

"Restitution!" he said in a ringing voice. Then he added, "That is, shorn of its flowery language. They demand that the human be returned to his own world, and that the kidnapper—that is the word they used—be handed over for justice—again, that was their word. As you can see, two deceits are embedded in the demand itself."

My own outrage was in accord with the further growls in the hall. One of the trolls on the dais benches stood up.

"There is something odd about this. It is all out of proportion."

The light-haired chair-troll rose to his feet. "Indeed!" he said. "We believe this is a deliberate provocation, a *casus belli* as it were—a pretext for war."

Chapter 28
A Desperate Plea

WHEN THIS SPEAKER sat down, the murmurings in the hall were even greater than before; they now containing the distinct quality of alarm.

Then a troll in the upper benches cried out, "Well, I say, if war is what they want, then war is what they will get!"

There were roars of agreement to this, but other voices as well, angry voices of disagreement.

I heard another rough voice say, "We must use this opportunity! We must put a stop to the spate of bullying that has been visited upon us by the human authority in recent decades!"

More cries. Then the voice that had called for war said even more fiercely, "We must do this! It is necessary if we are to survive as a free and self-determining people and not slaves of the human machine of domination."

More noise, into which another voice from the higher benches cried, "Those are fine words, emotional words. But, to speak of domination is to speak generally, conceptually. Domination? To what end? What do they want—beneath the words?"

Both chair-trolls rose to their feet, and the sound ebbed away.

The light-haired chair-troll spoke. "It is our contention—" he nodded to the dark-haired chair-troll, "and that of others on the council—that the human authority wants to utilize our diggings for their own mining operations, for minerals."

"And that," added the other chair-troll, "is merely the surface of their intent. We believe they wish to impose their will upon us in every aspect, to turn all of the Underworld into a subordinate, dependent realm, in which trolls become servants or slaves. They would as well 'mine' our knowledge and our culture."

"But—" A female troll spoke up now, and she sounded, more than anything, aghast. "That is—unthinkable! Do they not realize the consequences of such an action? The very balance between our worlds. The forces opposing and supporting each other—the Earth-power itself—"

The light-haired chair-troll replied. "I would say of that: they appear simply not to care. Theirs has become a world of technology, where wealth and power are of paramount importance. They have lost their true connection to the Earth-power. They are therefore, to our way of thinking, *mad*."

A tense near-silence followed this pronouncement; the murmurings were low and disturbed now. I looked around at the trolls in my proximity, and saw faces taut with bewilderment, fear, and outrage. And into this an anxious voice from the somewhere in top-most tiers said desperately, "Do we—do we have the strength, the resources, the—power to resist?"

All eyes turned to the chair-trolls, whose grave faces became if anything, still graver. They exchanged a look, one nodding to the other, who stood up.

"Such things are not easily determined. For my own part, I believe that we do not—not if all humans take this aggressive stance."

"But do they?" came a response. Some of the trolls close to me turned and looked at me so I blushed under their gazes.

Perhaps it was those looks that did it, for I felt a sting of outrage rising in me and, without really thinking, and despite a cringing sense of unwillingness to make a spectacle of myself in public, I got to my feet.

My knees shook slightly, but my anger and my love for Grendel, and through him for all these trolls, kept me standing.

"Not me!" I shouted, raising my fist. "And there are others," I added. Then a momentary doubt assailed me. "At least—I *think* there are others," I said in lower tones. But in another moment, frowning, I shook my head and cried out, "No! I *know*—" for in my heart at least I decided I knew. "There *are* others! Potentially."

Feeling my confidence drain from me, my own thoughts continued inside my head: *The organs of power tend to corrupt the human heart. But they are not all there is.* Taking a deep breath, I raised my voice again.

"The heart of the people—I believe—in many, possibly the majority, is better than that of the bureaucrats and the politicians. For we humans, we too—I truly believe—love this earth we share with you—though most are unaware of that last.

"Maybe they could be contacted," I concluded, and sat down.

I saw several of the trolls on the dais nod at this.

"That will not be easy—" one of them murmured. "Our presence in those realms—"

"A human!" cried a voice. "Cannot a human go? As our ambassador?"

Heads turned to me again, and I became uncomfortable as before.

"I am willing," I said, rising to my feet again. "But I don't know how much weight my words will have." I gestured to my body. "As you see, I am no longer of human scale. Some will be shocked. Others will be afraid. And those in the powerful positions will use that, I feel certain."

"Then—another?" came a voice.

My thoughts immediately went to Bruce, who was even now in custody somewhere in the Underworld. But would his treatment by troll officialdom have turned him against us? Then I remembered how he had looked at Crang, and decided it most likely hadn't.

"There is—another," I said. "Another human—who might be willing."

"That alone," another troll on the dais said, "is only a possibility. It is, to be frank, all too likely to fail. But there is another possibility. I think we all know of what I speak."

I don't, I thought, as I listened to the murmurs of agreement around me. They seemed familiar with this alternative, but they didn't sound happy about and, as I listened, I had the distinct impression that the idea of this other possibility had been collectively dismissed.

I shook my head, trying to clear it. My mind was buzzing with half-understood ideas. At last, however, I realized one point: they were saying they could not fight the humans. What exactly did that imply? Capitulation in *some* form. And what the humans wanted was to have Grendel sent up for punishment—probably slavery.

Oh!

And *now* I felt I had my bearings, the single concrete point upon which to build my position, my attitude.

The last troll's final statement had hung in the air as the low buzz of voices continued. I still felt they had dismissed the suggestion, whatever that was, and I felt anger and desperation rising up in me as I thought of Grendel's possible fate. I stood up.

"I would like to say something!" I cried.

Almost to my surprise, the hall quieted quickly, and the light-haired chair-troll nodded toward me.

"I know that I am—or, was, I don't really understand this, my growth and all that—a human. And I think I understand what you say about the evil modern industrial society has done to humans. And, having understood this, I want to say to you now—" I paused for emphasis "—that I turn my back on it—*utterly*!"

There was a smattering of clapping that died away quickly. I took a deep breath.

"And as for the interests of the world below, I would say two things. First, I have come here to live—if that is okay with you. And second, I have learned to appreciate already something both of the Underworld and its inhabitants—you trolls. And I make this vow: I will fight beside you, and for you, with whatever strength and ingenuity I possess. I will put them at the service of you all."

There was some cheering this time, but also some murmurs—humorous I realized after a few seconds. This puzzled me until I realized what I had said might have been taken as a double entendre. There were even a few hoots as well.

"But," I said, when things had died down, "I don't understand your lack of belief in yourself. I see you as strong, powerful, and courageous. You don't have technology, but there are other things surely; I don't know a lot about how those things work, but don't you have wards of some kind? And I agree with the idea of an ambassador to the humans. But surely there are other things, too."

There were some low murmurings.

"And," I continued, still on an adrenaline high, "someone just now said something to the effect: *If the humans want war, then war is what we will give them.* Well—again, I don't understand things that well—but, I mean, what about it? You say you're not sure if you're strong enough. But isn't that the wrong way to think? Isn't it better to stand up in defiance and *test* your strength?"

There were some loud cries of agreement to this, but not many. Other voices murmured their disquiet. The dark-haired chair-troll stood up, and the sounds died away. The troll gestured to me.

"War," he said, shaking his head. "You are human, and do not understand. You seem to speak of war as if it is something that is natural to us, something to be glorified and even desired." He looked at the other chair-troll, who nodded, then turned back to me.

"It is not we who fight wars. That is the human way. For them it is natural, to kill and seek glory in domination. They do not understand the nature of the twin systems, the duality that is and always was inherent in us. As playthings of our two-planet system, life was created, both on the earth and under it, from the interaction of the two sources of generative impulse: Earth-power and starshine. Yet, for whatever reason, humans appear not to understand this, though I think at one time they did, at least they felt it in their deepest nature."

"Yes," said the other chair-troll. "It is not *we* who are the monsters. It is almost never those who are so labeled that are. It is a symptom of arrogance and an excess of power that labels and condemns the others as monsters—a projection of their *own* monstrous nature, which they will not own or control. They need the scapegoat, and that—truly—is us."

There was a long and somehow terrible silence that filled the hall after this. I looked around and saw to my surprise that the trolls were not angry. Neither were they shamed nor cowed. They were merely sad, grieving it seemed, over the nature of both their predicament and the nature of the world itself.

The chair-trolls looked at each other, one nodded and the other spoke.

"It would seem," he said heavily, "that for the preservation of the peace, and to prevent the general loss, we must make some individual sacrifices."

"We must sacrifice," said the other, still more heavily, "some individuals. And it is only reasonable that this be those most intimately connected with the causation of this current dilemma."

Heads turned toward one location—toward Grendel.

I felt stunned, stricken, and suddenly unable to stand. I grasped the back of my bench, and collapsed onto it. Jake sat very close to me, as if in support, no doubt aware of my distress.

"Do you, Grendel, agree to this—to make a sacrifice of yourself, for the sake of your brethren and as payment for your indiscretion?"

I heard a roaring in my ears as I saw Grendel, whose head had been bowed, now made as if to stand. He seemed unable to do this, however, and instead he spoke from his seated position. But, when he spoke, it was in a firm voice: "I do."

The two chair-trolls seated themselves and there was a low murmuring throughout the hall. I felt as though everything was spinning. It was all going wrong, I realized, and so very quickly!

"*Wait!*" The shrill cry echoed through the hall, and it was only after a few seconds that I realized it was my own.

The response was a stunned silence. The chair-trolls turned their gazes to me. The light-haired troll stood and raised his hand in my direction. To my surprise, he was nodding and smiling.

"You speak out of consideration for love," he said. "And that is commendable. But this is for our very survival here in the Middle Realm. We are condemned to live, trapped between two hostile forces, and our choices of action must reflect that. Love alone is secondary."

I was momentarily confused by what these *hostile forces* might be, but I decided that didn't matter.

"*No!*" I cried, my voice even louder.

This drew rumbles from the trolls present, but the sound did not seem to be outrage at my temerity. There were some who appeared to be murmuring in favor—or perhaps out of respect for my having the nerve to speak out like this. In them, somehow, I felt Grendel's own spirit. These were the dreamers, I felt certain, and perhaps the would-be lovers, trolls who sympathized with Grendel and me.

As if to confirm this, one of these trolls cried, "What is life without love?"

There were outcries at this, both in agreement and against.

The light-haired chair-troll, however, said dispassionately in response to this, "I remind you that while the *idea* of love is valued by us, in terms of practicality, we all know that the vast majority of trolls live, and live well, without a personal love."

"Yes!" replied the same troll. "I know that. I am one who does. But I say this: Love for us is rare, yes. It is not something that comes easily to us. In that, however, Grendel and the few like him represent the best of us, not the weakest, and certainly not deserving of being sacrificed to the hateful humans to secure our pathetic safety! This is not right!"

There were roars in response to this, mostly but not all in support. I could feel their energy now, and suddenly being in a large hall filled with outraged trolls made me feel very vulnerable. What might they be capable of if this became a melee? And how would I, one demi-troll, and his small dog, survive such?

What if, in short—I cringed at the thought—that this was the sparking of a kind of Underworld civil war?

My mind blazed with the certain truth that a house divided in itself cannot stand. This in turn produced a feeling of desperation that, oddly, seemed to fill me with a preternatural sense of energy and purpose.

"*Wait!*" I cried again in my loudest possible voice.

This single word cut through the deep roars like a knife through butter. The noise subsided.

The chair-trolls on the dais both stood and made motions with their hands for everyone to sit down. When this was accomplished, one of chair-trolls gestured to me, hand out, inviting me to speak.

My heart was pounding, and I was terrified. Yet I was also filled with an almost incandescent sense of purpose.

"You are wrong!" I began in a loud, carrying voice. "You say *hateful humans*, and I agree with that in part, but not entirely, for it is only true for *some* humans. I descended with Grendel out of love for him. I left my life, my business, my home—all to secure that love."

I let that sink in before making my principal point, and was relieved at the almost total silence. They wanted to know what I had to say.

So, I continued, speaking even louder, "Your suggestion that love is secondary to safety and comfort—I tell you, I *know* that to be false! I stand before you as a living example of this!

"I still do not fully understand, but I think you are wrong in this. Horribly wrong! I am a stranger in a strange land, and that is a gift as well as a challenge. I see things through fresh eyes."

I paused again, before concluding. My chest was heaving, and tears were in my eyes. "And what I see here, in you, is something so wonderful, so precious and beautiful, that my heart has been turned toward troll-kind—with admiration, respect, and with love!"

There was positive murmuring at this, but amid this I heard someone half growl, "What is your point?" This brought renewed murmurings, many of agreement. What *was* my point?

"My point," I said in ringing tones, "is that I believe you are selling yourselves short! You are worth more than this! You are worth fighting for! And not only do I dedicate myself to your cause; I believe there are others among the humans!"

Suddenly I became aware that I had my fist in the air. I lowered it slowly, my face burning with embarrassment. I still remained standing, however. It seemed important, even though I was not sure what it was I was trying to say, exactly. But I was at least grateful that there had been no derision in the murmurings that followed my shooting my mouth off. Perhaps they appreciated the nerve of an eleven-foot demi-troll speaking out in this way, in their defense.

"But," came a voice from high up in the hall, cutting through the murmurs that continued, "for all its wonderful nature, for all that it does for us, what is love in the face of the weapons of the enemy, the humans?"

I had an answer, but I had to summon my nerve to speak again to that assembly. It helped, however, when a number of troll faces from around the hall turned to me expectantly.

"You say, *the enemy* and *the humans*," I countered, "just as if they are one and the same. But I tell you, *that is not true!* Among humans there is much appreciation for you—perhaps not consciously, but in the sense of love and respect for Mother Earth. And there is much valuing of love, and of peace. The enemy that you face is not the whole of humanity itself, but rather a minority, those who run big corporations for, who get caught up with the bottom line, with profits, and government officials who see their positions dependent on their society's economy, on finance and productivity. Ordinary humans are just swept along with this—I believe. And I believe that most humans are utterly unaware of how this way of living poisons the very flow of Earth-power."

I stopped talking, aware that my reference to this most sacred thing had produced a dead silence in the hall. My head span for several seconds as I tried to take in a new idea that was pushing its way into my consciousness. I took a deep breath and, as it were, stepped out onto the perilous.

"I might be wrong," I couldn't help beginning with. "But I believe that you are very wrong to decry and diminish love as being subordinate to power. What I say to you is: *What else do you think the Earth-power is?*"

I cringed inwardly after making bold pronouncement. I had no idea whether what I had said was true. I only was sure it *felt* true, so true, and at so deep a level that I had been able to shoot my mouth off like this.

There were several heart-stopping moments of utter silence, but then, incredibly, the entire hall erupted in roars of approval, agreement, and simple exhilaration. And oddly, I found this, more than anything confusing, and so I just stood there, heart pounding, chest heaving. It was both intoxicating and terrifying, the sense that at this moment I had pretty much the entire troll assemblage in the palm of my hand.

I must have been suffering from emotional overload now, for my mind more or less shut down. I sat down, aware that my limbs were shaking—while the hubbub continued around me.

I don't recall the next several minutes very clearly. I withdrew into myself, bowed my head and closed my eyes. Jake licked me and I held him close to me, cherishing his warmth and his reassuring support and presence. I heard no more speeches just then, but plenty of voices, the rumble of many exchanges, conversations, disagreements.

I was still sitting like this, aware only that things were quieter now, when Jake gave a sudden bark.

Looking up, I saw a troll approaching my box. He was dressed like a guard.

He bowed low to Jake and then to me in the fist-to-chest gesture, and said, "The consuls request you join them, in the council chamber."

Consuls? My mind reeled. *Those chair-trolls!* I blinked several times, trying to make sense of the guard's statement.

"Oh," I said at last, in a weary voice. I did not feel much interest to any meeting, I was so wiped, and too confused. Then I thought of something. "Will Grendel be there?"

I saw the guard's mouth twitch slightly, but he nodded. So, I put Jake down on the floor, got up, and followed the guard.

Chapter 29
Council of War

JAKE AND I were led to the exit stairs I had used coming into the hall, then along passages and up or down flights of stairs. Since the guard and I were both barefoot (and the characteristic tread of trolls, and in my case demi-trolls, being almost completely silent), the only sound was the rapid clicking of Jake's claws on the stone floor and the click-click, click-click, click-click when he descended stairs. I found the sound immensely reassuring.

Finally, we were ushered into a large, oval-shaped room with a long table at its center, around which were a number of chairs.

In the middle of one long side of the table sat the two consuls, and opposite them sat Grendel. The guard led me to the chair next to Grendel, and as I seated myself, I automatically reached out for Grendel's hand, which was reaching for mine. That contact was reassuring.

Then I remembered Jake, and lifted him into the empty chair next to mine. And, looking across at the consuls, I was reassured to see looks of benevolent approval in their faces. Jake immediately lay down with his chin on his paws, to watch the proceedings.

I looked around, and was a bit surprised there were only the four of us (and Jake) here; the guard having gone back to the door through which he had led us, and taken up his position standing there. *All those empty chairs*, I thought wonderingly, but then dismissed it as being not important. I looked back at Grendel, who was regarding me with an expression that contained both love and worry.

"It's not your fault, big guy," I murmured, leaning toward him, and squeezing his hand.

Then I looked across the table, and the taller consul began by addressing me, "What you said about Earth-power. What did you mean by that?"

I blinked and stared back at him, confused. For a second or two I had no idea what he was talking about. Then it came back to me.

"Oh! You mean about Earth-power being love?"

The consul nodded, but I only stared at him, frowning now.

"I don't understand," I said. "Is that a foreign concept to you?"

The consuls exchanged glances, then looked back at me. They looked uncomfortable. Finally, one of them looked at Grendel and nodded curtly.

"Ken," Grendel said. "This is a thorny problem for us."

"It is?"

"Yes. Since we came up from the ancient place, we have lived, in a sense, in exile."

"*What?*"

"We were driven out—that is the right word, though it is harsh."

"Driven out?" I repeated, incredulous. "How? By who—I mean, by whom?"

Grendel smiled ruefully.

"I know you think I quote too much—" he began.

"No, no! Who told you that?"

He looked at me, his eyebrows raised in surprise. I took hold of his hand.

"I *like* you quoting our poets. It makes me feel—I mean, makes us seem closer, somehow, even when I don't know the quote myself."

"Oh," Grendel said quietly, and a gentle smile grew on his face.

"But what was it you were saying?" I continued. "About you being driven out. By whom?"

"Oh. I was going to quote your poet, Shakespeare: *There are more things in heaven and earth, Ken, than are dreamed of in your philosophy.*"

"Hamlet? But you inserted the *Ken*, right?"

"Yes. In the original it was *Horatio*, Hamlet's friend."

"When he saw that ghost, right?"

"His father. But it was Horatio who saw the ghost first."

I nodded. "Anyway. So, you're saying there are other—what?"

"It is widely spoken of down here that you humans have gone the way of the machine." He shook his head sadly. "And it has given you wealth, and control. But it has also changed you and robbed you of the deeper elements of life. You don't see things for what they are, what they mean in themselves, but only what they can do for you. That is *instrumentalism*; you use things and then discard them, and with people too. That is very bad—for everybody."

There was a profound silence in the room after this. I looked at Grendel, but he seemed disinclined to continue. So, I looked across at the consuls. One of them looked at me speculatively, and then began to speak, in a quiet, sad voice.

"The blind willfulness of human beings is something awe-inspiring to trolls. But it is also easily perverted—misused.

"In seeking mastery over the world, humans set out to learn the nuts and bolts of its functioning. And they have succeeded, and at the same time failed, horribly. For the structure that they discovered was only what they looked for: the nuts and bolts. There is no soul, no *value* in such things, or in the discovery and mastery of such things, unless it is mastery itself, and the ease and riches it gives, that are all that are desired of life.

"But these things are not what lies at the heart of life, and it is all that is deepest in life, in the fullest sense—that you humans have forgotten. Though perhaps your friend here would not put it this way, I believe that is why Grendel made the perilous journey up from the world below to the world above, as a call to life, as it were, this forgotten thing, to remind you humans."

"Really? But how?" I stared at Grendel, but he appeared to be thinking about what the consul had just said. I looked at the consul. He raised his hands, palms up and out in a gesture of opening. "To stimulate by example the functioning of the human heart, to suggest the possibility of such a way of living, in opposition to that in which the brain dominates."

"The brain dominates?" I repeated, not fully understanding.

The consul smiled. "The human brain functions through local practical reason—though by *brain* I mean the rational, logical part of who you are. Reason is the language of nuts and bolts, which leads to utilitarianism and instrumentalism. But these things, on their own, are death to *true* life, to the human heart—though they do feed the heart's dark shadow, the ego. Vanity and pride are the language of the ego, and they lead nowhere; they are dead ends in the fullest sense.

"The language of the heart is the language of love and of beauty, and there is truth in those things as much as in the reasoning, the nuts and bolts of the world—nay, even more. For it is the nature of the reason to serve the heart. Reason teaches you *how to do* something, but the heart alone tells you the *value* of that something, its ultimate *meaning*, whether it feeds the human soul or poisons it."

At this point, Grendel stirred. He looked at me and smiled sadly.

"One of your poets," he said. "William Blake. He put that so well—*so well!* How does it go? Let me see."

"*When the sun rises, do you not see a round disc of fire somewhat like a guinea? O no, no, I see an innumerable company of the heavenly host crying Holy, Holy, Holy is the Lord God Almighty.*"

He looked at me. "Do you see? It is the rational person that sees the guinea sun—a guinea being a golden coin—the sun being observed as like that golden coin: round and gold in color. But the scientist goes further and describes the sun as a ball of hot gas. It is the poet and the lover, who sees deeper, who sees, as Blake says, a manifestation of the heavenly host. For that is what the sun truly *is*, in terms of what it means to the essence of humans, its value. And it is that *value* that is important."

I thought I understood that, so I nodded and Grendel, pleased, sat back and lowered his gaze, evidently returning to his ruminative state. Briefly I wondered whether his speaking out like this in front of the consuls was in some way inappropriate. But I dismissed this and turned to the consuls. They both nodded at me, and the one who had spoken before leaned forward.

"Very well put," he said. "In your modern society it is the rationalist and the scientist who principally guide human effort. And that has, not surprisingly, led to a worldview in which it is the physical, the material that is considered real and worthy of consideration. Thus, to a large degree humans fail to understand and appreciate, and to act in a way that reflects this, the true value of the world and existence itself." He shook his head sadly. "And so, the souls of humans have been starved for centuries—even as your technology and science have 'triumphed.'"

I nodded, blinking back tears of sadness and pain. "Yes," I said quietly. "I see that." And with that admission a wave of disgust and horror passed over me—as well as shame, for hadn't I been complicit, living in my suburban comfort? My life was a success story, and yet I knew all along that something was missing, and the closest I could get to identifying this was that I wanted a boyfriend.

There was another silence. I turned and, leaning toward Grendel, I said, "But, hey! Big guy! You said trolls were driven out, but you haven't told me—*who* or *what* was it that drove you out—and, from where? Earth? I mean, the Overworld?"

"Yes. And no."

I laughed. "Could you be more specific?"

"Our passage up was—easier, before. But that is not what I meant exactly. We were driven *up*, from the old places that exist further within the earth, where the Earth-power is stronger."

"Oh."

"We were different then, too. Like our cousins, the humans—we changed."

I began to feel my head swim. "Okay. But *who or what*, drove you—up?"

Grendel shook his head. "There was a—change. There are forces, powers if you like. Everything interacts, balances are achieved. We lived deeper within, and we had communion with the denizens of the Deep Realm—what your mythology calls fire lizards."

I blinked but dismissed the new term as a distraction. "What was the change?"

Grendel shrugged. "Who can say? The entire configuration of the four realms shifted at that time."

"*Four* realms?"

"Yes. The Deep Realm, the Underworld, the Overworld, and the Upper Airs. The last is where the Spirits live, washed in sunlight and moonlight. I have always thought it must be the most beautiful of existences."

"You'd fall," I observed drily.

He chuckled. "Yes. Of course. I suppose I dream too much."

Leaning toward him, I squeezed his hand and shook my head.

"But Spirits?" I asked, puzzled. "What are they like?"

"Oh. Spirits of the Upper Airs? I have never met them. They do not come down. Each to their own, as they say."

"What do you mean by that?"

"Well, each of the four realms has its own characteristic—or, you might say, representative—form. Each—for want of a better word—*gardens* its own region."

"And, what? Humans are the representatives of the Overworld?"

Grendel nodded.

I sighed.

"But now," he said, "they are encroaching, not merely polluting their own realm, but mining deeper and deeper in ours, pressing the boundary closer and closer to our dwelling places."

I nodded. Grendel looked at the consuls. He shifted in his seat and cleared his throat.

"Ken," he said, his voice slow and serious. "I was puzzled by what you experienced at the place of descent. It startled me, in fact. And when, after you and I had reconciled and I was brought before the council, they asked I relate everything of our experience together in detail. They seemed especially interested in your reaction at the place of descent." He smiled apologetically. "And they requested your presence at the meeting."

"Why?"

Grendel looked at the consuls, who looked at each other.

"We did not tell him, of course," the shorter consul said. "It is not our duty to explain our very thoughts at every turn."

"Oh," I said, feeling my face heat up, but irritated by this attitude toward Grendel.

"But now," the consul continued, "we will tell you—both." And he nodded at Grendel.

"Basically," said the other consul. "We wanted to see what would happen. A test. An experiment if you will."

"And?" I prompted.

"And?" The consul looked puzzled. "And what?"

"How did your experiment go?"

The other consul snorted. "Well, it is still going on!"

Oh!

"But now, we would ask that you relate exactly what you felt—and anything, anything whatsoever, however indirectly related—that you thought."

"At the place of descent?"

"Well, yes. And elsewhere, everywhere. In the Overworld, or here in the Underworld. You said you have a fresh eye. That is true, but of course, there is more than mere sight."

The other consul leaned forward, tapping the table in front of him. "It seems," he said. "You appear to have a connection—of what sort we cannot say. We would like you to share that with us."

AND SO, I did, and was slightly surprised at how long I talked, and how neither consul became even the least bit impatient. They were, on the contrary, rapt. I told them of my descent down the spiral staircase at one location, to the next level down. They seemed incredulous that I felt nothing different during that descent. I wondered whether that was a good or a bad thing.

When I had finished, I thought I saw a new light in their eyes, though Grendel looked a bit uneasy.

But now the shorter consul addressed Grendel.

"And you," he said. "In your report, the description of your experience at the place of descent you mention none of the ordinary symptoms common to our people in such places: nausea, a sense of toxicity of the very air. You understand that is distinctly curious."

"Yes," Grendel nodded. "I was surprised by that myself, but I did not think about it much. I was distracted—very happy to be with Ken again. I guess I thought I was otherwise focused."

"Do you think that was it now?"

"No."

"And, on previous occasions—what did you experience?"

"Oh. What you said. What everyone experiences—the nausea, the toxicity, all that."

"When were those previous occasions?"

"Oh, a number of times, right up to just before—" Grendel stopped, his mouth open, his eyes wide with surprise. The consuls looked at each other, and nodded.

"We believe that the difference arises as the result of your going above. There have been reports of similar effects, in the records from long ago. But they were never systematically studied."

"So," Grendel murmured. "You think that. Do you have an idea of how it happens?"

Both consuls shook their head, and one said, "No. The obvious likelihood is that direct contact with the starshine—principally in the form of moonlight—has imparted something that has changed you, made you hardier perhaps, in some way."

"Wait a minute!" I interrupted. I had been listening to the exchange, becoming increasingly perplexed. "How is it that trolls find those well structures toxic? I mean, *you* came from below—oh!" It hit me. "That was the change, then? You were driven up because you began to find the greater—what was it, Earth-power—intolerable?

"Yes," said the consul. "And now, perhaps you see our—what might be termed Achilles heel. There has been much written on that subject, but there has been no conclusion; but we need not go into all that."

I thought about this.

"Huh," I murmured. "I guess the question then is: why isn't it toxic to me? I mean, it was almost the opposite. I felt drawn to that whatever—influence that was rising."

The consuls nodded at this. They looked excited now.

"Yes, yes!"

"I don't understand." I looked at Grendel. He was looking at the consuls, his eyes wide with surprise and fear.

"Are you suggesting—?" he began and then stopped.

"What?" the taller consul asked him.

"Earth-power. That Ken go down to the Ancient Realm—and—perhaps—*below* that? And perhaps, talk with—*them*?"

"We believe it to be the only way."

I looked back and forth between Grendel and the consuls. I felt completely confused.

"What are you all talking about?" I asked.

All three trolls looked at me.

"A quest," one of the consuls said at last. "A descent into the Ancient Realm—to seek assistance from the denizens of the deep."

"For the struggle with the human authority?" I asked, incredulous. The consuls nodded.

A rush of excitement hit me, and I slammed my hands flat on the table. "Well, in that case, *count me in!*"

"But Ken—" Grendel began.

"No!" I said firmly. "I said I would put everything I had in with you trolls, and I meant it."

Grendel looked at me in silence for a long time. At last, he took my hand gently in his.

"Very well," he said quietly. Then, turning to the consuls, he added, "In that case the quest must include me as well."

Both the consuls smiled. "That was our idea," the taller one said.

There was a long silence, then, before the shorter consul added, "And we can help you to prepare. We have ancient records that you might find useful, and one or two old scholars who might have some suggestions, though—"

"I doubt it," murmured the other, and I realized this consul at least did not have a high opinion of such scholars.

"Very well," I said, making as if to rise. My blood was up and I wanted to get on with things. "How do we start?"

"But," said the second consul. "There is the other idea, suggested in the assembly." He looked at the first consul, who nodded.

"Of an ambassador—to the humans. Yes."

And now they both looked at me again. "You said there was another who might go in your stead?"

"Oh," I said. "Well, yes—Bruce. You have him in custody, I believe. He's headstrong, but good-hearted. I would trust him to the end of the earth."

"And someone to go with him," the first consul murmured. "In the stead of Grendel, here."

"Possibly—Crang," the other consul commented. "He seems to be— taken with the young human."

Both consuls smiled amusedly.

"And he is—let us be honest—one of our very best."

"Yes. But will he?"

"We can only ask him."

One consul turned to where the guard stood by. "Bring Crang and the human, Bruce, here, immediately."

The guard raised his arm in salute, elbow down fist shoulder high, turned and left.

"And now, if you two would care for some refreshment—" The consuls rose and led Grendel and I to an archway at the far end of the room.

IT WAS SEVERAL hours later that Crang and Bruce arrived at the council chamber. By that time Grendel and I had dined and bathed in what can only be described as Roman opulence. It transpired both Crang and Bruce were in favor of the idea of their going up, first as doppelgangers for Grendel and me, and then, possibly as ambassadors. I was impressed, for they both seemed eager for the challenge. I noticed Bruce kept looking at Crang with affection and something like a proprietary air; and Crang, while he looked at Bruce with a kind of sardonic hauteur, there was definite affection there as well.

And so, things were concluded.

"Very well," the first consul said. "Having agreed upon this, we must bring this proposal to the full assembly, but I have little doubt they will support the idea. They appreciate braveness, and a willingness to sacrifice."

I took Grendel's hand, squeezed it, and looked up at him. He smiled down at me with an expression of such deep love that I felt I was floating on it. *Nothing,* I felt, *can harm me now.*

Oh, I knew that wasn't literally true, but in another, subtler way it *was* true.

The consuls led the way back to the dais, and Grendel and I followed, for once holding hands in a very public manner.

"We can do this," I murmured to him without turning my head.

"Sure," he replied, and added, "together. It will be exciting—and perhaps, who knows, fun."

Yes! I thought. *That was it! Doing this together, facing challenges, it* would *be exciting. At least, I amended, it will be interesting!*

And, somehow, in that moment, I felt entirely certain—certain of, well, everything, but especially certain about Grendel and myself and what we would do *together.* And I was certain that we would succeed.

Well, almost.

But that was good enough when I was holding Grendel's hand.

ABOUT GORDON PHILLIPS

I HAVE LIVED all my life at the intersection of the head and heart, of art and science, and while this has resulted in a life path that is something of a meander, it has also made my life both quite enjoyable and very interesting. Academically, I have trained in several sciences and done research in them, publishing a number of scientific papers. I have also worked in various office jobs in the computer engineering field, where I found that cubicle life did not suit my temperament at all. In between these occupations I have also written articles and stories for several local and international community (LGBTQI) periodicals, co-authored a biography of a 19th Century historical figure, and published several novella-length stories in the erotic romance genres.

While all things interest me, from the physical functioning of our world and engineering control systems of all sorts, to the neurons that direct action in the brain, what particularly fascinates me is the manner in which our actions are directed by the mysterious functioning of the human heart.

For more information, visit gordonphillipswrites.com.

Made in the USA
Middletown, DE
28 April 2023